LISTENING
FOR
DRUMS

LISTENING
FOR
DRUMS

ROBIN STRACHAN

CAVEL
PRESS

Seattle, WA

CAMEL
PRESS

Camel Press
PO Box 70515
Seattle, WA 98127

For more information go to: www.camelpress.com
www.robinstrachanauthor.com

Cover design by Sabrina Sun

Listening for Drums
Copyright © 2017 by Robin Strachan

ISBN: 978-1-60381-611-3 (Trade Paper)
ISBN: 978-1-60381-612-0 (eBook)

Library of Congress Control Number: 2017941102

Printed in the United States of America

Acknowledgments

—᎐᎐᎐—

I N 2012, I WAS INTRODUCED TO the work of the Blackfeet Volunteer Medical Corps (BVMC), a group of healthcare specialists and other volunteers who serve the Blackfeet Indians living in and around Browning, Montana. While Blackfeet Volunteer Medical Corps physicians provide services for the people in the hospital's clinics, other volunteers repair houses and help out at the De La Salle Blackfeet School—whatever is needed most. As I learned more about the corps, I decided to sign up. It would turn out to be the experience of a lifetime.

Listening for Drums is the story of a young physician, Carrie Nelson, DO (Doctor of Osteopathic Medicine), who dreams of serving as a doctor on the Blackfeet Indian reservation, much to her father's and fiancé's dismay. This story is told entirely from Carrie's perspective as an outsider living among the Indians, watching, learning from them—loving them. What she sees and experiences is a window into the culture, history, and lives of the people.

In researching this book, I have read everything I could get my hands on about the Blackfeet, the Plains Indians, the Glacier Park region, Native American medicine, and Native American history. I have visited the area, read regional newspapers, met with Blackfeet tribal elders, and talked with many business owners and locals. It was a great honor to be permitted to walk behind the Blackfeet chief, Earl Old Person, during a ceremony at the campground. My fellow volunteers and I also attended a cookout and bonfire on the Blackfeet Chewing Black Bones campground. When I presented a painting I had done of their sacred Chief Mountain, our Blackfeet host Clyde Homeguns shared spiritual insights about his life and the significance of the mountain through dreams and symbols. It is an experience I will never forget.

The word 'medicine' in the Native American tradition has a very different meaning from what we commonly call 'medicine' in this country, with its pills, needles, and reliance on invasive procedures to repair and heal. Native Americans are the original physicians and pharmacists, using plant-based remedies. Many pharmaceutical products in common use today were discovered as a result of plant-based remedies used by Native Americans.

We often read about the mind-body connection. Native Americans take that to the next level and consider Spirit as an integral part of their practice of medicine. Without help from the Creator, there can be no healing.

Although I was told that a book about Indians, written by someone who is not an Indian, would never be accepted, I also was advised that no matter what I wrote, there would be controversy, even among different tribes of Native Americans. My intent in telling this story is to be respectful of the Blackfeet and to provide whatever assistance I can in helping them lead healthy, happy lives. I wish all Native Americans prosperity, good health, and the ability to live as they choose.

I want to thank two people, in particular, for their steadfast support. They are Catherine Treadgold, publisher, and Jennifer McCord, associate publisher, of Coffeetown Enterprises, Inc./Camel Press. From our first conceptual meeting about this novel in October 2014, through a series of spirited discussions and revisions, this book has been a labor of love. I owe Catherine and Jennifer a debt of gratitude for their sage advice and encouragement. They are incredible people who love books ... and writers. I feel lucky to be one of their authors.

Thank you, Elizabeth Kramer-Brent, PhD, my longtime friend, for your valuable feedback regarding characters, plots, and subplots of my novels. To Hal Brent, who was forced to put up with his wife test-reading this novel while on a romantic ten-day European cruise, thanks for your enthusiasm and interest in reading the manuscript yourself and providing a male perspective to all of my books. Thank you, Charlie Goldsmith, my dear friend from Denver, for reminding me who I really am, whenever I forget.

A big thank you goes to Karen J. Nichols, DO, Dean of the Chicago College of Osteopathic Medicine, for support of my work and for reviewing an early draft of the manuscript. Thank you, Laura Rosch, DO, for your dedication to helping others understand that plant foods are medicine, too. Finally, to my own physician, Kim Huntington-Alfano, DO, thank you for all you do to keep me tuned up and in great condition.

To Joseph Matheu, DO, "Medicine Eagle," founder of the Blackfeet Volunteer Medical Corps: your kindness, sense of humor, and gracious support are deeply appreciated. Your healing career has made a tremendous difference in this world and to the Blackfeet people. To Michael Ksycki,

DO, whose trauma and reconstructive surgical skills save lives in Browning, Montana: thank you for helping me understand how much more is needed.

To all of my fellow volunteers with the Blackfeet Volunteer Medical Corps: you are the best example of what it means to be caring citizens.

Also by the Author

Designing Hearts

Manifesting Dreams

Dedicated to

The Blackfeet Nation

Prologue

⚊⟍⟊⟋⚊

WITH THE EARLY MORNING SUN STREAMING through the windows of her room, Dr. Carrie Nelson peered outside and watched as her dog Annie played Frisbee with Dr. Jim Miller, Carrie's mentor and friend. She laughed as Dr. Jim sent the Frisbee flying and Annie caught it, midair. He might be a great doctor, but in this case, Dr. Jim had his work cut out for him. Annie was highly skilled—and insatiable—when it came to Frisbee.

Carrie had spent the past week volunteering at the tiny federal hospital on the Blackfeet reservation, located adjacent to Glacier National Park. This was her favorite place in the world, and she couldn't wait to return each summer. She was grateful to have such nice accommodations at the Millers' vacation home. Dr. Jim was a family physician from Kansas City who had founded a volunteer medical corps serving the Blackfeet. His wife Lois was head party-planner, chief cook, and bottle washer for the corps, to hear her tell it. From the sound of the Hoover upright roaring its way down the second-floor hallway, Lois meant business in whatever job she took on.

Carrie fluffed the pillows on her bed, straightened the handmade quilt, and hung up her towel. Then she rifled through her carry-on bag, making sure she hadn't forgotten anything for the long trip home to Philadelphia. Her suitcase was packed with just a few items for the week. She planned to leave everything else here, since she would be coming back to spend an entire year on the reservation. Her heart flip-flopped with excitement at the thought. Slinging her carry-on bag over her shoulder, she headed downstairs, where the aroma of coffee and bacon lingered in the air. Pouring herself a mug of strong black coffee from the carafe on the kitchen counter, she took a sip and stared out the window at the mountains rising high in the distance, ringed in a few white clouds. It was another perfect day at this visitors' paradise. Then she sat down at the dining room table and picked up the *Northwest Montana Glacier-Sun*. Someone—probably Dr. Jim—had folded it over to reveal the story on page one, illustrated by a photo of Carrie. What she saw gave her a jolt.

WINNER OF ROOSEVELT AWARD TO LIVE AMONG BLACKFEET
By James Harrington, Staff Writer

As she gazes out her office window at Blackfeet Community Hospital in Browning, Dr. Carrie Nelson surveys the panoramic view of the mountains and pauses as if allowing the Northern Rockies to inspire her next words. In fact, she says, the mountains provide her with a sense of something bigger than herself.

"I gain strength from them," she says. "When I feel overwhelmed by the challenges in my work, I remember how long those mountains have stood, and it gives me perspective."

Nelson, an osteopathic physician who hails from Philadelphia, initially visited the Blackfeet reservation as part of a volunteer medical corps directed by James Miller, DO, "Medicine Wolf," a Kansas City physician who founded the group 15 years ago. Nelson met Miller at a family medical conference and recruited her to the group, which now numbers more than 40 physicians and other healthcare professionals, along with a cadre of volunteers who undertake construction projects.

"Dr. Jim and I quickly discovered we had something very special in common: a passionate interest in healthcare for underserved Native Americans," Nelson said. "I just had to experience firsthand what he was telling me about. I'm eternally indebted to Dr. Jim for everything he has taught me."

Has there ever been a moment when the realities of practicing medicine in such a remote location have caused her to question what she is doing here? "Just the opposite is true," she insists. "I feel needed in ways I can't begin to explain. What I do here matters."

Since her first visit, Nelson has returned for two weeks of volunteer service each summer. This year was no exception. But as she was packing to leave the reservation, she received exciting news that she is the annual winner of the Roosevelt Award, a national medical award open to physicians in the United States. The award, which comes with a $50,000 stipend, is dedicated to Eleanor Roosevelt's humanitarian efforts on behalf of medically underserved individuals in the U.S.

"Mrs. Roosevelt was a huge inspiration when I was growing up.

I heard my grandmother, who is also a doctor, talk about Eleanor Roosevelt all the time. I can hardly believe I won the award this year," Nelson says. "I feel humbled that I was chosen. I thought I'd end up applying several times to even have a shot at winning."

For Nelson, the medical service project funded through the Roosevelt Award is one she feels particularly passionate about. "I always knew my project would focus on the Blackfeet and the ways that traditional Native American medicine can work in complementary fashion with the modern academic medicine I practice. I did my residency at Mayo in Rochester, Minnesota, where there is a renowned program in complementary and integrative medicine. This is the next step in my dream of understanding more, of doing more to help the people."

Nelson will remain at Blackfeet Community Hospital through July of next year, when she'll return to Philadelphia to work in her father's group practice and marry her fiancé, who is also a physician.

"Even though I won't be living on the reservation after next year, I'll be back as often as I can to continue my work on behalf of the Blackfeet," she said. "I feel as much a part of the people here as I do my own family."

Wow. That story had appeared faster than she would have believed possible. She had just shared the news of her award the day before yesterday with Margaret Blue Sky, RN, the Blackfeet Community Hospital's interim chief executive officer. Leave it to Margaret, who was the model of efficiency, to take immediate action. Margaret had been thrilled to hear that Carrie would be coming back. Only a handful of physicians were assigned to the tiny federal hospital, and there was only one general surgeon. To make matters worse, the lone obstetrician had recently been reassigned to a hospital on a neighboring reservation.

The young reporter for the local newspaper had visited Carrie's office later that day to ask a few questions. Carrie hadn't thought much about it, assuming that like most news on the reservation, the story would merit a quick mention, appearing weeks from now in the newspaper in what everyone referred to as *Indian Time*—when the spirit moved the process forward. She chuckled. Clearly, this was bigger news than anything else going on. Yet somehow, seeing the story in print made the prospect more real. Mixed feelings of excitement and nervous energy engulfed her.

Oh, how glad she was that she had summoned up her courage and applied for that grant! With three physicians in the family—her fiancé, father, and grandmother—she had no doubt there would be a celebration. Grabbing the newspaper, she tucked it into her carry-on bag to share with them later.

She was intent on keeping her news a secret until she could tell everyone at the same time: Tom McCloud, MD, her fiancé, who had proofread her project proposal several times and cheered her on; her parents, Lynne and Mark Nelson, MD; and her grandmother, Nanette Reed-Nelson, DO, one of only two women in her medical school class. Carrie smiled, picturing Gran, who would be especially excited to hear the news. It was Gran who had encouraged Carrie to follow her heart and dream big.

Chapter One

_⊸✢⊶_

A S THE RADIO ON HER BEDSIDE table at her parents' home in a suburb of
Philadelphia played a hit pop song on the iHeart network, Dr. Carrie
Nelson sang along. " 'Think again before you set me free … oh-oh-oh ….
There's more to me than what you see ….' "

She raised her arms and slipped a new dress over her head. How long
had it been since she'd worn anything other than hospital scrubs? Her voice
sounded muffled as the jersey fabric slid over her face.

She smoothed her hands along the length of the navy-blue wrap dress that
accented every curve on her lean runner's body. Around her neck, a single
strand of creamy, opalescent pearls—a gift from her father on her sixteenth
birthday—matched the earrings her fiancé Tom had given her for her twenty-
eighth birthday. She turned this way and that in the mirror to admire new
black pumps with a higher heel than she usually wore.

She was far more accustomed to wearing sensible shoes in her work as
a physician, especially with all the back and hip problems she treated. But
tonight, the heels made her feel alluringly feminine, powerful, and confident
in the way she carried herself. Tonight was a dress-up affair—a welcome home
dinner—and a celebration in every sense of the word.

She had flown in late the night before from Montana, having spent a
whirlwind week there, working in the hospital's clinic and enjoying the sights
and sounds of Glacier National Park. She loved it there in ways she couldn't
begin to describe. The time had flown by, as it always did when she was
working.

And now, she had big news to share—a professional honor that would
catapult her career forward while allowing her to continue to make a

difference in the lives of medically underserved Native Americans. It was a miracle, something she had never dreamed could happen. She pictured the pride in the faces of her family and Tom's broad smile as he congratulated her.

Even if their wedding and house-hunting plans had to be postponed for a bit, Tom would understand. She had hardly been able to contain herself from calling him right away. But this announcement was too wonderful not to share in person.

She blew out an anxious breath, anticipating the moment she'd tell them she had received a Roosevelt. The generous stipend would be more than enough to support her and further her work. Now she could spend the next year studying Native American medicine while continuing to work in the clinic at the community hospital. She had never felt more needed—or challenged— as she did while working there. The remote location of the hospital made it difficult to recruit physicians. Physician assistants and nurse-practitioners provided much of the care. After the hospital lost its only obstetrician, she found herself delivering babies, too.

She frowned, thinking of several high-risk patients. If any of them went into labor before she got back, Dr. Nate Holden, the hospital's general surgeon and head of emergency medicine, would have to step in. Where Nate was concerned, she had no worries. She'd trust him with her own life; he was that good.

Stopping to examine her reflection in the large mirror over her dressing table, she moistened her ring finger—the one that glistened with an engagement diamond encircled by smaller stones—and removed a stray fiber of mascara from under her right eye. Then, picking up a hairbrush, she ran it from root to tip through her shoulder-length blonde hair, now sleek and shiny from a cut and conditioning earlier in the day. It was a treat from her mother, Lynne, as part of the spa time they always scheduled whenever Carrie was home.

As they'd reclined in spa chairs, Lynne bubbled over with ideas for the wedding reception venue, bridal colors, flowers, menus, and favors. Carrie had felt a momentary pang of guilt. Of course, her mother couldn't help but have mixed feelings when she heard the news. After four years at Princeton, four years of medical school, and three more years of residency, Carrie wouldn't be returning to Philadelphia to join her father's practice—at least not right away. Even so, she felt confident that Lynne would swallow her disappointment and rejoice at this extraordinary turn of events. They could talk via Facetime to make wedding arrangements.

She walked over to her closet and assessed her appearance in the full-length mirror mounted on the back of the door. In it she saw a petite woman, cobalt-blue eyes prominent in a heart-shaped face with just a hint of amber-colored freckles. She had inherited the freckles and fair skin from her mother, whose hair was similarly gold. Their temperaments were alike, too, inspiring an extra measure of closeness.

Sliding a slim gold bracelet over her left wrist, Carrie tugged gently on the waistline of her dress and twirled, admiring the way the soft fabric swirled with her movements. " 'So go ahead and go-oh-oh-oh. You know you can. Some dreams don't go the way we plan,' " she sang.

"Very nice," a man said. "The singing isn't bad, either."

She pivoted to find Tom admiring her body, and she looked forward to later that night, when she would welcome him into her room. Clad in a charcoal-gray suit and light-blue dress shirt, Tom towered over one of the double sinks in the Jack-and-Jill bathroom that linked Carrie's room with his guest room. Although they had lived together during residency, they minded their Ps and Qs whenever they visited either set of parents. Her father tended to be conservative where the apple of his eye was concerned.

"You look nice, too," she said. "Ver-ry handsome. You smell good, too."

Tom straightened the knot on his burgundy tie and peered suspiciously into the large bathroom mirror as if not trusting that he could dress himself properly. Attractive in a bespectacled way, with dark hair that fell rakishly over his left eye, Tom McCloud, MD, always appeared rumpled, as if he had just rolled out of bed in a rush to get to his next patient. Like Carrie, he was a primary care physician. Carrie was a doctor of osteopathic medicine specializing in family medicine and osteopathic manipulative medicine—hands-on healing.

They had met while working on a pediatrics rotation together during their residencies at Mayo. She had been instantly attracted to his good looks and gentle manner. Her first impression was that he would make a great husband and father someday. Their relationship progressed from collegial friendship to dating and then to living together, culminating in their engagement last Christmas.

After they finished their residencies, Carrie headed straight for Montana, and Tom landed in a group practice in Bucks County, Pennsylvania, just minutes from her parents' home. She knew he held out hope that a spot would open up for him in her father's practice. It was bound to happen, sooner or later. She wanted Tom to be as happy as she felt right now.

While Carrie had a reputation as an emerging young leader in the profession, Tom had his own ambitions. His career aspirations included partnership in a lucrative practice and an appointment to teach at a school of medicine. It had occurred to her more than once that Tom was the offspring her father, Mark Nelson, MD, should have had. Tom had even said he wanted Mark's life.

She'd been contemplating the best way to make her announcement and decided on coffee and dessert—when everyone would be relaxed and receptive. Leaning against the door frame, she watched as Tom finished dressing. He pulled a belt through the loops on his pants before flicking off a piece of toilet paper pasted on a razor nick.

She had wanted him to go with her to Montana this summer, but he had declined, kissing her on the nose. "You live a charmed life," he said. "At least one of us has loans to pay off."

As if she didn't know how lucky she was. Carrie took a few more deep breaths, picturing the expression on her father's face—and Tom's—when they heard the news. Although Tom knew she had applied for the grant, her father didn't. She had wanted to tell him, but something held her back. It was almost unheard of for a first-time applicant to be selected. If she had told him and didn't get the award, she'd have to listen to him second-guess her choice of projects.

Even though her father had looked forward to having her join his practice, he'd be overjoyed that she had won a Roosevelt. She couldn't wait to show him and her grandmother the press clipping. Oh sure, he'd grumble about having to juggle schedules, but there was little doubt he'd agree in a snap to a change in her start date. *A Roosevelt. What were the odds?* She shook her head. Hadn't he told her often enough that in medicine, the sky was the limit if she applied herself and worked hard? And now, with a Roosevelt Award to further her work, she was starting her career in the best possible light. It could only bring accolades and reflect positively on his practice.

She had bitten her tongue numerous times today to keep from spilling the beans to Tom. Although he'd be excited for her, the thought crossed her mind that he might not be thrilled about having to find a short-term rental or continue to live with her parents. Her parents were more than happy to have him there. It would all work out. Things always did.

There was still so much she wanted to know about Native American plant therapies and other traditional remedies used by the Blackfeet medicine woman. She was fascinated at how these treatments could coexist with the modern academic medicine she had been taught—a holistic way of healing that enhanced patient outcomes. It was a big reason why Mayo had been her first pick for residency, since it offered a strong program in complementary integrative medicine therapies such as acupuncture and herbal remedies.

She leaned in to Tom, sniffing the citrus and bergamot aftershave he favored and she loved. He bent over to meet her five-foot-one-inch frame and kissed her, softly at first and then with more urgency. With one foot, he pushed the bathroom door shut and lifted her onto the bathroom countertop, evoking a surprised, delighted laugh from Carrie. She wrapped her legs around him as he continued kissing her.

"Rain check," she said finally, giving him one last peck on the lips. "And keep your hands to yourself under the dinner table. You know how my dad is."

Tom drew her close as she rested her head on his chest, thinking how great their life would be. She wanted three kids and a sprawling house with a big yard. They would look for a fixer-upper, one that could grow with them as a family. She'd get pregnant right after the wedding. They'd go through childbirth as a team, tackling middle-of-the-night feedings, teething, the terrible twos, peewee soccer, and Brownie Scouts. As physicians, they'd have to work hard to achieve any sort of balance in their lives and make time for each other. But hadn't they already been through so much together? She couldn't imagine marrying anyone else.

She returned to her room and sat down on the white chenille bedspread. Picking up the stuffed rabbit she had loved as a child, she held it up for Tom to see. "Look what Mom found in the attic. It's Peter Rabbit, my favorite toy when I was little."

"Poor bastard," he said. "I see you've been hard on the men in your life from an early age."

Carrie laughed and rolled her eyes at him. "Oh, stop. At least I've never pulled out your chest hair."

"Well, not on purpose." He raised his eyebrows.

She laughed and ran her fingers over the raggedy rabbit. Its nubby brown fur was rubbed off down to the cotton backing in spots. The black button eyes would never pass current toy safety laws. The rabbit's front paws were wrapped in dirty surgical tape that was beginning to unravel.

"And may I also say that your wound dressing technique clearly improved after going to medical school." Tom smiled and laid a large hand on her shoulder.

"I didn't even know Peter Rabbit was still around until Mom handed him to me this morning," she said and sniffed the toy, which smelled of cedar and stale attic air. "We were looking for her wedding veil. I'm definitely going to wear it."

"I look forward to seeing you in it. Hubba-hubba!" Tom pulled her to her feet. "I'm starving."

Downstairs, the dining room table was set for five with a starched white tablecloth, her mother's best china, Waterford crystal, and the good silver. Carrie leaned over to kiss the rose-scented cheek of her paternal grandmother, Nanette Nelson, the first of three generations of Nelson physicians.

"Hi, Gran."

As usual, Gran looked gorgeous, her fine white hair upswept with two silver combs. "Hello, yourself," she said. "Howdy-doo, Tom."

Tom laid his cheek against Gran's before pulling out Carrie's chair. "Wow," he said, surveying the array of dishes on the table, "this is quite a spread."

A honey-glazed ham studded with cloves and adorned with pineapple rings and maraschino cherries graced the center of the long table. Carrie breathed in the smell of roasted red potatoes with garden-grown rosemary and her mother's yeasty homemade rolls. "Mom, this looks amazing," she said. "I could smell those rolls the whole way upstairs."

Dinner conversation was predictably lively that evening, with three generations of Nelson physicians debating politics in academic medicine and whether Medicare rates would increase. As usual, Mark led the discussion. He was brilliant and ambitious, a renowned cardiologist and faculty member at the University of Pennsylvania's Perelman School of Medicine—also his alma mater. Carrie had followed in Gran's footsteps and attended the esteemed Philadelphia College of Osteopathic Medicine, where Gran had been one of only two females in her class.

As they ate, Carrie noticed that Tom was quieter than usual. She assumed it was a natural reaction to the verbal sparring that frequently took place between her father and Gran, who rarely saw eye to eye on anything. In fact, he could be downright dismissive of his elderly mother—something that deeply troubled Carrie, since Gran was a respected internist who had been in primary practice for nearly sixty years. It was likely that half the adults in Bucks County, Pennsylvania, had been delivered by Gran during her long career. She had been a female pioneer in the field of medicine at a time when few women dared to dream of becoming doctors.

As her mother brought a three-layer coconut cake to the table, Carrie blew out another long breath and replaced it slowly. She cleared her throat. Now was her moment to announce her biggest news ever.

But before she could utter a word, her father held up his wine glass and tapped it with his dessert fork. "I'd like to make a toast to Carrie and Tom," he said. "Both have done exceptionally well in their training. They're a credit to the profession."

Everyone clinked glasses as her mother and Gran echoed his words of praise. Then he reached into his jacket pocket and dropped a set of shiny silver keys in front of Carrie. He tossed the second set to Tom, who caught it with one hand.

Tom's face reddened. "Thank you, sir."

Carrie's eyes darted from her father to Tom and then to her mother, who appeared tense yet pleasantly expectant. Gran's face, however, had a pained expression. Noting the speed of Tom's thank you for the keys, Carrie knew it hadn't been a surprise.

"These are keys to the front door of the building and your new offices. Carrie, I'll expect you at employee orientation on Monday morning," her father said, grinning broadly. He took a gulp of wine and waited, as if expecting applause. "Tom, I realize that you may need a little longer to make the transition from where you're working now."

She hadn't expected her father to preempt her remarks with a bombshell of his own. "I guessed what the keys were for, Dad," she said, managing a smile. "Thank you. But the thing is … you sort of beat me to the punch. I have an announcement to make." She started to speak, but he interrupted her.

"Just a minute, Carrie, we're not quite finished yet." Her father turned to Tom, whose face was nearly as red as his tie. "There is another announcement I hope will make you even happier. Your turn, son."

Tom reached for Carrie's hand. She allowed him to take her now-cold fingers. He looked sheepish as he handed her another key ring. "I hope this makes you as happy as you make me," he said.

"What is this?" Carrie studied the decal on the key ring as a deafening roar started in her head.

"It's the keys to the house I just bought for us. Since we're going to be working together here, I thought it was time for us to have a real home nearby. Your dad helped with the down payment."

"What did you say?" Carrie had five seconds of vertigo. When the feeling passed, it was replaced by clear-headed indignation. "I thought we were going to look at houses together."

He didn't seem to hear the warning note in her voice. "It's a great place— near the lake. Brand new. There's only one office upstairs, but we can turn part of the basement into office space for you, if you decide you need it."

"Tom, one thing at a time here. Give me a moment." Carrie sat back in her chair. How could this be happening? It was like watching a series of train cars derail, one at a time.

Carrie felt cornered and ready to bolt, but she managed to stay put. She could feel the heat of an angry flush rising in her chest and creeping up her neck to her face.

"The thing is … I've just received a Roosevelt Award to continue my research on the reservation for a year. It's a … a *Roosevelt*," she repeated.

"I'm sorry if I didn't make myself clear," her father said, his face also changing color by degrees. "I just handed you the keys to my practice. I need doctors now, not in a year."

"Dad, didn't you hear me?" she pleaded, trying to keep the anger out of her voice. "It's a Roosevelt Award. Only one is given out each year to a physician doing groundbreaking work with underserved populations."

"All right then, congratulations. But I still expect you at the office on Monday morning."

"Carrie, that's terrific news," Tom said, pushing his glasses up higher on the bridge of his nose. "But I just bought a house for us. There are Indians here, too. Surely, you can do your research closer to home."

Aghast, she stared at both of them. Tom had been there while she spent countless hours writing and rewriting her project proposal. A change in location wasn't possible. The Roosevelt application included a detailed proposal with a description of the location and population to be served, along with measurable outcomes and a project timeline. The proposal had been written for Browning, Montana, and couldn't be replicated elsewhere without compromising the integrity of the project. She'd have to turn down the award if she didn't complete the project as written. Tom knew everything about the grant and its criteria.

As new thoughts and questions whirled through her mind, each more troubling than the last, Carrie realized that her joyful plans were being derailed by the two men she had thought loved and supported her most. Her throat ached with the effort of holding back tears, along with feelings of frustration and anger caused by other people wanting to control her life and her work.

How could Tom purchase a house without talking with her first? They were supposed to be equal partners in their careers and personal lives. She thought an engaged couple should select their first home together. Why had he behaved as if he had not received a job offer from her father? Clearly, he *had* known and feigned innocence, since a real estate transaction took time.

Although she had made the decision to surprise Tom with her announcement tonight, it had never been an act of deception. She had wanted to tell him—had scarcely been able to keep such a big happy secret. But she also had wanted Gran, her mother, and father to hear the news at the same time. They had all been part of her life and her career choice to be a DO. How could she have guessed that Tom would do something as outrageous as buy a house without telling her? He had known for over six months that she had applied for the Roosevelt. What did he expect her to do? Say, "No thank you" to the greatest achievement of her professional life thus far? It was her chance to build a name for herself in osteopathic medicine. She also wondered what her father or Tom would have done if either of them had received the award. Of course, they would have expected her to go along with their choice.

She sat very still in her chair, making every effort to remain cool, which was far from what she was feeling. She was a physician accustomed to difficult discussions. She knew that no good could come from an angry outburst—not now. It was better to negotiate from a position of strength.

"Dad, the timing on this award isn't ideal for you and your practice. I realize that," she said in the steadiest, strongest voice she could muster. "For any inconvenience this causes you or your patients, I apologize. I didn't really expect to be given this award when I applied for the grant." Her hands shook.

She wanted to confront him—to ask how he could possibly think it was okay to loan Tom money to buy a house without her knowledge. How could he fail to understand how important this award was to her and her career as a physician? She didn't understand the anger that was directed at her.

She couldn't trust herself to look at Tom, although she could sense his eyes on her. Staring down at her hands, willing them to be still, she looked up to find Gran watching her, encouraging her to be brave and follow her heart. Gran was her rock, her inspiration.

"I thought that another year would be acceptable to you. I've already told my colleagues and patients on the reservation that I'll be back. I want to study complementary Native American medicine with their medicine woman and then write a book. It's just for another year. I'll be back next July."

"Is that so?" Her father stared her down, his tone icy. "Carrie, I don't understand what could possibly be going through your head." He plunked his glass of wine down on the table so hard, red wine sloshed over the rim onto the starched white tablecloth.

"Dad ... Tom ... doing this work on the reservation has been my dream. This award came as a complete surprise to me. They informed me just the other day, before I left to come home. I hope you can find it in your hearts to understand and to be proud of me as a doctor."

Her father's lips were a thin white line. "I don't much care if you saunter off to Montana every summer for a couple of weeks, or if you go there on your vacations to help out. But I've been holding this position open for you. Perhaps it has escaped your notice that I have a business to run in addition to my medical practice and teaching responsibilities."

"What Carrie is saying is that she'd like to finish what she started at Mayo with the intention of using that knowledge to benefit our patients," Tom said, placing his hand over hers as it lay in her lap. "I'll be glad to cover for her. I know how much she appreciates this opportunity, and we intend to make good on your generosity and confidence in us."

A red haze clouded Carrie's vision. She yanked her hand out of Tom's and looked directly into Gran's eyes, as blue and determined as her own. In them, she saw what she now knew was the truth. There would be no discussion, no give-and-take on this issue. It was either her father's way or the highway. Tom had purchased a house for the two of them without her input. But she, too, had not told him about the award and her decision to return to Montana. What did it mean that they were selectively choosing to communicate important information with each other? What did it mean to her career as a physician?

She looked hard at Tom. "We'll discuss this house business later." Making direct eye contact with her father, she continued, "Dad, if I don't do this now, I may never get the chance."

Her father's face, perpetually pink with rosacea, was now mottled lavender, the veins visible in his temples. "Carrie, it's time for you to get serious about your career," he said in biting tones. "I appreciate that Tom has his head on straight."

She leaned forward, matching his steely look with her own. "This is *my* decision, not yours, and it is what I am going to do."

His gray eyes were piercing as he spoke the words Carrie knew could never be forgotten. "Take your place in the practice or begin paying back the tuition I've invested in your education. I'm sending you a bill."

Her mother's eyes flew open. "Mark, you don't mean that," she said to her husband in genuine horror.

As the pleasant family meal disintegrated in what had become an unfortunate pattern over the years, Gran spoke. "Mark, I will write you a check for her entire tuition, if that's what it takes. She has received one of the most prestigious awards a young physician can get. I am so proud of her. She deserves to follow her dream."

"Isn't this about your dream, Mother? Stay out of this." He pushed back his chair from the table with a loud scraping sound and rose to his feet.

Tom's forehead was covered in beads of sweat. "Carrie, I don't get it," he said. "It's the perfect house for us."

"You're right, you don't get it, and neither does my father." Despite an urge to storm out of the room, she maintained her composure. "Did it ever occur to you that picking out a house for us without my input might not be the best way to go?"

She looked to her mother for support, wondering whether she was as complicit in this matter as Tom and her father. If so, it would add salt to the wound. Surely, her father hadn't loaned Tom money for a house without consulting his wife. The truth showed in her mother's eyes, in the splotches of rosy color on her cheeks. Carrie bit her upper lip and looked away. They had all made plans without a moment's thought to her wishes. She could scarcely believe what had just happened.

Finally, her mother spoke. "I agree that consulting you about a home purchase would have been a better way to handle this. But I've seen the house, and I do believe it's a place you'll come to love." She turned to her husband.

"Mark, there has to be a compromise position in the matter of when she starts work."

"I'm afraid compromise isn't an option," Carrie said, rising from the table. "I've upset you, Dad, and that was not my intention. I hope those keys will still open the door to my office when I get back from Montana next July."

She looked across the table at her father, who refused to meet her gaze. Then she walked around the table to her mother and leaned in to kiss her cheek. "Dinner was great, Mom. I'm going upstairs. It's time for me to think of the next steps in my life and what this all means."

It would take some time to digest what had just happened. Instead of a toast of congratulations, her exciting news had been met with anger and belittlement. Lynne shot a beseeching look to Gran, whose eyes remained calm and reassuring. As Mark stormed out of the dining room, followed by a thoroughly baffled Tom, Gran remained calm, and her eyes shone with undeniable pride.

Placing her napkin on the table, she rose to her feet. Taking Carrie's hands, she kissed her on the forehead and said, "I love you, my dear, and you make me proud to call you my granddaughter. I will send a check to your father tomorrow. It's official: now we are both pioneers."

They left the room together, arm in arm.

Chapter Two

⁓ᐞⵣ⁓

T HE CHOCOLATE-BROWN STALLION SHOOK ITS MANE and tail, stomping its hoof on the asphalt as Carrie turned her Subaru SUV into a nearby parking space. The sight of such an enormous animal so close to her car was still enough of a novelty that her lips parted in an automatic smile. The horse was tethered to a sign pole in front of the Blackfeet Community Hospital. Here on the reservation, horses were a primary mode of transportation, particularly during summer months. It was this aspect of frontier life meets modern world that had captivated her from the first moment she set foot on the reservation.

Peering at her reflection in the rearview mirror, she secured her hair in a low ponytail and patted concealer over the bluish circles under her eyes, the result of too many sleepless nights. If she wasn't being roused at all hours to deliver a baby, she was worrying about what would happen with Tom. She hadn't taken an easy breath since the blow-up at dinner ten days ago.

Baggy green scrubs concealed her slender frame. On her feet, she wore cushioned black clogs suitable for long hours of standing on hard surfaces. They were utilitarian, but she liked that they made her appear taller.

Stepping out of the car, she took in deep breaths of the sweet-smelling mountain air and gazed at the Northern Rockies, perpetually capped in snow. The sight of these magnificent mountains never failed to inspire her with a sense of wonder and magic. Whenever she saw them, even in photographs, her worries lessened, her stress level dropped, and anything seemed possible. After the uproar at home and the subsequent agonizing phone calls with Tom and her mother, she sorely needed the sense of inner peace the mountains provided. With the sun high overhead now, the air temperature was rising, promising another picture-perfect day for visitors to nearby Glacier National Park.

Catching sight of Dr. Nate Holden sprinting from his car to the front entrance, she raised her hand in silent greeting. Nate waved back, flashing his toothy grin before disappearing inside. Judging by his speed, a patient was in trouble.

Unlike Carrie, who was supported by the Roosevelt stipend, Nate was a full-time employee at the federal hospital serving the Blackfeet Indians. Highly skilled and well respected, he had moved to the reservation after working as a trauma surgeon in Kansas City. In addition to being DOs, Carrie and Nate had one other significant thing in common: both had been inspired to come to this remote wilderness location by their mentor and friend, Dr. Jim, who had founded the volunteer medical corps.

As she made her way across the hospital lobby, she smiled and greeted the young Blackfeet receptionist sitting at the front desk, receiving a polite half-smile in return. Over the years, as she volunteered at the hospital, Carrie had experienced her fair share of double-takes and curious stares from patients and hospital staff members alike. No one had been discourteous. It wasn't their way. Yet with her blonde hair, fair skin, and blue eyes, Carrie was only too aware of how out of place she must appear to these dark-skinned people.

As she rounded a corner and continued down the hall toward the clinic, she heard a ping. Glancing down at her phone, she saw a cryptic text message from Tom. *Flying into Great Falls. Pick me up at 4:00.*

She let out a sigh. Great Falls was at least a two-hour drive from Browning. She texted back, *Can't take off work that early. Rent a convertible & enjoy the drive! Can't wait to see you!* No doubt having to find his way here by himself wouldn't make Tom happy, but it couldn't be helped. He had many good qualities; flexibility wasn't among them.

They had toured the new house together before she left Philadelphia, with Tom leading the way like a novice realtor desperate to make his first sale. The house had neutral colors—sand and cream—Tom's preference. There were four bedrooms and three bathrooms, all painted white. She didn't hate the house. It was just that she had wanted something with more character, something less pre-fab. The large country kitchen featured granite countertops and stainless-steel appliances.

As they walked around the gleaming kitchen, Tom pointed out that it was designed for a serious cook. "But there's no rule that says you can't use it, honey. Ha ha."

It was exhausting keeping up with his litany of excuses for everything he had decided to do without her input. He had meant well—of course he had. So she tried to keep an open mind. But she couldn't quite shake the disillusionment she felt.

As she boarded the first leg of her flight back to Montana, Tom had said he would join her in a week so they could talk. This would give them time, he said, to think about their plans for marriage. She didn't expect the discussion to be any easier than the heated debates they'd had in recent days. Ever since the dinner fiasco, she'd wondered whether Tom's decision to purchase the house was more than just a momentary lapse in judgment, an ill-fated surprise. Did he think she would go along with whatever he wanted, taking a passive, secondary role? A talk clarifying expectations was long overdue.

Although he had seemed the ideal partner early in their relationship, as supportive of her career as she was of his, Carrie sensed that his attitude toward her "extracurricular career plans," as he called them, had done an about-face. While he had never been wildly enthusiastic about her passion for working on the reservation—even if it was just for two weeks in the summer—it was only after their engagement that he had become more outspoken, citing career concerns and safety issues, then disappointment that she was willing to be apart from him.

"Come with me, then," she had suggested. "We don't have to be apart. You'll have the time of your life and get a chance to give back to people who don't have everything that we have. Plus, it's gorgeous there."

Her interest in Native American medicine had been influenced and nurtured by Gran, who had given her a cherished copy of a book about Native American remedies. A Quaker, Gran hailed from a long line of female healers and midwives who used plant-based remedies in their work.

"It's time this belonged to you," Gran had said. "I think you'll find it useful on the reservation."

Tom had chuckled when Carrie showed him the leather-bound book, a second edition reprinted in the early 1930s. "Looks like something your grandmother would own," he said, flipping the brittle pages in such careless fashion, Carrie took the book away from him.

The offhand comment might have been a thinly veiled jab at the bond she shared with Gran. She knew that Tom agreed, at least tacitly, with her father that her focus on holistic medicine was more of an interest than a passion. In fact, Carrie's decision to follow in Gran's footsteps had been a bitter pill for her father to swallow. He had expected Carrie to go to his medical school. His disapproval lessened considerably when she got her first pick of a residency at Mayo. He was even more delighted when Tom proposed marriage, for in this bespectacled young man with his conservative outlook on life, her father saw an ally.

Pushing thoughts of him and Tom out of her mind, Carrie entered the clinic and greeted her favorite nurse, Peg Bright Fish, who wore her cinnamon-colored hair teased into a style that resembled swirled cotton candy. Today, Peg was dressed in pink scrubs decorated with tiny red hearts. The good-natured nurse was as smart as a whip, and her sense of humor was legendary. While other nurses on staff treated Carrie as an outsider who would leave soon enough, Peg was warm and welcoming, genuinely glad to have another doctor on board.

"Morning, Peg," Carrie said. "I just parked next to someone's horse."

"That's Tall Boy—the horse, I mean. He belongs to Vernon Eagle Spotter. I've already validated their parking pass." Peg handed Carrie a clipboard and a mug of coffee.

Carrie chuckled. "Is Dr. Jim around? He left the house this morning before I had a chance to talk to him."

It was a stroke of luck that Dr. Jim and Lois had insisted she continue staying at their home while she worked on the reservation. She had met the kindly doctor at a family medicine conference during her last year of medical school, and they'd bonded instantly, thanks to their shared interest in healthcare for Native Americans. His enthusiasm for the volunteer corps he had founded was a major factor in Carrie's decision to go to Browning in the first place. Her weeks here had been all Carrie needed to decide where to study Native American medicine. It was Browning or bust.

"Dr. Jim's in the ER all day," Peg said. "They're shorthanded, as usual."

"I just saw Dr. Holden on his way over there. He was in a big hurry."

"One of the braves got thrown from a horse at the campground," Peg said. "Compound fracture. I heard the drums."

Carrie paused, pondering the matter-of-factness of Peg's statement. Messages were shared by drums on the reservation. Even if she had no idea what they were communicating, she loved the way they sounded.

Taking a cautious sip of steaming coffee, she leaned against a countertop. "Peg, we need to round up anyone with belly issues. Dr. Jim recruited two GI specialists to be here next week."

"Colonoscopies for everyone," Peg said, flashing a smile. "Yes, Doctor." She picked up a ringing phone and answered, "Peg Bright Fish, RN."

Carrie deposited her purse in the bottom drawer of her desk and donned her white coat, a going-away present from her colleagues at Mayo. She smiled at the royal-blue lettering on the lapel, *Caroline Nelson, DO, Family Medicine.* Thank goodness, her friends hadn't made good on their threat to have *Medicine Woman* stitched on the coat instead.

She had taken her fair share of good-natured ribbing over her decision to come here. Although most people thought her desire to serve in such a remote location was commendable, not everyone understood why she was so driven to learn more about Native American medicine. Only Gran understood that the time Carrie spent on the reservation was the natural next step in a well thought-out career plan.

"After all the time she spends on that reservation, I half expect my daughter to show up to work wearing leather garments she's made herself and beating a drum," her father often joked to family and friends. "Next thing we know, she'll expect me to add a sweat lodge to our ancillary services."

At times like these, Carrie exchanged longsuffering glances with Gran, who shook her head at her son's attempt at humor. Her mother, ever the diplomatic doctor's wife, took the middle ground. Gritting her teeth, Carrie remained silent, grateful that her father had agreed to her plan to spend two weeks on the reservation immediately following residency—to "live the dream," as he put it. She had learned, sometimes with regret, that his benevolence could be highly suspect and only went so far. After that, he expected her to come home and take her place in his practice. He had a set of rules for his life and expected everyone around him to follow them.

"Don't keep me waiting or I'll fill your spot," he would say in a voice that she'd guessed was only half-humorous. She now knew that he had not been joking.

She had seriously miscalculated the ramifications of her announcement about the award. She had never expected him to react so negatively, and the depth of his anger had shaken her to the core. She couldn't help but wonder whether something like this could result in a permanent schism, following the same pattern as whatever had caused her father and Gran's decades-long conflict. Although he was quick to judge and often carried a grudge, he was still her dad. She loved him. She was not at all sure this situation with her father would turn out well. She had decided, however, to continue to work on the reservation and hope for the best.

Arranging the stethoscope around her neck, she glanced up at the clock and gulped half her coffee. It was time to get to work. "Okay, who's first?" she asked.

"We've got a baby in Room Two with a fever and cough," Peg said.

Carrie rapped lightly on the door of the examination room and greeted the young Blackfeet mother holding her infant son Mingan. The baby's chubby cheeks were rosy. As her hand hovered over his back, she could feel the fever rising from his skin. She guessed it to be a little over a hundred and two.

"Hello, I'm Dr. Nelson," she told the young mother, who smiled politely but didn't respond. The baby's grandmother, who wasn't much older than Carrie, stood nearby. Inserting a digital thermometer into the baby's ear, Carrie took Mingan's temperature: 102.3. Then she shone a light in his eyes and ears while he screamed, a raspy sound that concerned her as much as the fever. "Let's see what's going on with Mingan. At least when he's crying I can see into his throat."

She directed the light into the baby's mouth and inserted a tongue depressor in and out quickly. Mingan gagged and coughed, then screamed even louder. She listened to his heart and lungs and knew that they were dealing with a classic case of bronchiolitis, a common respiratory illness that caused the airways to become inflamed and fill with mucus. Without treatment, the condition in a baby this young could become serious, requiring hospitalization, even a respirator. In that case, he would need to be airlifted to another facility.

"It's good you brought him to see us today," Carrie said. She prescribed an antibiotic, careful to give directions to both mother and grandmother. However, she made most of her eye contact with the baby's mother as she gave further instructions.

The young woman nodded. "Twice a day, every twelve hours," she repeated like an obedient child.

She *is* a child, Carrie thought. This in itself was a concern. "If he gets any sicker or his fever goes any higher, bring him back here or go straight to the emergency room. It's better to be safe and let someone have a look at him."

"He was fine yesterday," the young mother said. She seemed to be a responsible young woman. Didn't every new mother experience fear at her baby's first serious illness?

"Babies run fevers quickly, and their fevers can get high. I know it's scary, but you're his mom. If you're worried, bring him back." She patted the young woman's arm. "Good job, Mom."

After they left, Peg smiled. "I liked the way you talked to Momma. Sometimes our teen mothers try to hand off their babies to their mothers or grandmothers. You kept her in charge."

"Thanks, Peg. Coming from you, that means a lot. Now, who's next?" Carrie asked with a grin and slung her stethoscope around her neck. "I'm on a roll."

At five thirty, as she entered notes on her last patient, she thought back to her interaction with the elderly man she had just treated for complications of diabetes. Despite efforts to engage him in conversation, he was aloof, answering her questions in monosyllables or shrugs. She suspected he would have preferred a male Blackfeet nurse-practitioner or physician assistant rather than a young White female doctor. She was learning not to take it personally.

Stretching her arms high over her head, she rolled her head in circles and bent from side to side to relieve the tension in her neck and between her shoulder blades. She was used to a hectic pace, but Blackfeet Community

Hospital tested her time management skills in entirely new ways. Patients frequently showed up late or not at all, or they showed up without an appointment, a phenomenon known as *Indian Time* that created chaos in scheduling. It had been one of those days.

As she prepared to leave the hospital, intending to shower and change before Tom arrived, she heard her name on the hospital's intercom system. "Dr. Nelson to the emergency room. Dr. Nelson to emergency."

She hurried over to the ER, where Dr. Jim was waiting for her at the front desk. Tall and lean, in his late-sixties, Dr. Jim had an ever-present twinkle in his eye and a heart of gold. "Carrie, sorry to do this to you," he said. "I know you're on your way out, but we just had a pregnant woman come in. I think she'd be more comfortable with a female doc."

"Sure thing," she said. "I hope Indian Health Services can send another OB soon."

"Don't hold your breath." Dr. Jim offered a quick smile. "See you later at home. We're looking forward to meeting Tom."

Carrie greeted her patient, who was thirty-six weeks pregnant—nearly full-term—and appeared quite ill. Her face, hands, and ankles were noticeably swollen. After quickly assessing the young woman's condition, Carrie knew she was dealing with a case of preeclampsia. The only treatment was immediate delivery of the baby. Given the mother's condition and her health history, the baby would need to be delivered by caesarean. She directed the nurse to summon Nate Holden to do a C-section.

"Your blood pressure is on the high side. That's why you have such a bad headache," she explained to the patient, whose name was Peta. "The swelling in your face and in your hands, ankles, and feet tells me that it's time for you to have your baby." Her tone was gentle, yet firm. "How long have you been feeling this way?"

"Since my last appointment," Peta answered.

"How long ago was that?" Carrie tried to keep concern from creeping into her voice.

"Monday," Peta said. Four days ago. "I have another appointment with the nurse next week. I thought I would wait," Peta said, "but then I got this bad headache."

"Waiting is never a good idea when you're expecting and don't feel well."

"I've had swelling in my ankles for all my babies," Peta insisted.

"Your baby needs to be born today," Carrie said, gently laying her hand on her patient's shoulder. She said nothing else, knowing there could be complications.

Within a few minutes, Nate arrived. Golden-brown curls escaped from under his surgical cap, and he had at least two days growth of beard on his square jaw. At just over six feet, he towered over Carrie as they stood together conferring about their patient.

"Glad you caught this," he said. "We lost a young mother a few months ago—same problem. Care to scrub up? I could use the extra hands. It's been a long day."

"Of course." Carrie was delighted. "I guess that's just another benefit of working here. I get to do more."

"You may regret saying that." A wide grin made the dimples pop on either side of Nate's mouth. "Glad you understand how it is around here. We jump in where we need to. Let's scrub up."

Within the hour, Nate and Carrie delivered Peta's healthy baby girl. As Carrie removed her surgical mask and gown, a wave of satisfaction flooded over her. Before leaving, she stopped by the recovery area to check on the new mother, whose vital signs were now in a healthier range.

A glance at the clock on the wall made Carrie's heart drop. *Tom!* No doubt, he was wondering what had happened to her. She hadn't been able to get to her phone before heading into the operating room. She reached for her white coat and retrieved her phone from the pocket. She scrolled through a series of progressively more agitated messages. *Where are u?*

"Darn it." She quickly called his number. This wasn't a good way to start their weekend together, but they were both doctors, and maybe he could understand. She hoped so.

He picked up after the first ring. "I've been wondering what happened to you," he said. "I had to figure out how to get here."

"I'm really sorry, babe. I had to assist with an emergency C-section."

"You did what?" Tom's voice was incredulous. "What kind of place is this?"

"It's an Indian reservation, Tom. The hospital just lost its OB." She didn't think it was a good time to tell him she might get called over the weekend to deliver babies. "The surgeon has been busy all day and asked if I'd assist." When Tom didn't respond, she took a deep breath and said, "I need to get my purse. I'll meet you outside."

She saw his rental car. It would have been funny if horses had been standing in the parking lot, but by the look on his face, Tom would not have found it humorous. "Hi," she said, moving into his arms and offering her face for a kiss. "How was the drive?"

"There sure isn't much between Great Falls and this place." He shrugged.

Carrie blinked. The drive between Great Falls and Browning was stunning, with great expanses of mountain and incomparable rustic views. Tom appeared rumpled and out of his element in pleated khaki trousers and a button-down blue shirt.

"Things happened pretty fast, as you know they do in situations like that," she said, realizing there was no need to apologize. They were doctors, used to a last-minute change of plan. "Why don't you follow me back to the house? You can say hello to Annie and take her for a quick walk while I shower and change. Carrie's dog, Annie, had accompanied her to Browning. Dr. Jim and Lois are looking forward to meeting you."

"I thought the two of us could have dinner by ourselves," Tom said. "We have things to talk about—a wedding date, for starters."

"What days are you free next August?" She smiled up at him. "There's a lot to plan between now and then if we're going to have such a big wedding and reception. My mother has been dreaming about it since the day I was born." She took his hand and held it in hers.

At that moment, Nate left the hospital. Still dressed in his surgical scrubs, he offered Carrie a quick salute. "Appreciated your help today!"

"Thanks for giving me the chance," she said to Nate. Turning toward Tom, she said, "Allow me to introduce you to our surgeon, the guy who seemingly can fix anything, Nate Holden. We're fortunate to have someone with his skills here. Nate, this is my fiancé, Dr. Tom McCloud."

"Nice to meet you, Tom," Nate said, flashing his usual sincere grin. The two men shook hands.

After Nate left, Tom raked a hand through his hair. "What's the draw for him? Why would a surgeon come all the way out here?"

"People desperately need the skills he has to offer, and he likes the area," she said. Tom looked doubtful and more than a little perturbed as he watched Nate get into his car. Things were going from bad to worse. "Oh, come on, Tom. I'm sure he fishes or skis. That's a big reason people come here. Don't you think it's gorgeous—these mountains, all this sky?" Carrie's eyes were animated as she indicated the expanse of scenery. She held onto his hand, squeezing it. "I want you to have a good time this weekend. You deserve a break."

Tom retrieved his hand. "I drove through the center of town and I have to say it: I was surprised to find a hospital out here in the middle of nowhere."

Carrie looked back at the one-story building, feeling the same sense of pride that others did in this tight-knit community. Though small, the facility was attractive and surprisingly modern. "Nice, isn't it?"

Tom shook his head. "Carrie, you're turning into your grandmother."

These were fighting, hurtful words. Carrie's smile faded, and the light in her eyes went out. "I only hope I *can* be as good a doctor as Gran someday." Her voice sounded fierce, even to her ears. She took in a deep breath to restore her composure. "I don't want to argue about why I'm here and what I'm doing."

"Me, neither." Tom opened the driver's side door to his rental car. "Let's get going. I'll follow you."

Carrie unlocked her driver's side door. The thrill of delivering a baby under challenging conditions had been replaced with a sense of foreboding. As she fastened her seatbelt, she tried not to panic. Everything felt wrong. Why was he acting like this? Where was the Tom she had fallen in love with? She started the engine and pulled out of the parking spot.

In her gut, she had always felt the *knowing* even before she could analyze what it meant. This intuitive part of her fit in well with her work as a physician, diagnosing conditions before they became bigger problems. She knew that she loved Tom and that he felt the same. Somehow, they had started down very different paths in their lives. How could she continue to entertain thoughts of a life together with him? She loved him and knew he felt the same. But right now, she couldn't imagine marrying him.

Chapter Three

_-_\\'_-_

A S SHE PAUSED IN FRONT OF a convenience store gas pump that Sunday afternoon, Carrie could hear the sound of multi-tonal drums coming from the Indian campground. In an instant, she calmed down. Twisting her hair into a messy topknot, she inserted her credit card and pushed the button for regular unleaded. It felt wonderful to be outdoors running errands with Annie. No matter where they went, the old dog was just glad to be with her.

Tom had left Browning just after dawn. It had been a weekend fraught with tension and unspoken words. She didn't feel free to speak what was on her mind for fear of escalating the tensions between them. As a result, he had done most of the talking, leaving no doubt as to what he expected or how he felt. She had expressed remorse for not letting him know immediately about the award and her thoughts on returning to the reservation. However, nothing she said made any difference. He did not once mention her award or its impact on her career. Their time together left her profoundly sad and a little afraid. She had invested almost three years in this relationship and envisioned a future that included a home of their own and a family.

"It seems you have some thinking to do," he said as he threw his carry-on bag in the car. "We're supposed to be embarking on a life together. That means we need to be in the same place." He added, "I can't live here."

She had already committed to a year at Blackfeet Community Hospital. She needed that much time to complete the Roosevelt project. It would have been irresponsible to leave the hospital when it still had no obstetrician.

"I'm sorry, but I can't leave. Not until next summer," she said, biting her lip. She searched his eyes for some possibility of compromise. "Tom, this isn't black and white. It's not that easy. Why can't we make this work for both of us?"

Tom had no answer. As she watched him drive away, headed back to Great Falls to catch his flight, she blinked back tears. Then she turned away, unable to watch the tail lights of his car as they faded in the distance. She hoped that after he had a chance to think, he'd call to say he was open to a compromise. She went into the house, heartsick yet relieved that he was gone. This feeling was more troubling than the sadness that enveloped her.

Now, as she stood lost in thought at the gas pump, the drumming slowed, becoming louder, more compelling. She pondered the changing pitch and rhythms, and wondered what the drummers were saying this time. Above the drums, she heard voices rise in song.

"Listen, girl."

Annie, the Australian cattle dog mix Carrie had adopted a few years earlier, poked her head out the window and cocked it from side to side. Only the tip of her pink tongue was visible beneath a slight overbite. She thumped her long tail on the backseat and danced in place. The sound of drums grew louder and abruptly stopped.

In just a few days, Indian Days would begin. The annual powwow was one of the biggest in North America, a time when Browning burst at the seams with visitors from all over the world. There would be arts and crafts, sporting events such as bareback riding, authentic tipis, drumming, singing, and dancing. Even this early in the week, there was more traffic on the main street than usual. It was hard not to get caught up in the excitement.

Shading her eyes with one hand as she looked into the distance, Carrie felt her pulse quicken at the sight of the mountains with their picturesque blue-gray peaks and dusky-lavender crags dusted in white. In fact, it had snowed heavily a week ago—not an unusual July occurrence this far northwest. But now, the late afternoon sky was an intense periwinkle blue with billowing white clouds that left their shadows on the ground. Prairie grasses—jade, emerald, yellow-green, and gold—waved in the late afternoon breeze. The outside temperature would soon begin to cool as the sun began its slow descent. But for now, it was an arid ninety degrees. Summer wildflowers in red, yellow-orange, white, and blue dotted the grassy landscape. The view was Photoshop-perfect, a scene that she returned to in her mind's eye again and again whenever she heard the word *heaven*.

"Oh, beautiful for spacious skies, for amber waves of grain ..." she sang under her breath.

Scrubbing her windshield of the resin-like remains of dead bugs, she paused to contemplate the meaning of the familiar song. Surely, the lyrics to

"America the Beautiful" were conceived in a place just like this. "For purple mountain majesties, above the fruited plains."

"Don't go too far," she warned Annie, opening the car door. Left to her own devices, Annie had a tendency to roam.

The old dog was everything Carrie had ever wanted in a friend: loyal and devoted with enough sass and good humor to be fun. With a yawn, the barrel-chested animal hopped down from the backseat, stretching out her front legs in a yoga-like downward-dog move. She loped over to the grass to relieve herself before sniffing a lacy plant with white flowers growing through a crack in the cement. It was wild carrot, sometimes called Queen Anne's Lace, a plant known for its healing properties and tantalizing, carrot-like aroma.

"Does that smell like carrots? You *love* carrots." In response, Annie sneezed twice. "Bless you!"

In a field down the road, a half-dozen horses munched on the lush green grass. It was disappointing that no buffalo were visible in the fields, although she looked for them each day. She smiled at the sight of a young chestnut mare standing just outside the fence, observing the slow-moving traffic.

"Stay," she said as Annie's herding instincts began to kick in. The dog sat on her haunches, ears perked, her bright eyes following every flick of the horse's mane and tail. "She got herself over that fence. She can get herself back in."

In contrast to the beauty of the emerald pasture and the expanse of grassy plain, most areas of Browning showed the effects of extreme poverty, as if located in a third-world country. This point had been driven home the first time she was warned not to drink the water on the reservation. Most Blackfeet were desperately poor, living in ramshackle houses and trailers in a region known for the relentlessness of its endless winters.

Winter will be here soon. She hadn't expected to be staying on the reservation over the winter. She had assumed she'd be ensconced in a secure job that came with a lucrative salary and predictable hours. Admittedly, the prospect had never brought much excitement. She enjoyed the challenges of practicing medicine on the reservation. There were the same difficult medical cases, but almost no back-up specialists. Physicians worked by sheer instinct rather than the measured manner possible at medical centers in large cities. It was the sort of career she had always imagined.

This was what her father and Tom struggled to understand—why she preferred an unpredictable and often harsh life to the financial security awaiting her in an upscale suburban practice. She sighed, contemplating the differences between what she wanted in her career and what Tom desired. Medicine to him meant financial stability and peer recognition. The disparity in their goals hadn't seemed to matter, until recently.

How had Gran managed her career, along with marriage and motherhood?

Her husband, a truck driver, had died young, leaving her with seven-year-old Mark and a busy family practice. But from all Carrie knew, the marriage had been a happy one. Maybe the next time they talked, she could ask Gran how to broach this issue with Tom.

She tried to put aside the anxiety that never seemed to go away. It was as if she was in a constant state of hyperawareness. She bit her lip, processing what Tom had said last night as they sat up until the wee hours of the morning, talking in low voices to avoid disturbing their hosts. Although her parents were happily married, she had seen enough of her mother's acquiescence—to anything and everything her father wanted—to know that this was her mother's answer to quelling discord. She couldn't—wouldn't—marry Tom if he wasn't able to compromise and accept her choices, too. Perhaps a little time apart would clarify the situation. For now, all that mattered was the work.

She thought about her phone call to Gran earlier that afternoon. Dear, resilient Gran looked forward to hearing every detail of Carrie's experiences on the reservation, and Carrie had savored the calm steadiness of her reassuring voice. Gran delighted in descriptions of the scenery, chuckled at the story of the horse in the parking lot, and commiserated with tales of disrupted schedules as patients showed up late or without an appointment. She was thrilled that Carrie's responsibilities included delivering babies.

"That's mostly left up to the specialists these days. It wasn't like that when I started out. We had to do it all." She paused. "And how did Tom like the place?"

The way she phrased the question told Carrie that her astute grandmother already suspected the truth. "Not much, I'm afraid," she answered. "We didn't exactly fight, but we didn't get along, either. He's mad that I didn't say, 'I'm coming home with you.' Clearly that was what he expected me to do."

Gran clucked her tongue. "Him Tarzan, you Jane."

"The part that bothers me most is that he's acting more and more like Dad. Both of them put down what I'm doing because it's not what they would do."

"I suspect Tom is a little jealous of you."

"Of me? Our careers have followed the same trajectories. He's a really good doc. He'll have his choice of whatever he wants."

"Yes, but he wasn't a Roosevelt winner. You've upped the ante on him."

"I really thought he'd be thrilled for me. I'll have to think about what you just said—about his being envious, I mean." She picked at her nail. "I'd be happy for him, if the situation was reversed."

"Well, give him a little time and see if he comes around. I'm proud of you for standing your ground. I was fortunate that your grandfather was a natural-born compromiser."

"I'm lucky to have this chance. Even after this year is over, I want to keep coming back, whenever I can."

"I'm not surprised to hear you say that. You've wanted this since you were a little girl."

"I wish you could be here, too."

Gran sighed. "How I would love that. It's enough to know you're where you need to be. What you're doing matters, and don't let anyone tell you any different. I'm an old-timer. There were so few women practicing medicine when I was your age. You're to be commended for all you're doing, studying Native American remedies for the value they offer."

At eighty-four, Gran still had a practice she ran out of her two-story white farmhouse in Bucks County. Gran's property was as pretty a spot as you could find anywhere, with its ancient trees, rolling hills, and fertile soil. She had a large greenhouse where she grew vegetables, flowers, herbs, and roots year-round—many used in plant-based healing powders and tinctures.

"Each plant has a purpose," Gran always said. "It's a tribute to learn what it has to offer." From bee balm to sage, Echinacea, ginger, St. John's wort, thyme, rosemary, arnica, comfrey, and other less well-known plants, she knew the best uses.

As far back as Carrie could trace her family's roots, the women were healers and midwives. Knowledge passed from mother to daughter, each generation of young women intent on preserving the tradition. Gran had been the first to be admitted to medical school. But she also had taken the benefits of the education she received from her mother and grandmother and used plant-based therapies in her practice. Carrie was carrying on the tradition. In his own way, so was her father, even if he would never see it that way.

As a child, Carrie spent weekends with Gran, sitting at the kitchen table with her crayons as she saw patients in her home office. She had watched in fascination as Gran snipped and dried herbs for teas, mixed ingredients for healing salves and aromatic oils, and concocted tinctures for everything from eczema to depression. As a result, Carrie had a strong sense of the value of roots, herbs, and flowers in healing the body.

If a patient wanted to try an herbal remedy generally recognized as safe, Carrie helped them find information and directions for its use. Many times, patients wanted a spiritual component to their treatment plan as well. This, too, was something she understood and supported. This particular aspect of healing—the psycho-spiritual—was at the heart of Native American medicine. It was this holistic approach to medicine—body, mind, and spirit—that Gran had modeled.

"When Indians say the word 'medicine,' they don't mean it the way we do—pills and shots and operations," Gran explained one day. "Their medicine is about worshipping nature—plants, animals, birds, fish, rocks, and soil. Even the wind, water, and fire mean something to them. If they get sick or hurt, they look to the Creator for help and get back in touch with the spirit in nature."

"How do they do that?" Carrie asked as she pulled up a stool and tossed her Little Pony backpack onto Gran's kitchen table.

"They use plants the way I do. Sometimes they go into their sweat lodge. That's a place where rocks are heated over a fire, and then water is poured over them to make steam. They pray and sweat out whatever's ailing them."

Carrie could only imagine what her father would have to say about this. But then she remembered he often went to the sauna at his health club. "Dad goes to a sweat lodge, too."

Gran chuckled. "He wouldn't call it that. But you're right, doodle-bug."

It was Gran's motto—"The body heals with help from the mind, heart, and spirit"—that Carrie adopted as her own. But Mark wasn't a fan of his mother's natural healing techniques, which he pooh-poohed as "witch-doctoring."

"I don't approve of anything that isn't evidence-based according to accepted medical journals," he declared. Although he had grown up watching his mother's remedies help people for miles around, he had rejected her work.

"My work *is* evidence-based," Gran insisted, pulling herself up to her full height, just shy of five feet. "I'm board-certified in internal medicine, just like you are! And I can clearly see the results when people get well."

When he finished his cardiology residency, Mark turned down his mother's offer to work together and elected instead to join another group practice—just as Carrie had done, in a way. Gran was delighted when Carrie chose to attend her medical school instead of Mark's. But Gran hadn't lorded her victory over her son. She'd never stopped worrying that he would miss out on opportunities to deepen his connection with his daughter. She well understood the distance that could come between a parent and child.

As his group practice flourished, Mark and his partners invested in two buildings with other medical services, including radiology, laboratory, ambulatory surgery, and outpatient pharmacies. Medicine became big business for him. Now a prominent and wealthy man, he was even more condescending toward his mother's practice, especially her investigations into plant-based therapies.

"Weeds and seeds," he sneered. "People heal because they weren't seriously hurt or injured to begin with."

Gran's response was matter of fact. "They heal because we use plants known for their healing properties and allow nature to take its course. Where do you think digitalis and aspirin came from?"

Whenever she made a point, Gran's azure-blue eyes grew even more intense. As quick-witted as ever, she could still hold her own in a debate with her son, and often won decisively. Her white hair, pulled securely into an elegant twist, was as well-controlled as her emotions. Strong-willed, brilliant, logical, and still fearless, she had been one of the first women in her conservative community to earn a living—and to wear pants. She had faced this kind of medical scrutiny all of her life and knew how to handle young, upstart men—even her son.

Gran never turned away anyone who needed her help, even if they couldn't pay. This, too, had been an important influence on Carrie in understanding that practicing medicine was about caring for people first. Grateful patients supplied Gran with fruits, vegetables, meats, eggs, cheeses, and homemade baked goods. Repairs were made to her home and her ancient Ford station wagon. Two patients even helped pick her out a new car when it was time, and they chose a good one. When she wanted a greenhouse to grow more herbs, one appeared as if by magic.

"You'll have to unlearn what your grandmother taught you when you go to medical school," her father advised Carrie as she prepared to take the medical school admission tests. He was wrong, but it was unlikely he'd ever admit it.

Carrie loved her father with all her heart. But the legacy of generations of women healers ran strong and proud in her bloodline. It was troubling that he found it so easy to dismiss Gran, a well-respected and successful physician.

"You have a choice, you know. You can be an MD like your dad or a DO like me," Gran suggested one day during Carrie's sophomore year of high school as they worked together in the greenhouse. "You'll have the same medical training and have to pass all the licensing boards, but you'll also have additional training in musculoskeletal manipulation. It's hands-on medicine, the way I believe medicine was intended."

Following in Gran's footsteps fit Carrie's idea of medicine and caring for patients. Except she knew she was expected to attend Mark's school. That was his plan. But after researching the holistic philosophy of osteopathic medicine in its modern academic setting, Carrie knew what course her life would take. She would become a DO like Gran.

She hesitated to tell her parents any of this. Her mother would be supportive. But if she told her mother and not her father, it would put them at odds. So Gran was the only person Carrie confided in when she applied to the Philadelphia College of Osteopathic Medicine. One of her father's longtime partners was a PCOM graduate, and she hoped this fact would buffer his inevitable reaction when he learned of her plans.

All her life, Carrie had done everything he expected of her. In this case, she was determined to follow her own counsel. As a fallback plan, she applied to Penn and got accepted. Disappointment followed when PCOM waitlisted her. Her letter of acceptance eventually arrived. Ecstatic, she sailed into the kitchen to show her mother the letter, not realizing that her father was home early. When she saw him, she stopped short.

"What've you got there?" he asked. "It looks official. Is it about orientation at Penn?"

"Actually, it's my acceptance letter—from PCOM," she said, handing him the letter. Her stomach felt as if a swarm of bees had taken up residence. "I wasn't sure I'd get in."

"I had no idea you were planning to apply there." Her father's voice was clipped. "Why would you do that, when you've already been accepted at Penn?"

"Dad, I think osteopathic medicine would be a better fit for me. I've been thinking about this for a long time. I decided to apply and see if I could get in before I mentioned it. I want to learn how to give treatments like Gran."

"You applied there without telling me or your mother?" He raised his eyebrows at his wife, who appeared both surprised and accepting. "I can't believe you'd even consider turning down admission to Penn. I'm on the faculty! What am I supposed to tell my dean?"

"Just say I wanted to learn manipulation, too."

Pushing his chair away from the kitchen table, her father gave Carrie a withering glance. "If I were you, I'd give more thought to this plan of yours."

For days, Carrie did not attempt to engage him in discussion. After two weeks, nothing had changed. She wondered how long his silent treatment would go on. When he did speak to her, his tone was curt and dismissive, cutting her to the quick.

"You'd think I committed treason," she said as she set the table for dinner. "Some fathers would be proud that I got into two great medical schools. Some fathers might even say, 'I'm proud of you.' "

"He *is* proud. It's just that he had other plans for you." Her mother stopped tearing garden lettuce and wiped her hands on a terrycloth towel. "Yes, I know—they were his plans, not yours. But he's always had your best interests at heart, even if they sometimes look more like his own. He can be very single-minded and forget about other people and their lives."

"I know what I want to do with my life, Mom."

"He's hurt because you don't want to go to his medical school. He thought that school would be a good fit for you and your talents."

Carrie did understand. She had known all along how much it meant to him that she would follow in his footsteps. She could only hope that in time, a truce could be called. A month after she started medical school, she shared everything she was learning in the anatomy lab and her classes, and he began to come around.

The next four years passed in a flurry of classes, endless study, challenging clinical rotations in every medical specialty, and nerve-wracking board exams. She considered specializing in cardiology like her father, but decided on family medicine because it was most useful in rural and remote areas. After landing a coveted residency at the Mayo Clinic, Carrie began to notice that her father's attitude toward her career choice began to soften. When she graduated second in her medical school class, he quietly congratulated her and presented her with the keys to a new Subaru.

"There's a place for you in our group practice when you're finished with residency," he said, kissing her on the cheek.

She held him close, choosing for the moment to say nothing. It was not the time to talk about her ambitions as a physician. He was a stubborn man. In this way, at least, she was just like him. She didn't want to compromise the full scope of her goals, either, and wondered if they would ever see eye to eye.

Chapter Four

⁀ゝ|ノ⁀

WITH ONE MORE GLANCE OVER HER shoulder at the mountains, Carrie called out to Annie. The old dog trotted back to the car and propelled herself onto the backseat, settling on a well worn fleece blanket chewed to threads in one corner.

Carrie leaned into the open window. "Be back in a sec. I'll bring you a cookie."

She walked inside the convenience store to the refrigerated case and pulled out a bottle of her favorite peach-flavored tea. Grabbing a box of dog biscuits, she headed to the register to pay. A pretty clerk with a nametag that read *Betty Spotted Fawn* waited at the front counter.

"Beautiful day," Carrie said, retrieving a wad of bills from the pocket of her faded jeans. She handed the clerk a ten. Noticing a display of Glacier Park postcards on a nearby rack, she selected two and laid them on the counter.

With a trace of a smile, Betty Spotted Fawn nodded her response to the fair-haired stranger. The Blackfeet were circumspect, not prone to idle chitchat. Nevertheless, Carrie found these Plains Indians gracious, quick-witted, and like Peg, full of dry humor.

She observed four Blackfeet men standing in a semicircle in one of the aisles. Their coarse black hair was tied back with leather strips or tucked behind their ears, and they wore ragged jeans with barely legible stenciled tee shirts. It was hard to know whether they lacked better clothing or were simply following the grunge style so popular with young people. They carried cold sodas, packaged cold cut sandwiches, and large bags of salty potato chips—dietary gifts from their white brethren, she noted with a wry glance. She thought of the high incidence of diabetes, hypertension, obesity, and alcoholism she had encountered here. In this way, at least, residents of Browning were not much different from other Americans.

Taking a sip of her tea, she got back in the car, handed a biscuit over the backseat to Annie, and started the engine. As she entered the main street of the business district, she passed a hotel built onto the side of a casino. Today, the gravel lot was overflowing with cars, pickup trucks, campers, and motorcycles. With Indian Days scheduled to start on Thursday, Browning was turning into a perpetual party. Once the festival started, however, no sales of alcohol would be permitted on the reservation. Despite efforts to curtail drinking among Native Americans, it was an unfortunate reality that alcoholism was rampant.

As she drove by the powwow grounds, the sound of drumming intensified. Towering white tipis with wood pole supports stood alongside camping tents, small trailers, and hastily built lean-to's constructed of plywood and blankets. Vendors were setting up shop around the campground, offering everything from handmade crafts and cheap trinkets to the usual assortment of carnival food. She saw a Blackfeet man drinking discreetly from a paper bag between his knees.

Here and there, scruffy dogs without collars roamed or rested in the shade. Dogs were considered family here, free to come and go as they pleased. From her perch in the backseat, Annie let out a nervous, high-pitched yawn and poked her wet nose between the front seats, nudging the back of Carrie's arm. She reached back to ruffle Annie's velvet ears, offering reassurance. Whatever strangeness she might be experiencing living and working here, she could only imagine what Annie must be feeling.

She found it ironic that she had been born and raised in Philadelphia, the birthplace of America. There, the cracked and now silent Liberty Bell rang out, celebrating liberty and justice for all. Yet, throughout history, those concepts had never seemed to extend fully to Native Americans. There was little doubt that the City of Brotherly Love had played an important part in forming her values. It was the place where Caroline Nelson, age seven, learned that although in theory all men were created equal, not all men were treated as such.

"White folks pushed the Indians as far west as possible, out of the way of their progress," Gran explained one weekend as they baked molasses cookies for Carrie's second-grade class. The children were learning about the Indians who had lived in southeastern Pennsylvania, the very land on which their modern-day homes were built.

"Did we push the Indians away, too?" Carrie hoped not. She knew that both sides of her family had roots dating back to the earliest colonial settlers.

"We're Quakers. We supported the Indians' right to live as they wanted. Our family has always acted on our beliefs."

Carrie pondered this before announcing at dinner that evening, "I want to do something to help the Indians. I'm going to be their doctor."

"That's an admirable goal, my love," Mark answered, eyes twinkling.

"I'll go where they live. Daddy, you can come with me."

"Carrie, why don't you and I make Indian pudding this weekend?" Her mother stood up from the table and retrieved an old cookbook. "Your American Girl doll, Felicity, lived during those times."

As Carrie grew older, her commitment and concern for those less fortunate also expanded. In high school, a talent for debate coupled with well informed opinions on social justice led to spirited discussions with many in her family's wealthy circle of friends, but especially her father. Although he was proud of her spunk and intellect, he and his headstrong daughter butted heads regularly.

"Carrie, I'm *glad* you're concerned about the welfare of others. I think it's *admirable* that you want to take actions to support your beliefs. But surely, you recognize that your status in life is one of privilege. You don't always understand the bigger picture, honey. The poor will always be with us."

"They may be poor, but they don't have to be sick, too," she insisted, and signed him up to help at a health fair.

Her decision to volunteer on the Blackfeet reservation that summer after her first year of residency added another layer of conflict to their already troubled father-daughter relationship. Her father's reaction was predictable. His eyes narrowed as he cut into his porterhouse steak. Glancing up at her over his glasses, he cleared his throat. "I think your time would be better spent on more serious pursuits."

"I want to learn more about Native American medicine so I can write about it and use it," she said. "This way, I can begin to gather all the information I need, and do some good at the same time. They're desperate for physicians there. It'll enhance what I'm learning at Mayo."

"You're going through a very idealistic time in your life," he said. His condescending manner set her teeth on edge.

But Gran beamed with delight. "Oh, how I wish I was young enough to join you!"

"I applaud your professional curiosity," Mark said with exasperation. "It's nice that you want to serve the disenfranchised. But remember, this country is doing all it needs to do to take care of the Indians, and what do they do in return? Drink and squander opportunities to live the American dream."

"Whose American dream *is* that, Dad?" Carrie asked, exasperated. "They were the first Americans, and I disagree that our government has lived up to all its promises."

"Mark, Carrie," her mother interjected as the storm between her husband

and daughter threatened to derail yet another family meal. "Let's agree that this is a complicated subject and mistakes were made. There aren't easy answers to anything in this life."

Gran shook her head. She later confessed to Carrie as they sat together in her kitchen that Mark's refusal to accept Carrie's choices as equally valid to his own was a source of deep sadness for her. Nor, it seemed, was she permitted to hold an opposing viewpoint. The situation was made even more volatile, Gran admitted, because Mark blamed Gran for interfering in Carrie's life. Anything Gran said in her defense only stoked the fires of a decades-long battle.

It was no secret that he harbored long-standing resentments toward his mother. Gran acknowledged there were reasons for this, even if nothing she said or did was ever likely to change his mind. It had all begun after the sudden death of her husband, when Mark was a child. Over the years, he had buried his emotions and painful memories and avoided talking about what had happened that terrible night. Gran's attempts to scale the wall her son erected between them were rejected soundly. But now she worried that his festering resentments threatened to poison his relationship with his daughter. Mark was free to believe whatever he chose. But where Carrie was concerned, Gran would not remain silent.

"Son, she's still young. Let her explore those interests now."

"Mother, with all due respect, you and I have had these discussions before. This is about what I am offering my daughter."

"I understand that. But what else is she being offered?" Gran's eyes were clear and direct.

"I have an established, respected practice that I've worked long and hard to build," Mark continued, ignoring Gran's question. His face was flushed with indignation. "It's time she took her rightful place. It's time for her to get serious about her career."

Carrie could see that even her mother felt the sting of that remark, well aware that Carrie's passion was strong enough to prevail. On this score, her father would have to hold his own. Lynne looked across the table at him, her expression composed yet firm, sending a strong message of her own. Just as Carrie resembled her mother, she also shared Lynne's thoughtful manner of speech and facial expressions that communicated far more than their words.

"It seems Carrie has given a great deal of thought to this. It's important to her."

"I'm done trying to talk sense into her." Mark waved his hand, dismissing the topic—dismissing Carrie. "She thinks complementary medicine is so wonderful. If it's so great, why isn't everyone using it? Huh?"

Carrie and Gran exchanged long-suffering glances. The practice of Western medicine was in its infancy compared to Native American and Asian health practices. Carrie thought about reminding him that it hadn't been until after the Civil War that sterilization of surgical instruments began saving lives. Native Americans, on the other hand, already had effective methods for preventing and combating infection. But she held her tongue, knowing it wouldn't change a thing.

"As for the Indians and the way they live, this isn't about tyranny and oppression anymore," Mark continued. "That's all in the past. This is about how these people *choose* to live."

"Dad, they choose to live on land they believe is sacred. They live where the government told them to live, where they were forced to go. Now they're the caretakers. They still have a lot to offer, if we care enough to listen and learn from them."

More and more, she could hear in his words how far he had strayed from his Quaker upbringing. Quakers were peacemakers who believed in taking loving action to help others. She bit her tongue rather than speak inflammatory words that would incite more anger. "I want to learn from them. And while I'm at it, maybe I can do something to make their lives better."

He blew out a frustrated breath and met his daughter's level gaze. As if noting of the strong set of her jaw and the intense expression in her eyes, he let out a long breath. "Very well," he said.

Carrie was only too well aware of how much like her father she had become—determined to be the best. There was nothing she couldn't do—nothing, in fact, that her father wouldn't wish for her, if it was his to offer. She knew how proud he was that she had been *summa cum laude* at Princeton, then second in her medical school class at PCOM, where she excelled in her coursework and clinical rotations. Even with such a demanding academic schedule, she had still managed to lead and participate in community service projects. He shouldn't have been surprised at her plan to do more with Native Americans, unless he hadn't been listening. She had talked about serving on a reservation for years. She had always fought for the underdog. In this way, she was just like her grandmother.

EVERY DAY AFTER CARRIE RETURNED TO Montana, her mother called, wanting to know how Carrie's life was going after the derailed dinner. It was clear that her mother felt terrible that their family time together had ended in such a wretched battle of wills. Whenever she called, Carrie always asked about her father, even though she suspected he rarely asked about her. Conversations always began with her mother crying and apologizing. Carrie wished her mother would find some way to make peace with herself and what had happened.

"Your dad isn't here right now," Lynne always said.

Carrie wondered if he was really absent. If he was avoiding her, how would they repair their relationship this time? Was it possible that he had disowned her? If so, would her mother be forced to choose between her daughter and her husband? It was a dreadful time for Carrie. She was grateful that work took up so much of her time. But at night, she slept fitfully, waking with her mind fully engaged, replaying the scene at dinner and wishing it had all turned out differently.

She had asked her mother during one call, "What if he treats me the same way he treats Gran?"

"That is inconceivable to me. He loves you more than you could ever know," her mother said. "We all have to give him time."

There wasn't much Carrie could do until her father was ready to talk. It also wasn't healthy for her to obsess about a situation out of her control. She decided to make the best use of her time and concentrate on her work and her patients. She had a year to complete her Roosevelt project and formulate a plan of action for the rest of her career.

Sunlight streamed through the trees ahead as Carrie turned onto the gravel road toward the rustic log home owned by Dr. Jim and Lois. Driving slower now to avoid deep ruts and loose gravel, she realized there was another important question: whether she could count on the good counsel of the two men most responsible for convincing her to come here. Stopping the car by the side of the road, she foraged through her purse until she found a dog-eared photo taken two summers ago in front of the hospital in Browning. In the picture, she wore green hospital scrubs and sunglasses. A stethoscope was slung around her neck. She looked—and remembered feeling—as if she could take on the world and come out on top.

Standing on one side of her was Dr. Jim, also dressed in green scrubs. On her other side was a young Blackfeet man in a University of Montana sweatshirt. Their arms were around Carrie's waist as they huddled together for the photo. Dr. Jim squinted, never comfortable in the limelight. The Blackfoot man, handsome and gregarious, wore a toothy grin a mile wide.

Chapter Five

__\\\|\/__

As she continued along the partially paved road bulleted with potholes, Carrie thought about the differences between Mark Nelson, MD, and Jim Miller, DO. Although both were fine physicians, the only other characteristic they had in common was their love of golf. Carrie had gravitated toward Dr. Jim as a kindred spirit. Despite a thriving practice in Kansas City, Dr. Jim was passionate about his service to the Blackfeet Nation, and was respected by all who knew him.

"The Blackfeet made me an honorary member, you know," he said. "My Blackfeet name is Medicine Wolf. The Wolf part of the name is a tribute to Lois, too, I think, since wolves often mate for life."

"Just call me Mrs. Wolf." Lois rolled her eyes after hearing the story too many times to count. "When I want him to come home these days, I just howl."

Over the years, Dr. Jim's volunteer medical corps had been embraced with open arms, growing larger each year as he recruited more doctors. Travel conditions permitting, volunteer physicians visited throughout the year, offering more specialized medical and therapeutic care—services that were sorely needed and gratefully accepted. In such a remote location, it was difficult to recruit physicians. A few long-time dedicated doctors worked there, trading bigger, more prestigious assignments for time in the rugged outdoors. But nurse practitioners and physician assistants still provided most of the health care.

Just before she left for Montana, Carrie had received the book on Native American medicine from Gran, and immediately called to thank her. "Was this your mother's book?" she asked.

"Sure was. It was her reference on weeds and seeds," Gran quipped, earning a hearty laugh from Carrie. "I want you to have it so you'll remember *everything* you've been taught. There are common herbs and other plants that the Indians use for healing. Some you'll already know from working with me in the greenhouse."

At that moment, Carrie could have sworn she was surrounded by the aroma of her grandmother's homemade castile soap and primrose oil, a fragrance she always associated with love. "I'll treasure it," she said.

"When you get to Montana, ask someone to introduce you to their medicine woman," Gran advised. "You'll need to understand her ways."

Carrie already knew that Gran's stamp of approval was critical in helping many a new physician be accepted by the locals. If Gran didn't approve of a young colleague, her long-time patients wouldn't trust that person, either. Carrie would likely need it to gain the trust of at least some of her Blackfeet patients.

"Gran, I bet you and the medicine woman would get along great."

There was a chuckle on the other end of the line. "If I ever get the chance to visit, I'd love to find out."

IF SHE WAS COMPLETELY HONEST WITH herself, Carrie had to admit that she'd chosen Montana for her project because she'd felt drawn there. From the time she had set foot on the reservation, she'd had a sense that irresistible forces were in motion. Even so, she worried that the decision would turn out to be a mistake, rooted in stubbornness and naiveté.

On the night she called Dr. Jim to share the news about the award, Carrie had a dream about a gray wolf, its face silvery with age. In the dream, she rose barefoot from her buffalo hide sleeping mat and pushed open the flap of her family's tipi to face the she-wolf. Their eyes met in a silent greeting.

"Why are you here?" Carrie asked. "What message do you have for me?"

The wolf spoke, its voice that of an older female. "It is time."

Then the animal turned and disappeared into the woods. Carrie awoke, certain that she had seen the place before. The wolf was as familiar as family. *Time for what? What does it mean?*

SHE BRAKED TO A STOP, WATCHING as a cow meandered across the rutted road to a pasture on the other side. There were few fences marking property here. Most land was open range. There was a saying common in these parts: "Hit a cow and you just bought it." Annie's curious brown eyes followed the cow as she crossed the road. She woofed out a warning to Carrie.

"I see her."

She continued driving, slower now, until the steel mailbox with the red flag marked *The Millers* came into view. Turning into the dirt driveway, she parked and waved to Dr. Jim, who was sweeping the porch and walkway in a futile attempt to keep it free of ever-blowing dust and grit. She watched him, noticing the slight stoop to his shoulders that age brought. How long would he be able to keep up his exhausting schedule, split between his practice in Kansas City and his service on the reservation?

Annie galloped toward Dr. Jim, who leaned his broom against the porch rail and knelt down to scratch behind her ears. Standing, he wrapped an arm around Carrie's waist and gave a little squeeze. She leaned in to him, grateful for this small gesture of affection.

"Are you feeling better now?" he asked. "I told Lois I thought you needed a hot meal and some relaxed conversation tonight."

"That's exactly what I need," she admitted, letting out a long breath. "You know, Tom isn't always like that. I can't imagine what you must be thinking."

"Where he's concerned, you are the *only* one whose opinion matters." He held open the front door for her. "You had a baptism by fire at the hospital last week. I'll help you out this week until the volunteers arrive. You'll be the boss of me."

"As if." She let out a self-conscious laugh. "I'm lining up patients needing GI docs and the orthopedic specialist."

"I recruited a hematologist-oncologist, too."

Wafting from the kitchen doorway was an irresistible smell of roasting meat and cinnamon apples. Carrie took a whiff. "Lois, whatever you're cooking smells wonderful."

"I thought you two deserved a decent dinner," Lois said. "As hard as you both worked last week. I decided to pull out all the pots and pans."

As she bustled off to the kitchen, Dr. Jim smiled in her direction. "You can't control her. You can only hope to contain her."

Carrie's heart contracted at the love she saw in his eyes for his wife of forty years. Theirs was a model of a successful marriage—just as her parents' was, in its own way. She hoped to emulate their accomplishment someday. Her brow knitted as she thought of Tom. Until this weekend, she had been able to envision their life together. Now she was hard-pressed to imagine any detail of day-to-day life with him. She knew that where her father was concerned, her mother was in charge of the household and kept the marriage running smoothly. Carrie wanted a more equal partnership with a fair measure of give-and-take, something like what Dr. Jim and Lois had.

Anyone who knew Lois understood Dr. Jim's devotion to her. High-spirited and good-humored—her auburn hair styled in a no-nonsense bob— she looked ten years younger than her sixty-two years. Never one to sit on the sidelines, she was a hard worker whose down-to-earth, gracious manner put everyone at ease. While Dr. Jim built a practice in Kansas City and later started the volunteer medical corps, Lois raised their children, kept track of details, and made sure he didn't take himself too seriously. The Millers were a team.

These days, they spent as many weeks as possible at their Glacier Park retreat. They jokingly claimed it was their final resting spot. Yet Carrie rarely saw them resting.

"It's just the three of us for dinner tonight," Lois said, carrying a tray of iced-tea glasses. "Well, four … Annie, too, of course. I made her a hamburger and rice casserole."

"You're spoiling both of us," Carrie said. As she sat on the sofa, sipping sweet tea, she caught sight of a new painting over the stone fireplace. "Where did you get that? It's gorgeous."

"Jim and I found it today at the heritage center. Seems like we can always find reasons to spend money there." Lois let out a hearty laugh. "The artist is John Leathers' father, Earl."

"I didn't know John's father was an artist."

John Leathers was the Blackfeet school superintendent—and the handsome younger man in the photo she always carried with her. It was clear from this painting that his father had considerable artistic talent. She admired the oil painting with its lovingly rendered figure of a Blackfeet elder with his long feathered headdress, sitting majestically on a black horse. The spectacular 'Shining Mountains' rose in the distance.

"The man on that horse is rumored to be John's grandfather. He's a member of Tribal Council." Dr. Jim stood next to her.

"The mountains look so luminous, just like they are in real life." At that moment, Carrie decided to purchase one of Earl Leathers' paintings. His work was sure to increase in value in coming years. When she returned to Philadelphia, she'd have a daily reminder of the reservation and her time here.

She ran upstairs to her room to change for dinner. Pulling her hair into a French braid, she touched mascara to her eyelashes and fastened on the pearl earrings Tom had given her last year for her birthday. Then, looking at the engagement ring on her finger, she twisted it around and around, deep in thought. Most of their discussions this weekend had centered on when to get married. Carrie wanted to wait until after she returned to Philadelphia so they could consult her parents. Tom wanted to move forward more quickly. In the end, he had agreed not to make any more decisions without her. She was holding him to that promise.

With a glance at the clock on the bedside table, she picked up her cell phone and dialed her parents' home number. It was nearing eight o'clock in Pennsylvania. But after four rings, the answering machine clicked on with its customary private-professional message. "This is the Nelson residence. We are unavailable to take your call. If you are a patient and this is a medical emergency, please hang up and dial 911. Otherwise, leave your name, number, and a message at the sound of the tone."

Carrie impatiently tapped her foot on the floor, waiting until she heard the high-pitched sound. "Hi, Mom. Hi, Dad."

She paused, hoping her mother would pick up. But on a Sunday night, her parents were probably having dinner at the country club with friends. She left a message and went downstairs, where Dr. Jim met her with a glass of chardonnay.

He eyed her with a mixture of fondness and amusement. "So, after everything you've been through since you got here, are you still glad you came back?"

She took a sip. "Oh, yes. But there's still a lot I don't know about the people—how they view me, for starters. Am I naïve to think I can do this? I don't want to let you down."

"That isn't possible. I couldn't be more proud if you were my own daughter."

Gratitude swelled in Carrie. "I only hope I can be half the doctor you've been for them," she said, knowing that might take years.

"You'll be even better," he said with an understanding smile. "Whether or not they show it, they appreciate that you're here. The women are glad to have a female doctor."

"I sure hope so. This blonde hair is a dead giveaway I'm not a Blackfeet."

The uncertainty on Carrie's face caused Dr. Jim to pause. He reached out and touched her cheek. "You are needed and wanted here. The blonde hair is a big attraction. Trust me."

She slid into one of the dining room chairs, her eyes taking in the array of food on the table. From popovers to roasted chicken, mashed potatoes, and a big green salad, Lois had prepared a feast. Dr. Jim winced as he eased into his chair.

"What's bothering you?" she asked.

"Old age." Dr. Jim laughed. "I was hoping you'd work on me."

"I'd be glad to." She paused. "Do you …? I mean is that something I can do comfortably here with the people? The touching, I mean."

"Too much about medical care is impersonal these days," he said. "The Indian people trust hands-on healing. We've been able to keep quite a few folks from surgery using manipulation. If I were you, I'd offer it every chance you get."

"My grandmother uses it on all of her patients," Carrie said. "She says she can tell more about a patient's condition by placing her hands on their head and back than from any X-ray or test."

After dinner, Lois served coffee and apple cobbler with vanilla ice cream. Carrie had just taken her first bite when they heard a knock at the door. Lois glanced at Dr. Jim. "Were you expecting anyone?"

He went to the door, a mischievous glint in his eye. "I have a feeling I know who it is."

Carrie registered the visitor's identity by his voice even before she saw him. The man was a Blackfeet, taller than most of the Indians she knew, his thick black hair brushing the collar of his shirt. He was undeniably handsome, his smile genuine. Soulful eyes the color of dark chocolate. He wore a pair of pressed khakis and a navy-blue dress shirt, open at the collar. His moccasins were handmade—a labor of love from his older sister, the town's moccasin-maker.

"John!" She leaped to her feet as the man covered the distance between them in a few long strides. Then his arms were around her shoulders and she was returning the hug. His lips grazed her cheek respectfully.

"Carrie," he said, "it is good to see you. I was away for a month or I would have stopped by sooner."

"How did you know I came back to the reservation? I haven't had a chance to call or email you yet."

Dr. Jim coughed politely. "Carrie, news travels fast here."

"But how ...?" Carrie looked from one man to the other and back again at John Leathers.

He smiled broadly. "The drums," he said. "I knew the minute you got here."

Chapter Six

⟶⟍⟋⟵

Sleep came in fits and starts that night. Carrie tossed and turned, willing her busy brain to be still, blaming insomnia on the three cups of coffee she drank as John recounted tales of the Blackfeet people. He had shared little-known folklore, Blackfeet myths, and stories of his life growing up on the reservation. In many ways, his childhood sounded similar to hers, filled with family, faith, and expectations of high achievement.

"My mother's father is an elder. He encouraged me always to remain true to my heritage. But he also expected me to get an education. There was never any question about that."

John attended the De La Salle Blackfeet School on the reservation before graduating from Browning's public high school. From there, he went to Boston College on a full scholarship before spending two years exploring Europe. When he returned to the states, he taught secondary English at a high school in Missoula while earning a master's and a doctorate. He was well-educated and highly influential—a man who got things done.

"I know your grandfather. You're a lot like him," Dr. Jim said.

John's smile was humble, and he flushed at this unexpected praise. "Thank you," he said. "You could not have said anything that would please me more."

His college plans led some of his school friends to view him with suspicion, he explained. They even mocked him. "Peer pressure makes it difficult for some Native American kids to excel, or even remain in school."

Carrie had been told by Peg that it was common for young people on the reservation to hide special gifts or talents so as not to appear different. But the bigger challenge was that unemployment on the reservation was high. Many students and their parents didn't see the point of an education.

"I'm determined to change that," John said. "Grandpa told me it was my job to go to college and serve our people. He expects me to make sure Blackfeet children get an education. But he also wants them to learn the old Blackfeet ways. He and just a few other elders still speak the language."

"Was it tough being the grandson of an elder?" Carrie asked, mopping up the last of the melted ice cream and cobbler before pushing away her dessert plate. "You were probably held to a higher standard and expected to behave yourself. Am I right?"

"Like most kids, I did things that could have gotten me in trouble. I borrowed my uncle's truck when I was nine." He looked sheepish. "It's lucky I never got caught. I would've faced far worse punishment at home. But when my students get in trouble, I am not without sympathy." He grinned.

As Carrie listened to him share challenges he faced as an educator on the reservation, she couldn't help wondering about his personal life. In sharp contrast to so many other Blackfeet men his age, he was educated and had traveled abroad. This made it difficult for him to connect meaningfully with women from the tribe who might never have finished high school.

Two years ago, when she had visited, he had been dating a fellow teacher from another town. His family hadn't approved of the woman, who was Cherokee. Perhaps he would tell her more later, in private.

As if reading Carrie's mind, Lois winked. "John, is there still a young lady in your life?"

"Lois, let the man alone." Dr. Jim rolled his eyes. "I apologize for my wife, John. She thinks everyone's business is hers."

"I do not." Lois had the grace to blush. "Just the people I care about."

"I am still with Gali," John answered, putting down his coffee cup. "Of course, my family would prefer that I marry Naomi Prairie Hen, the daughter of my mother's best friend. If I marry Gali, my grandfather and my parents will be upset. But I cannot imagine marrying Naomi." The look on his face discouraged further discussion.

After John left and Dr. Jim went upstairs to bed, Carrie and Lois remained at the table. "From the first time I met John, I felt as if I knew him," Carrie confided. "I feel completely comfortable with him, even though we come from such different backgrounds."

"Maybe you two were siblings in a previous lifetime." Lois yawned and picked up their empty dessert plates while Carrie gathered coffee cups. "The Blackfeet believe in reincarnation. Maybe you were once a member of the tribe."

"Well, that would certainly explain my interest in anything having to do with Indians." Carrie thought for a moment before adding, "But Jeez, you'd think I'd stay as far away from entitled white people as I could, instead of coming back in this life as one."

"You've never once acted 'entitled,' dear." Lois took the empty coffee cups from Carrie and dunked them in soapy water before stacking them in the dishwasher. "John knows you care for his people. He's an important man here. Listen to what he says, and you'll be fine."

"I will." Carrie pressed her lips to Lois's cheek. "Thanks again for a great dinner and for being so understanding about Tom."

"I wouldn't fret too much. Life has a way of working things out." She squeezed Carrie's hand. "Sweet dreams."

Carrie considered the wisdom in Lois's advice as she pulled a Philadelphia Eagles nightshirt over her head, brushed her teeth, and smoothed on the moisturizer Gran had made for her. It contained clary sage, an essential oil known for its calming, antiseptic properties. She was exhausted, but unable to relax as she nestled under the heavy comforter, thoughts parading through her head. In addition to her troubles with Tom, she faced other challenges. Beyond their health concerns, there was so much she needed to understand about her patients in order to help them. The Roosevelt project came with its own daunting set of expectations.

She thought of Lois's advice about John. "He can teach you what you need to know."

As she listened to the howl of a lone wolf in the distance, Carrie's last thought before drifting off to sleep was, *I'm counting on it.*

MONDAY MORNING DAWNED IN PALE HUES of rose, peach, and yellow as the sun made its gradual, stunning ascent over the mountains. Within a matter of minutes, the sky changed to the palest of powder-blues, the mountains now a deep lapis lazuli color. Carrie watched the sunrise from her bedroom window, still feeling the effects of her stressful weekend with Tom. He had emailed the night before, a message that was anything but apologetic. She hadn't yet decided how to respond.

His message read, "I can't believe you're choosing an award over our relationship."

She re-read the email, frowning at the negative tone of his message. Coming from a man she thought she would marry and who would be a partner in her life, it struck her as downright chauvinistic. Had the tables been turned, with Tom the winner of the Roosevelt, he would no doubt expect her to be understanding and wait for him. In all the times she had talked with him about her Roosevelt application and the many times he had reviewed or proofread her work, he had never once expressed concern that the project was written for Montana.

The truth finally hit home: he hadn't believed in her enough to think she could win, so there was never going to be a problem about where she would live or work. Somehow, this was even more of a betrayal than his reaction to her decision to accept the award.

Dropping her nightshirt to the floor, she pulled on fleece pants and a sweatshirt and laced her running shoes. Threading her ponytail through the back of a Phillies ball cap, she called out to Annie, whose tail wagged in anticipation of a run. She did a few stretches to warm up her leg muscles and set out at a leisurely jog, with Annie galloping along just steps behind.

They ran past the hospital, picking up speed by degrees. Along the highway, they passed a pond dotted with whitecaps. A bald eagle soared overhead, its wingspan creating a shadow the size of a small aircraft on the ground below. The eagle coasted over fir trees before dipping onto the pond, splashing diamond-like water droplets as it landed on the surface. Moments later, it took off again, flapping upward, gaining speed. Its talons clutched a flopping silver fish, iridescent scales flashing in the bright sunlight.

With the stiff breeze slapping her back, Carrie hit her stride, feeling the serotonin high that predictably came with running. As tempting as it was to take off across the field to the pond, she knew that snakes and animals hid in the grasses. It was important to follow the advice she would give patients and avoid doing anything that could invite injury. She turned to make sure Annie was close behind and saw her trotting more slowly now, her eyes alert to all the movements across the field.

"Hurry up, slowpoke!" she called out, and Annie raced to close the gap between them.

Slowing her pace, lungs aching from the exertion of running at such a high altitude, she stopped for a moment and bent over slightly, hands on her knees, to catch her breath. Shading her eyes with one hand, she looked out to the Northern Rockies stretching before her, rising so high into the atmosphere that on stormy days, the earth and sky seemed to merge together. Some days, the summit was nearly invisible through the misty clouds. These 'Shining Mountains' stirred her soul, reminding her why the Indians worshipped nature. Out here, she would create her own meeting place.

Home again, she eased into a steaming bath and lay back in the tub. She'd managed to put aside thoughts of Tom's email during the run, but now she considered how best to respond. She was starting to see that Tom valued his own wishes above their relationship. Could she marry a man who treated her desires as secondary? What was the best way to express her needs without arguing or appearing selfish?

Female physicians faced special challenges in meeting the needs of their patients while balancing a marriage, home, and children. It could be done, but required a continual process of give-and-take on the part of husband and wife. Since Carrie and Tom were both physicians, their relationship was likely to demand twice the sacrifice and compromise.

She got out of the bath and sent Tom a quick, careful text. *I'm disappointed by your last email. We need to continue talking about this.* Then she threw on a clean set of scrubs and headed downstairs, where the aroma of freshly brewed coffee and toast filled the air, along with the smell of wood smoke from the fireplace. Dr. Jim and Lois were drinking coffee and reading the newspaper when she appeared in the kitchen doorway.

"Good morning," she said, stretching her arms over her head. "That coffee smells great ... although I probably shouldn't have indulged so much last night. It took me a long time to get to sleep."

"Carrie, that was decaf," Lois said, and Dr. Jim chuckled. "Surely you don't think people as old as we are drink regular coffee, at least not that late at night," she added with a grin. "Maybe it was the wolf that kept you awake. Lord, that's a mournful sound."

"It's unusual to hear them this close." Dr. Jim looked up from the paper. "One must still be hanging around. Better keep an eye on Annie or she might run off and join the wolf pack. Won't you, girl?" He ruffled the fur on Annie's head.

"I don't think I've ever heard a real wolf before." Carrie sat down at the table. "I didn't think they came close enough for us to hear them." She poured half-and-half into her coffee. "I guess they do whatever they want."

She glanced over Dr. Jim's shoulder at the front page of a newspaper. As in so many small-town papers, local writers provided a version of the news that could be humorous at times. "From the police blotter," Dr. Jim announced, clearing his throat. "A pickup truck was reported stolen. It was not."

Carrie and Lois let out hearty laughs. He continued, "A woman called the police to report that her husband went to town. There was no further explanation."

"Oh, my." Lois buttered a slice of toast. "Worse things happen than what gets reported. We just don't read about those."

Carrie accepted the paper from Dr. Jim. Today's front-page story was about North American Indian Days and the crowning of the new teenage Miss Blackfeet. A pretty sixteen-year-old, Sinopa, posed in front of a white tipi with the new Tiny Tot Princess, a four-year-old named Nuttah.

"What a cutie," she said, her eyes softening at the tiny Blackfeet girl with her baby-toothed smile. "It's lucky that I can be here for the festival this year."

After breakfast, she watched as Dr. Jim popped two over-the-counter pain relievers. She could tell from the way he moved that he was in pain. Glancing at her watch, she said, "Before we head over to the hospital, why don't I see what's causing the pain in your back? I have some time this morning."

"I'd appreciate that." He stood up from his chair and groaned. "I'll get your table out of the car."

"You will *not*. Just sit down and finish your coffee. It isn't that heavy."

She removed the portable manipulation table from the back of her car and set it up in the living room. Dr. Jim sat at the edge of the table while Carrie ran practiced hands over his neck and down his spine, searching by touch for the area she knew was likely the source of his discomfort. She continued working, moving his limbs and asking him to offer resistance until she felt the muscle release.

"Ah, that was it," Dr. Jim said. "You've got the touch."

"Whatever you were doing to cause that, please stop." She helped him into a sitting position. "Take it easy for a while."

"Will do, chief."

Lois sat on the arm of a nearby chair. "Is everything all better?"

"This one knows her stuff," Dr. Jim said with a grin. "I feel like a new man." He pumped his fists in the air.

"Just listen to her and behave yourself," Lois said, wagging an index finger at her husband. She clucked her tongue. "Honestly, he still thinks he's in his twenties."

"Why don't we ride together to the hospital this morning?" Dr. Jim suggested. "I'd like to consult with Nate about something before he gets too busy."

"Sounds good," Carrie said. "I was glad he asked me to assist with the surgery on Friday. That's not something family docs get to do much anymore."

"I'm sure he appreciated your help," Dr. Jim said. "He's the only surgeon for miles around."

"Were you surprised when he decided to move here?"

"Shocked would be more like it. He was on staff at the big medical center in Kansas City. It's the kind of job young surgeons salivate over. But he had a couple of pretty bad experiences there. One night, he called to say he needed to make a change."

"What happened?" Carrie considered scenarios that could drive a successful young surgeon to an Indian reservation. Surely, it was more than love of the great outdoors.

"You'll have to ask him. It's quite a story, but it's not my place to tell. By the way, the nurses are all in love with him," Dr. Jim added with a laugh.

"You expect a surgeon to have an ego. So far, I haven't seen that in him," Carrie said. "He's really nice."

"That he is. We've known Nate since he and our middle son were in kindergarten. He's stayed the same good guy we've known for years."

As Dr. Jim drove to the hospital, they talked about some of the more challenging aspects of practicing medicine on a reservation. "It's impossible to keep to a schedule here. If you're hung up on punctuality, you're in the wrong place."

"I've noticed a lack of clocks."

She'd intended the observation as a joke, but Dr. Jim cocked his head, carefully considering his answer. "The Indians live in harmony with the rising and setting of the sun, the changing seasons, planting and harvesting, and the like." He slammed on the brakes to avoid hitting a dog darting across the road. "That's how they measure time. It's a completely different way of living, very spiritual. We're the ones who get stressed out."

"Yes, but people also have trouble getting to the clinics. I hear that all the time."

"Some of these folks live off the beaten path and have to travel on horseback. A few have motorcycles. But just try getting your obese grandmother onto a horse or motorcycle." Dr. Jim shook his head. "It's even more of a problem when roads are muddy or when there's heavy snowfall. During the winter, folks have no easy way to get to the hospital."

Blackfeet Community Hospital was a one-story earthen-colored building adorned with red Native American symbols around the exterior and tasteful local art displayed throughout. A large metal sculpture had been erected in front, depicting wildlife common to the area. Although there were only about two dozen beds, the facility boasted two operating rooms, an inpatient pharmacy, a family practice clinic, inpatient addiction treatment center, outpatient dental and optometry services, a women's health center, diabetic clinic, and an emergency room. With no intensive care unit, patients requiring that level of care were stabilized and sent by helicopter to Kalispell or Great Falls.

Dr. Jim stopped by the ER to find Nate, who was already in surgery. "If you remember, when you were here last summer, we didn't have a surgeon," he told her. "Now that Nate's here, he handles the trauma cases. People have a better chance of surviving with that level of care."

"He seems able to do it all."

"I brought him with me to do a reconstructive surgery. He stayed a few more days to hike and fish. That was all it took to convince him."

"Do you think he's happy?"

"He seems to be thriving. I was worried for a while because his fiancée wouldn't move here with him. Then they broke up a few months later."

"Not an outdoors kind of girl?"

"That would be putting it mildly. Marisa was nice enough." Dr. Jim shrugged. "Sometimes people discover they have different goals and values in life. Better to find that out before the wedding. It's not a disgrace." He squeezed her arm. "I need to double-check logistics for the volunteers. After that, I'll be over to help you in the clinic."

BETWEEN PATIENTS, CARRIE DECIDED TO CHECK on Peta, her caesarean patient, and the new baby. Both were scheduled to be released today. When Carrie popped her head behind the curtain, she saw Peta sitting in a chair, nursing the tiny newborn swaddled in a pink flannel blanket.

"May I see this beautiful little girl?" Carrie asked.

Peta looked up at Carrie and smiled as she stroked her daughter's forehead. "She is a good baby."

"She's so pretty! Are you feeling better now?" She picked up her patient's chart and reviewed it, noting that Peta's blood pressure was in a healthy range and that she was progressing nicely after the surgery. "Dr. Holden and I had to hurry up and bring this little one into the world. But everything looks fine. What's your baby's name?"

"KoKo," Peta said, switching the baby to the other side to nurse. "It is my mother's name. This is my first girl."

Carrie stood by, observing as the baby latched on. Peta was clearly an old pro. "I'm glad you're doing so well with breastfeeding. That will help her a lot, and you, too. Is there anything I can get for you before I go? Are you in any pain?

Peta shook her head no. Then she raised her eyes to Carrie's. "Medicine Owl said you make good medicine—you and the other doctor who gave me KoKo."

"Medicine Owl?" Carrie did not know anyone by this name, and then realized that Peta was talking about the medicine woman. Her stomach flipped with excitement.

"Medicine Owl tells my sister that you and the other doctor, the curly-haired man, belong here with the people."

Carrie was overwhelmed with surprise, gratitude, and pure joy. "Thank you for telling me. I haven't met Medicine Owl yet, but I want to." She couldn't wait to tell Gran about this extraordinary compliment. "My grandmother is a medicine woman, too."

"She taught you how to make good medicine."

"Yes, she did." Carrie smiled. "She taught me everything that matters."

Chapter Seven

‑‑\|/‑‑

ON A GORGEOUS FRIDAY EVENING IN mid-July, with most of the medical corps volunteers and their families in town and Indian Days in full swing, Carrie accompanied Dr. Jim and Lois to the powwow grounds to watch competitive dancing. The sacred campground was the hub of Indian Days, featuring a small stadium and bleachers. Over the loudspeaker, the voice of the announcer could be heard, introducing each event.

They walked around the festival, stopping to look at booths selling trinkets, jewelry, leather garments, and other carnival fare. As they entered the stadium, Carrie saw Nate sitting on one of the bleachers. It was the first time she had seen him in anything other than scrubs and sporting two days' growth of beard. Tonight he looked dashing in dark navy jeans and a white dress shirt open at the neck. Although she found Tom attractive and sexy, Carrie's first thought upon seeing Nate was that he was the most handsome man she had ever seen. With his light-brown curls, show-stopping blue eyes, and muscular physique, he could have been an actor playing the part of a television surgeon.

"Carrie, over here!" Nate's face lit up when he saw her. He beckoned her to join him on the bench. Dr. Jim and Lois stopped to talk with a group of volunteers, leaving Carrie and Nate alone.

"I'm not used to seeing you in anything other than scrubs," she said. "I almost didn't recognize you."

"You clean up well, too," he said with a grin. "Did your fiancé leave already?"

She grew quiet. "He was just here for the weekend."

"So, is he okay with you staying here for a year?"

"No," she said without hesitation. "But there's a long line of people not happy with me over that decision. My father is mad that I didn't start working in his practice like he expected me to. My mother is just now able to speak to me without crying. The truth is Tom came here to talk some sense into me. It just happened to sound more like an ultimatum."

"That bad?" Nate looked at her. "They should be proud of you." He smiled. "I am."

"Thanks." She smiled back. "My grandmother is proud of me, but that's a story for another time. The bottom line is that I made a choice that may end up ruining my life—or so I'm told. My father may never speak to me again, and my fiancé is telling me I have a decision to make, and we know what that is."

"Hmm. If it's any comfort, my mother still cries on holidays when I see her. And my fiancée, Marisa, broke up with me over my coming here. Hindsight being twenty-twenty, I think it was probably for the best. She would've hated these long hours. I'm doing far more surgeries here than I ever did back home."

"I bet. You probably see a lot of broken bones from falling off horses … or cliffs."

"You'd be amazed how many gunshot and knife wounds I get." He shook his head. "I also see my fair share of limbs that need to be removed—complications of diabetes, stuff like that. Tumors, bowel resections, bypasses, what have you. It keeps me on my toes and staying abreast of the newest techniques. If I were in a bigger hospital, I wouldn't get to do as many different procedures. It's great to be able to use everything I've been taught."

"I think so, too." Carrie and Nate exchanged smiles of understanding. "I hope you'll call on me again some time to assist. I enjoyed my surgical rotations."

"You bet. Hey, do you want to walk around a little?"

They strolled over to join Dr. Jim and Lois in an area where Blackfeet competitive dancers were lining up behind their chief and the governor of Montana. Dancers of all ages stood solemnly in line for their turn to proceed into the inner circle. Some of the men wore long-feathered headdresses. Everyone was decked out in brightly colored costumes, beads, and moccasins. As the drumming began, Carrie felt each beat in her chest, thumping in perfect rhythm with her heart. Members of the medical corps were thrilled by the invitation to walk with the tribal members.

"It *all* has a deeper meaning, doesn't it?" she asked Dr. Jim in a low voice as she and Nate joined the volunteers in line to go into the inner circle. "What they wear, what they sing, the dance steps, even the number of feathers *means* something. I can't get enough."

"Sometimes I forget to breathe." Dr. Jim saw the chief and raised his hand in greeting. The chief wore traditional leather garb with a long-feathered headdress and mirrored sunglasses—the only accessory that indicated he lived in this century.

"As dry as it's been, I wonder if they'll do a rain dance tonight," Lois said in a hopeful voice.

The aggrieved look on Dr. Jim's face made Carrie laugh. "If they do, our hike to Iceberg Lake could get rained out," he said and glanced over at Carrie. "You think I'm kidding?"

As the evening wore on, the Blackfeet performed a variety of traditional and elaborate "fancy dances." The fancy dances, Carrie knew, were created after the Indians' traditional religious dances had been banned. The symbolic meanings of the dances were veiled, a way for the Indians to maintain their beliefs and practices without raising undue suspicion.

These ceremonial dances, so different from the silent worship of her family's Quaker faith, fascinated her. In the Quakers' austere meeting house, congregants sat quietly, contemplating their connection with the Divine. No one spoke unless spontaneously led to share an insight. Everything about the Blackfeet ceremonies was colorful and full of sound. Carrie was mesmerized by the drumbeats and songs, flowing dance movements, and the display of brightly colored clothes, beads, and long-feathered headdresses.

She had read in a Montana guidebook that feathers play a significant role in Native American spirituality, expressing the idea that divine life exists in all living things, including birds, animals, and plants—even in the essential elements of rocks and gemstones. But it was the singing and drumming that fascinated her most—human voices and drumbeats that communicated ancient stories and deeply held beliefs. When she heard these drums, she could easily let herself go into what she could only describe as a different state of consciousness. Through these songs and dances, the Indians were divinely inspired to give voice to their beliefs, just as the Quakers did in their meeting houses.

Dr. Jim was well versed in Blackfeet lore. "Indians didn't readily accept Christian dogma," he explained to her in a low voice. "The church did everything possible to try to take away their spiritual practices. The fancy dances were the result of the Indians' determination to keep their traditions alive."

"Blackfeet spirits can't be broken," Carrie said.

She remembered one of John Leathers' stories that underscored the cruel treatment Indians had endured. In days past, Catholic priests removed Indian children from the reservation and forced them into boarding schools, determined to make proper Christians out of them. "The children were disciplined harshly and their hair was cut off—a sign in the Native American tradition that their parents were dead."

Although Dr. Jim and Lois were staunch Catholics, they were upset by this aspect of Indian history. "The church hasn't always followed its own teachings," Lois stated in her most tactful manner. "Frankly, that story makes me mad."

Yet through it all, the Blackfeet retained their dignity and sense of identity and pride. Carrie found this a wonder, given what she saw as atrocious treatment at the hands of the U.S. government and the Cavalry. Even after treaties were signed, solemn promises made to the Indians had not been fulfilled. It was the Blackfeet people's resilience, their insistence on maintaining the tenets of their culture, that allowed their Nation to survive. Now she hoped with all her heart that, even if it was just for the next year, she might play a small role in helping the people lead healthier lives.

After snapping photos of Blackfeet women in ceremonial garb, she replaced her cell phone in her purse and looked across the inner circle. John Leathers was there with an older, scruffier man. She waved and received a nod in response.

While the drummers and dancers took a break, Carrie and Nate walked with the others over to where John stood. The older Blackfeet man next to him was intoxicated, alcohol fumes permeating the air. John's girlfriend, Gali, was nowhere in sight. Carrie was disappointed. She had hoped to meet her during Indian Days.

John said, "This is my brother, Mike."

Carrie's trained eyes took in Mike's overall physical condition, noting signs of malnutrition in addition to alcoholism. Without a word, Mike turned and shuffled off, his gait unsteady. No one spoke for a moment, watching him weave his way out of the stadium.

John's dark eyes followed his brother's departure with an expression Carrie couldn't quite decipher. There was a lengthy silence before he asked, "Will you be on the hike tomorrow? Dr. Jim asked me to be the guide."

Carrie's face brightened. "I wouldn't miss it for anything—well, other than work. Nate, what about you?"

"I'm on call in the ER tomorrow," he said. "I'd sure like to go with you guys. Have fun. Oh, and take bear spray with you."

"I'll be sure to do that," she said, flashing a quick grin. "Do you suppose it's like an umbrella? If you carry a canister of bear spray, you're less likely to need it?"

Nate laughed. "Chances are good that you won't run into any bears. But from what I've seen, it's better to err on the side of caution."

"Says the surgeon who sews people together again," Dr. Jim remarked. "Don't take chances."

Carrie smiled. "I'll remember that. But I'm sure I'd set a new land speed record if I did see one."

"Don't make the mistake of thinking you can make a run for it," John warned, his expression stern. "Animals are always faster than you are."

"Not to frighten you unnecessarily, but there are grizzlies, mountain lions, wolves, badgers, and even wolverines close by," Dr. Jim pointed out. "It isn't unusual to find, um, evidence of their visits."

"I learned quickly not to put food on the porch in the wintertime to keep it cold," Lois added. "It's like inviting a critter to dinner. The first year we were in the house, I learned that the hard way. My refrigerator was full so I put my beef tenderloin outside. It quickly disappeared."

Carrie nodded. "Good to know for after you're gone. Although I don't cook. I mean at all. If they were foraging around my place, the local wildlife would find me a disappointment."

"Before Jim and I leave to go home to Kansas City, I'll fill the freezer," Lois said. "There's plenty of pasta and canned goods in the pantry." She looked meaningfully at Nate. "Perhaps you could show Carrie some of those gourmet cooking and grilling skills I've heard so much about."

"Sure thing. We need doctors too bad to lose one to starvation."

"Very funny," Carrie said. "I'm not that clueless."

After eighteen hours of sunlight, the day was coming to an end at ten o'clock. Her eyes took in the tranquil reddish-orange glow of the setting sun over the mountains, a scene that normally brought a sense of serenity and well-being. She loved that it stayed light so late into the evening. But tonight, the sight of the glowing sunset brought no peace. Her gut was telling her that her life was taking another sharp twist.

Lois yawned. "I'm getting sleepy. Carrie, if you're not ready to go back yet, maybe Nate could drop you off later."

They heard a buzz coming from Nate's pager. He glanced at it and frowned. "My fun is over for tonight." His eyes met Carrie's. "It was good to see you. Enjoy the hike tomorrow."

"I will. See you at the hospital." She watched his retreating figure, thinking that he reminded her of someone.

"He works so hard," Lois said. "I worry about him being alone here."

She heaved a deep sigh and shot Carrie a meaningful look. "His fiancée, Marisa, was a spoiled brat, in my opinion. Nate had a valid reason for coming here. Sometimes things happen, and people need to make sacrifices for the ones they love. Marisa refused to give an inch. That's no way to start a life together."

Chapter Eight

—⁂—

WHEN CARRIE OPENED HER EYES THE following morning, bright sunshine was seeping through the slats of the mini-blinds in her room, promising another gorgeous Saturday. Today, the volunteers were taking a ten-mile hike to Iceberg Lake—five miles over and five miles back. The hike was anything but easy, even for experienced hikers. Iceberg Lake, an alpine lake fed by mountain streams, was encircled by thousands of acres of forests, mountains, and glaciers. Snow lay on the ground year-round and perpetual ice floes dotted the lake's spectacular turquoise-green surface. She had heard that brave visitors occasionally attempted a swim in the lake, but most got out as fast as their feet touched the bone-chilling water.

After a shower, she brewed a cup of tea while standing at the kitchen sink, surveying the vast land behind the house. Four horses galloped across the prairie, their manes flying in the wind, legs moving so fast, they were a blur. As stunning as she found the sight just outside her kitchen window, it was also unsettling, as if she had just taken a step back in time.

She glanced at her iPhone, seeking some kind of reassurance that she hadn't just time-traveled. She saw her mother on the recent call list and quickly touched the number, looking forward to hearing her mother's voice.

"Hi, Mom. Somehow I missed your call. I must have been in the shower."

"I was just thinking about you," Lynne said. They chatted for a few minutes about weather and activities there. "By the way, Tom came over for dinner last night. He told us all about his trip to see you. I must say, from the sound of things, you're practically working in one of those M.A.S.H. units."

"Hardly," Carrie said. She frowned, wondering what else Tom had told them. It irked her that he had direct access to her father. Where Tom was concerned, everything was fine with her father.

Her mother was silent for a moment. "We'll take good care of him until you come home."

"He's a big boy, Mom. How is he doing with the house?"

"Fine. We sent some furniture over to help fill up the rooms. Of course, when you get back, you'll want to put your stamp on the place." She paused, waiting for a response.

"Mom …" Carrie began, then stopped. She doubted her mother knew that Tom had issued an ultimatum. "He made it clear what he expects me to do. He's put me between a rock and a hard place. Please do not pretend that all is well."

"He's being a man, Carrie. Men always have to growl a little bit. It's part of their genetic makeup."

"Mom, this is more than a little growling. He wants me to come home now."

"He'll start working with your dad in a few weeks. That will keep him busy. Before he knows it, you'll be home for the holidays."

"Maybe. We'll see what the weather brings. I can't promise that."

"I think Tom hero-worships your dad. He's the son your father never had. That's why they get along so well."

"And I don't hero-worship him? I've always looked up to Dad."

"You know what I mean. It's a guy thing."

"Maybe it's because Tom is a lot like Dad," Carrie said, not intending it as a compliment.

"As soon as you get back, you and Tom can make plans and put your lives back on track," her mother said before changing the subject. "Are you keeping up with your running? Make sure you're eating properly. Do they have grocery stores there?"

"I can probably shoot most of the protein I need." Carrie rolled her eyes. "Come on, Mother. We have two real grocery stores here."

"Don't make fun of me," her mother said with an easy laugh. "I may be thousands of miles away, but I'm still your mother. I'm glad you have a nice place to live."

"The Millers have a beautiful home. The truth is, I've loved every minute of every day I've spent here," Carrie said. "I'll miss it when I have to go."

There was another long silence. "We all miss you. Gran and I talk about you every day."

At the sound of Gran's name, Carrie's nose itched, a sure sign she was near tears. "I just got an email from her. How's her hip?"

"She's still limping around. She acts as if it's nothing, of course."

"I wish she had let me give her a treatment when I was there the last time." Gran hadn't wanted to focus on her own health while Carrie was visiting. She swallowed the lump in her throat. "I need to get going. Love you, Mom."

"I love you to the moon and back, sweetheart," Lynne said.

Carrie's eyes welled up. It was her mother's favorite way to say good night or goodbye. She wiped her eyes with the hem of her tee shirt and glanced at the clock on the kitchen wall. John would be here soon. He had offered to drive her to the lodge, where the volunteers were carpooling to the hiking site. She put on a two-piece bathing suit under jeans and a tee shirt and applied a liberal coating of sunscreen. Stepping into her hiking shoes at the bottom of the stairs, she opened the front door. John's black Jeep was parked in the driveway.

"Hi," she said as he lowered the driver's side window. "Lois is fixing all three of us lunches to take on the hike. Thanks again for going with us. I'm sure you have better things to do than supervise a bunch of out-of-shape hikers."

"It's a nice walk up to Iceberg Lake. When we finally get there, the water will feel good."

"I thought it was freezing."

"You'll have to get in and see for yourself."

As they drove to the lodge to meet up with Dr. Jim and the other volunteers, she said, "It was nice to meet your brother last evening. I would've guessed he was your brother. There's a resemblance."

"Mike was not in any condition to be introduced to anyone," John said after a moment.

"Is he much older than you?"

Mike had looked to be at least ten years older than John. Carrie knew alcoholics generally had other health issues in addition to their addiction. As she stared ahead at the road, she watched John's profile out of her peripheral vision. His expression didn't change, although his hands tightened on the steering wheel.

"Mike is two years older. He's been like this since he was a kid. Being a doctor, you can surely see that he's killing himself."

"You've never said anything about a brother before. I only knew you had a sister."

"There's not much to say. My parents tried to get him to stay in school, but he dropped out sophomore year. If he hadn't, he probably would have been expelled." John shrugged. "He is unemployed and living with some of his friends on the rez. I don't see him that often." He let out a long breath. "I was sorry to see him last night."

"If I can do anything to help, I'd be glad to," Carrie said and stopped. It was up to the alcoholic to stop drinking. It also was none of her business, unless Mike was her patient. Depending on what he was drinking, he might already have irreversible organ damage.

"The way things are going, it's only a matter of time. My parents need to prepare for the worst."

John parked in front of Glacier Park Lodge, a historic hotel that was a favorite of volunteers and their families. Dr. Jim was in the lobby with a clipboard, trying to corral the rowdy group that included a dozen doctors and at least twenty-five construction volunteers who were helping with renovation projects on the reservation. Wives and children of the doctors often helped out on the construction crew.

Seeing Carrie and John, Dr. Jim said, "Glad you're here. We're about ready to leave. Did Lois send a sandwich for me, I hope?"

"Oh, was that one yours?"

The forlorn look on Dr. Jim's face brought an immediate apology to her lips. "I'm sorry. I couldn't resist. She made your favorite—peanut butter and banana."

Dr. Jim playfully yanked Carrie's braid. "Okay, smart-aleck, let's go. You're in charge of supplies."

He got into the front seat of John's car, leaving Carrie to sit in back with two cases of bottled water, a tarp, and the first-aid kit. John's car led the volunteer caravan. Along the way, they passed acres of burned trees—the result of the last wildfire.

"I knew that fire was terrible, but this is way worse than I thought." Carrie took in a sharp breath. Television news footage didn't do the devastation justice.

"This has been another bad fire season." John removed his sunglasses, surveying the scene as they drove. "Active fires are getting more frequent and severe."

"How big of a factor is weather?" Carrie asked, looking in dismay at the trees, blackened like burnt matchsticks. "Not enough rain means more fires, right?"

"Climate change and weather both have a role in the number of fires and how long and fast they burn." John raked his lower teeth over his upper lip.

Dr. Jim shook his head. "People can debate climate change until the cows come home, but here, you can see the consequences. More forest fires and fewer glaciers left. The proof is right here in this park. Carrie, when this fire was burning, it jumped from one side of the highway to the other. The road wasn't closed. Lois and I were driving home from having dinner with friends in St. Mary. We could feel the heat of the fire through the car. There was no other way to get home."

After a moment of silence, John said, "When things are as dry as this, people don't realize they can't idle their vehicles over dry grass. Just like that, a spark can start a fire and wipe out thousands of acres. It doesn't take much to kill an entire forest."

"I know a lot of Blackfeet men have to fight the wildfires. Do they get called out a lot?" Carrie asked.

"They don't just fight fires on the reservation. They get called out to fight fires all over the Northwest. It's dangerous, but at least it's paid work." John's expression was grim. "My father was a firefighter before he began painting full-time. Painting is safer."

When they arrived at the trailhead, Carrie handed out extra bottles of water to all the hikers. After checking her backpack to make sure she had insect *and* bear spray, as well as plenty of sunscreen, she zipped up her light jacket. It was noticeably cooler at this altitude, and the clouds overhead were heavy with precipitation. The ground was wet from an earlier shower. She bit her lip, remembering the rain dance from the night before. *Works like a charm.*

It was a five-mile hike up the mountain—challenging even for the teenagers and experienced hikers in the group. The first ten minutes were brutal—a steep uphill ascent over rocks that were sharp and unevenly spaced. The trail leveled off after a quarter mile, but there was still a significant grade. Even though she was in good shape, the altitude caused Carrie to feel breathless. She was careful to drink water and to loosen her jacket when the sun came out. Even when the terrain made it tough going, the view was breathtaking everywhere she looked. Keeping this group together would be a chore. People were stopping every few yards to take photos.

Two hours in, the hikers stopped to rest at a large flat rock overlooking a waterfall and fast-moving stream. Friendly ground squirrels investigated their backpacks, hoping for handouts. As Carrie and John sat together on the edge of the rock, she gazed out over the waterfall, enjoying the soothing sound of the rushing water. After a rest, they trudged on, stopping now and then to take more photos and catch their breath.

After what seemed an eternity for the tired hikers, they reached Iceberg Lake, a magnificent expanse of blue-green more like turquoise glass than water. Even this late in the summer, crusty snow lay on the ground, shin-high in places. The mountainside adjacent to the lake was covered in snow.

Chunks of glacial ice dotted the surface of the lake, a microcosm of the panoramic grandeur of glacier days gone by. The view was so pristine, so pure, that Carrie sent up a silent prayer for the future of the glaciers. If, as John had told the hikers, only a fraction of the original glaciers remained from the time that Glacier National Park was founded in 1910, there was good reason to worry that they could all disappear. The prospect filled her with dread and sadness. What would Glacier National Park be without glaciers?

She had little doubt, however, that climate change or not, the temperature of Alpine Lake was barely above freezing. She stared in dismay at the ice on the lake. She was hot and tired, and had looked forward to wading by the shoreline. One look at the surface of the lake was enough to convince her it wasn't a good idea. Icy water lapped at her feet along the shoreline. She squatted, running her fingers back and forth through the water until they ached. John dipped his hand in the water and flicked some at her.

"I guess we can't swim, after all," she said.

"Sure we can." John squinted at her in the intense sunlight. "We can wade around until you get used to it. It is warmer in the shallow areas."

"Warmer, you say? Ha!" Carrie laughed. "John, I don't think I .... Wait, what are you doing?"

"Race you to the other side." John grinned and waded into the water up to his knees, motioning for her to join him. "It feels great."

"I'll take your word for it." Carrie watched anxiously as he walked farther into the icy water. "Is there another warmer lake where we can swim?" she asked. "Um ... like someplace else?"

"This is it." His grin was a mile wide. "This is the cleanest water in the world! The first plunge takes your breath away, but you'll get used to it."

"John, we aren't polar bears. This water is cold enough to stop someone's heart. I don't want to have to do CPR on you."

"You think I'm a little crazy?"

"A little." John's playful side was amusing, but she still didn't think it was a good idea. "I'll just stay here on dry land in case you need medical attention—assuming you survive, that is."

John moved swiftly from the shallow rocky area into the water and dove in, swimming with powerful strokes until he reached the glacier. He held up one hand in a victory salute. As she watched him swim back to shore, Carrie rubbed her cold arms, thinking the air temperature was dropping by the minute. From dry land, the other hikers cheered him on. John swam back to shore much faster this time while Carrie watched his every move. What if he hit a hidden piece of ice and struck his head?

She stood on the shore, calculating the amount of time it took for a person to go into shock in water this cold. She glanced over at Dr. Jim, who was laughing and cheering along with the rest of the group. He walked over to her and put an arm around her shoulders.

"Don't worry," he said. "The Blackfeet come from tougher stock than we do."

As John got to his feet and made his way out of the water, she handed him a towel. "That was quite a feat."

"Nothing to it," he said, towel-drying his hair. He shook off water droplets like a bear shedding water from its thick coat. "The water felt good." He hopped from one foot to the other as he wrapped the towel around his shoulders. His clothing was soaked.

She shook her head in a mock reprimand. "Human beings aren't intended to be in water that cold."

"I have been swimming in lakes like these all my life," he said, smiling at her. "You worry too much."

Carrie began pulling lunch items out of the sack Lois had packed for them. "I guess it's true that medical people always imagine the worst. I once treated a guy who nearly drowned after falling through thin ice on a pond. That was an accident. You went into icy water on purpose. Who *does* that?"

John assumed a stance of warrior power and threw back his head, laughing. "The Blackfeet!"

After a break for lunch, the hikers began the five-mile downhill descent to the park entrance and their cars. John and Carrie kept to the rear of the group this time, making certain no one got left behind. A few of the volunteers had developed blisters and were showing signs of exhaustion. As the group descended the mountain, Carrie decided to ask John the question that had been on her mind two nights ago.

"I hope you don't think I'm butting into your business. Do you suppose you and Gali can ever be together openly?"

John walked along for about a minute before responding. "I hope so."

"But you're not with her this weekend."

"I will see her tomorrow. I go to Heart Butte as often as I can." He held out his hand to help her over a patch of rough rocks.

"She wasn't with you the other night at the campground," Carrie persisted.

"She came here for Indian Days last year, but it did not go as well as we hoped with my family. This year, she stayed away."

"I like her name, Gali. Is it a nickname?"

"It's short for Galilahi. The name means 'beautiful.' " John walked a few steps ahead of her, checking the path and kicking away loose rocks.

Carrie repeated the name slowly. "It's lovely. You've said before that your parents would prefer that you marry a Blackfeet woman. What if you insist on marrying Gali? Do you think your family could eventually learn to love her? And if you had children, what grandma or grandpa can resist a grandchild?"

"You don't understand," he said, with an edge to his voice. "This is nothing personal against Gali. She would likely never be accepted fully on the reservation, and that means our children wouldn't be, either. Of course, my mother would love grandchildren. But this is a reservation. The children who are not full-blooded will always be outsiders. That is what concerns my grandfather."

Carrie walked along in silence. It was difficult for people of different races to marry, no matter where they lived, it seemed. Judgments based on skin color, nationality, and religion seemed a part of human nature. "You've said there is another woman your mother prefers."

"My mother wants me to marry Naomi Prairie Hen, her friend's daughter. There you have it. It doesn't matter what I want." John shrugged. "I've thought long and hard about marrying Naomi Prairie Hen, but it would be a marriage of duty, not love. I will always want Gali."

Carrie was silent for the next mile, thinking that she was not the only one whose parents had different views of what their children should do, who they should marry, and where they ought to live. Somehow, she didn't feel quite so alone now with the events transpiring in her life.

Chapter Nine

⁓\⎮⁓

IT WAS NEARING FIVE O'CLOCK WHEN John dropped the two exhausted doctors off at home. As Carrie and Dr. Jim dragged themselves up the front steps, they found Lois on the porch swing cross-stitching a holiday dishtowel. Annie snoozed at her feet. Lois looked up, taking in their bedraggled state.

"Hail to the alpine climbers. Yodelayheehoo! You two look done in," she said. "I say we're all three going over to the lodge for dinner tonight." She accepted a kiss from her tired, sweaty husband. "Jim, after hiking ten miles, you have my permission to eat whatever you want."

Easing herself onto the top step with a moan, Carrie hugged Annie, burying her face in the soft fur on her neck. "Were you a good girl?" she asked and received a sloppy kiss in response. She looked over at Dr. Jim. "She was able to go outside by herself when we lived in Minnesota. There was a doggie door on our rental house."

He stretched out his long legs and leaned back, closing his eyes. "If I thought it was a good idea to have a doggy door in these parts, I'd install one. But you might come home to a critter in the kitchen that looks nothing like Annie." He yawned. "Doggie doors aren't a good idea in a national park."

"We'll figure out something," Carrie promised Annie. She stood up and headed down the steps, Annie close behind. "I think I'll walk around the back with her—let her roam a little."

While Annie sniffed to her heart's content, Carrie investigated the indigenous plants around the house. She recognized bear grass, a plant John had told them got its name after an explorer saw bears tumbling around in a patch. In reality, the bears had no particular fondness for the stuff. There was bee balm, also called wild oregano; Echinacea, a more common flower used to combat colds and flu; and other flowering plants she vaguely recognized and suspected had medicinal value. She just needed to figure out what they were. She took photos with her phone so she could compare them to the pictures in the book Gran had given her.

Annie stayed close at Carrie's heels as they circled the perimeter of the house. Then Annie growled, baring her teeth. She nudged Carrie's leg hard, herding her back toward the porch.

"What's the matter?"

Carrie froze in place, her heart thumping in fear. In the field, about two hundred yards from where they stood, she saw what appeared to be a large gray dog crouched in the grass, its pointed ears visible. In an instant, she realized it was a wolf. The fur on Annie's neck stood on end, and she growled again, a low warning sound. Carrie reached down and held tightly to Annie's collar.

"Annie, stay!"

It took all her strength to lead Annie by her collar up the back steps into the house. It had been a close call. Even in the backyard, Annie would need to be on a retractable leash in the future.

Dr. Jim was in his favorite easy chair with his feet up, a beer in his hand, when Carrie and Annie came into the house. She poured fresh water for Annie and joined Dr. Jim and Lois in the living room. The fear she had felt seeing the wolf was gone, replaced now by curiosity. Safe or not, she wanted another look.

"I poured you an iced tea," Lois said.

"I think I just saw a wolf," Carrie said, reaching for her glass.

"It's possible." Dr. Jim stood up with difficulty from his chair and went to the living room window, peering outside. "You sure did. I see it from here."

"What did Annie do?" Lois asked.

"I grabbed her collar too fast for her to take off after it."

"You'll need to keep a tight rein on her when you're outside, especially if she likes to run." Dr. Jim held out his arm toward Annie, who settled at his feet.

"I was hoping she could play outside. But with all the stray dogs and now a wolf …." She turned over in her mind ideas of how to protect Annie. There would be no unsupervised time outside, not now, not ever. She resolved to get advice from John about coexisting with wolves and to learn more about their habits in the wild.

"Are you joining us for dinner tonight at the lodge?" Dr. Jim asked. "We're leaving in a few minutes."

"I need to shower first. You guys go ahead. I'll join you in a bit." She wanted to go back outside and see if the wolf was still there.

After her shower, she walked outside—this time without Annie—intent on seeing if the wolf was still in the field behind the house. The animal was even closer than before. Her breath quickened as she backed slowly away, watching the animal. They studied each other from a distance. In their backyard in Pennsylvania, Carrie had once surprised a red fox that scurried off into an adjoining field. But this was Montana, a land that was still considered America's frontier. In Glacier National Park, species roamed free in their natural habitat. It was people, not animals, who were out of place here.

She stood transfixed. She had never seen a wolf this close. It was still watching her, and yes, she could see that its face was a silvery color, meaning that it was an older animal. She shivered, but with excitement rather than fear. Was it possible? Could it be the wolf from her dream?

ON SUNDAY MORNING, CARRIE RAN INTO Nate at the hospital while she checked on a few of her patients who had been admitted. The ER was even busier than usual. Festivals tended to cause an increase in illnesses and injuries, some severe. This year was no different. She saw the tension in Nate's shoulders and the strained expression on his face as he hunched over, reviewing patient notes on a surgical case.

"Good morning," she said softly, not wanting to startle him.

"Hi." He turned and offered her a watered-down version of his usual smile. "How was the hike? You don't look any worse for wear."

"It was spectacular. You've got to go sometime. Dr. Jim is moving pretty slow today. To be honest, I could hardly get out of bed this morning."

Nate smiled and leaned against a counter. "Can you stick around a little while? I've got a hot appendix to remove, and someone needs to check on the kid in that room over there. He's got a belly ache, but I think it was just the three corn dogs he ate."

"Sure thing. My schedule's light today. Your only trouble is you need to grow another set of hands."

He shrugged. "It's the nature of what I do."

Carrie smiled. "When do you get an entire day off?"

"As a matter of fact, I have next Saturday off. I wondered if you'd like to come over for dinner. I'll throw a couple of steaks on the grill."

"I'd like that. I'll throw something made by someone else into a bag and bring it." She batted her eyes.

He erupted in a laugh. "You really can't cook, can you?"

"Nope." Carrie took in Nate's overall appearance, liking what she saw.

As his eyes met hers, she brushed a wisp of hair away, feeling slightly off balance. He had the most extraordinary eyes, the color of sapphires, full of intelligence and warmth, with just a hint of mischief. She had never seen eyelashes that long on any man. She caught sight of a tuft of golden chest hair peeking above the V-neck of his scrub top and felt her face grow warm.

They stood together for a moment without speaking. When the silence became awkward for her, she said, "Okay, well, thanks again for the dinner invitation. I'm looking forward to spending more time with you." Her cheeks flamed. "I mean, away from the hospital. Like at the festival. The other night."

"Same here. It'll be fun." There was a buzz. Nate glanced at his pager and frowned. "Okay, okay, I'm coming." He offered her a quick smile. "See you around."

She was glad he had invited her to dinner. She needed to cultivate friendships here or it could be a long, lonely year. She and Tom had always had friends of the opposite sex. It would be okay to have dinner with Nate. There was a ping on her cell phone that caused her to jump. Glancing at it, she saw a text message from Tom. *Haven't heard back from you yet.*

Carrie texted, *At work. Talk to you later.* To lighten the tone of her message, she added *XOXOXO*

He replied, *Heading outside to mow the grass. This house is a lot for one person to take care of. Hope you're having fun.*

She bit her lip and considered calling him. But what would be the point, other than to offer moral support? It wasn't like she was in any position to help with the house. He had brought this on himself, but that didn't mean she didn't feel sympathy—or guilt. Of course that was the point of his text. She did not feel good about the course of their relationship.

She called him as soon as she left the hospital, but he didn't answer. He didn't return her call that evening, either, although he texted again to say he was going out to dinner with her parents at the club and would talk with her later. She went to bed that night with a heavy heart.

Their last phone conversation was replaying over and over in her head. After listening to her talk about her day, he had made a sarcastic comment.

She took a deep breath and said, "Tom?"

"Yeah?"

"I feel like we're not really talking. You're making jokes, and all I hear in your tone is contempt for what I'm doing. It hurts me. I don't want this to drive a wedge between us."

"Whose fault is that? Not mine," he snapped. "You're, like, twenty-three hundred miles away. That's your choice, by the way."

"I don't mean that we're not together in the same place. I mean we're not connecting the way we did before. You never ask me questions about my work."

"I care about you. That's all that matters."

A stunned, sick feeling settled over Carrie. "Do you, Tom? I'm completely invested in knowing what you're doing. I want to share this experience with you, too. I'm working really hard to help these people. It's so fulfilling .... The least you could do is act interested. Because I think if you did care about me, you'd be interested in what's important to me, too."

"Carrie, you need to realize that what you're doing for these Indians means nothing in the long run for them. They have existed for hundreds of years without you. They'll still be there when you go. You're not Mother Teresa, you know. You're not going to save them."

A tear seeped out of the corner of Carrie's eye and trailed down her cheek, dripping from her chin onto her scrub top. "Tom, I know that I can't *save* them. I *am* helping them as their doctor. I'm learning more about their ways so I can do more to help them in the future."

"And then what?"

"I'll want to continue as a volunteer, helping Dr. Jim arrange the medical corps each year, coming back to the reservation for a week or two in the summers. You don't have to come with me, if you don't want to. I won't ask that of you."

"We're getting married. What about what I ask of you? You'd go to Montana without consulting me when we're married? Is that what you're saying?"

"Not without consulting you? Of course, I'd consult you. We could make it work by planning ahead."

"And what if I said I didn't want you to go? Would you go, anyway?"

"Tom, since when did my work in Browning become such a difficult situation? I want to understand why you object. How can we compromise on this issue?" She kept her tone reasonable, speaking in a quiet voice. "This is important to my career. If this kind of professional opportunity came along for you, I would understand, and I'd want to help and support you."

"The way you're helping and supporting me now?" Tom's voice was clipped and cold. "I've got stuff to do here—stuff I'm doing all by myself while you're out there doing what? I'm not sure what it all entails as far as being a doctor."

She took in a ragged breath. "Your attitude is uncalled for, Tom. I think maybe we're done talking for tonight."

"For once, I agree with you." Tom hung up.

Thoughts of the future, once so exciting, now caused her stomach to drop. This heavy feeling was familiar. A few times in the past she'd faced situations or people that called for her to be wary or to detour. Never had it hit with such sickening force. She couldn't ignore the signs her body was giving her. She shook her head, willing the uncomfortable thoughts to go away. It was common to have cold feet before getting married, wasn't it? Marriage to Tom would be secure. They would have their careers in common. He would be a good father to their children. Why, then, was she so troubled?

* * *

"I ACTUALLY HAD TO LOOK AT the calendar to figure out what day it is," Carrie confessed to Peg on Friday morning.

The week had blown by at warp speed. Between her morning runs, hectic work days, and evening activities with the volunteers, her time was completely filled. The best part was that the visiting specialists had been able to see every patient. Although it was customary for doctors to spend an average of eight to ten minutes per patient, she had been able to invest much more time with some people this week, thanks to the volunteer physicians. From infants and toddlers to the elderly, the doctors saw patient after patient, many with conditions exacerbated by their poor diet and living conditions.

She listened attentively as patients described their symptoms, often in halting and scant detail. In some cases, they gestured or pointed toward the afflicted part of their body. In the process of diagnosing their illnesses, she often indirectly learned of their troubles, too.

In an email to Gran, she wrote,

> The past two weeks have been incredible. It's wonderful meeting these people, taking time to find out a little more about them and their families during visits. The Indians are quite matter-of-fact, even stoic, about illness or the severity of injuries. They tell me they haven't felt well or have been in pain for days or even weeks. What worries me is that, in addition to transportation challenges or a lack of knowledge or understanding about their conditions, patients take dangerous chances when they delay coming to the clinic. The need is so great here for physicians. I'll feel guilty when I have to leave them.

It was the relationship-building process of caring for people that was the best part of being a family physician. From Gran and her father, she knew that relationships developed over many years and across generations so that long-time patients became lifelong friends. This wonderfully intimate doctor-patient relationship would surely enhance her life as much as it did the lives of her patients.

As usual, patients continued to be late for appointments, causing predictable back-ups in the schedule. She got interrupted often—sometimes in the middle of the night—to deliver babies, a duty she embraced as a privilege. As she brought the most recent newborn, a healthy boy, into the world and handed him to his young mother, her heart filled with joy. This job was everything she had ever dreamed it could be—and more. Although she was accustomed as a hospital resident to working at breakneck speed and without much sleep, she realized that she was being challenged in entirely new ways. Each unexpected complication forced her to be flexible, changing course in an instant to tackle the situation at hand.

"Why didn't that patient go directly to the emergency room?" she asked Peg when she entered an exam room and found that her next patient, a middle-aged woman in excruciating pain, had suffered three smashed fingers when her grandson accidentally slammed a metal screen door on her hand. To make matters worse, the injury was two days old.

Peg explained, "She couldn't get here because her husband wouldn't come home from Indian Days, and she couldn't leave the grandkids. Her husband finally came home and dropped her off in front of the hospital. The ER is busy right now, so they sent her over. I think she needs you, Dr. Carrie."

The stoic patient regarded her with grateful eyes. "I know it hurts," Carrie said in a soothing voice as she gently examined the torn and broken fingers. "I'll give you something right now for pain."

"Tell X-ray to hurry up with this one," Carrie told Peg. "She's lucky at least one of those fingers wasn't severed. I'd like Dr. Jim's orthopedic specialist to look at this before he leaves."

After Peg helped the woman into a wheelchair to transport her to X-ray, Carrie sat in silence in the examination room. She felt shaken at the level of pain she had just witnessed and the reality of the patient's helplessness, forced to cope with no transportation or backup child care.

The brave and long-suffering nature of the Blackfeet patients manifested itself in another way. Carrie noticed that all her patients waited patiently for their turn to see the doctor—an uncommon attitude in areas where medical care was more readily available. If someone needed help more than the patient next on the schedule, no one complained at having to wait a little longer. Not a single person tried to move ahead of someone else. Entire families arrived together, supporting their loved ones for as long as it took. She knew that patients experienced less stress when they had family members with them.

By the end of that week, she still hadn't had a chance to meet the medicine woman. She wondered if, when they finally met, Medicine Owl would be willing to share her tried-and-true remedies. Or would she consider them a tribal secret? Peg would be happy to accompany Carrie to see the medicine woman—but only after an invitation was extended.

"She will tell you when it's time," Peg said.

Carrie tried to bide her time and be patient. *This is Indian Time.* But she was only too aware of the amount of work necessary to complete her research project. She had started a narrative for her eventual outcomes report. She could only hope that she'd get to meet Medicine Owl soon.

THAT EVENING, SHE SAT ON THE back porch swing with a mug of chamomile tea, engrossed in the book Gran had sent her. She turned the brittle pages with care. The book was astonishing in its detail of plants, their care and uses, how to prepare them for ingestion or application, and potential side effects. She already knew that a medicine man or woman had a veritable pharmacy of natural remedies at their disposal to treat every condition. But the variety of plants used was nothing short of amazing. Lost in the text of the old book, she had no idea that an hour had passed when she looked up to find Dr. Jim coming up the steps.

"That book looks like a classic," he said, settling in beside her. He set the swing into motion with his foot. "How old is it, anyway?"

"It was originally published in 1898. This edition is from 1930, if I recall correctly. It's all about plant and herbal remedies. My grandmother gave it to me."

"I'd almost forgotten your grandmother is a medicine woman." Dr. Jim smiled as the sound of drums started up in the distance.

"I like that you called her that. She'd like it too."

They sat together in silence, listening to the captivating sound of drums in the distance. As she was transported to a deeper place, Carrie wondered whether she might someday understand the drummers' messages. Perhaps if she emptied her mind and listened intuitively. Being away from the Quaker meeting house for so many years had left her less able to sit in silence more than a few minutes. Yet the sensation of silent communion was familiar and enjoyable.

As she relaxed, enjoying the back and forth motion of the porch swing, the drumbeats became as meaningful to her as spoken words. If she opened her heart and embraced the silence, the message of the drumbeats was clear.

When she spoke, it felt like the 'amen' to a silent prayer. "The drums help me hear my own thoughts."

"I know what you mean." Dr. Jim let out a deep sigh of contentment. "This is the only spot in the world where I can relax and think."

"I don't think I've ever seen you relax." She laid her head on his shoulder. "When will you and Lois be back?"

"We'll be here for two weeks in mid-September, then not again until next June. We'll keep up that schedule until I retire in a few years. But even then, we'll continue to winter in Kansas City. If your bones ache in the cold and you're not able to participate in all the winter sports, this isn't the most comfortable place to be."

"I'll miss both of you." By this time next week, when all the volunteers went home, she and Annie would be left on their own for two months before they saw Dr. Jim and Lois again.

"I guarantee you'll be too busy at the hospital to even notice we're gone."

Dr. Jim leaned back on the swing and closed his eyes for a moment.

Carrie watched his face with concern before putting the book aside. She curled one leg under her on the swing. "Dr. Jim, is everything okay?"

"Of course," he said. "I'm just glad that everything is working out for you here. I feel better leaving the reservation this time."

"It'll be weird without you. You're *always* here when I'm here."

"You'll do fine. You're a natural at this."

"I don't know how I can ever thank you enough for introducing me to this place and for letting Annie and me stay at your home. Thanks for making this whole experience possible. I've decided that after my Roosevelt commitment is over, I want to come back at least a couple of times a year to help out."

Dr. Jim stared off into the rays of the setting sun for a moment. Then, patting her on the knee, he rose to his feet. Removing his glasses, he cleaned them on his shirt before answering. "You're a gift to these people," he said, his eyes growing moist. "I'm counting on you to carry on my work."

Chapter Ten

⸺✦⸺

A T FOUR O'CLOCK THE NEXT MORNING, Dr. Jim and Lois packed up their rented minivan for the two-hour drive back to Kalispell International Airport, about a hundred miles west of Browning. Carrie threw a blanket around her shoulders and went outside to see them off. As their vehicle rounded a curve and disappeared, she experienced a moment of fear so intense, she wanted to run after them. She breathed in and out until the panic subsided.

"It's just you and me now," she said, stroking Annie's head. "We'll be okay. I promise."

In the distance, a wolf let loose a ghostly howl, bringing Annie's ears to full attention. Like a shot, they scurried into the house, Carrie taking the stairs by twos. She launched herself back under the covers and motioned for Annie to join her under the heavy quilt. The dog burrowed far under the covers and settled on top of Carrie's feet to warm them.

The rest of the day was spent doing laundry and working around the house. She intended to keep the place shipshape while the Millers were gone. She had offered to pay rent, but they wouldn't hear of it.

"Save your money. We're just happy to have someone living here while we're gone," Dr. Jim said.

In the end, they reluctantly agreed to allow her to pay for the utilities. This meant most of the Roosevelt stipend could be used to repay her father for her medical school tuition, although he hadn't gotten around to sending her the bill. Did this mean he had softened and decided he was being unreasonable? It was more likely that her mother had put her foot down and told him she wouldn't stand for it. Nevertheless, Carrie intended to pay him back every cent.

Feeling drowsy, she sprawled on the sofa and watched an old *Lassie* show while she waited for the last load of laundry to dry. An hour later, she woke from a sound sleep and rushed upstairs to dress for dinner. She thought about putting on a sundress, but didn't want to look as if she was dressing for a date. She settled on her best jeans and a periwinkle sweater that made her blue eyes pop. Then she hurried to Glacier Family Foods to pick up a bottle of wine to take to Nate's house.

While she was at the store, she called him. "I'm looking at some mighty fine huckleberry pies and a chocolate layer cake," she said. "What's your pleasure?"

"I got this," he said. "Just bring yourself."

It was exactly six thirty when she arrived at his house, located near the hospital in the opposite direction of the Millers' home. It was a small one-story tract house with cream-colored siding. The best compliment Carrie could come up with about the home's curb appeal was that it had a stunning view of the mountains. A spindly tree was staked in the front yard, and the grass was spotted with brown patches. Nate's late-model Chevrolet SUV was parked in front. Holding the wine in one arm, she knocked on the front door.

Nate greeted her with a quick one-armed hug. He wore khakis that hugged his muscular thighs and a long-sleeved gray V-neck shirt that showed off well-developed chest muscles.

Carrie handed him the bottle of merlot before registering that there were plates of appetizers arranged on the coffee table. "Wow, you really went to a lot of trouble just for me."

"Not just for you. I invited John and Gali, too. I thought it would be nice to get to know her."

"Oh, good. I've looked forward to meeting her. And John is fun." Carrie picked up a toasted pita chip and dipped it in hummus. "Mm, this is delicious. Where did you get it?"

"Made it."

"You *made* this?" Her eyes widened. "It's the best I've ever had."

"Hummus is easy," he said. "I've got bruschetta, too."

"You're a man of many talents."

"Most of them useful," Nate said, shrugging. "My mom taught my brothers and me how to cook. She didn't want her future daughters-in-law to curse her for raising meatheads."

Carrie laughed. "Well, you're going to make some lucky woman very happy."

"What can I get you to drink? Beer? Wine? I make a mean dirty martini."

"A glass of wine is fine—whatever you have open." She tasted a perfectly seasoned piece of bruschetta. "If this were me entertaining, you'd get takeout pizza or my mom's spaghetti sauce."

She peeked into the kitchen. The cheap cabinets and countertop were chipped and scratched, but spotlessly clean. The living room, though tiny, showed a remarkable shabby-chic style. Colorful pillows provided splashes of color on the sagging brown sofa. Occasional rugs in bold patterns partially covered the pockmarked tile floors. Carrie admired a whimsical blown-glass sculpture on the 1960s-style coffee table. This was a man who had his domestic act together.

He handed her a glass of red wine. "So, overall, how have your first few weeks been?"

"Fine. Everyone is alive, and the nurses are still speaking to me. Peg Bright Fish covers my butt a lot."

"I hear you're cool as a cucumber under pressure, and the patients like you," Nate said. "That comes from the nurses, by the way."

She was about to tell him about Medicine Owl's compliment to both of them. But there was a knock on the door. Nate hurried to answer it. "Hey, buddy!" he said as he shook John's hand. "We're glad you two could join us. This must be Gali. It's really nice to meet you. Let me take your sweater."

A stunning woman dressed in an elegant full-skirted chocolate-brown sundress stood beside John in the foyer. She was an inch or two taller than Carrie, with silky, long dark-brown hair that swung freely as she moved. She had high cheekbones and brown eyes fringed in dark lashes. Her silver jewelry was simple and elegant, and she had a slender, curvaceous figure. John was right: Gali was beautiful. She was also friendly and approachable, and Carrie liked her immediately.

"Thank you for the invitation to dinner," Gali said to Nate, her voice polished and musical in its dialect. Carrie offered her hand, and Gali took it, cradling it between her hands for a moment in a gesture of friendship. John offered Carrie a quick brotherly hug before accepting a beer from Nate.

"Did you read the story in this morning's paper about the Grizzlies?" Nate asked, referring to the University of Montana's football team. "Don't you have a senior who'll be going there to play?"

"Two of our seniors have been scouted by the athletic director there," John said. "My Indians will do well this season, I think." There was pride in his voice. "Both boys are interested in going on to college, but one needs to get his GPA up. He may be a great running back, but that's not enough." He winked at Carrie behind Nate's back as if to apologize for leaving her out of the discussion. She relaxed at this sign of solidarity.

"The Grizzlies' schedule is tough this year," Nate continued. "They'll need luck—and for their junior quarterback to stay healthy and get some playing time." He picked up a plate of raw steaks and indicated with a nod of his head for John to follow him outside to the grill.

With Nate and John occupied, Carrie and Gali were left alone. "John said you live in Heart Butte? Is that where you're from?" Carrie asked.

"I'm from Missoula. But the Heart Butte High School needed a math teacher. By then, John and I had met at a state education conference and started dating. I was glad to move a little closer to him." She smiled. "I'm assistant principal now, too."

"I'm sure John could use a good assistant principal here who also teaches math."

Gali smiled in a noncommittal way. "Perhaps someday. We have many things to work through."

They talked easily together, Gali asking questions of Carrie that showed she was sincere in wanting to know more about her. They had similar experiences as good students with strong backgrounds in math and science. Soft-spoken and articulate, Gali was the kind of person Carrie would choose as a friend.

Nate and John came back inside, bearing plates of grilled meat and roasted asparagus and red peppers. Gali looked up to meet the adoring eyes of John, who sat beside her on the sofa. Their eyes met just long enough for Carrie to see that they were deeply in love. Their feelings for each other were so palpable, her heart ached. She wondered if she and Tom had ever looked at each other that way.

"Carrie, I met Gali when I did a workshop about infusing Native American culture into curriculums," John said. "Gali and I do that workshop together now." Again, their eyes met.

Nate was watching, too. In his eyes, she saw longing. Was he lonely living and working on the reservation? Did he regret coming here, thus bringing his engagement to an abrupt end?

Nate served the meal family-style. As Carrie and Gali continued their discussion, he and John debated which ties were more effective in fly-fishing, and on which bodies of water each fly worked best. It was a surprisingly animated discussion filled with passion. Carrie realized that she was having a wonderful time and hoped they could get together again soon.

Over coffee and dessert—a delectable chocolate mousse topped with whipped cream that Nate insisted was easy to make—he filled in background information about himself. From the time he was a teenager, he had known he wanted to be a surgeon. Like Carrie, he was drawn to the idea of helping underserved people. His last job at an urban medical center in Kansas City had seemed the perfect place to hone his surgical skills while serving a diverse patient population.

"Working in such a big place was challenging, but I learned a lot." His eyes clouded over and he appeared lost in thought for a long moment. Shaking his head, he took a swig of beer. "After a couple of unfortunate incidents, I decided to look for a place where I could do the work I'm trained to do while getting away from the politics and problems inherent in a big public hospital. I had been here with Dr. Jim, so this place was high on my list. Now it feels as if I was led here."

"I feel the same way." As on other occasions, Carrie found Nate to be genuine and touchingly sincere. She wanted to ask more about his experiences on his last job, but he didn't seem open to sharing details. Maybe one of these days, he'd confide in her.

"I'm sure a lot of people wouldn't understand what we do here or why. But this is more than just treating everyday illnesses or injuries," Nate continued, looking at Carrie. "It's about giving people something the rest of the country takes for granted. When I'm preparing to do surgery, I think, 'I can fix this.' "

For Carrie, accustomed to having to defend her love for this work to family and friends, it was a breath of fresh air to spend time with someone like Nate. He understood what motivated her. "After I came here the first time, it was all I could think about," she said.

Nate nodded. "Same here. The best part of this whole experience is the overwhelming sense of ... I don't know, feeling valued, I guess. Oh sure, there's too much to do at the hospital and no way to do it all, but working here matters. Your skills are tested in ways you could never have foreseen."

"That's true," Carrie said. She exchanged smiles with Gali. "The minute I get to work, I know the day won't necessarily be easy and anything can happen. If I were working for my dad in his suburban practice, I wouldn't be delivering babies. That's for sure."

"I've never felt so strongly that what I do matters the way it does here," Nate said to Carrie.

They continued talking for two more hours. As the clock neared ten o'clock, John cleared his throat. "Although school is out for the summer, I still have a board meeting to prepare for. I think we'd better be on our way. Our thanks to you, Nate, for a wonderful meal."

"Yes, Nate, it was delicious. I'd better get going, too." Carrie would have liked to stay longer. As he leaned in for a good-night hug, she kissed him on the cheek. "Thank you," she said.

John took Carrie's hand and leaned in for a brotherly hug. Then Carrie and Gali embraced and touched foreheads. As they did, Carrie felt certain that in this lovely Cherokee woman with the kind eyes and gentle manner, she had met a kindred spirit.

CARRIE WALKED INTO THE HOUSE a little after ten fifteen and greeted Annie, who had been left alone with only the television for company all evening. The truth was that Annie was a couch potato. Carrie attached her leash, and they walked outside into the cool night air. While Annie sniffed all the night smells in the front yard, Carrie thought about the four people she now counted as friends: Peg, Nate, John, and Gali. Smiling to herself, she thought about all the aspects of her experience here that she loved: her work, time in nature, her research project, and now good friends, too. Feeling serene and relaxed, she went back inside and made herself a cup of tea. There was a slight chill in the house, so she lit a fire in the fireplace and curled up on the sofa.

Her cell phone rang, startling her. She leaned over and picked it up, seeing Tom's name on caller ID. "Hello," she answered. "I was just sitting here, enjoying the peace and quiet. What's going on with you?"

"Carrie, we have to talk."

She carefully set her cup of tea on a coaster on the coffee table. "Okay," she said. "Let's talk."

"I'm thinking this situation really isn't what I want in life—you in Montana and me here. You've clearly decided to keep going with your life, independent of me. I need to make a life, too."

"I thought you had a life. But go on. I'm listening." Her mouth felt dry.

"I hate to do this on the phone, but I'm ending our engagement. You can keep the ring, of course. I gave it to you as a token of my love. I do still love you very much, you know. But this isn't working for me. You had a chance to come home weeks ago, and you chose to stay. Where does that leave me?"

"Tom, your choice for me was to come back to Philadelphia and give up the Roosevelt Award. I was supposed to choose what *you* wanted for *you*. I wasn't given a choice about what I wanted or even a chance to discuss what could possibly work for both of us. What about the way these decisions have been made sounds fair?"

"Life isn't fair. This also isn't just about your life. It's about mine. We want different things."

"I can't disagree with you on that." Her heart rate had slowed, and her breathing was shallow. "I was hoping we could weather this challenge together. But I don't see that happening now."

"You could have made a different choice," he said again. "This is all your doing."

"No, Tom. It's *our* doing," she said, taking a deep breath. "If we aren't meant to be together, it's better to know that now."

"Carrie, you're being stubborn and unreasonable."

Now she understood. He wasn't breaking up with her. This was an attempt to force her hand—to inform her that the next move was hers. Return to Philadelphia or forfeit the engagement. He could then claim he had no responsibility for the breakup. It was all going to be her fault.

"I respect your decision and will always wish the best for you. Good night, Tom," she said. "I'm grateful for the love we shared."

Chapter Eleven

THE BREAKUP WITH TOM LEFT CARRIE sad and more than a little shaken, even though she told her mother and Gran that she felt certain she had made the right decision. There was never any question that Gran would understand. But to her surprise, her mother did, too.

"He could have handled this situation differently," she said. "Anything would be better than the way he did it. I'm sorry, honey."

"This means, of course, that I might be giving up my chance to have a husband and children," Carrie said. "But it just didn't feel right."

"I wish I could console you in person." Her mother sighed. "In my opinion, one year is not too long to ask someone to wait, particularly when it may help your career. It's a great opportunity for you." After a moment's silence, she added, "I can't pretend to agree with how your dad and Tom have behaved. But now, I just want to know, are you okay? Do you want me to come out there?"

"Mom, that's good of you to offer. But I'm so busy, we'd hardly have any time together. Thanks, but I think I just need to buckle down and work on my project and concentrate on my patients. Thanks for always being there for me. I'm sorry if I've disappointed you. I know how much you looked forward to planning the wedding."

"Disappoint me? Oh, no, Carrie. I hope I have supported you enough through this situation. I'd be disappointed if you knuckled under and married someone you didn't think was the one for you. Marriage is tough enough without compromising who you are as a person. I sometimes go along with things I don't agree with, where your father is concerned. But in the end, we either compromise or agree to disagree."

"I thought Tom had better sense than that," Gran said when she heard the news. "He'll regret this the rest of his life." She paused, then added, "I wouldn't be surprised if he asks for your forgiveness."

"It's no use, Gran. I've made my decision. Even so, I can't help but worry that this will make things even worse with Dad."

"Well, it won't make them better. That's for sure." Gran let out a long breath. "If I were you, I'd stop worrying about what your father thinks and just live your life to the best of your ability. Your dad and I don't see many things in the same light, it's true. But I do know my son. He'll chew on this until all the flavor is gone. Then he'll have to figure out what to do with a wad of grievances that won't quite go down and that keep him from happiness. I've made my peace with the events of my life. He'd be happier if he learned to do the same. He always tells you to grow up. Well, he has some growing up to do, too."

BY THE FIRST OF AUGUST, CARRIE's life had a comfortable rhythm to it. She felt more confident on the job, even on days when there were too many patients and too few hours to get everything done. She had begun talking every few days with the hospital's doctor of pharmacy, an older man who was part Native American and appreciated plant-based therapies. He understood the ways plants used by the medicine woman interacted with modern pharmaceuticals, and said he would work with Carrie to assess how prescription medications and Native American therapies could work in tandem. With this stroke of luck, she felt confident her Roosevelt research study was well underway.

Her biggest concern wasn't professional. She worried that Annie was left alone so much. After admitting her concerns, she was delighted when Peg volunteered her husband, Ken, to check on Annie throughout the day. Judging from the addition of a few new toys in Annie's collection, he was intent on spoiling her.

"It's such a help having Ken check on Annie. She's getting older, and I can't make her wait all day to go outside."

"You just *think* Ken is doing you a favor." Peg snorted. "You're actually the one helping him. He's been bugging me to get another dog. I told him to adopt one of the strays hanging around our house. Annie's his special girlfriend."

Carrie took Annie for as many runs as possible, determined to make up for the time she couldn't spend with her during the day. At night, before darkness fell, they took walks around the fields behind their house. Carrie looked for the wolf every day, but hadn't seen the animal in almost a week. She wanted to believe it was more curious than predatory. Still, she didn't let her guard down. She hadn't yet asked John about the best course of action.

In fact, she hadn't seen him since the dinner party at Nate's. She knew that he made the fifty-mile round-trip drive to Heart Butte several times a week, and that Gali came to his home whenever she could. They kept to themselves. Carrie had enjoyed their company and wanted to invite them for dinner. But to do that, she needed to learn to cook something.

"Cooking is easy, Dr. Carrie," Peg said. "You just read the directions and follow them. If you can deliver a baby, you can bake a chicken."

"I know when a baby is ready to come out. It isn't as clear figuring out when a baked chicken needs to come out of the oven."

Peg laughed until tears rolled down her cheeks. "I'll help you. We'll start with something easy."

To Carrie's surprise, John showed up at the house the following Sunday, looking handsome in jeans and a blue-and-white plaid flannel shirt. He wore hand-tooled cowboy boots. In his hands, he held a broad-brimmed leather hat with a braided leather band.

I figured you'd be over in Heart Butte with Gali," she said.

"Not today. I thought you might like to go horseback riding."

"I'd love that! Can I bring Annie or will she scare the horses?"

"The dog can come. She'll like where we're going."

Carrie changed into jeans and boots, grabbed a light jacket, and called out to Annie, who bounded to the front door. "Where are we going?"

"Not too far. There is someone I want you to meet. Or rather, I should say, there is someone who wants to meet you." They got into the car. "Buckle up. Where we're going, there aren't many paved roads."

"I've been meaning to tell you how much I like Gali."

"She likes you, too."

His mood was pensive as the Jeep bounced along the dirt road. Just ahead, Carrie saw a weathered, dark-brown barn and about a dozen horses grazing inside a pasture area. Behind the barn were low hills leading to the mountain range. "Who owns this place?" she asked.

"My dad's youngest brother. He works for the U.S. Department of Agriculture. We're allowed to ride the horses whenever we want."

"It's too bad Gali can't come with us. Was she busy?" She felt vaguely uncomfortable riding out into the hills with John. It occurred to her that their being along together might start rumors, adding to his parental woes.

John pulled the Jeep behind the barn and parked in the shade of an old tree. "I won't have a chance to see her this weekend. We had some family matters last evening. They aren't over yet, unfortunately, so I stayed in town." He walked toward the barn. "I'd like to get us saddled up and on the trail. We need to get there and back within a few hours."

"Okay, tell me what I can do to help." Carrie stood by uncertainly as John opened the double doors to the barn, which smelled of horses, old wood, manure, and musty vegetation.

She followed him to the back behind the stables. He dragged two saddles down from the wall and dropped them on the barn floor. As she started to pick one up, he stopped her with a hand on her arm.

"Leave it," he said. "It is too heavy for you." He carried a saddle pad and brown leather saddle outside, where two horses—a huge, dark-brown stallion and a smaller chestnut-colored mare—stood near the gate. Approaching them, he reached out to pet the larger horse. "You and your lady friend are the lucky ones today."

The horses whinnied and stamped their feet as John took the time to stroke each of their noses and flanks. He ran his hand down the bigger horse's neck. "This big guy with the white star on his forehead is Poncho. The mare, Sally, will be your horse. She's gentle, but she loves to run. She'll follow Poncho's lead, so there is no need to be afraid if she suddenly picks up speed."

He started putting the bridle on Poncho, talking softly to him and running his hand down the long nose. "You are a good boy. Easy, easy," he said, stroking the horse's withers.

He inserted the bit into Poncho's mouth and slid the crown of the bridle over the horse's pert ears, one at a time, while Carrie reached up and touched Poncho's sleek shoulders. John threw the saddle pad over the horse's back and expertly centered it, then arranged the saddle and fastened the cinch straps, tightening them gently. "You can help me with Sally and her saddle," he said.

"You don't realize how big horses are until you're standing next to them, trying to put a saddle over their backs," she puffed. There was no way she could lift the saddle high enough to arrange it over the horse's back.

John grinned. "I'll do it. You would have to grow several inches."

She smiled back. "I beg your pardon. I'm five foot one. The way you said that … you sounded like my dad. From the time I was little, I wanted to do things all by myself. I'm not used to needing help with anything."

"Why doesn't that surprise me? It is not a sign of weakness to ask for help. I'll give you a boost up."

Carrie's leg muscles, developed through years of running, were strong. She put her left foot into John's hand, and he lifted her high enough that she could easily swing her right leg onto Sally's back. He waited until she was settled before effortlessly mounting Poncho.

"Stay close to me," he said, making a clicking sound as he nudged the horse forward.

Carrie hadn't ridden a horse since her first summer in Montana, when the volunteer corps rode into the high plains. Even so, she found it easy to keep up. Now and then, she glanced back at Annie, who was alternately running and trotting along behind, looking happy to be included. Within minutes, both horses were cantering side by side across the field toward the foothills. "What a good idea this is! Thanks for inviting us."

The strong breeze lifted her hair, blowing it every which way. Riding so high on Sally's back, she could see for miles. The landscape resembled an impressionist painting with its broad swaths of color. As they drew closer, the details came into focus. It was like watching a scene take form from initial sketch to finished painting.

"Let's stop so Annie can take a break and have some water," she said.

They brought their horses to rest beneath a tree near a stream. John dismounted and helped her off Sally's back. Carrie stooped and ran her sweaty fingers through the icy water, then wiped them on her jeans.

"John, I have a wolf that visits me. It's around a lot. I'm worried about Annie."

"But not about yourself." He smiled and cocked his head, watching her.

"Why does it sit there in the same place, watching? I assume it's looking at Annie and planning something."

John's eyes grew more serious. "Keep an eye on her. You don't keep livestock or chickens. Wolves are more likely to prey on sick or injured animals—weaker ones that can't move as fast. They thin out herds that way. Ranchers don't like them."

"Do you think the wolf could be watching Annie, knowing she's old and vulnerable?"

"Hard to say. Annie still moves pretty fast. As long as she doesn't provoke the wolf, she'll be fine. Wolves are smart. It actually may be more curious about *you*." He smiled. "I can see that it troubles you, though. If you're afraid, call the park service. They will send a ranger." John helped her onto Sally's back and mounted Poncho, clucking his tongue to the big horse.

"I'm glad you didn't tell me to get a weapon for self-defense," she said, half-joking. "I can't do that."

He looked serious. "You don't strike me as the kind of person who could kill something that lives in the manner of its birth, as is its right. The wolves were here long before people came."

"You're right. The truth is that I'm becoming less afraid." She looked off into the distance. "The wolf and I are learning to coexist."

"Well, just don't try to feed it by hand. This isn't *Dances with Wolves*."

Carrie laughed. She had almost forgotten what a good sense of humor John had. He had been so serious of late. They continued riding along in silence.

Finally, John spoke again. "I do have something to discuss with you. It is difficult for me to talk about." He rode with his eyes straight ahead. "It is about my brother."

Carrie already suspected what John was going to say. "I'll help if I can."

"He was taken to the hospital Friday evening. It is why Gali and I aren't together this weekend. My parents are upset. They asked me to figure out what to do."

"The hospital must have released him fairly quickly or I would have seen him on inpatient rounds yesterday morning."

"My parents took him back to their house, but it would be better if he was in the hospital for treatment. Mike was found unconscious by the friends he lives with. He could have died. If he continues staying in that house with those friends, he *will* die." John sucked on his top lip. "I believe that is his preference. He does not care to live."

Carrie let out a long breath. "Are you asking me for medical advice?"

"I guess so. My mother wants him to see a doctor, and she knows you're here. She prefers that Mike live at home where she can make sure he eats and stays out of trouble. I don't agree."

"Sounds like something a mother would say. Does she comprehend how serious this is and what it will take to help him recover? Is he experiencing withdrawal now?"

"My father gave him whiskey yesterday, but hid the rest of the bottle. He'll dole it out a little at a time, as necessary. Dad knows it isn't the best course of action. Mike will drink anything he can get his hands on—even mouthwash. To tell you the truth, I'm not sure he can recover. No one I've known has ever stopped that behavior. They just die."

"John, he can get better, if he wants to. But he has to want to stop, and he has to deal with the other issues that cause him to drink. He has to stay away from friends who drink or use drugs. That's the really hard part. Otherwise, you're right. He'll start drinking again."

"We cannot let this go on much longer," John said. "My big brother is killing himself."

As they rode Poncho and Sally higher into the foothills with Annie close behind, the air became cooler. Even riding on a horse, Carrie found herself laboring to breathe at this higher altitude. "Who are we going to see, John?"

"We are nearly there. Medicine Owl lives just a little farther."

"Medicine Owl!" Carrie felt her heart starting to pound with excitement. "One of my patients mentioned her name to me. Medicine Owl told my patient she approves of my work. I've wanted to meet her."

"She would not have asked that I bring you if she did not approve. You have found favor."

"I'm so honored. You must know her well, since you were the one she asked." Carrie wanted to learn as much as possible about Medicine Owl before meeting her. As usual, John wasn't offering much in the way of additional information.

"Everyone knows her." John turned to look over his shoulder at Carrie. "She is the oldest woman on the reservation."

"How old is she?" Carrie couldn't imagine an elderly woman living so far in these hills, miles from Browning. "Does she stay up here all the time?"

"She is well into her nineties, I think. She says she has seen more moons than anyone else. I believe her." John looked thoughtful as he urged Poncho onward. Carrie looked behind to make sure Annie stayed close.

They reached a flat area surrounded by ancient fir trees listing to one side. Carrie saw a tiny hut that amounted to little more than large planks nailed together. She doubted it offered more shelter than a tipi. Through the tin roof, a pipe rose, letting off a thin plume of white smoke. "In a heavy snowstorm or winds, how does this place manage to stay upright?" she asked.

"It's been here for years." John helped her down from Sally's back and fastened the reins of both horses to a tree. "We can walk from here. Annie can come with us. Medicine Owl will like the dog."

"John, are you *related* to Medicine Owl?"

"She is a relation to all."

"Oh, of course. Is there anything I need to know before we meet—some special way to greet her?" This meeting was so unexpected. What if Carrie said or did something wrong, without realizing?

"It will all be clear." John knocked lightly on the front door.

A few minutes passed before an elderly Blackfoot woman appeared. She was so tiny that even petite Carrie felt tall next to her. She had kind eyes and a sweet expression, and she walked with a hand-carved stick that was taller than she was by at least two feet. She waved them in with her hand without speaking a word. Carrie's stomach roiled with nervousness. Should she introduce herself first?

"Medicine Owl, this is Dr. Caroline Nelson." John made the introduction and then stood back to allow the two women to greet each other.

"I'm glad to be here," Carrie said, taking Medicine Owl's small hand. "Thank you for inviting me. Please call me Carrie."

"I have wanted to speak with you." Medicine Owl gestured with her hand, inviting Carrie to sit on a pine bench. The old woman sat on another bench across from Carrie. She summoned Annie by holding out her fingers and rubbing them together. Annie went immediately to Medicine Owl and sat at her feet while the elderly woman patted the dog's head. John stood by the door, arms crossed. He might have been a royal guard on sentry duty, his bearing was so regal.

The cabin was small—just one room. Other than the two benches, the only other furniture was a rough table and chair, wood stove, and a low bed, barely inches off the floor, covered in a large buffalo hide. There was a small stand in the corner with wood and stone figurines, wood sticks, and feathers. Carrie glanced around and saw displays of feathers and dried herbs hanging from the walls and posts. *Gran would love this as much as I do.*

"You have brought your medicine to our people. There is much more you need to know about ours," Medicine Owl said. "You are here to learn our ways. I will teach you."

"There is so much I don't know. Thank you."

"You have knowledge of plants, I am told."

Carrie looked quickly at John, who nodded. She wondered who had shared this information with Medicine Owl. "Yes, my grandmother is a doctor. She has taught me about plants from the time I was a little girl." Carrie felt flustered. She cleared her throat. "My grandmother wants me to learn about the medicine wheel."

"We have a big medicine wheel on the reservation." Medicine Owl raised her arms high to show that the wheel was large. "Lives-with-Books can show you."

Carrie was confused for a moment and then smiled as she realized Lives-with-Books must be John's Blackfeet name. When Medicine Owl glanced at John, he nodded.

"Come," she said. "I have a medicine wheel over in that corner."

Medicine Owl rose slowly and made her way to a small stand near a wood stove. Carrie knew a little about the medicine wheel from the book Gran had given her. She had read that Native Americans believed nature expressed itself in circles and cycles, never in straight lines. Birds' nests were round. Eggs were ovals. The earth, sun, and moon were spheres. Spring, summer, autumn, and winter evolved perpetually in the overarching cycle from birth to death. Now, as she examined the medicine wheel, it occurred to her that there might even be cycles to lifetimes, with spirits returning again and again. This insight felt like an essential truth.

Medicine Owl explained that a medicine wheel was arranged with its directions of north, south, east, and west. "Every living thing—people, animals, plants, even rocks and gemstones—are connected in this wheel. By creating a medicine wheel, a person can learn how to live with the great Creator."

"Heart, mind, body, and soul," Carrie said.

Medicine Owl's medicine wheel had a hand-carved wood bear on the west point. North was a light-colored stone wolf. At the center was what appeared to be a dragonfly. An eagle marked the eastern point.

"Our medicine is not like yours," Medicine Owl explained. "When I tell you about our medicine, it is the Great Spirit, the life force that lives here." She indicated the center of her chest. "We must find our own way to be healed with help from the Creator."

Carrie nodded. "And I must know myself in order to practice good medicine."

Medicine Owl nodded again. "Your path takes you on a long journey. You learn many lessons. You are here with us to continue your journey." Medicine Owl pointed to the dragonfly. "This is a totem. Bear is a totem. Wolf is a totem."

"Do I have a special totem?" Carrie looked into Medicine Owl's kind dark eyes.

"Think on this. You already know."

Carrie was silent, considering what animal held deep meaning for her. "I ... I'm not sure."

"Is there a wolf that comes to you?"

Carrie felt shivers run down her spine. "I do have a wolf that visits me."

"She watches over you." Medicine Owl walked slowly back to her bench and resumed petting Annie, who rested her head on the old woman's knee and closed her eyes. "You are kin."

Carrie sat down again on the bench opposite Medicine Owl, her head full of questions. The love she felt at that moment for this woman was so strong that she was nearly overcome. It was as if she was seeing a beloved family member after many years apart. She scarcely knew where to begin. "I want to understand more. I want my medicine to work with yours."

"You understand more than you know." Medicine Owl reached behind her and pulled out a long, grayish-white feather. "This is yours, for your journey."

"What do I need to do next?" Carrie's eyes glistened with tears at the special offering from the wise woman.

"You are already one with us," Medicine Owl said. "We will speak again."

Chapter Twelve

꙳

A S SHE WALKED TO THE HOSPITAL Monday morning, a car horn tooted behind her. Startled, she turned to see Peg pulling up in a tan Chevy Blazer the exact color of the road dust that covered it. Peg rolled down the window on the passenger side. "Can I give you a lift to work?"

Carrie opened the passenger side door. "Thanks!" She climbed up into the truck, using the door frame to propel herself into the high seat, and fastened her seatbelt, remembering that Peg liked to drive fast. "How was your weekend?"

"I spent most of it over at the Little Flower," Peg said, referring to the town's historic Catholic Church.

Staunchly Catholic, as were so many on the Blackfeet reservation, Peg was second in influence only to the parish priest—or so it seemed. She served on the board of the parochial school, too. Clearly, the church relied on Peg's good-hearted efforts as much as the hospital did.

"You're such a hard worker, Peg. I don't know how you do it all."

"The man upstairs sees fit to give me a good life. I'm just returning the favor. I hear you went to see Medicine Owl."

Carrie's eyes widened. "Did the drums tell you that?"

Peg chuckled. "No, I heard it from Nadie Leathers. Her son, Mike, had some trouble this weekend, and I stopped by with a casserole. You may have heard about it already."

"Yes, I did hear what happened ... from John." Carrie decided not to elaborate. "I enjoyed meeting Medicine Owl. I think she can teach me a lot about her medicine so I can write about how it works with mine."

"She is coming back into town soon to stay for the winter. Then you two can see each other more often," Peg said.

"It would be nice if Dr. Holden could meet her, too," Carrie mused. "I saw him over the weekend and wanted to tell him about Medicine Owl, but I didn't get a chance."

"You saw Dr. Nate over the weekend? At the hospital?" Peg hit a bump in the road and Carrie's bottom lifted off the seat.

"No, not at the hospital." Carrie was hesitant to say anything else. She had stopped by Nate's house, at his invitation, for a glass of wine and a shared pizza. They sat outside on the patio until the sun went down, sharing stories of their lives before Browning. She had hoped Nate would tell her more about what had brought him to Browning, but he didn't.

"I thought all Dr. Nate did was work," Peg remarked. "It's a relief to hear he makes time for a social life." She glanced sideways at Carrie. "You two should be good friends."

"I think we're already friends, Peg."

"Well, I'm glad. Oh, I know you're engaged and all that. But you're here on this reservation, and he's here, too. It just makes sense."

Carrie decided to come clean. Peg would probably hear about her breakup with Tom at some point, anyway. "I'm not engaged anymore. Tom wanted me to come home, and when I told him I couldn't, he said he was ending things."

"He broke up with you? He must be crazy or stupid."

"Thanks." Carrie chuckled. "It's for the best, I think. I was starting to have second thoughts about him, too."

"So, now you can stay here with us!" Peg said, elation in her voice. "I bet Dr. Nate was glad to hear you're free."

Carrie twisted her mouth in an expression of reproof. "I haven't exactly told him yet. I'm a little embarrassed, I guess. Peg, please don't get any ideas about the two of us. Rebound relationships are never a good idea, and I value his friendship too much to risk that. Remember, I can only stay until next July. After that, I need to head home to Philadelphia. That is, if I ever want to repair my relationship with my dad."

"I know," Peg said. "I have to remember that. You're such a blessing to us, but this isn't your home. We worry that Dr. Nate will leave us, too." She clucked her tongue. "It was a miracle when he came here. Miracles don't always last, though."

Carrie wondered how Indian Health Services could ever replace Nate. They seemed to be having enough trouble replacing the hospital's obstetrician. "I agree. He's so good at what he does. What *would* we do?" She intended it as a rhetorical question, but hearing Peg's deep sigh, she turned toward her. "What is it, Peg?"

"You don't know how many people we lost before he got here," Peg said in a subdued tone. "My mother died from peritonitis from a ruptured appendix. If Dr. Nate had been here, that never would have happened."

"I wish things had been different for your mother." Carrie reached over and squeezed Peg's hand.

Peg held tightly to Carrie's hand. "She's in a better place."

"I believe that, too."

Peg rounded the next curve without slowing down while Carrie gritted her teeth, pressing her foot against an imaginary brake pedal. "You should think about attending Little Flower," Peg said. "I know you aren't Catholic. There's still only one Creator upstairs."

"That's true. Little Flower is such a beautiful church," she said. "I'll make it a point to join you sometime."

As they approached the hospital, Peg parked in the lot, turned off the motor, and reached for her lunch sack. "We're glad you're here, Doctor. Not everyone who comes here likes it, and most of them don't make the effort to be part of life on the reservation."

"It helps that I want to be here. I wish it could be longer than a year. But after that, I'll be back to help whenever I can." Carrie stepped out of the vehicle and smoothed her hair into place. "I could never stay away from this place."

"I just hope a year of working in that crazy clinic of ours don't change your mind. We might see you running for the hills."

Carrie wasn't surprised to find that their first patient that morning was Mike Leathers. "While you check vitals, I'll review his medical history," she said to Peg.

"He's a nice man, but he's been like this a long time. I hope you can help him."

"I hope I can, too." Carrie reviewed the notes from Mike's recent emergency room visit. Helping someone with an addiction was never easy, and it usually involved at least a few failures before the person was ready to make changes— if the addictive behavior didn't kill the person first. She took a deep breath and knocked on the exam room door.

"Mr. Leathers? I'm Dr. Caroline Nelson. It's nice to meet you."

He nodded, saying nothing. Carrie leaned against the sink while she asked questions about his ER visit. Mike Leathers closely resembled John, but today he looked old enough to be his father. His black braid had a salting of gray at the temples. His limbs were emaciated, the muscles slack and undefined. His stomach protruded visibly through the exam gown. His skin had an unhealthy pallor, and there was a faint smell of alcohol on his breath. His hands were shaking.

"May I call you by your first name?" Carrie asked.

He hesitated before saying "Yes" in a voice that reminded her of John's.

"How are you feeling today?"

Mike Leathers raised his shoulders in a shrug and looked down at his feet as Carrie approach, pulling her stethoscope out of her pocket. "Let's see how your heart and lungs sound. Take a deep breath for me. Again. And again." As her fingers rested gently here and there on his chest, torso, and back, he flinched. "Breathe in and out as deeply as you can," she said quietly. "Relax and pretend I'm not here."

It was a joke she made often with patients who seemed overly tense or anxious. It usually evoked at least a smile. But the expression on Mike's face did not change. "Your heart and lungs sound fine, no congestion. I see from your records that you were in the emergency room on Friday night. I'm concerned about that. Tell me what happened."

"I did not know what happened until I woke up."

"You are fortunate that you woke up," Carrie said, making eye contact. "You're also anemic. That means your blood doesn't have enough red blood cells. That is usually the result of not eating properly. I'm going to order more lab work today, and after I review those, we'll see where we stand. In the meantime, let's talk about the real problem: whether or not you think you have a problem with alcohol."

"I do not drink more than others I know," Mike said, brushing off her attempt at a discussion. She had expected this.

"Mike, do you think you have a problem with alcohol, either occasionally or on a daily basis?" Carrie stood directly in front of him. When he didn't make eye contact or respond, she continued, "Okay, let me rephrase this. Do you understand that you can die from drinking too much alcohol? Because that is what will happen if you keep drinking so much and so often."

Mike's lips twitched. "It is not my choice to die."

"Would you allow me to help you?" Carrie waited until he raised his eyes to meet her steady gaze. "I can arrange for a stay in our inpatient addiction unit, as well as counseling and other services that may help you stop drinking and even improve your life. But you have to want this, and you have to work at it. You wouldn't be doing it alone."

"How can anything improve my life? You do not know anything about my life." Beneath the soft-spoken yet abrupt response, Carrie heard despair. He was depressed, self-medicating with alcohol to mask the pain of the disappointments and hardships in his life.

"You're right. I don't know anything about your life," she said, sitting down in the chair opposite the examination table. "But as your doctor, I do care about you, and I understand that drinking too much is a sign of other things that aren't good: unhappiness, frustration, fears. We all have things in our lives that bring us pain and make us feel out of control. Alcohol, for many people, is a way of trying to make things better. But drinking too much alcohol will only make things worse."

She was relieved when he nodded in response. "You cannot continue to drink alcohol, even a little. If you want to get better, you must stop completely."

Mike's body language spoke volumes, letting Carrie understand the level of frustration, even pent-up anger, he felt at his life. But he remained silent. Finally, he said, "I do not think I can stop drinking."

"I believe you can. I believe you are a strong man." Carrie's expression was encouraging as she took his hands in hers, studying his fingers and seeing further evidence of malnutrition and liver damage—hopefully reversible, to some extent. "It will have to be a choice you make each day not to drink. You can take it one day at a time."

Mike nodded. There was a long pause before he said, "Yes."

"Okay, then, you and I are going to create a plan together. We'll use medication for a while. It is very effective. But here's the thing: you cannot drink alcohol at all. Stop using mouthwash that contains alcohol, too. This is how we'll begin the process of helping you stop. But I also want to help you deal with some of the troubles in your life."

"There are too many." Mike's ragged sigh spoke volumes. Carrie's heart went out to him.

"Today, you begin." She offered her hand to help him off the examination table. "It'll be important for you to avoid friends who want you to drink with them. I know that part is hard, but it has to be that way. Are you able to live away from your roommates who drink?"

"My mother wants me to stay at home," he said. "That is not something I want. But she will not hear of anything else. It is easier to do as my mother wishes."

Carrie could barely disguise the smile that crossed her face. "Mothers usually get their way. At least, my mother does," she said with a chuckle and was rewarded with a glimmer of a smile, the first she had seen from her patient.

She knew that Mike Leathers had a difficult road ahead, and that recovering from alcoholism would be a lifelong challenge. She hoped there could be some reversal of his liver damage. The trick would be for Mike to find something else to keep him occupied and content. Without steady employment, he had too much time on his hands. He wasn't married, had no children, and all his friends were likely to be alcoholics or drug abusers, as well.

"Do you have any hobbies or activities you enjoy?"

Mike shook his head no. His lack of interests or activities that didn't involve drinking was the first hurdle. He would have to find healthier outlets for his energy and emotions. It was a long shot, but perhaps through counseling, medication, and the care and concern of family members and friends, he could build a better, healthier life for himself.

She was glad his parents insisted he move home where they could keep an eye on him. Not all families cared enough to take such an active role in an adult child's recovery from alcohol or drugs. She hoped they wouldn't give up the first time he backslid. It was an inevitable part of recovery.

"I'll arrange for you to be in the hospital for a time so we can get you sober. Then you'll go home and meet with a counselor daily while you take the medication as directed. I'll check on you every day." She patted his shoulder and headed to the door. Turning to say goodbye, she watched him for a moment. He sat on the table, shoulders hunched, head hanging low. "Mike?"

He looked up, his eyes lifeless. The medication and counseling she offered could help, but there was something more he needed. Without hesitation, she spoke the words he needed to hear most. "Go see Medicine Owl."

It was turning out to be Leathers family day in the clinic. That afternoon, Carrie met Violet Hightower, John and Mike's first cousin. Violet was a cheerful, pretty woman in her early thirties with dark-brown hair that flowed in heavy waves down her back. As Carrie checked her patient's blood pressure for the third time and found it still too high, Violet announced, "I will blow up like a geyser."

"No, ma'am, you most certainly will not," Carrie said. "Not while I'm here, you won't. Are you feeling particularly nervous?"

Violet shrugged. "Everyone in my family has the high blood pressure. My father had it. His brother had it. Now my son has it."

"I want you to sit here quietly and let me check it again in a few minutes. I also think we need to do an EKG. I'm noticing some elevation on your lab report that tells me your kidneys are working very hard. You aren't diabetic. That's good. But when I look at your family history, I see that your father and his brother have passed on. What caused their deaths?"

"My father died of a heart attack," Violet said. "My uncle died of a stroke. My Aunt Nadie is the only one left. She is fine, I think."

"Has anyone in your family had kidney disease ... that you know of?" Carrie asked.

The appearance of notes indicating frequent urinary tract infections and sharp flank pain, in addition to her enlarged abdomen, caused Carrie to wonder if Violet's kidneys were affected with polycystic kidney disease, commonly called PKD, a genetic disorder usually passed from generation to generation. The disease could result in kidney failure. She hoped her suspicions were wrong, since a cure and treatments for PKD were still under investigation. Violet had two sons, ten and eight. If she had PKD and one of her children already exhibited signs of high blood pressure, he would need to be carefully watched for signs of the disease, as would the other child. Carrie had treated other patients with PKD and felt confident that she could manage Violet's care—up to a certain point. She knew that the typical Blackfeet diet of processed foods was no help.

"We need to get your blood pressure under better control, first thing. But it would help your kidneys if you ate more fruits and vegetables, whole grains like oatmeal, and not so much meat or packaged foods," Carrie told her.

"My husband likes his meat and potatoes."

"Could you try to cut back on the red meat or substitute chicken or fish? You can include a little meat in recipes as an ingredient. Just don't make meat the main part of what is on your plate. That will help you so much."

Violet let out a good-humored groan. "More vegetables ... more stuff my husband and kids won't like."

Carrie smiled. "You can have a little low-fat milk, cheese, and yogurt, but don't overdo it on cheese, either. It would be best if you could stop using the salt shaker, too. If you stop using salt, you'll lose your taste for it. I did."

Violet let out a frustrated breath. "My family does not like vegetables without cheese sauce," she said. "I thought cheese was okay because now the kids eat broccoli."

"It's wonderful that you feed your kids vegetables. It's a challenge to find healthy meals that children like. Just do the best you can. One vegetarian meal a day is a great way to start. We can arrange for you to talk with our hospital dietician. She can give you recipes your kids will like."

Violet hung her head in dramatic fashion. "My kids? My kids only like Fritos."

Carrie chuckled. "Fritos are my favorite snack, too. Make sure you're drinking more water, not soda pop. Choose decaf, whenever possible. I'd like you to get regular exercise, even if all you do is walk a little more or do some bending and stretching in the house. Breathe out stress, like this." She demonstrated deep breathing to release tension.

"I will try," Violet said. Then her face clouded. "Will I die young like my father and uncle?"

"We'll do everything possible to help you make wise choices so you can stay healthier." Carrie touched her patient's shoulder in a reassuring way. "I want you to have an EKG this morning before you leave. We'll also schedule an ultrasound so I can take a peek at your kidneys." Carrie paused, remembering the frequent flank pain Violet complained about. "By the way, have you had any more pain here?" She pointed to either side of her mid-to-lower back.

"I have that pain always," Violet said. "I take something to make it not hurt so bad."

"I want you to be careful about what you take for pain and how much," Carrie said. "Pain relievers can cause other problems. But once I see a picture of your kidneys, I'll have a better idea of what is going on and what you can do. I'd like to see you again after I look at your test results."

The hospital didn't have a nephrologist specializing in high blood pressure and kidney disease on its medical staff. The closest specialist was in Missoula, nearly four hours away. Carrie knew it would be up to her to manage Violet's care. She resolved to look for a continuing education seminar about kidney disease as soon as possible. Better yet, she'd call Gran, who had additional training in nephrology.

After Violet left the office with a prescription for a higher dosage of blood-pressure medication, Peg said, "Dr. Carrie, you know what is going on with Violet, don't you?"

"I've got my suspicions, but I don't want to worry her, in any case. I suspect PKD—polycystic kidney disease. If I see cysts on her ultrasound, I'll have to talk with her about what that might mean for her and her children."

"Is there a cure? Medicines you can give her? I hate to see her on dialysis."

"There's no cure for PKD yet. There's research going on that is likely to produce treatments, eventually. It's a complicated disease. Many PKD patients are able to get kidney transplants. But a transplant can't happen here."

Watching Peg's face fall, she explained, "She'd need someone willing to donate a kidney, and she'd have to go away for the surgery and pre- and post-op care."

"You are giving her a death sentence then." Peg's voice was flat. "I can't see anyone here giving her one of their kidneys—not on the reservation. What about her children? Will they have the PKD, too?" Peg was genuinely distressed now.

"It's possible that one or both of them could have it, if we find out that Violet is affected. It's a genetic disease. Her kids might have it; they might not. Her little boy already has high blood pressure, Violet said, and that's a strong indicator."

Peg was silent for a moment. She lowered her glasses and peered over them at Carrie. "Nadie Leathers may have the PKD, too."

"If Mrs. Leathers still doesn't have any symptoms at this age, the gene that causes it may not have been passed down to her. It's highly possible that her two brothers who died weren't so lucky." Carrie wrote an order for an ultrasound for Violet and then paused, pen in midair. "If Mrs. Leathers doesn't have the disease, then her children won't, either."

This would be the best possible outcome. If Nadie was healthy, then

John, Mike, and their sister would not have inherited the disease. But Peg was right. In a place like Browning, a diagnosis of PKD was likely to have a very different outcome than it would for someone who had access to bigger hospitals offering transplant services and clinical testing sites.

"I believe you can help her, Dr. Carrie."

Carrie paused, feeling the weight of high expectations on her shoulders. "I'll do what I can."

Chapter Thirteen

—◦✶◦—

"**N**ATE, WAIT UP!"

Carrie was on her way out the front door when she saw Nate sprinting down the hall from the ER. He appeared ready to lift off. The white coat he wore over green surgical scrubs billowed out behind him like wings.

"Hi, Carrie," he said, a smile lighting up his entire face.

He wore an operating-room cap over his golden-brown hair, but a few stray curls managed to spill out. Carrie felt a flutter in her midsection. Even when he was haggard from long hours of surgery and lack of sleep, Nate was undeniably sexy. He was also oblivious to the effect he had on women.

"I haven't seen you all day," she said as she caught up to him. They started down the hall, Carrie taking two steps to every one of Nate's.

"I've been living in the OR. Hey, are you up for a game of 'mystery meal' from the kitchen?"

"Actually, I was on my way home." Noting the disappointed look on his face, she added, "But now that I think about it, I missed lunch today. Or at least that's what my stomach is telling me."

"How are things in the clinic?"

"Fine." She shrugged. "I wish everyone cared as much about patient notes as I do. I'm a doctor, not a detective. What does 'cold' mean? That the patient *has* a cold or that the patient *is* cold? How about you? I heard you had to fix another victim of a knife fight."

"That was my first case this morning. He'll live to see another brawl. After that, it was a fibroid tumor, then a gall bladder," he said. "Never seen stones that size in one person before." He shook his head. "No wonder the poor woman was in pain."

While they waited for the kitchen staff to serve up their meals, the doctors discussed bile ducts and rare gall bladder removal complications. As with most physicians, graphic medical discussions had zero effect on their appetites. Nate covered the entire surface of a roll with a packet of butter and took a huge bite before digging into his brown gravy-covered supper.

"What is that?" Carrie asked, taking a spoonful of vegetable soup. "Some kind of beef?"

"I have no idea." He cut into the gelatinous mound with his knife and cautiously stuck a forkful into his mouth. He chewed and swallowed, still looking uncertain, and then shrugged. "Whatever it is, it isn't likely to digest anytime soon. So at least I won't be hungry right away."

Carrie laughed. "How can someone who cooks as well as you do eat that slop?"

"I eat to live when I'm here. Does your fiancé like to cook?"

Carrie's eyes shot open. "Oh." She felt the color crawl up her neck. "No, he doesn't. I mean, he isn't my fiancé anymore. We, uh, broke up."

"You did? When?"

"Right after I had dinner at your house, actually. I got home and he called to lower the boom. It was more of the same. I'll spare you the tiresome details. The long and short of it is that it's over."

Nate put down his fork. "Are you okay? That was a couple of weeks ago. Why didn't you say anything?"

She met his gaze. "I'm fine. I didn't say anything because … well, I guess I didn't want you feeling sorry for me. The poor girl got dumped and all that. Actually, I got the impression he was doing the whole tough love thing. He said it wasn't working for him. But then, when I agreed, he seemed to backpedal. I let him end it. It was easier that way. But the truth is, I'm relieved." She sat back in her chair, surprised that she had actually said this.

"I don't get it. You were on a short leash here already. You were planning to leave next summer. All he had to do was wait a year. Doesn't it take that long to plan a wedding, anyhow?"

"Yes, it does. I don't get it, either." Carrie made another attempt at eating her soup. "The turning point for me, I think, was when I realized that he actually expected me to turn my back on a Roosevelt. As if! He proofread every section of that project proposal. He supported me the entire time I was writing it." Imitating Tom's voice, she said, " 'This is great stuff, Carrie. You're gonna set that committee on fire with this, babe.' " In frustration, she beat the handle of her spoon on the table, causing it to flip out of her hand and land on the floor. "But he didn't think I'd win. He didn't believe in me."

Nate leaned over and retrieved the spoon. "I'm not sure you know your own strength," he said in a mild voice. "No more cutlery for you." He sat back in his chair. "I haven't known you for long, but I do know that you're one of those people who will accomplish anything you set your mind to. I can't wait to see the end result."

"Thanks," she said, meeting his eyes. "That means a lot, coming from you." She paused, reflecting a moment. "Why does love have to be so hard? Sorry. That sounded like a country song."

"I'm not sure it has to be like that. But don't listen to me." Nate opened a pint of milk and drank half of it. "I'm clearly not an expert."

Carrie crunched a saltine. "I have never pretended to be anybody other than who I am. I was always honest with him about what I wanted to do. But then, suddenly, he wanted me to be someone else. That should have been a clue, right? Or maybe I just didn't want to see it."

Nate speared another forkful of mystery meat and wiped it back and forth through his mashed potatoes. "If my experience means anything, I'd say yes."

"He's been heavily influenced by my dad. They were a united front."

"Okay, so, onto the next question. Is there any chance you'll take him back?"

The question was posed in a conversational tone. Yet Carrie knew it held more weight than that. She looked off into the distance, trying to imagine under what circumstances this might ever be a possibility. "I don't believe so, no."

"After you leave, would your dad be okay if you came back here for a month or so a couple times a year? Maybe you could negotiate something into your contract with him … like a compromise, so you can work in Philadelphia and be here, too. Knowing you, you'd work circles around his other docs."

Carrie pushed away the soup. "There's no way my dad would go for that. I can probably swing a week each summer and maybe fall, too, if I have enough vacation time. But that's about as far as my dad's benevolence as an employer goes. I'm not having happy thoughts about going back there. But what really bothers me is that I don't want to end up letting down Dr. Jim. He's counting on me to keep the medical corps going."

"What is it *you* want?"

The question hung in the air between them.

"This. I want this," Carrie said, squaring her shoulders. "But I want more, too." She looked away so he couldn't see the tear forming in the corner of her eye. She didn't know him well enough to say that the end of her relationship with Tom likely ended her dreams for marriage and a family, at least for the foreseeable future. She had invested three years in Tom, and now she was back to square one.

"Occasionally, I think about how long I'll be here," Nate said. "I wonder where I'll go. Maybe New York City or Chicago—someplace with lots of options." He wiped his mouth with his napkin. "I can't go back to Kansas City, and that isn't something I think my parents will ever completely understand. It's more than just being under contract here or wanting some of my loans repaid because I work in a remote area."

There it was again. His reluctance to go into detail led her to wonder if there was something he felt ashamed to talk about. Not wanting to appear nosy, she chose her next question carefully.

"However long you stay here, you've made a difference. You have to believe that." Her eyes met his. In them, she saw the truth of that statement. She rested her elbows on the table. "I feel as if you and I are going through the same stuff: trying to get the people we love to accept our choices."

"Yes, but if you think about it, we're also in the same boat as John," Nate pointed out. "His family can't accept that he loves Gali. It seems that no matter where you come from, families are the same. They have their own ideas about who you are and what you should do. You end up being judged for the choices you make—choices that you have every right to make. John is being pressured to give up the woman he loves. We're being pressured to give up the work we love."

"I hadn't thought of it that way."

"I can stay here as long as I want," Nate said. "To tell you the truth, I love it. And it isn't just the challenges of the work. It's the place, the people. I can't just desert them."

Carrie's expression softened at the sincerity in his eyes. "I'm relieved that the hospital won't lose you anytime soon. Whenever I come back, I expect to see you here."

"There's a good chance you will." Nate picked up his spoon and started in on a dish of chocolate pudding. Then, glancing at his watch, he finished the last two bites and stood up. "I need to check on my gall bladder patient."

"Take care, Nate." Carrie smiled at him. "I'm glad I ran into you."

"Me, too. See you around." He stood up, but didn't move away. Instead, he remained still, his eyes focused on hers. His expression tugged at her heart, made her want to reach out and touch him, comfort him, assure him that whatever had happened in the past, it would all be okay. What was it about this man that brought out all her most caring instincts and vulnerability?

Watching his back as he left the cafeteria, she knew how much she'd miss him when it was time to leave the reservation. She hoped he'd find another woman to love: someone who accepted him for all of his special qualities, a true partner who respected his work and understood that his ability to heal others was as much a part of him as those glorious blue eyes. Returning her tray to the kitchen, she headed home to Annie.

* * *

Annie's enthusiastic greeting nearly knocked Carrie off balance. She regained her footing and knelt down to hug her animal as Annie's tail wagged a mile a minute and she covered Carrie's face with kisses. She couldn't help laughing as Annie fetched a new rope toy.

"What is this? Did Ken bring you another new toy?" Carrie fastened the leash to Annie's collar. "You're a lucky girl that a man loves you unconditionally."

Annie wagged her tail. They went out the front door and down the long driveway. While Annie relieved herself on the dry grass, Carrie retrieved the day's mail. Although it was still August, the evening air had grown noticeably cooler. Some nights, the temperature dipped into the forties by sunset. She glanced through the short stack of mail, which included a sales letter from an insurance agent, an envelope of coupons, and a supermarket insert. No matter how far you roamed, junk mail looked the same.

She poured a bottle of water into Annie's bowl and refreshed her kibble before sinking onto the sofa. Kicking off her shoes, she turned on her iPad. There she found an email from her mother.

> Dad and I just got back from the city. He took me to Bookbinders for the fish soup. It's still one of our favorite places. It was just like a date—only now that we've lived together for almost thirty-five years, we finish each other's sentences. There are no surprises, but we still have fun. I've broached the subject of a Montana adventure one of these days. It will be good for him to broaden his horizons. XOXOXO We love you. Mom (and Dad)

She wearily massaged her own neck and thought of her parents, still in love after all these years. Would she ever experience that kind of forever love? As she considered this question, another thought occurred to her. After she returned home to Philadelphia, she and Tom would be working together again. They'd see each other every day. Would they eventually drift together again as a couple? She chewed on a rough cuticle, wincing as she drew blood.

That night, as she lay in bed, reviewing unfinished business, she heard the cry of the wolf. Annie stirred in her sleep, and from her dream state let out a muffled woof. Rolling over onto her side, Carrie propped herself up on one elbow, listening intently. She wondered if it was *her* wolf and whether the animal had a mate. She thought of her dream several months earlier.

"It is time," the female wolf had said.

It was time for so many things: building her career, completing the Roosevelt project, making peace with her father, marriage, family, and a home of her own. They couldn't all happen at once. Or could they? That night, she dozed fitfully, her sleep punctuated by wild, confusing dreams that included Nate, Medicine Owl, her father, the Leathers family, and even Peg. The common thread running through these snatches of images was the old gray wolf. *My spirit animal.*

ON FRIDAY MORNING, PEG KNOCKED ON her office door. "Dr. Carrie, the ultrasound is back on Violet Hightower."

"Thanks. Let's hope for the best." Carrie looked at the report and bit her lip. "It's what I suspected. Look at all these cysts."

"Will Violet need dialysis soon?" Peg stood behind her and made a tsk-tsk sound as she studied the ultrasound. "This can't be good."

Carrie shook her head. "Her kidney function is still within an acceptable range. If we can get her blood pressure under control through diet and medication—maybe some weight loss, too—then it might be possible to keep her off dialysis for quite a while."

"I don't like the idea of dialysis on someone so young," Peg said. "It would be hard on Violet and her kids."

Carrie noted information on Violet's electronic patient record and joked, "Well, I doubt Nate feels confident doing a kidney transplant."

"Maybe he could." Peg looked hopeful. "Dr. Nate, he can do anything."

"I'm afraid not," Carrie said. Peg's face fell, but she nodded. "Kidney transplants require a team of experienced surgeons and nurses. Plus, you need other experts to ensure the likelihood of success. Then there are expensive anti-rejection meds, special labs, biopsies, and things like that to make sure the patient isn't rejecting the new kidney. We can't do that here."

"Well, there's one thing I can do." Peg looked determined. "After work, I'm going to Little Flower to light a candle and pray for Violet. Do you want to come with me?"

"You go to Little Flower and pray. I'll talk with Medicine Owl and my grandmother. Between all of us, maybe we can figure out a plan to keep Violet healthy."

Chapter Fourteen

—◦—

CARRIE'S LAST PATIENT OF THE DAY also happened to be one of her favorites. The elderly woman named Dancing Bird smiled a sweet, gap-toothed grin that showed more gum than teeth. As Carrie took her health history, Dancing Bird answered some questions and ignored or simply smiled at others.

Finally, Carrie gave up. "Okay, enough questions."

"You have nice teeth," Dancing Bird said. "You are not married yet."

"Not yet," Carrie answered. "Someday."

"Soon." Dancing Bird raised her eyebrows and smiled. "I know."

Just how Dancing Bird could know this piece of information was beyond Carrie, so she smiled and said, "That might take a miracle."

She pressed with the pads of her fingers on the old woman's ankles and knees, noting acute puffiness and white spots where her fingers made indentations in the delicate skin, indicating fluid retention. "Are you taking your medication at the same time each day?" she asked, rather than asking her patient whether or not she remembered to take her medication.

Dancing Bird waved one hand dismissively. "I take your medicine every day for years. It does not make me younger."

"Nothing can do that. But the medicine helps your heart and keeps you from getting sicker," she said, taking the old woman's hands and noting swelling in her fingers. "Have you been eating more salt than usual?"

"I don't know," Dancing Bird said. "My granddaughter cooks the food. Her husband likes salt." She shrugged. "I eat what I want."

"I see." Carrie listened to her patient's heart and lungs, concerned that she heard congestion in the lungs. Dancing Bird was eighty and showing serious signs of congestive heart failure. "I'm going to increase your medication a bit. It would make me very happy if you would ask your granddaughter to use less salt in her cooking. Just tell her your doctor says it is not good for anyone in the family to have too much salt. Don't sprinkle more salt on your food. Promise me?"

"Yes, yes," Dancing Bird said. "I will take your medicine. But I will still eat *some* salt." Pure mischief showed on her wizened face.

It was impossible not to smile back. Although she had met Dancing Bird only a few times, Carrie felt as if she had grown up knowing her. It was that way with so many of the people she met here. With the utmost care, she made adjustments to her elderly patient's spine using soft tissue massage along her back and shoulders. Gently, she manipulated the muscles, easing strain on the vertebrae. The old woman seemed to enjoy the process, relaxing under Carrie's touch, even sighing with relief a few times.

When she finished the treatment, she helped Dancing Bird from the table to a standing position, her hands supporting the old woman under her arms. To her surprise, Dancing Bird leaned into her. Carrie recognized it as a gesture of gratitude, and yes, affection. She held her patient close for a moment.

"She is a 'wise one,' " Peg said as Dancing Bird left the office with her grandson, a man of about fifty. Carrie could see that he cherished his grandmother, and her thoughts automatically turned to Gran.

"A wise one? I'm not sure I understand exactly what you mean by that."

"My mother used to go to her for help."

"What kind of help?" Carrie's forehead wrinkled.

"My mother needed advice about my father. He was depressed because he had no job," Peg said. "Dancing Bird has special gifts. She knows many things from above." Peg pointed upward in reverent fashion.

Carrie made a mental note to remember this about Dancing Bird. Native Americans were deeply in touch with their inner lives, and intuition was highly valued. In this culture, spiritual beliefs were as closely aligned with their physical lives as the breaths they took.

"I wish I had Dancing Bird's abilities," she said. "I'd love to know what's going on with someone's body that I can't see with my eyes or feel with my hands."

"What is going on that you can't see ... is the spirit," Peg said. "That's where true healing happens."

"Well, the spirit part isn't something you find in medical books." Carrie let out a long breath. "But I believe it's there all the same."

"You find it right here," Peg said, touching her heart. "Dancing Bird's heart has taken on many people's troubles."

That evening, Carrie emailed Gran.

I don't think I'll be creating a medicine wheel for each patient, but I'm learning more and more about how the Blackfeet people view their bodies and souls. Their medicine is about the spirit found in nature—the same spirit they know within. They understand there is no separation between body and soul. We lost that somewhere along the way in Western medicine. Now, when I listen to a patient's symptoms, there is a point when I wish I had Medicine Owl there with me. I would ask, "How can we work together to help this patient?"

Peg ushered Violet Hightower into Carrie's office and shut the door to give them privacy. Unfortunately, Violet had come to the clinic alone. It was always better when a family member or friend came along to offer another listening ear. Unfortunate news sometimes frightened patients so they were unable to hear or comprehend all the information the doctor shared. Carrie remembered Peg's comment that Violet's husband wasn't supportive.

"Violet, I wish I didn't have to give you this information," Carrie said, coming around the desk and pulling a chair closer to her patient. Violet's hands were folded on her lap. She appeared calm but wary.

"I've reviewed your test results. There's a reason for your high blood pressure and the pain in your back. You have a condition called polycystic kidney disease. 'Poly' and 'cystic' mean 'many cysts.' It's called PKD for short. Let me show you what your kidneys look like." Carrie stood up and pointed to the images on the computer screen. "These are your kidneys. Do you see all of the bubbles on them? Those are fluid-filled cysts."

Violet stared impassively at the images. She pursed her lips, saying nothing. Carrie tried to think of how to explain the disease and its possible effects without frightening or confusing her. The reality was that Violet could do well. It was impossible to predict the course of the disease.

Finally, Violet spoke. "Is this what my father and uncle had?"

"I can't tell you that for sure, but I'd say that it's likely. It is a disease passed from generation to generation." She had almost said 'parent to child,' but thought better of it since she didn't want Violet to immediately fear the worst or feel guilty if her son had the disease, too. "Here is the good news: knowing that you have PKD will help you stay healthy. You can take positive steps with your diet, and you can exercise and drink more water. We can also help you learn to meditate to relieve stress."

"What about my sons?"

"We want to manage their blood pressure levels, too, just like we watch yours. If we see a problem, we can get pictures of their kidneys and see what's there," Carrie said. "There is no reason to worry. Let them be kids. If either or both of your boys have PKD and they have any pain, we may want to limit contact sports like football and hockey."

Violet's face became more serious. "I will see Medicine Owl."

"That's a great idea." Carrie smiled. "See what she has to say. We can work together."

"I will. Thank you, Dr. Carrie."

After Violet left, Carrie thought about all the transplant centers dotted across North America. Patients in other areas had ready access to specialists. If Violet lived anywhere else but on an Indian reservation in such a remote area of the country, if she had insurance and the same access to specialists and high-level medical facilities, she could even have a transplant. The thought that her patient—a young wife and mother—might die for want of something that many others took for granted brought a heaviness to her step.

WHEN CARRIE BUMPED INTO NATE THAT evening just outside a patient's room, she had an inspired idea. "Hey, why don't I buy us a real meal?"

"Do you mean a real meal as in food that doesn't come out of a box or the freezer?" Nate grinned and rubbed his hands together in anticipation.

"I mean real food that doesn't come with microwave instructions," Carrie added. "Preferably as far away from the hospital as we can get."

"I can leave now," Nate said. "Why don't we change out of our scrubs and put on real clothes, too?"

"Does seven o'clock give you enough time to get ready?" Carrie asked.

"I'm a guy, Carrie. I only need five minutes to shower and throw on something clean. For you, I might shave."

"How thoughtful. Just a reminder: I'm not a guy, and I need more than five minutes."

"You're definitely not a guy," Nate said with a grin. "I'll pick you up a little before seven."

The comment sounded flirtatious, yet she hesitated not to give it more credence than it deserved. This was Nate, a new friend and colleague. She drove home and attached the leash to Annie's collar. There was a strange odor in the air outside the house, a wild-animal smell. The hair rose on the back of Carrie's neck. Annie stopped to sniff the breeze, one leg poised in midair. After they went inside, Carrie peered out the window, looking for movement outside. There was no telling what kind of creature had been near the house, or where it might be now. Was it her wolf?

Feeling decidedly uneasy, she showered and changed into dark jeans and a white blouse before opening her jewelry box to find her pearl earrings. As she reached into the top drawer, her fingers found the engagement ring she had tucked inside. Instantly, her mood shifted to sadness. She remembered the joy she had felt on Christmas Eve last year, when Tom proposed. It had been just the two of them sitting together on the sofa in front of a crackling fire at her parents' house. He had popped a bottle of Champagne, poured two flutes, and handed one to her. Then he had gotten down on one knee and handed her the black velvet box. She smiled at the memory, remembering the love in his eyes.

She would make sure he got the ring back the first trip she made to Philadelphia. There was no reason to keep it, since it only brought unhappy memories. She recalled her conversation with Dancing Bird, who had said she would marry, and soon. *I can't imagine how. It takes time to meet someone and build a relationship.*

She opened the front door and smelled the same rancid wild scent in the air. How close had the animal been to the house? It might still be nearby, watching her. As Nate's car pulled into the driveway, she locked the front door and ran to meet him. To her surprise, he got out and opened the passenger side door for her, an act of chivalry that surprised and pleased her.

As they headed out the main highway to the restaurant in East Glacier, about twelve miles away, Nate turned on satellite radio to a smooth jazz station. "This was a good idea—to get away for a while. We have to enjoy the local restaurants while we can. Most close in September."

"That's right," she mused. "I've never been here any time other than summer. What's it like living here in the winter?"

"Peaceful," he said. "I'm sure a lot of people would go stir-crazy, but not me. Oh sure, it's tough not to have dining and entertainment options year-round. When the restaurants re-open in the spring, everyone gets excited."

"Don't you get lonely?"

He was quiet for a moment. "Sometimes. It isn't always easy being alone with your thoughts."

She considered this remark. When had she ever been truly alone? "I guess I'll find out. Fortunately, I'll have time to work on my project and write my findings."

"If there's anything I can do to help, I hope you'll ask me. It sounds interesting."

"I will. Thanks."

They rode along in silence for a few minutes. Finally, Carrie asked, "Nate, when I got home this evening, I took Annie outside, and there was definitely the smell of a wild animal around. Did you notice it?"

"Probably deer."

"I thought there might be a bear or a mountain lion nearby ... or a wolf. I have one that visits me, you know."

"I did *not* know that," he said. "Be careful. There's a lot of land between your house and those foothills."

"It's unnerving to think there might be something big and fierce like a bear roaming around the house."

"You're twelve times more likely to die of a bee sting than a bear attack."

She chuckled. "There's comfort in that, I suppose."

"We live practically next door to Glacier National Park. There are wild animals everywhere, even if we don't see them or know they're there." Nate turned off the main highway. "This is where they live. We're their guests."

"But how likely is it that a mountain lion or bear would come so close to the house?"

"Where you are? I'd say it's a sure thing. But remember, most animal attacks are defensive. Bears don't prey on people. They're peaceful, but they'll attack if threatened, or if they have cubs. Grizzlies ... well, they're more aggressive, it's true. Last fall, a woman was brought into the ER after being mauled by a grizzly. She was out walking and didn't realize what was happening until the bear came at her from the side. It was bad."

Carrie flinched. "Did she survive?"

"She's doing fine now, but I honestly don't know how she made it. Strangely enough, most bear attacks on people aren't fatal. Believe me, if a bear wants you dead, you're dead. They disable whatever they perceive as a threat and then move on fast. They don't look upon humans as food. After attacking this woman, the bear ran away. She managed to walk a mile to get help, which in itself is amazing. I fixed what I could, just to stabilize her, and then we sent her by helicopter to Great Falls. Without a strong will to live, she wouldn't have made it that mile to her neighbor's house."

"I can't even imagine something like that." Carrie shuddered. "I worry more about Annie than myself."

"You're a good mama," Nate said, parking in front of the restaurant, a local favorite.

They headed to a back table with a votive candle and worn, unmatched chairs. Nate pulled out her chair and sat down, enjoying the casual ambience of the place. Their server handed them menus and took their drink orders. Carrie studied the daily specials while Nate opened the menu, scanning the left side.

"Are you having a salad for dinner?" he asked politely.

"I am *not*," she said. "I'm having a real dinner, and so are you. This is my treat, and I want you to get whatever you want. Don't choose something off the left side of the menu just because your mother taught you not to be greedy when a girl is paying. After weeks of whatever it is we eat at the hospital, we're going for real food tonight. Right side of the menu all the way."

He gave her a friendly nudge. "The next dinner is on me, pal. Seriously, though, I'm glad we have a chance to catch up. By the way, Peg said something yesterday about a kidney transplant. I was in a hurry and didn't get the gist of it. Do you know what she's talking about?"

Carrie smiled. "Leave it to Peg to take matters into her own hands. I have a female patient presenting with cystic kidneys. It's advanced."

"That's tough. We can offer dialysis here. That's about it."

"Darn it. I was hoping you'd say, 'Sure, we could do a transplant, you and me. I'll book both ORs.' " Carrie grinned. "I'm kidding."

Nate chuckled, his dimples popping. "I'm flattered you think that might be remotely possible. Even if we had the facilities and the personnel, there's no money to do that here."

"Yes," she said, "but if we could do it, I'd trust you to know exactly how to proceed."

"I appreciate your confidence." Nate sipped his water. "I also trust your judgment on a plan for her care."

"There's no cure yet, Nate. Treatments are being investigated, and there's a lot to be positive about, but you know how long it takes to get drugs tested and approved. All I can do is monitor BP and kidney function, advise her on diet, and treat problems as they crop up."

"And may I point out for the second time since I've known you that it was *you* who figured out there was something serious going on with this patient and investigated? She's had this condition all her life. It was getting out of control. Now you're on top of it."

"Maybe it isn't even what I think. I'm not an expert on everything. Other diseases produce cysts, too."

"I'm guessing you're spot on with this diagnosis," Nate said.

"Well, just for the record, this is one time I'd be glad to be wrong." She frowned. "She's my patient and I want her to have the same treatment anyone else can get who has this disease. I want her to have a chance to take part in clinical trials and have a transplant, if she wants one."

His eyes met hers. "Carrie, you have to accept the limitations. We'll never be able to offer what bigger hospitals can."

"Doesn't it get to you sometimes?" she asked.

"Of course … when I allow it to. But that's why you and I are here to begin with, right? We want to provide more than what these people have had in the past. We do what we can to the best of our abilities." He looked into her eyes. "You've already made a difference. I … we … just wish you could stay longer than a year."

Their server came to take their orders. After hearing the daily specials, Carrie ordered cedar-planked salmon with a side of steamed broccoli and a roasted sweet potato. Nate ordered a steak, medium rare, with green beans and a baked potato with sour cream and butter.

As they ate, they discussed the hospital and what was likely to happen when a permanent CEO was found to replace the interim. Nate wanted an outsider with a business background. Carrie hoped the interim CEO—a registered nurse who had been running the hospital for over a year—would get a fair shot at the job.

"I won't be here long term, so my opinion doesn't really count, I suppose." She took a bite of sweet potato.

"Of course, it counts. And you'll be coming back from time to time."

"Nate, I hope I'll be coming back. The reality is it might be harder than I think to continue as a volunteer."

"Are you sure you don't want to stay on permanently? Look at all we have to offer," he said, tongue in cheek.

"I do want to stay." She made direct eye contact. "I'm torn about this. I know what my dad is offering is really great. His practice is like the premier practice in that area."

"But look what we have: incomparable mountain views, wolves in your backyard …."

"There's that, yes." She smiled. "Working here is everything I've ever wanted. I feel needed here. But to think about staying on … well, it's a lot to wrap my mind around. I want other things, too. Just because Tom and I broke up doesn't mean I've given up on the whole work-life balance thing." She stared at her hands. "I wonder if I'll regret ending things with Tom. What if I blew my shot at having kids? Relationships are about compromise. Was I just as unwilling to compromise as Tom?"

He sat back in his chair. "I have no right to say this, but I'm going to say it, anyway. I'm the poster boy for unsuccessful relationships. No one I've dated since high school has understood what makes me tick, and I'm tired of trying to be someone I'm not. Don't compromise on who you are. Make sure whoever you love knows who he's marrying."

"That's the problem. Tom figured out who I am. I didn't meet his requirements." She took a sip of her wine.

"Ah, Carrie, don't do this. Don't do what I did and think there's something wrong with you for wanting what you want. You have this incredible gift. You're a fantastic doctor. Compromise is fine, unless you have to stop being who you are."

"Nate, I want kids. I'm running out of time." Was the chardonnay loosening her tongue?

He shook his head. "You'll have kids. You can be with someone who understands you, too. That's the only way." He raked his hands through his hair. "What am I saying? I broke up with a woman who was beautiful and funny and popular. She would have made a great home for us and been a terrific mother. I chose work on an Indian reservation over her. I'm a surgeon who works all the time and has nothing to offer a woman."

"I wouldn't say that. You give a hundred and fifty percent of yourself to everything you do. Heck, you even cook." She grinned. "Maybe Gali has a friend she could set you up with."

"How did we end up on this subject?" Nate's ears reddened. He swallowed the remaining ice water in his glass. Then he looked bashfully at her. "Did you say this dinner included dessert? Because I think apple pie à la mode is calling my name."

"I hear my name, too. But I think it's the huckleberry cobbler."

For now, the discussion of relationships was over.

Chapter Fifteen

⁓⌇⁓

ON THE FOURTEENTH OF SEPTEMBER, CARRIE woke from a strange dream to the sound of tiny hammers tapping on the windows. Disoriented, she lay quietly in the dark before realizing what was making the strange sound. Stepping gingerly out of bed onto the cold floor, she shivered and peered out the blinds at the still-dark sky. Sleet pelted the house and ground. The sky was overcast, swollen charcoal gray with precipitation that had the potential to turn into many inches of snow, heralding the arrival of winter. With Dr. Jim and Lois scheduled to arrive back in Browning later in the day, she hoped the weather wouldn't prevent them from flying into Great Falls.

She planned to welcome them home by making dinner—the one recipe in her repertoire: her mother's spaghetti sauce. She looked forward to conversations with Lois over tea and freshly baked cookies at the kitchen table, and to late-night talks with Dr. Jim. There was so much she wanted to tell him about all she had learned from the medicine woman.

Over the past two months, she had spent at least one evening each week with Medicine Owl, learning how the dear woman managed health care for tribal members. She had learned more than just common plant remedies—some even Gran hadn't heard of. In many cases, foods like corn were considered medicine. Without mentioning specific names of patients, Carrie and Medicine Owl talked about high blood pressure, a common health problem on the reservation, and one about which Medicine Owl had strong opinions. Carrie learned that the advice she gave patients was no different from what Medicine Owl told anyone who came to see her.

"I recommend more vegetables and fruits, less meat," Medicine Owl said. "I say 'Use garlic and onions and herbs to season foods, no salt.'"

In addition, she recommended hawthorn leaves, berries, and flowers for cardiovascular diseases, purslane with its red stems and green leaves—often scornfully referred to as an invasive weed, corn in any form, and even honeysuckle prepared as an herbal tea. She also warned against stress. "That is not as big a problem on our reservation as it is in your world," she said. "More quiet, more time in nature, less talk."

On one visit to see the medicine woman at her son's home in Browning, Carrie knocked on the door of the rundown one-story home and waited. When Medicine Owl's face appeared at the door, she indicated with a nearly imperceptible nod of her head and a warm smile that Carrie was invited to enter. The interior of the tiny home was modest, the furniture comfortable yet worn.

"Thank you for seeing me today, Medicine Owl. I have come to ask for your help with a patient who needs more than I can offer. I have asked her permission to talk with you."

"Tell me who it is. I will tell you if I have already seen her." Medicine Owl sat down on a hard-backed chair and waited.

"Violet Hightower."

Medicine Owl nodded, almost imperceptibly. "Yes, I have seen her."

"Her kidneys are covered in cysts. This disease—PKD is what we call it—is passed down between the generations. I am concerned that her son may have it, as well."

"I am aware of this disease," Medicine Owl said. "I have given Violet a ginger-lemon tea to help her kidneys. I told her she cannot do the sweat lodge. She needs to drink more water. I also told her to eat more buckwheat."

"I agree."

"For now, we will create a medicine wheel for Violet Hightower and her family."

Carrie's eyes lit up. "Thank you, Medicine Owl."

Once again, she became aware of the extraordinary honor bestowed on her, being taught by the tribe's medicine woman. For the next hour, Carrie and Medicine Owl constructed a medicine wheel for the Hightower family. On it, they arranged feathers and totems of animals, including a bear and a dragonfly. Medicine Owl prayed over the wheel while Carrie watched and listened.

When the ceremony was finished, Carrie stood and put on her coat. "Thank you for teaching me about the power of the wheel," she said. "I understand now."

Medicine Owl grasped her hand and walked with her to the door. "At the new moon, we will meet again."

Notes: I met today with Medicine Owl. The Blackfeet medicine woman often refers to the medicine wheel in her work, calling it the *sacred hoop*. The wheel is used by Blackfeet and many other tribes for health and healing. She says the medicine wheel can be an actual wheel shape or a piece of art such as a painting or sculpture. The wheel has four directions—north, south, east, and west—that signify elements of nature such as the sky, earth, or a tree with its arms outstretched. Everything is arranged in a circle like the cycles of nature. These directions also represent life—the spiritual, physical, mental, and emotional dimensions. Plants, water, fish, fowl, animals, and even rocks, minerals, and gemstones are included in this circle of life, and all are believed to have an important role in healing.

* * *

"YOO-HOO, ANYBODY HOME?" LOIS CALLED OUT in her singsong voice as she pushed open the front door. Annie barked in excitement and hurled herself against Lois's knees, nearly flattening her. "Oof! Good grief," Lois said as she righted herself against the door frame. "Yes, yes, hello, old girl. The other old girl is here now."

"Lois!" Carrie rushed from the kitchen, where she was making dinner. They collided in a hug. "I've missed you so much!"

"I've missed you, too. Goodness, I smell something wonderful. Carrie, are you cooking for us?" Lois's eyes were as wide as her smile.

"You could say that. I'm not sure what else you could call it. Actually, I'm making my mom's foolproof spaghetti sauce. Even I can't screw that up," she said and looked down at her shirt, which was dotted with spots of reddish-orange sauce.

"You'd better pre-soak that shirt," Lois advised as she took off her coat and hung it in the closet. "Better yet, let me do it."

Carrie ran out to the porch to greet Dr. Jim as he carried two suitcases up the front steps. He looked uncharacteristically grouchy. "We have perfectly good clothes here already. I don't know why we need to bring more." When he caught sight of Carrie's beaming smile, he dropped both suitcases and enveloped her in a tight embrace. "Hey, something sure smells good! I'm as hungry as a grizzly after the spring thaw."

"Spaghetti and salad, garlic bread, and ice cream sundaes," she supplied. "Nate is joining us. I think he needs sustenance."

Carrie grabbed one of the suitcases from Dr. Jim, who appeared out of breath. His color wasn't good. With another concerned glance at her old friend, she returned to the kitchen where Lois had uncorked a bottle of cabernet sauvignon and poured glasses for the three of them.

Dr. Jim tasted the wine and then headed upstairs with his glass. "You two catch up. I need a quick nap."

This was unusual, coming from Dr. Jim. Carrie exchanged glances with Lois, who watched him with concern as he made his way up the stairs. "Is he okay? He looks exhausted."

"He's not sleeping well. He's had a lot on his mind lately." Lois lifted the lid of the pot containing the spaghetti sauce and gave it a quick stir. "This smells good. What can I do to help?"

"Why don't you just sit down and relax? I've got this under control. It's not as good as what you'd make, but at least it will fill us up."

Carrie started a pot of water for pasta. Then she slid a loaf of garlic bread on a cookie sheet into the oven. As she set the dining room table, she hoped her efforts at preparing dinner would be acceptable. It was intimidating to cook for Lois, of all people. Her meals were legendary.

"With your schedule, I'm guessing you're too busy to do much cooking after work. I say that's why God invented frozen meals." Lois sipped her wine as she sat at the kitchen table. "Anyhoo, food is food."

"My food is just food. Yours sets the gold standard." Carrie blew a strand of hair from her eyes and began tearing romaine lettuce. "A salad, I can handle," she said with a sheepish grin.

Lois leaned back in her chair. "You young women have so much more to worry about than I did when I was your age. When Jim and I were first married with young kids, I stayed home. Most everyone did in those days. Not that it was easy, mind you!" She shook her head. "Three little kids and Jim at the hospital all the time? I thought I'd lose my marbles. Nowadays, you do it all: career, marriage, family, and all the other stuff women do. It's a tall order." Lois studied Carrie's face and her expression softened. "I was sorry to hear about the breakup with Tom. But don't you worry. You'll meet someone even better. You're a smart, caring, beautiful girl."

"Thanks, Lois," Carrie said. "I guess I worry about the old biological clock ticking away. It takes time to meet someone, and then you have to develop the relationship a while to even know if you want to be with the guy long term. You try to figure out whether he'll be a good father and husband. Oh, and working all the time doesn't leave much room for a social life, to begin with."

"You still have time," Lois said. "When I met Jim, I knew just like that he was the one." She snapped her fingers. Getting up from the table, she walked over to where Carrie stood.

"But how did you know?" Carrie said, frown lines deepening. "That's what scares me. I thought Tom was the one, and I couldn't have been more wrong."

Lois took a moment to consider her response. "I think there can be more than one person who is right for us, depending on where we are in our lives.

I had a serious beau before Jim, and Jim was dating my best girlfriend. But one night, we looked at each other, and I swear, everything just clicked. We were married less than a year later. I think there are reasons for everything. Tom was probably perfect for you … while you were both in residencies. And then, you learned more about what you *didn't* want in a relationship. That helped you figure out what you did want. It didn't work out this time, and that's okay." She touched Carrie's face reassuringly. "Sometimes happiness finds us just when we least expect it. In fact, I wonder whether life might have some wonderful surprises in store for you yet."

They were interrupted by the sound of Nate's voice in the foyer. He came into the kitchen and stopped short, looking confused. "Hey, Lois, I thought you and Dr. Jim just got here. You've obviously been here long enough to do some serious cooking. Something sure smells good!"

"We *did* just get here," Lois said. "Carrie cooked an Italian feast."

"Carrie *cooked*?"

"Now, don't sound so surprised." Lois laughed.

"Yeah, why do you sound so surprised?" Carrie asked indignantly.

"You know why." Nate gave her a peck on the cheek. "Is John coming, too?" he asked.

"He had other plans," Carrie said. "It's my fault. I asked him at the last minute."

"He's in Heart Butte, I bet."

"I don't know where he is. He's like the wind." Carrie handed Nate a glass of wine. "What about you? Have you seen him lately?"

"I played basketball with him the other night, but we concentrated on beating the heck out of each other. There was no talk."

Carrie laughed. "I want to have them over for dinner some night soon. I'll try to get better organized and call everyone ahead of time."

"Do you think John's girlfriend will move to Browning to be with him?" Lois asked.

"At this point, I don't think that's even a remote possibility," Nate said. "His mother doesn't know he's still seeing her."

"Oh ho ho, I bet Nadie does *too* know!" Lois howled with laughter. "Nadie Leathers doesn't miss a trick. She won't confront him or the girl, but if she doesn't approve, John won't have any doubt how she feels. Her silence speaks volumes."

Carrie thought of her father's prolonged silences whenever he disagreed with her. "Don't mess with Mama Bear, eh?"

"John is still straddling that line between being true to the Blackfeet Nation and doing what he wants to do, which is to be in love with this fantastic girl."

Nate picked at the end crust of the garlic bread as Carrie laid the hot cookie sheet on the stovetop.

"I wish he could have a normal relationship, without all the drama," Carrie said. "He works so hard, and he's such a good person. He deserves to be happy."

Nate looked troubled. "Sometimes it sucks being a guy."

Carrie and Lois burst out laughing. "Whaaat?" they both said at once.

Nate looked offended. "It does suck being a guy."

Dr. Jim walked into the kitchen. "Sounds like I missed a good joke. And I agree with Nate. Sometimes it does suck being a guy."

"Oh, you don't know how good you have it." Lois rolled her eyes.

"I *do* know how good I have it." He leaned over to kiss his wife's forehead.

"We were just talking about John," Carrie said. "I asked him to dinner, but he had other plans."

"Hope we can see him while we're here." Dr. Jim eased into a chair at the table and poured himself a little more wine. He looked rested, but Carrie could tell something wasn't right.

"Dr. Jim, I've been spending at least one evening a week with Medicine Owl," she told him.

"How do you rate?" Nate broke in, eyes wide with surprise. "I still haven't met her."

"You will. It all started after we delivered Peta's baby by C-section in July. Peta told me that Medicine Owl thought what we did was good. I guess she knew Peta wouldn't have survived without your help."

"And yours. You took one look at her and knew she was in trouble."

She smiled. "Okay, so we *both* had a hand in saving a life—actually two. Then John took me to see her—at Medicine Owl's invitation, no less—while we were horseback riding a couple months ago. Nate, you'd really like her. She has such a commanding presence."

"It's important to tap her knowledge now, while you still can. She's ninety-four—or maybe even older than that. Wow, that's really something, Carrie." Dr. Jim shook his head in wonder. "I'm glad you're able to spend that kind of time with her."

"I enjoy it. Actually, she reminds me of my grandmother."

Carrie added a diced tomato, carrot, and celery to the salad to make it more colorful before draining the spaghetti in a colander. So far, so good. As Nate picked at the garlic bread when he thought she wasn't looking, she gazed out the kitchen window, assessing whether snow might be on its way.

Her hands tightened on the edge of the sink. There, in the field, right where she always saw her, was the she-wolf, so close Carrie could see the whites of her eyes. She almost called the others to the window to look, but remained silent. This was personal, between her and the wolf. She kept sneaking peeks out the window until the shadows darkened and the wolf disappeared.

Tossing sauce into the bowl of pasta, she said, "Come and get it. I've got extra sauce for on top." She blew strands of gold hair out of her eyes. "I hope this tastes okay."

"I feel lucky to be invited," Nate said, digging into the pasta.

"Luck is exactly what you'll need." Carrie gave him a sidelong glance that caused him to laugh out loud.

She loved seeing him so relaxed and carefree, away from the constant pressure he faced at the hospital. Yet even when he was stressed, Nate had a razor-sharp wit and playful sense of humor. Quick with a smile or a joke, he was known for his kindness toward colleagues.

"I have Moose Tracks ice cream for dessert," she announced. Moose Tracks, an incomparable mix of fudge and peanut butter cups swirled into vanilla ice cream, was sure to be a hit with everyone. Maybe next time, she'd bake a pan of brownies to go with the ice cream—from a mix, of course. That she could handle.

Dr. Jim helped himself to more sauce for his pasta. "Haven't talked with you in a while, Nate. Had any interesting surgical cases lately?"

"When I married a doctor, I should have known I'd never enjoy another meal without a discussion involving bodily functions or fluids," Lois complained.

"Everything has been routine lately, except for a gunshot wound and a nasty foot amputation. Guy got his foot caught in a piece of farm machinery." He shuddered and looked apologetically at Lois. "Actually, I can't stay very long tonight because I've got a hysterectomy scheduled for six a.m. and then a colostomy reversal at eleven. So please don't think I'm rude if I eat and run."

"Well, if you leave too fast, I'll assume you don't feel well after eating my cooking," Carrie looked anxiously around the table, making sure everyone's plates and salad bowls were full.

Lois chuckled. "If you're going to start cooking in earnest, I can give you some of my recipes to try out. I'm pretty sure Jim married me for my meatloaf. It's still his favorite meal, even after all these years."

"Lois, I'm pretty sure Jim married you for many other reasons," Carrie said with a knowing laugh. "I'll probably never be able to hold a candle to your cooking. But at least, if I make anyone sick, I'll know how to treat their symptoms."

Lois chortled. "Atta girl. Always look on the bright side."

ON SUNDAY AFTERNOON, CARRIE ARRIVED HOME from delivering twins to find John Leathers sitting at the kitchen table with Dr. Jim and Lois, drinking coffee and enjoying a slice of freshly baked banana bread. He wore faded jeans and a green Glacier Park sweatshirt. "Hello," he said, standing to greet her as she came in the front door. His hands were stuck in the side pockets of his jeans. "I'm sorry I wasn't able to join you for dinner last night."

"Well, it was my fault for not asking you earlier." Carrie plopped into a kitchen chair and let out a huge yawn as she unfastened the braid holding back her hair. She had been at the hospital since daybreak, even missing her morning run. Although the delivery had gone well, the young mother had been in labor all night. Carrie knew her presence calmed the frightened girl. Annie bounded over to John, who crouched down to give her a good rub. "I'm glad you stopped by," Carrie said. "I've been wondering how things are going at home."

"My brother is doing better. My sister has been coming over to my parents' house when my mother isn't able to be there. We don't want Mike to be alone."

"It's really good that your entire family is supporting him."

Dr. Jim and Lois remained silent. Carrie knew they understood that as Mike's physician, she couldn't divulge patient information. But John didn't seem to mind if they knew.

"My brother nearly died a few weeks ago. We're helping him stay sober," he told them. "It's been a difficult time for the family. My mother has been beside herself with worry. Even my father hasn't been himself. He hasn't finished a painting in weeks."

"There's a reason why families go into counseling when one of their own has alcohol or drug problems," Dr. Jim pointed out. "It's real hard on everybody."

"My parents don't expect much. Mike has been drinking for over twenty years." John picked up his coffee cup. "Since he got out of rehab, he hasn't taken a drink, as far as we know. But he has begun eating too much, especially sweets. You won't be happy with his weight when you see him again, Carrie. I've been trying to get him to play basketball with me."

Carrie remained carefully silent on medical matters pertaining to her patient. "I can tell you that family support means a lot," she said. "Eating sweets helps raise his serotonin levels, and burning off those calories is a good thing."

"He needs work that keeps him occupied." John sat down again, resting his forearms on the table. "In the meantime, my father is encouraging him to draw. Mike has real talent. He could be as good as my father."

"That's it!" Carrie said, brightening. "That's exactly what Mike needs."

Chapter Sixteen

"**A**RE YOU STICKING AROUND FOR THANKSGIVING?" Carrie asked Nate one evening as they ate supper in the hospital dining room. "I've been looking at air fares online. If you're going anywhere, you'd better buy now."

"I just did," he said. "I'm going back to Kansas City to see my family." Pulling apart his sandwich, he examined the contents and made a face. "I haven't been back in a long time. Your mother isn't the only one who cries over a prodigal child. What about you?"

Carrie put down her fork, pushing away the remains of her tuna salad. "I don't think so. My dad still isn't speaking to me. I try to call when I know he's home. He won't come to the phone. I'd love to see my mom and Gran, but I don't want to go if my father refuses to talk to me."

"If you go there, he's going to have a hard time not talking to you," Nate pointed out. "You could just show up, you know, beard the lion in his den and all that."

"You don't know my dad. Maybe I'll ask Gran for her advice. Just showing up might make things worse." She took another bite of salad. "Will you see your ex while you're in Kansas City?" For some reason, the idea of Nate seeing his ex-fiancée bothered her.

"Nah. On the rare occasion I go back there, I stick pretty close to home. I hardly let anyone know I'm around. I don't go looking for trouble."

"Trouble? What kind of trouble? Nate, this is none of my business, and you don't have to answer. But why are you here? It sounds like you had a great job."

"I did." Nate set the sandwich back on his plate. "Some things happened. I couldn't stay there anymore."

Carrie listened, concerned that he had made a mistake that cost the life of a patient. "Do you want to talk about it?"

He looked away. "I suppose some people might say I'm a coward. I thought the choice was clear, at least at the time."

"What happened?" Carrie's eyes widened.

"A guy walked into the emergency room with a burn on his arm. Nothing major. Meth lab, probably. It was pretty obvious he was high on something. He was triaged and put into a room to wait his turn. Let's just say he didn't feel like waiting."

"He had a weapon?"

"A knife. He took a nurse hostage. To get her out of harm's way, I said I'd take care of him right away. I gave him a strong sedative—told him it would kill the pain and give him a good high. He dropped the knife pretty fast."

"Smart." Carrie leaned her elbows on the kitchen table. "I feel lucky that nothing like that has ever happened to me." Having worked in a Philadelphia inner-city hospital during her medical training, she knew that many of her colleagues risked their lives to do their jobs, especially in emergency medicine. It wasn't only on television medical shows that doctors and nurses faced grave danger.

"Actually, that time wasn't so bad. It was the second incident, about two months later, that convinced me I needed to leave. Montana seemed far enough away."

"Something even worse than facing down an addict with a knife?"

"I was working on a young male with multiple gunshot wounds. The guy was in bad shape, and I was trying to keep him alive until I could fix the worst injuries in the OR. I heard a commotion in the hallway—shots fired, lots of screams. Suddenly, I felt something against my head." He pointed to his left temple. "A rival gang member was holding a gun to my head. He said to step back or he'd kill me. He was the one who had shot up my patient. He was there to finish the job."

"Oh my God."

"I tried to protect my patient by covering his body with mine. The shooter got me in the back of my right thigh—just missed the femoral artery. Even so, I lost a lot of blood. Then he did what he came to do—killed my patient with a point-blank shot to the forehead. Blood and brains spattered everywhere. I'm an ER doc, a trauma surgeon. I've seen it all. But I swear, I'd never seen so much blood in one place before, and a lot of it was mine. While I was still on the floor, he held the gun to my head and said, "Don't move. If you tell anyone what I look like, I'll hunt you down.""

"That's awful." Carrie shuddered. "What did you do after that?"

"As soon as he left, I managed to get up off the floor. The patient was dead, of course. There was still a lot of chaos happening with security chasing the guy, police everywhere. I was taken to surgery to have the bullet removed. Then I answered questions and described the shooter. The police caught him. Right after that, I got the first death threat. After three more threats, I resigned and came here."

Carrie shook her head. "I don't blame you for leaving. And I think coming here was brilliant. No one would think to look for you in this place."

"I've got to admit, it's hard going back, even to visit my parents. I'll always be watching my back."

"You're lucky you're not dead. And if my opinion counts for anything, you're not a coward. Far from it. Nate, you risked your life twice by protecting a nurse and then by throwing yourself over your patient to protect him."

It all made sense now. Not knowing what else to say, she got up and walked around to the other side of the table. As she did, Nate rose to his feet. They were silent for a moment, studying each other. Then Carrie went with her first instinct, which was to wrap her arms around him. And then he was returning the embrace.

As she stood on the back porch with Annie one afternoon in mid-October, Carrie surveyed the snowy field behind the house, hoping to see the wolf. Breathing in the frigid air, she heard drums in the distance. The rhythm was familiar. She had heard it before, although she couldn't pinpoint exactly when.

In the fading afternoon light, the mountains were luminous. Their majestic heights were ringed in low-hanging clouds that she knew meant it would snow again tonight. As she took deep breaths, one after another, she felt her heart rate slow and her breathing become more measured, less shallow. She allowed Annie more length on the retractable leash, giving her room to roam.

When it was time to go back inside, she said, "Come, Annie."

It was at that moment that Carrie saw the wolf about a thousand feet away, heading toward her. The animal moved slowly, giving Carrie time to send Annie inside the house. With a rapidly beating heart, she returned to the top porch step within a few paces of the door, knowing that she could make a hasty retreat, if necessary. Still, she felt no fear. The wolf stopped, leaving enough distance between them that Carrie understood the animal meant her no harm. They stood watching each other as Carrie felt the first inner stirrings of renewed joy and peace.

The phone in her pocket rang. The caller ID said *Dr. Nanette Nelson*. Carrie bowed ever so slightly and bade the wolf a silent farewell before turning to enter the house. "Hello."

"Hello, dear. I haven't heard from you yet this week. You must be extra busy."

"Gran! I was just about to call. I have something important to ask."

"Is everything okay?"

"Yes. But I need your advice … about Dad."

"You don't think your mother would be a better one to ask than me?"

"Not this time. I was thinking about getting a flight back to Philly for the long Thanksgiving weekend, and Mom would say to come, even if it wasn't a good idea. Dad is still avoiding me. What if I just showed up? Do you think he'd have to talk to me?"

"I think it's a good idea to reach out to your father and try to clear the air. Why don't you write him a letter first? That way, you can let him know how you feel, and he'll have time and distance to consider your words. Then you can call and say you're coming home to talk to him."

"That's a great idea. I'll do it."

That evening, Carrie sat down and put pen to paper. She did a first draft to practice her best penmanship and then started with a fresh sheet of stationery. A letter to her father about something this important needed to be handwritten, not typed. She spent an hour writing down her thoughts, crossing out sentences, and rewriting them before she finally put the letter aside. No matter how hard she tried, the letter sounded angry. And why shouldn't it? She still felt angry at the way he had reacted to her news about the Roosevelt Award. And that whole business about giving Tom money to buy a house without her knowledge? She blew out an angry puff of air. It was a good idea to sleep on what she had written and try again tomorrow.

The next evening, and the next, she sat at the kitchen table and wrote letter after letter to her father, expressing her feelings about winning the Roosevelt, letting him know that she understood his disappointment that she hadn't been ready to come to work for him, but that this was the opportunity of a lifetime, and that they needed to talk. As she reread each letter, she could see that the tone still didn't convey her true feelings. As she wrote, the anger and hurt bubbled to the surface until she had no choice but to crumple the sheets of paper. Strangely, this exercise was getting her nowhere. And with the anger came a sadness so intense, she often cried herself to sleep.

"Dancing Bird, I'm glad to see you looking so well."

The tiny elderly woman who had won Carrie's heart with her sweet smile and gentle nature looked chipper and happy to see her. With her silver hair fastened in one long braid, Dancing Bird perched at the edge of the examination table, her small brown feet barely visible underneath the voluminous exam gown.

Listening to Dancing Bird's heart and lungs, she realized that her patient's health had improved. Her weight had dropped a few pounds, the result of less fluid retention, and her lungs sounded clear. Even so, Carrie knew that a chronic condition like congestive heart failure could suddenly take a turn for the worse.

"I am not using the salt shaker." Dancing Bird's voice was filled with pride in her accomplishment. "My granddaughter, she tells her husband he must lose the weight, too. She says no more potato chips."

Carrie grinned. "I'm glad everyone in the family is trying to eat healthier."

"We cannot live on just lettuce, Doctor," Dancing Bird said, suddenly becoming more serious. But then her face crinkled into a beaming smile. "We like lettuce with ranch dressing."

"A little ranch dressing is one of life's great pleasures," Carrie agreed. "Dancing Bird, I have wanted to ask you a question. I was told that you *know* things."

"I see things, hear things. I know them *here*." The old woman patted her chest.

"Those are special ways of knowing," Carrie said. "I have to use my hands or my stethoscope, or look at blood or X-rays to know things about people."

"You can see and hear things, too, in your mind and heart." Dancing Bird touched Carrie's brow and then her heart. "I see things in the past and the future." She touched her right ear. "I hear the words."

"Dancing Bird, it must be wonderful to have those gifts. What do you see?"

"You have had a life here before. You have returned to complete your spirit's purpose."

"Oh! I didn't mean about *me*." Carrie paused, considering whether to continue along this line of questioning. In the end, curiosity got the better of her. "Are you saying that my spirit's purpose is taking care of people here?"

"You have chosen this life to serve the people. You were one of us."

"But I am not a Blackfeet in *this* life."

"No, but you were a healer then, too. You are doing much good." Dancing Bird patted Carrie's cheek with her arthritic fingers. "You are a loving spirit. I think there is another loving spirit here who will care for you."

A small, delighted laugh escaped Carrie's lips. "Dancing Bird, I think *you* are someone who cares about me."

"You are learning more about our ways. That will help you remember what you knew before."

Carrie's brow furrowed. "What else do you see?"

"You are alone much of the time and this makes you sometimes sad."

"My family lives far away." She hadn't intended to admit how much she missed her family, but the words came out, anyway.

Dancing Bird patted Carrie's face. "You will not be alone always. Spirit hearts must find each other, wherever they are." She closed her eyes for a moment as if viewing a scene. "We find our spirit friends and complete the journey. That is all I have to say about that."

NATE WAS AWAY FOR A WEEK at a surgical conference in California. On his first day back, Carrie found him, his back turned to her, examining snack options in a refrigerator. "Good morning, Dr. Holden," she said.

He whirled around. "Oh, hey! I was just about to come find you. I wondered if you're free on Saturday night for dinner. We could drive over the mountains. There are some nice restaurants I haven't tried yet."

"That sounds great."

"I'm not suggesting this just because it's obvious you've lost weight," he said, studying her with concern. "Are you okay?"

"I've been busier than usual with this project, and I forget to eat." She shrugged.

"Are you sure that's all it is? You aren't wishing you could leave here? Second thoughts about spending the winter? It would be normal to feel that way."

She smiled and shook her head. "No. I'm fine being here for the winter." She looked down at her feet, aware that Nate was watching her. "Okay, so I'll just say it, since you sort of already know. My dad isn't talking to me ... I mean at all. I wish he'd just let this whole thing go, once and for all. I'm pretty sure he's also mad that Tom and I broke up. I'm to blame, even though Tom was the one who ended it, technically. Tom is Dad's golden boy now—the son he always wanted, to replace the daughter who's such a huge disappointment."

"I'm sure he doesn't think that about you." Nate's eyes were full of sympathy.

"Yes, but he's never gone radio silent on me for so long before, and it really bothers me, you know? Gran suggested I write him a letter, then call. The trouble is that I can't seem to actually get the stupid letter written. Nate, instead of time making things easier, it's actually getting worse. I'm scared that Dad won't forgive me the way he won't forgive Gran for whatever it is she did."

"We can talk more about this later. I believe it will all turn out fine," he said. "Just so you know, I'm here if you need anything. I mean *anything*."

She reached out and touched his arm. "I know that."

THE NEXT TIME CARRIE SAW MEDICINE Owl, the sight of the tiny woman with her gentle smile and kind touch brought immediate tears to Carrie's eyes. She quickly wiped them away with the hem of her shirt. "I'm sorry. I don't know what's gotten into me."

Medicine Owl led Carrie to a bench. "Sit, daughter. I will make you heartbreak tea."

A laugh burbled its way up as Carrie dabbed at her eyes. "Heartbreak tea?"

"You don't think people here have their hearts broken?" Medicine Owl began the ritual of making a pot of tea. She opened small cloth bags and allowed Carrie to sniff them before spooning the dried herbs into the teapot.

"I smell lavender and something else, something sweet."

"Yes. Sassafras, a little chamomile, and rosewater. Too much is not good. A little is just right."

"How did you know what I was feeling?"

"I know more than you think," Medicine Owl said. "I know your heart needs healing. It will take time and prayer. The body heals with help from the spirit. We will begin today."

Carrie sipped her tea as the medicine woman prayed and chanted. Then Medicine Owl picked up a small drum and began to beat a steady rhythm, her eyes closed, entering a trance. As Carrie listened to the drumbeats, she saw a vision in her mind's eye—a tipi and Indian people in a circle around a campfire, taking turns smoking a long pipe, talking in low voices. She heard the words and understood their meaning. But it wasn't English they spoke. She opened her eyes to find Medicine Owl sitting on a bench across from her, watching.

"Tell me what is in your heart," she said.

Looking into Medicine Owl's kind eyes, Carrie knew that no matter what she shared, there would be acceptance. But how was it possible to put into words the depth of sadness that engulfed her over this estrangement with her father? In the past, there had been times when he became frustrated with her—when she'd made choices he couldn't accept. Never had he ignored her so completely for months, refusing to talk with her when she called. It was as if he had cut her off from his life.

Taking in a deep breath, she began, "I have been trying to talk with my father for months. But he doesn't want to. My mother always says he can't come to the phone, but I know. He wants nothing to do with me. I tried to write him a letter, but ...." She shook her head. "What can I do?"

Medicine Owl nodded, listening. "He wants you to leave here."

"Yes. He has been angry with me for staying on the reservation. But I need to finish my work here. I had hoped he would forgive me by now."

"As you have forgiven him?"

Carrie let out a deep breath and shook her head. "It's hard to get past what happened. It would help so much if I could hear that he accepts what I'm doing, even if he doesn't completely understand."

"This work that you do is important." Medicine Owl nodded her head. "You don't think he understands why you want to be here with us?"

"I won an award that I thought would make him proud. I was so sure!

Instead, it did just the opposite. He was angry and disappointed in me. It seems I'm always doing the wrong thing."

"Ah, yes. Someone must be wrong so someone else can be right. But you see, daughter, there is no wrong way and no right way. There is just one way."

Carrie frowned. "I don't think I understand what you mean, Medicine Owl."

"There are many ways of living and all are good. There is no real separation between us. We are all as one, created from the same Great Spirit. Yet we think this thing is right and that thing is wrong. This person is right and that person is wrong. But you see, that is our mistake. We choose to be separated from each other, which means being separated from the Great Spirit. And so we suffer."

"I think I understand. But every time we make a choice that upsets someone else, they have their own reaction. We can't control that. I don't choose to be separated from my father. It's his choice."

"You have told him how important it is to have his blessing for this work?"

"I .... Well, no. Actually, I haven't said that ... not exactly. Do I need his blessing to do what I feel I'm called to do? Isn't that like asking for permission?"

"Sometimes we try so hard to do what we believe is right for ourselves, we forget a greater truth: that it doesn't matter. These things all pass. What matters most is who we are with each other. What affects one of us affects all of us. That is why forgiveness is so important to peace. When you forgive someone, you heal the cause of your pain and the pain of others everywhere. There is peace." She raised her arms and lowered them in an enormous circle.

"But if I forgive my father, what if he still doesn't forgive me?"

"With forgiveness, there is peace. Let it start with you, daughter. This is your Medicine." Medicine Owl placed her hands on both sides of Carrie's face.

Carrie nodded and touched her face to Medicine Owl's.

Chapter Seventeen

◦◦◦

On a twenty-eight degree night in mid-November, Medicine Owl and her helpers prepared the sweat lodge for Carrie. The structure consisted of a small dome covered in blankets and canvas. Large stones were heated on a blazing fire outside until they glowed. Then Medicine Owl's helpers lifted and moved the stones inside the domed cavern using a series of lifts. Clad in a light robe, Carrie followed Medicine Owl inside the lodge, curious and only a little apprehensive. She watched with fascination as Medicine Owl poured water over the hot rocks. Clouds of steam rose, surrounding them. The medicine woman chanted as the steam created an intense sauna effect. Carrie wasn't sure how long she could stand the heat. The prayers and chanting went on until the heat began to dissipate.

Medicine Owl pointed outside. "I like to roll in the snow. It is your choice. But you must drink water after you sweat."

Screeching as her overheated body hit the snow, Carrie dropped and rolled, laughing at the strangeness of the experience. The entire process was exhilarating. As she drank the water Medicine Owl offered her, she smiled. "Much better," she said.

That night, she slept nine hours. Waking the next morning, she felt rested, carefree, at peace. Even more surprising, she looked forward to experiencing the sweat lodge again.

"It was amazing," she told Nate. "You should try it."

"I hear it's hotter than hell in there."

"It's hot all right. As you perspire, you begin to feel clean, inside and out. Afterward, I felt totally drained—in a good way. I haven't slept that well in years. The steam cleanses you of toxins and makes you feel … alive … new. I can't quite describe it."

"Did you *have* to roll in the snow?"

"You don't have to, but I wanted to."

"I'm impressed," he said, grinning. "Next thing you know, they'll be making you an honorary tribal member. Doctor Golden Hair."

On Thanksgiving Day, Carrie joined Peg and her family for a traditional turkey dinner with all the trimmings. The affair rivaled anything her mother might have prepared. Peg and Ken had four grown children and ten grandchildren—six under the age of three. As everyone sat down to eat dinner on folding tables, Carrie could feel the Bright Fishes' love for each other, and the love and acceptance they extended to her.

She had woken that morning feeling homesick, thinking of her family gathered around the dining room table. In addition to an enormous turkey with chestnut stuffing, there would be mashed potatoes as light as air, sweet potatoes with a brown, sugar-pecan crust, traditional green beans with fried onions, a dried corn casserole, and of course, pumpkin and Pennsylvania Dutch dried apple pies. Around one o'clock, she called and talked with her mother and Gran.

It was only natural, she thought, that a traditional family holiday would bring sadness when she was so far away from her family. Yet she had to admit that joining the Bright Fishes and playing with their babies and toddlers helped to allay the blues. Peg even put her to work as her assistant.

"Just watch what I do," she said. "I'll show you how to make gravy—my way." While she was at it, she taught Carrie how to whip potatoes with milk until they rose into peaks and dot them with butter that ran down the sides in golden rivulets. "See? Cooking is not so hard."

Peg's two daughters and two daughters-in-law giggled, fascinated that a woman knew so little about cooking. As Carrie's cheeks reddened, Peg held a finger to her lips. "Dr. Carrie has been in school for many years, learning how to save lives. She had no time to cook. Hush up."

Everyone complimented Carrie on her first attempt at whipped potatoes and gravy. As they piled their plates with holiday fare, even Annie got a plate of turkey and mashed potatoes. After finishing her second slice of homemade pumpkin pie, Carrie helped with the dishes, putting off the moment she had to leave. But as other family members said good night, she knew it was time to go home to the Millers' empty house. She lived there, but it wasn't her home. Not really.

Peg reached out to stroke Carrie's hair. "Thank you for being part of our family tonight," she said. "When you get home, put this in the refrigerator for dinner tomorrow night." She tucked a bag of food into Carrie's arm. "I gave you extra sweet potatoes and pie."

"Thank you, Peg," Carrie said, putting her arms around her favorite nurse and holding her close. "I am so lucky to have you in my life."

Peg touched her forehead to Carrie's. "Oh no, Dr. Carrie, we are the lucky ones. You have come so far to be here, to take care of us. My family is safer now. You are the daughter of my heart."

THE FOLLOWING MONDAY, CARRIE'S FIRST PATIENT of the morning turned out to be Mike Leathers. True to John's words, Mike had put on a few pounds. But the extra weight filled out his face, making him look years younger and considerably healthier than the emaciated man she had seen during earlier visits. She knew that recovering alcoholics often self-medicated with sugar and other starchy treats in an effort to replace the good feelings they got from alcohol. In this case, as long as Mike was healthy and continuing to exercise, she couldn't begrudge him a few sweets.

"So, tell me how you're doing." She pulled a chair closer.

"Fine. I have been to the sweat lodge."

"Do you think that helps?" Carrie did not share that she, too, had been to the sweat lodge and couldn't wait to go again.

"Yes. Medicine Owl gave me tea."

Carrie wondered which herb or root Medicine Owl had recommended. She'd have to make sure it didn't interfere with the medication Mike was taking. "So, what else is going on in your life?" she asked. "You look great, by the way."

My father and I work together. We draw and paint."

"I'm glad! Art is a good way to spend your time. I notice from your posture that you appear to have some discomfort." She indicated his upper back. "That could be caused by hunching over while you work. Let me see if I can give you some relief." She had some extra time today, so she worked on his neck and upper back while she kept up an easy flow of questions. "Do you draw every day?"

"Yes. I start in the morning and continue all day and into the night."

"I have no artistic talent to speak of. I'd love to see one of your drawings."

Mike pulled a square of white paper out of his pants pocket and unfolded it. Carrie gasped. "Mike, this is beautiful." She studied the wolf, drawn in pencil with obvious skill, lovingly rendered to the slightest detail. "I have a wolf that visits me," she said, meeting his eyes. "This looks just like her."

"You know it is a she-wolf?"

"I'm sure of it." Even if Medicine Owl hadn't told her, she had sensed all along that the wolf was female. She was certain it was the wolf who had talked to her in her dream.

"Wolves are good," Mike said. "When they kill, it is for food or to protect other wolves, especially their pups. They are one of the smartest animals in the wild. Wolves were hunted until there were hardly any left. But now they are back."

It was the most Carrie had ever heard Mike utter at one time. She sat down again on the chair and handed the drawing back to him. "Sometime I would like to hear more about wolves. I'm glad you showed me this drawing. I'm sure your father is very proud. Do you paint in oils, too?"

"Watercolors," he said. "My brother gave me a set of watercolors, brushes, and paper. I draw and paint every day. I like to paint animals."

Carrie smiled at the enthusiasm she heard from the serious, sad-looking man she had feared might find little joy after he stopped drinking. "I hope I'll get a chance to see some of your paintings in the museum. I would like to buy one."

He looked surprised, and then a small, shy smile crossed his face. To Carrie, it was like watching a flower bloom. "Yes, I think that is possible," he said.

THAT EVENING, SHE REACHED ACROSS THE miles to Gran. "I miss you," she said. "I wish you could come here."

"I miss you, too," Gran said. "I know you're doing a wonderful job and this is what you're meant to do, but I'm your grandmother, and I worry about you. How is life on the reservation?"

"Work-wise, everything is great. But I can't seem to shake the blues over what happened in July. Gran, I don't want my relationship with Dad to become—"

"Like my relationship with him," Gran finished. She let out a sigh.

"Medicine Owl says to work on forgiving him."

"Those are wise words." Gran was silent for a moment. "I have had to do that, too."

"And did you feel better?"

"I once read that not forgiving someone is like carrying a bee around in your pocket. Every time you put your hand in that pocket, you get stung. The other person is not. They don't even know what you're feeling."

"Have you ever thought that it was like that with Dad? That you needed to forgive him for all the times he has said hurtful things to you?"

"He's my son, and I love him. There is nothing he could ever do or say that I couldn't forgive. But I'm still human, so yes, I often have to work at forgiveness."

"After I did the sweat lodge, I felt better. Of course, just because I'm trying to forgive Dad doesn't mean that he'll automatically call me. But maybe someday, that will change."

Gran let out a breath. "I'm guessing you'll be coming back to Philadelphia for the family medicine conference in March? Perhaps you can sit down with him then."

"I hope so."

"I meant what I said, Carrie. I worry about you being alone so far from family."

"I have folks here who care for me," she said. "I work with great people. I have John watching over me. Of course, I run into Nate just about every day at the hospital. Medicine Owl is my friend."

"That's not exactly what I meant. Let me say my piece. When your grandfather died, I never looked at another man. When he was taken so suddenly, a big part of my heart went with him. What happened with you and Tom was terrible. But I thought you showed great courage. Even your mother understands now why you had to break off the engagement."

"She does? She still talks as if I may have given up my chance at love and happiness."

"My son does what he thinks is best, full speed ahead and damn the torpedoes. Your mother is as upset about what happened as you are."

"Gran, I want a family of my own. Can that ever happen? I might be running out of time."

"I'm an old woman, but I still know something about love. And what I'm saying to you now is don't put all that you have to offer a good man on a shelf while you concentrate solely on work. It isn't healthy. Medicine Owl gave you heartbreak tea for a reason. I'm pretty sure the breakup with Tom is part of the heartbreak you carry around."

"Yes," Carrie said in a small voice. "Yes, it is. Medicine Owl said people here have their hearts broken, too."

"It's a universal pain. I'm sure she knows from her work that hearts do heal. I believe that everything will be okay with your dad. I also believe you can find love again."

Afterward, with Annie's head resting on her lap, Carrie curled up on the sofa. Channel surfing produced nothing worth watching, so she turned the TV off. She needed to find something else to think about other than what was still missing in her life. Gran's comments led to thoughts of Nate. Although she had to admit she was attracted to him—who wouldn't be?—he was a colleague at the hospital. As she knew only too well, dating someone at work, especially in a hospital the size of this one, was complicated. They would be the subject of gossip. If their relationship fizzled, there could be tension. She might lose him as a friend.

A nearly full butter-cream moon illuminated the fields and hills outside. Long shadows on the snow shone in muted shades of blue and purple. A light snow was falling, making conditions perfect for snowshoeing or cross-country skiing, which had taken the place of her morning run. She had found a cross-country trail around a nearby lake and went as often as she could make time. With the night beckoning to her, she yearned to see the wolf. Somehow, the animal always brought a sense of comfort and company, just as Annie did.

A bit after nine o'clock, she quietly stepped outside onto the porch, breathing in the night air, hoping the she-wolf would sense her desire to meet again and appear. But if the wolf did come, Carrie never saw her. It wasn't until bedtime, as she nestled under the quilt, that she heard the creature's mournful howls. The sound was full of longing, a feeling she knew well.

As CHRISTMAS APPROACHED, CARRIE REGRETTED NOT purchasing a plane ticket home to Philadelphia for the holidays. Despite the rift with her father, it was the time of year for gatherings with family and friends, cross-country skiing on the trail near her parents' house, naps by the crackling fireplace, and an endless supply of Christmas cookies. She thought of sipping hot Hershey's cocoa topped with gooey miniature marshmallows while listening to favorite Christmas carols from her father's collection of vintage vinyl records. There would be ice-skating in the park, holiday movies with friends, and impromptu gatherings with people she had known since she was a child. For the first time ever, she wouldn't be part of it.

It was tradition that during the days leading up to Christmas and throughout New Year's, she and her mother would sit at the kitchen table every evening with cups of tea and a plate of cookies, dunking them until they had a half-inch of cookie crumbs on the bottom of their cups. Gran always joined them on Christmas Eve for seafood pasta swimming in olive oil, butter, and garlic, followed by even more cookies. After the meal, they'd turn on Christmas music, open presents, drink wine or her father's favorite Maker's Mark Manhattans, and talk by the fireplace until they were too sleepy to stay up anymore. Oh, how she loved listening to Gran's stories about her patients and seeing the unique homemade gifts they brought her: tatted lace, a clove-studded orange pomander, a handmade rug or afghan. Many times, these gifts were payment for services rendered. But more than that, they were gifts from the heart, extended to Gran in appreciation for her care.

Tears filled Carrie's eyes and dripped down her face, dampening the front of her sweatshirt. She scrubbed at her eyes with her fists, unwilling to be sad on such a gorgeous day. With the sun shining and fresh snow, it was healthier to play with Annie. In nature, she would find solace and strength. She would reclaim her spirit there.

Annie wagged her tail, always ready for fun, and waited patiently by the front door while Carrie smoothed sunscreen on her face and bundled up in layers with thick socks, ski pants, a heavy waterproof jacket, hat, a wool scarf, and ski gloves. Two feet of dry powder had fallen overnight, and she intended to make the most of it. It had taken her thirty minutes just to clear the porch and front steps that morning, enough time to assess that the snow was ideal for snowshoeing or making snow angels, but far too dry to build a snowman.

When she stepped outside, the snow was so stark-white, it nearly blinded her as she gazed out over the field next to the house. Squinting, she pulled protective sun goggles out of her pocket and grabbed her snowshoes and poles. Sitting on the bottom step of the porch, she fastened the snowshoes to her boots and carefully side-stepped out into the yard.

With Annie leaping through the deep snow as if mounted on a pogo stick, they headed across the field behind the house, the leash stretching as far as possible. The sun was high overhead, creating glints like diamond dust on the crystalline snow. The sky was a brilliant azure with wispy white clouds, and the mountains were a vivid navy blue. She couldn't imagine a more beautiful day to be outside. While others were in church, she was in God's country, experiencing her very own heaven on earth. In nature, one really could feel the Great Creator.

This profound moment of being one with nature evoked another feeling: a sense that everything would turn out for the best. Events had a way of unfolding in what she believed was divine order. She was in one of the world's most beautiful locations, doing the healing work she loved, meeting new people, and making a difference. Although it was normal to feel homesick when you were away from family at the holidays, there was no need to give more power to these emotions than they deserved. As she stood facing the mountains, she raised her face to the sky to give thanks for all she had.

"Great Creator, thank you." She had heard Medicine Owl use these words, and they resonated with her.

High above, a bald eagle soared, its broad wings powered by wind drafts that carried it aloft. She craned her neck as far back as it would go, following the eagle's flight pattern until it finally landed in the uppermost branches of the tallest ponderosa pine. She noticed the remains of animal tracks and studied them, trying to determine which animal had left its mark. In the deep snow, animals foraged for leaves, grass, and other remains of warmer weather bounty. About a quarter-mile from where she stood in a thicket of trees, she searched for other signs of life in this winter wonderland. But the only thing she saw was a white hare bounding across the snow.

Glancing behind her, she smiled, watching Annie leap through the tracks made by her snowshoes. With a snuffling sound, Annie lowered her head into the snow and came up with a face full of snow and a white beard. Carrie laughed out loud in delight at Annie's antics.

"You look like Santa Claus! Or is it Santa *Paws*?"

Annie woofed three times, as if saying, "Ho, ho, ho!"

Despite all the effort they were expending, they hadn't gone very far. She could still see the house from where they stood. The deep snow made it slow going. Breathing hard from the cold and exertion, she turned back, broadening the path she had made so that Annie could run more easily. As she placed one snowshoe in front of the other, planting her poles for balance, she stopped now and then to search the field, hoping to see the wolf. But there was no sign of her.

When they returned to the house, Carrie peeled off all her layers and curled up on the sofa in her thermal underwear, a thick pair of L.L.Bean socks on her feet. She turned on her laptop and opened email. There was a message from her mother, which she skipped over for a moment, more intent on reading the email from John.

It was a forwarded electronic message from the state health department regarding strep throat. That and influenza were becoming a serious public health threat. She was getting more worried about the flu this year, having read that the flu shot might not cover the most virulent strains. She replied to John's email.

> Some of your students have already tested positive for strep. I'm more concerned about flu as the weeks go by. Please continue to encourage students to get their flu shots. It offers some protection, at least.

Now she opened her mother's email.

> The Christmas tree is up, the presents are wrapped, and your gifts have been sent. A box should arrive by little brown truck early this week. We wish with all our hearts that you could be here for Christmas and hope that you can spend the holidays with friends there. Gran has been a little under the weather this week, but seems to be improving. Dad says that at her age, she shouldn't be seeing people who have contagious illnesses. But you know she won't turn anyone away who needs help. Wishing you could be here.
> —Much love, Mom

She had agreed to join Peg and Ken Bright Fish for Christmas Eve service at Little Flower Catholic Church. Perhaps she should stop by Nate's house today and drop off his gift. He had seemed a little down after returning from Kansas City. Christmas would be a tough holiday for him, too, without his family.

She opened the garage door and dragged a small fir tree from the roof rack of her car. Putting up a tree was usually a two-person job, even if it was small. The needles dug into her arm, and she felt a sharp sting on her cheek. She positioned the metal tree stand on the garage floor close enough to the wall that she could lower the trunk into the stand. Huffing and puffing with exertion, she was almost finished when her cell phone rang, startling her. Bobbling her cell phone in her haste to answer, she saw that it was John calling.

"Hello, John. I'm glad you called. Thanks for the email."

"Hello, Carrie. I talked with Medicine Owl yesterday. She would welcome a visit from you."

"My schedule has been more hectic than usual. I'll try to go tomorrow. Actually, I've been planning to talk with her about this flu that's going around. I'd like to know what she recommends." She paused. "While I have you on the phone, I was wondering whether you and Gali will be here over Christmas. Maybe we could get together for a little cheer some evening. Or will you be with your family?"

There was a long pause. Finally he said, "I'll be with my family. Gail will be with hers."

"Oh?" she asked. "That doesn't sound positive. Is everything okay?"

"I wouldn't say that," he said. "I haven't had as much time to drive to Heart Butte. There have been a lot of fires to put out. Most are still smoldering."

"At work or at home?"

"Both. I need to look into getting a new heating system at the elementary school, although our janitor thinks he can keep the old boiler working through this winter. Last week, six seniors got themselves in trouble over a prank involving a goat. They put the goat in their science teacher's car."

Carrie laughed. "Never a dull moment for the school superintendent. Did you suspend them? Who was more surprised—the teacher or that poor goat?"

"It was a draw. If I suspend the boys or take away their ability to play sports after school, they'll get into other trouble. I prefer to keep them in the building as long as possible. I made them write letters of apology to the farmer who owns the goat, to their teacher, and to their own parents. For boys, that is the worst punishment I can dole out."

"Nothing worse than the dreaded letter of apology," Carrie agreed. ·

"What are your plans for Christmas?" he asked.

She paused. "I'll go to church with the Bright Fishes. A quiet Christmas is okay with me."

"Nate will be alone for Christmas."

Carrie wasn't sure what to say, so she settled for "I'm sure I'll run into him at some point."

John was quiet for a moment before continuing. "Actually, the reason for my call, other than to say hello, is to ask if you would do a special health class for our high school girls about birth control and sexually transmitted diseases—sometime after the first of the year."

"Sure." With her knees screaming from squatting on the garage floor, Carrie lowered herself into a sitting position. If it had been anyone but John, she might have asked if she could call him back. But he was a tough man to catch, and she couldn't count on him to return calls right away.

"I see so many teenage moms in the clinic, some with more than one child," she said. "Even if they already have a baby, maybe they'll accept birth control advice before getting pregnant again, at least until they're older."

"The girls will like you," John said. "My secretary will call after the holidays to arrange a time."

"I look forward to it. And John …?"

"Yes?"

"Merry Christmas. I'm glad I'm here, and I'm grateful you're my friend."

"I feel the same. Merry Christmas, Carrie."

Chapter Eighteen

⁓⥾⥿⁓

FOR THE NEXT HOUR, CARRIE UNPACKED yards of twinkling white lights and Native American Christmas ornaments she had purchased at the Trading Post. The figurines were made of terra cotta, rough pine, leather, glass, and beads—perfect for her first Christmas on the reservation. She even found a gold star for the tree topper. In the middle of the star, an angel walked with a bear.

As she unstrung lights, she heard a knock on the front door. Glancing through the peep hole, she saw Nate carrying a package wrapped in shiny green paper with an enormous red bow.

"Hey, there!" she said, opening the door. She was delighted to see him. "I tried to call you a few times. I was beginning to think you fell through the ice or got devoured by a bear or something."

He stamped the snow off his boots and removed them before coming into the house. "No such luck," he said, handing her the gift box.

She raised her eyebrows at him. "Thanks. I have a present for you, too." She handed his gift to him. "What do you mean, 'no such luck'? Do I need to be writing you a scrip for an antidepressant?"

"I don't know what I mean. Never mind." He studied the Christmas tree. "That isn't a very big tree," he said, pointing out the obvious.

"I didn't think I could handle a bigger one." She shrugged. "While I was lugging it into the house, I realized why it's a good idea to have two people doing this."

"So, why didn't you ask me?"

"I thought you were too busy. Anyway, it's already up. Would you like to help me decorate it?"

"I'm not too busy, Carrie. You can always ask." Nate stood back to assess the tree. "It's crooked." He loosened the stand while she held the tree in place, tightening the screws again until it was perfectly straight. Standing back, he looked at the tree to make sure it wasn't leaning. "That's better." He carried the tree into the living room and positioned it in the front window. "Now I'll do the lights for you since you're so short."

"I'd appreciate that. But the word is 'petite,' not 'short.'" She sorted through the new ornaments, already fond of each of them. "Nate, what are you doing for Christmas?"

"As little as possible," he said. "I guess I'm not much in the holiday spirit."

"I had a case of the blues this morning, but I'm determined not to let it ruin my Christmas. I wondered if you'd like to join us—the Bright Fishes and me, that is—for church on Christmas Eve? It would do both of us good, I think." She gave him a hopeful look.

Nate brushed loose pine needles out of his hair and off the front of his sweater, weighing the question. Finally, he said, "Sure, why not?"

He strung the twinkle lights on the branches in record time, and then they hung the ornaments. When the tree was decorated to their satisfaction, Carrie handed him a Dr. Pepper. "Thanks for helping me. Have you eaten? I could throw a frozen pizza in the oven."

"Actually, the reason I stopped by, other than to give you your Christmas present, was to see if you wanted to try the restaurant over at the Izaak Walton Inn," he said. "They have good food. We could enjoy a decent dinner and get out of Dodge for a while."

"I'd like that," she said, thankful not to have to eat alone.

That evening, as Nate drove to the Walton Inn, a scenic hotel in nearby Essex, they spoke again about the experiences that had led them to Browning. Dr. Jim had been a major influence on Nate, mostly by example. "It wasn't just that he was my friend's dad and I grew up respecting him. Dr. Jim was our family doctor, and he's so good at what he does. I applied to his medical school because I knew I wanted to learn about manipulation, too. I liked the idea of helping a patient avoid surgery if at all possible."

Nate had trained in emergency medicine and general surgery in Kansas City at the same medical center where the shooting in the ER had taken place. Although he had enjoyed the work and the frantic pace, he said it was easy to get burned out working so many hours under such stressful conditions. Still, he'd had no plans to do anything different—until the two life-threatening incidents occurred in such rapid succession. When he made the decision to leave, he had also begun to want a different life.

"I wanted more balance, more time to do something other than work," he explained. "If I was going to get married and have kids, I wanted to be the kind of dad my father was."

"Do you think you'll ever be able to go back to Kansas City without feeling so anxious, maybe five or ten years from now? Whoever is responsible for the death threats might have given up by then."

"The way these gang members are killing each other, it's more than likely that the person responsible won't even be alive in five or ten years. But it'll be a long time before I can relax when I'm there."

"So, you're planning to stay here long term? You're so important to the people here."

"That's the plan. Will that still be the case three to five years from now? Who knows. What about you?"

"As much as I hate to admit it, I don't relish the thought of joining my dad's practice. Oh sure, it's secure and pretty much nine-to-five with a few Saturdays thrown in. He pays well, there are generous benefits ... pretty much everything you could ask for."

"Except it isn't what you're asking for," Nate supplied with a quick laugh. "You're different, Carrie. I haven't known you that long, but you don't seem as if you'd be happy in that environment."

"I'm more like my Gran. She always marched to the beat of her own drummer. She and my dad don't get along at all."

"How come?"

Carrie looked out the window at the snow-covered fields and endless trees. She thought back to what she had been told regarding the long-simmering tensions between her father and grandmother. She knew very little. The subject seemed to be taboo.

But she remembered something Gran had said a few years earlier: "My son had a rough childhood. It's tough for a little boy to lose his daddy so unexpectedly."

"I don't know the entire story," Carrie said. "When I asked my mom, she said it was complicated, and she didn't understand it, either. Maybe Dad resented his mother for working so many long hours at a time when most mothers didn't. That's what doctors do."

When they arrived at the Izaak Walton Inn, Nate shut off the engine. "Sit still," he said, and ran around to open her door.

Charmed by his good manners, she allowed him to take her hand to help her out of the car. As they walked toward the hotel, they passed historic train cabooses made available as rentals. Open year-round for cross-country skiing enthusiasts, the historic resort hotel included a rustic lodge with a dining car. When Nate held the front door to the hotel open for her, she said, "Thank you," and felt her face warm at the light touch of his hand on her lower back.

When their server arrived to take drink orders, she asked for a glass of chardonnay. Nate ordered a beer. Then he said, "You always say how important I am at the hospital. We need you, too." He shrugged his shoulders and smiled, embarrassed. "It seems like the two of us have had similar challenges. We care about the same things. Can't we just hang out here a while and be happy?"

"Compared to what you've been through, my challenges seem small." She pressed her hands flat on the table. "I mean both of us have ended engagements. That's stressful. But you had bigger issues to worry about, like personal safety." She didn't add the next thought that came to mind. *Both of us also deserve someone who will be supportive.*

Carrie studied the amber liquid in her long-stemmed glass, lit by the glow of the nearby fireplace. Then she raised her hand in a toast. "To the next phase of our lives," she said. "Whatever that may bring."

He smiled and touched his bottle to her glass. Rubbing his chin, he put down his bottle and placed his forearms on the table. "You really are something else." He shook his head. "You're the only woman I know who would leave what had to be a great opportunity with your dad to come here, of all places. And the thing is ... you actually seem to be thriving. You're so sure of yourself. How did you get to be so wise?"

"I come from a long line of wise asses," she said to lighten the moment as heat suffused her cheeks. She added, "That isn't exactly right. I don't have it all figured out. I have no idea where I'm supposed to be in this world. For now, it's here, I guess. Like you, I don't know about the next three to five years. It's important to do something meaningful in life and to keep exploring. If you want something, you have to go for it, right?" As Nate nodded, she continued, "I'm paying the price for that with my dad. But a career can't just be about making a lot of money or being a big shot. I want to make a difference doing work I feel passionate about. But I also want to love where I live and be with the people who are most important to me. I guess I want it all."

"Doesn't everyone? We work hard here, but we also live in one of the most fantastic places on earth. We should be able to enjoy life."

"Agreed. In one sense, I'm relieved that I don't need to worry about what Tom thinks anymore. But it was pretty rough at the end, and I'm working on healing."

She told him what had happened, beginning with the many months of sniping comments and Tom's disrespect for her career goals. "I couldn't trust him any longer. He kept it a secret for at least a month that my dad had already offered him a job. He bought a house with money my dad lent him, and I was just supposed to fall in line with that plan."

"He bought a house without consulting you?" Nate's eyes widened.

"Right. That was the final straw. But now I wonder if I used it as an excuse to break up with him." She stroked her upper lip. "I'd been feeling uncertain for a while. I knew what I wanted for my life and career. He wanted something completely different, but he wasn't willing to compromise at all. It takes sacrifices to make a relationship work, but it can't just be about one person's sacrifice. I would have had to give way more than Tom was willing to do for me. She paused. "So, let me ask you this: do you think that if you're doing what you love, and you're where you want to be, everything will fall into place?"

Nate didn't answer right away. "I guess we'll find out," he said finally. As their server came back to the table, he asked, "Are you ready to order?"

She looked over the menu. "I'll have a Caesar salad and the glazed wild salmon. I might have the huckleberry cobbler, too."

Nate winked. "I like a girl who isn't afraid to eat."

CHRISTMAS EVE DAWNED WITH A SKY of purplish-gray clouds and falling snowflakes the size of silver dollars. Sticking out her tongue to catch the lacy flakes, Carrie stood in her boots in the snow, flannel pajamas under her down coat, her hands encased in mittens as she held Annie's leash. She breathed in the frigid air, which promptly froze the lining of her nose and sinuses. Annie was predictably slow about doing her business, more interested in the smells beneath the snow.

It would be a shorter day in the clinic, but there were still sick patients to see, especially with strep throat and a particularly vicious strain of respiratory flu going around. This particular viral strain was accompanied with lower respiratory issues that could lead to pneumonia, especially in children, the elderly, and anyone with compromised immune systems.

She hoped the hospital census would remain as low as possible on Christmas Day when she made rounds. Fortunately, this already looked to be the case. Nate had two surgical patients still hospitalized, but he said he would manage their care.

The day passed easily, and Carrie and Peg even had time for a bowl of Peg's famous three-alarm chili. "Ken and I are glad you and Dr. Nate want to join us at church tonight," Peg said. "The early Mass is at five o'clock. There is another at midnight. We go to the early one."

"I'm looking forward to it. I've heard the service is beautiful."

"You should not be alone on Christmas. It isn't right." Peg lowered her head and peered over the top of her reading glasses.

"Thanks to you, I won't be." Carrie had a feeling Peg was going somewhere with this comment.

"Maybe after church, you could give Dr. Nate a little holiday cheer," Peg added, lowering her glasses even farther down her nose. As Carrie laughed, Peg added, "Now don't look at me like that."

* * *

THAT EVENING, STEPPING QUIETLY INTO THE sanctuary at Little Flower Catholic Church behind Ken and Peg, Carrie slipped into the church pew and pulled down the vinyl burgundy kneeler. She prayed for several minutes, giving thanks for all that had happened in the past year, and for the work and the people that had led her to Browning. So much about her time seemed providential: the friendship with Dr. Jim that had led her here, the support of John Leathers and Peg, even her working relationship and growing friendship with Nate. She lived in a stylish, comfortable home for which she paid no rent. She enjoyed time in the outdoors with her beloved dog. She had a wolf who thought she was special.

She smiled to herself. It was an achievement and a great honor to find favor with the medicine woman. It was almost too much to take in sometimes. And now that she was here in church on Christmas Eve with people she cared about, all was right with the world.

Nate arrived a few minutes later, smelling of the outdoors, wood smoke, and a hint of spicy aftershave. Carrie sniffed appreciatively as he slid into the pew beside her. She handed him a song sheet of carols.

He bumped her arm in a purposeful way. "Thanks for saving me a seat."

He slipped off his jacket to reveal a heather-blue fisherman's sweater with a blue dress shirt and dress pants. She had never seen Nate in anything except jeans or scrubs. He looked so handsome. Maybe Peg was right. A little holiday cheer might be nice.

"Glad you could make it," Carrie whispered, inching closer to Peg so that Nate would have more room. "I had almost forgotten how beautiful this church is."

As the priest spoke the first words of the Mass and the congregation responded, Carrie was swept up in the beauty of the Christmas story and the beloved music and lyrics to "Silent Night" sung in this historic church. The Mass had a strong Native American flavor, the result of Blackfeet traditions that had infused the church with a culture all its own.

During the sign of peace, she extended her hand to Peg, who squeezed it. "Peace be with you," Peg said and held her close.

Fresh tears welled in Carrie's eyes. "And also with you." She returned the embrace, feeling the motherly energy that Peg exuded. She turned to Nate. "Peace," she said, smiling, and held up two fingers in a V, the universal sign of peace.

"Peace, Carrie." She saw that his blue eyes also glistened with unshed tears. He squeezed her hand and released it. "I'm glad I came tonight," he whispered.

After Mass, Carrie and Nate took a walk through town. They left their cars parked near the church and strolled down the quiet street blanketed in white. Here and there, lights twinkled in houses and buildings around town, reminding Carrie of a wintry fairytale.

"This is what the North Pole must look like," she said. "I half expect to see a sleigh with eight tiny reindeer land in the middle of the street."

Nate burrowed his hands deeper into his pockets. "Moose are more likely. Hey, did you open your presents yet?"

"No. Did you?"

"My family opens our gifts on Christmas Eve. I haven't touched any of mine yet."

"In my family," she said, "each person is allowed to open a few gifts on Christmas Eve. We save the rest for Christmas morning." A small knot formed in her chest as she thought of everyone sitting in front of a blazing fire in the old stone fireplace. Her mother always served hot apple cider with sticks of cinnamon as they opened their gifts. She had an idea. "Why don't you go get your gifts and bring them over to my place? We can open presents and enjoy the tree you helped me put up. Come on, it's Christmas Eve."

"That's a good idea. Be over in a half hour or so."

They walked back to their cars and cleared them of snow. Carrie wanted to start a fire in the fireplace and warm a pan of apple cider before Nate arrived. She hoped he would enjoy the book on Native American medicine she had ordered online for him, along with a new blue-wool cap and matching scarf she found through an online outdoors retailer. While she waited for him to arrive, she took Annie outside for a few minutes of star-gazing.

The snow had stopped for the moment. The night sky was a clear indigo with dots of white light. From far off, she heard the faintest of drumbeats.

"Pa rum pa pum pum," she sang softly. "Me and my drum."

When Nate arrived, they walked together into the house, shedding their boots, coats, and gloves in a heap by the front door. Annie was only too happy to have him scratch her tummy while Carrie garnished glass mugs with cinnamon sticks for the apple cider. She arranged a plate of assorted cookies, compliments of the nurses in the clinic.

"The nurses took pity on me and gave me some of their Christmas cookies," she said. "Otherwise, we'd be eating Oreos."

"I got some, too. They never forget about us, do they?"

She handed him a mug of cider. "Okay, so I want you to open a gift first. You're the guest."

He rubbed his hands together and picked up a large, heavy box his parents had sent. "I have a feeling I know what these are." His voice was full of glee. He tore into the wrapping and opened the box. "Hockey skates. Yes!"

She smiled. "A boy and his toys."

"Your turn." He drank from his mug, watching with eyes newly sparkling with life.

She opened the largest box from her parents. Inside was a slightly smaller box. Inside that box was a still smaller box. She continued opening smaller and smaller boxes until all that was left was a red envelope with a silver bow. "I wonder what's in there?" she said.

"Cash," he guessed. "Always the right size and color."

"Oh my gosh!" She tore into the envelope and saw that it was an airline gift card loaded with more than enough credit to purchase a round-trip ticket between Great Falls and Philadelphia. "I hope my parents aren't under the impression that I don't have enough money to buy a plane ticket," she said with a laugh. "But man, those flights are expensive!"

"It's from your mom *and* dad," Nate pointed out. "Maybe your father is missing you, too. Will you be able to get back there anytime soon?"

"There's a family-medicine conference there in March. I could use the ticket then," she said. "I've been asked to do a breakfast speech at the conference about my Roosevelt project, so I definitely need to go."

"I'd like to hear your presentation sometime." He took a sip of hot cider.

"Thanks. I'll take you up on that and practice on you. My school is also honoring me at their alumni reception during the conference." She shrugged and grinned. "Plus, I need the continuing education credits. Okay, you open another gift," she said, biting into a chocolate chip cookie rich with butter and brown sugar.

He opened a flat package that contained several pairs of heavy socks. "Just what I needed," he said. He waved one foot in the air. A small hole was visible under his big toe.

"I got socks, too," she said, opening the box from Gran, who had knitted her three pair of cashmere socks as soft as kittens.

Nate reached under the tree and pulled out the gift he had given her. "I didn't know how you'd feel about being here over Christmas, and I wanted you to have a little piece of home." The twinkle in his eye told her he couldn't wait to see her reaction.

Tearing open the wrapping paper, she lifted the box lid and burst out laughing. "Okay, so I should have guessed what this would be." Inside was a Philadelphia Flyers hockey jersey. She pulled it on over her blouse and stood to model it for him. "I may not play hockey, but at least I can look like I do," she said. "Thanks, Nate. I'll wear it with pride."

He opened the box she had given him, ripping off the paper with the wild abandon of a small child. When he saw what was inside, he looked up at her. "These are really nice—my favorite color, too. Thanks."

He wrapped the soft scarf around his neck and pulled the cap over his curls. Then he picked up the book and studied its cover, deep in thought. Seeing the look in his eyes, she knew it had been the perfect gift.

"Thank you," he said. "Until I got here, I didn't realize that what we do is only one way of practicing medicine. What the people have had all along is valuable too."

"I know. They have this belief in something bigger, something they can align with for good health."

"It makes more sense to me the longer I'm here," he said. "I didn't get that before."

"Nate, do you ever feel that there was—I don't know quite how to describe it—this larger hand guiding you here?" she asked, wrapping her arms around herself. "It seems as if my entire life, everything I thought about and cared about, all that I was interested in … was intended to lead me to this place. It all feels so familiar, and yet not familiar, at the same time." She shook her head and leaned forward. "I think I once knew something important, and I forgot it. Every day I'm here helps me remember who I really am."

He took in a sharp breath and leaned forward until she saw herself reflected in his eyes. "Sometimes I see things, dream about them. Does that sound crazy? I think I may have been here before."

She nodded solemnly. "That makes perfect sense to me."

Chapter Nineteen

—◦◦◦—

JANUARY BROUGHT STRONG GUSTS OF WIND that created snow drifts as tall as one-story buildings—high banks of white that blocked visibility. The wind blew so hard that you had to hold on to metal poles and trees "to keep from getting blown clear into Canada," as Peg put it. As a result of impaired vision due to blowing snow and high drifts, there were three car accidents. Two pedestrians were struck by cars. Fortunately, the injured survived, thanks to Nate and the emergency room staff. Carrie stopped snowshoeing in the early morning darkness along the main road to the hospital.

She watched people lumber through the deep snow, their faces covered by woolen scarves and shoulders draped with blankets. They appeared more like Sasquatches than humans. Adding to the hardships were intermittent power outages. Those who normally used gas or electric heat had to depend on stoves and fireplaces. For elderly patients or those with special health concerns, a power outage presented particular challenges, especially if electricity was needed for a medical device. Carrie knew that space heaters were often used. With this secondary heating source, devastating house fires could occur. So far, the town had been lucky.

"I worry about babies, little kids, and old people the most," she said to Peg. "Their homes aren't built well, to begin with, and they don't look weatherized. There's just no sure way for people to stay warm."

"Dr. Carrie, you have to realize this is our life. This weather is all we've known."

Like so many aspects of life in Browning, she had to admit Peg had a point. In fact, she had started sleeping in layers of clothing, starting with Gran's cashmere socks, thermal underwear, and flannel pajamas. "Good thing I have no man in my life," she joked in an email to her Mayo friends. "Otherwise, he'd never see an inch of skin on me until June."

While January winds howled, the clinic was bursting with flu and strep cases. On Wednesday morning, Carrie looked up from the nurses' station to see Violet Hightower and her young son, Louis. Violet had brought him in for a throat culture. After checking Louis's blood pressure, which was higher than it should be, and noting tenderness in the middle of his back, Carrie suspected that the ten-year-old had inherited the gene from his mother that caused polycystic kidney disease.

"We can find out for sure by looking at his kidneys, the way we did with yours," she told Violet. "But that is entirely up to you and your husband. Whether or not Louis has the disease, I still recommend a low-salt, low-fat diet, and more vegetables than meat. We'll work on getting his blood pressure down. I'd like to see him again in two weeks."

"Okay," Violet said. "My Aunt Nadie says her blood pressure is normal."

Carrie was relieved to hear that Violet had questioned other family members. She hadn't expected to hear that. "I'm glad you've talked with Mrs. Leathers. Are others aware that there is PKD in the family?"

"I have told a few of them. If there is nothing that can be done, what is the point?" Violet shrugged.

"They need to know so that I can monitor their health, advise them on diet. Would you consider going with your son to Missoula to see a kidney specialist? I can refer you to someone there."

"Will this kidney specialist have a cure?" Violet asked.

"No. There is no cure ... not yet. I do believe there will be, one day. Maybe you could ask Medicine Owl what she thinks."

As soon as the words were out of her mouth, Carrie realized that this was exactly what Violet needed to hear. The mind was a powerful healing force, and what Violet needed most now was belief that her body could resist further harm by believing in something bigger than the disease.

CARRIE MET WITH MEDICINE OWL AT least once a week. She watched as the medicine woman crushed plants, often using each part—flower, leaves, roots, and seeds. Sometimes she burned the plant and inhaled its smoke. These experiences reminded Carrie of the many times she had watched Gran in her greenhouse, making tinctures from plants or extracting oils. She kept detailed notes on these visits:

> I met with Medicine Owl, who showed me how to make a poultice from the crushed roots of the bitterroot plant. She uses it for muscle

cramps. Bitterroot in tincture form is given for fever, cough, sore throat, and stomachache.

A tincture of osha roots or seeds is used to treat poor circulation, fevers, cramps, and bronchitis. When the roots of the osha plant are burned, the inhaled smoke can be used to relieve headache and eliminate sinus infections. Tapping on the area of sinus pain stimulates circulation and often provides relief.

* * *

THAT WEEK, CARRIE ADDRESSED A GROUP of junior and senior high girls about the realities of teen pregnancy and the responsibilities that came with infants. She knew some of the girls were already mothers, having delivered one of their babies last summer. She discussed birth control and safe sex, in addition to the importance of regular preventative healthcare.

"We combine health and phys-ed. But our classes are taught by the gym teacher," John told her. "He isn't exactly well-versed in women's issues."

"For girls, understanding their bodies is really important. If they learn how easy it is for them to get pregnant, they might come to me first for birth control, before they get involved with a boy. I wish they'd wait, but teenagers never think it can happen to them."

"You don't have to be a teenager to find yourself with an unplanned pregnancy," John pointed out. He tapped his pen on the desk in a distracted fashion.

Carrie watched him for a moment. "How is Gali?" she asked, changing the subject. "I've been hoping she'd be in town one of these weekends, and the three of us could get together."

"She is well. I have been going to her home the past couple of months because it is easier than having my mother notice that she is at my house."

"Isn't it strange that we can be grown adults with lives of our own and still be afraid to upset our parents?" Carrie smiled. "I still struggle with wanting my father to accept my life and be proud of me."

"I'm sure he is proud, on some level. People here like you. Do you know they call you Doctor Golden Hair?"

Carrie laughed. "It's certainly better than Doctor Who Stings with Needle."

"My family appreciates all that you are doing for my brother and for Violet, my cousin." He had never told her he was aware of Violet's health condition.

"Violet is a wonderful person," she said. "I've enjoyed getting to know her."

"This disease that is in the family, this polycystic kidney disease ... is it something that we all should know more about? Should my mother find out if she has it, too?" John's dark eyes showed concern. "I would want to know in case I had children."

"John, this disease has no cure yet. If your mother wants me to confirm whether or not she has the disease, I would be glad to see her. But all that can be done at this time is to manage high blood pressure and other issues such as infections, if they occur. I recommend a more vegetarian diet, more water throughout the day, and exercise." She held her arms up. "Beyond that, it's up to the Great Creator, who knows more than we do."

"I am surprised to hear a doctor say something like that."

"We should say it all the time," Carrie insisted, her passion for the subject evident in her voice. "The body heals because of the energy it already has and its innate ability to heal itself. We can help it along with medicines. But even I know the medical profession has its limits."

"My brother goes to the sweat lodge. I think it has helped him. But you have helped him, too."

"That's nice to hear. I've always talked about alignment in terms of the spine and the muscles and how they support good health. But now I believe it's about more than that. We align with something bigger, an energy that flows through everything, that is in all of us. I'm learning from your people how to practice medicine in a different way."

JUST AFTER NINE O'CLOCK THAT EVENING, Carrie received a text message from Nate. *Need your professional services.*

She texted back, What's the matter?

A moment later, he called. "Could you meet me at the hospital?"

"What's going on?" Carrie asked. "Where are you?"

"I'm sitting outside the hospital with ice and a pressure bandage on my chin—a little hockey accident. John drove me. I need sutures."

"I'll be there in a few minutes," she said and hurried to change out of her pajamas and into scrubs. She pulled on her coat and jammed her feet into boots. Then she drove to the hospital, hoping that the injury wasn't too severe and that she could do a good job stitching Nate's chin. It would be a shame if Nate's handsome face were marked by a noticeable scar. *All I'm doing is suturing up a trauma and reconstructive surgeon. No pressure there.*

When she got to the hospital, she saw him, along with John and Mike Leathers, in the waiting area outside the emergency room. Nate stood up. The front of his jersey and the pressure bandage were bloody. "I decided to wait out here. I don't want anyone but you touching this."

She chuckled. "You know, I don't do sutures every day."

"I trust you."

She thought he looked pale, vulnerable, and a little scared. "Okay, come with me," she said, taking his arm. She smiled at the Leathers' brothers. "Hi,

Mike. John, if you guys want to go home, I can drop Nate off at his house after I'm done taking care of this."

"Okay." John stuck his arms in his jacket and stood up. "I'll talk with you tomorrow, Nate. Thanks, Carrie."

Once in an exam cubicle, with a nurse assisting, she tilted Nate's head back and inspected the deep laceration. "How exactly did you do this to yourself?" she asked. "It looks like someone kicked you in the chin with the blade of their skate. It's pretty deep, bud."

Nate's skin was pearly white. She laid a cool hand on his forehead and made calm, direct eye contact. "This won't take many stitches, but I'll need to clean it out first and numb it up. Have you had a tetanus shot recently?"

Nate shook his head and mumbled. "I can't remember. I guess you'd better give me one, along with some penicillin."

She cleaned out the wound with saline solution and antiseptic. "Okay, that looks good," she said, peering into the laceration. "I'm going to numb you up now—just a few quick little stings."

Beads of sweat formed on Nate's face as she injected the needle a few times into and around the wound, just enough to relieve any pain during suturing. She had excelled in suturing in medical school and felt confident that she could do a decent job. Still, it wasn't a procedure she performed frequently. She stitched six neat sutures and tied them off. When she finished, she leaned over him, assessing his color, which she would have termed ghostly. "All done. That wasn't so bad, was it? You won't even be able to see the scar."

Nate let out a breath. "Can I look?"

She pulled out a mirror and handed it to him as he studied her handiwork. "Six stitches, all in a row. What do you think?"

"I couldn't have done it better myself. Thanks," he said. His eyes met hers and lingered.

Carrie felt her heart thump. Looking into Nate's blue eyes, she felt something strange and familiar—as if this moment was a repeat of an experience somewhere in their past. In another place and time, it might have ended in a kiss. She quickly came to her senses. "Let me cover the wound so you don't accidentally bump those stitches when you put on your jacket."

Helping him to a sitting position, she applied a nonstick pad and fastened it with tape. "There. Now stand and drop," she joked, picking up the first syringe the nurse handed her.

Nate lowered his pants to reveal the top of his left hip and buttock. Carrie concentrated on the syringe. She swabbed the spot with an alcohol square and gave him a tetanus shot followed by another shot of penicillin to prevent infection. "That'll do it."

"Great." He leaned against the table, looked at her, started to speak, and then stopped.

"What?" she asked. "Are you sure you're okay? Do you need to sit a few more minutes before you try to walk? You're sort of pale."

"Thanks for doing this, for coming so quickly when I called."

"You're welcome. Let's agree that if I ever take a hockey skate to my jaw line, you'll be there for me, too."

Nate laughed. He slid his arms into his jacket. "I owe you one."

"Seriously, how did it happen?" she asked in the car on the way to his house. "Tell me what offensive move was important enough to cause that kind of injury."

He laughed. "Any hockey move can cause a bloody mess, Carrie. And actually, for your information, it was a defensive move, and I scored."

"There's that, at least." She looked ahead at the road and drove slowly. Heavy snow falling sideways made it difficult to see much beyond the headlights. At least, the fresh snow provided traction.

"Hey, it was the winning goal," he said, looking slightly offended. "It was only when I saw all the blood on the ice that I realized why my chin was killing me."

Her intuition told her that he'd paled because all the blood reminded him of the day he'd been shot. By now his color had returned to normal, but she'd check on him tomorrow.

"I've never known a hockey player who didn't have scars and broken bones," she said. "But if you're looking to show off an impressive scar, I don't think this one will qualify."

It was snowing harder now. In the headlights, she saw three deer leap from a field on the right side into the road. She braked with care, throwing one arm protectively over Nate's torso as she guided the car through a skid.

"I've never had anyone do that for me before," he said after a long moment.

"You'd have done the same for me if I was gravely wounded." She chuckled, removing her arm.

"I mean it. You always put others before yourself."

"I think my father and my ex-fiancé would disagree with that, but thanks. Tom once said I'm hard on the men in my life." Carrie kept her eyes on the road.

"He only said that because you weren't doing what he wanted you to do."

"It's the story of my life." As she stopped in front of Nate's house, she reminded him, "Try to get some extra rest tonight, okay? I didn't like your color when I was working on you. This was a trauma to your body, even if you are a big deal hockey player and macho man. Oh, and by the way, don't you dare take out those sutures by yourself."

He laughed. "I *am* a surgeon, you know."

"Have one of the nurses do it. Or better yet, let me remove them when it's time," she said as he prepared to get out of the car. "If you have any problems, call me."

"Yes, Doctor." He leaned over and kissed her lightly on the cheek. "See you soon."

It was nearly midnight when Carrie pulled into the garage, exhausted from the long day but still wired from stress and very much able to feel Nate's lips on her cheek. She had a sense of being slightly off-kilter, and it had nothing to do with his accident or having to stitch up his wound. She wondered if her heightened sensitivity might be due to the fact that she hadn't had any physical contact with a man since July. If there was more to it than that, she dared not think about it.

Any time she spent with Nate gave her a jolt of electricity, a sensation bordering on recklessness, as if they were just a step away from acting on impulses both dangerous and thrilling. As they grew closer as friends, the sexual tension was increasing. Romantic notions about Nate weren't a good idea. For one thing, they were each recovering from broken engagements. But the main reason was that she would be leaving Browning when summer came. It would be harder to say goodbye if she was in love with him.

There were so many qualities in Nate that she admired. She was drawn to him in ways that were complex and deep. Now a trusted friend, he understood what motivated her life and work. She loved Nate's dedication to his career, his kind heart, and generous spirit, and she hoped he felt the same. She resolved once more to guard their friendship and avoid any romantic complications.

Most of the time, she was so busy at the hospital there was little time to think about the occasional pangs of loneliness she felt at home in the evenings, with just Annie for company. She remembered all the nights with Tom during residency, when they would leave the hospital and go home for a few hours of lovemaking. There would be wine and slow, passionate kisses that ended any thoughts of sleep, even when they were exhausted. She had been so attracted to him that for a time, their physical relationship was all that mattered. Yet, there had been something important missing. In many ways, Tom had seemed ideal. But those were surface qualities. When it came to the values that she held most dear, he had not lived up to her faith in him. How would she know for certain when she met the right man, the one for keeps?

That night, as she snuggled under the comforter with Annie warming her feet, Carrie wondered what it would be like to kiss Nate. There had been a few times recently that she found herself studying the contours of his mouth, the curve of his upper lip, the adorable dimples that appeared when he smiled.

Occasionally, he would touch her arm as they passed in the hallway and allow his hand to linger there for just a moment before letting go. Whenever he did, she was only too aware of the intense feeling it produced in her.

As they had sat together, opening their Christmas gifts, she'd wanted to touch his face, had known on some level that he would welcome it. But it wasn't a good idea. No, it was safer to be Nate's friend and colleague. She could get hurt by caring too much, and so could he.

It had also occurred to her that Nate was accustomed to a more traditional woman. When she looked in the mirror these days, she saw a plainer woman with lank layers of dry, flyaway hair and no makeup—a woman dressed more for utility. For comfort on long days, she had taken to wearing a sports bra that flattened out her chest under her scrubs. At the very least, she resolved to get her hair styled as soon as possible. She might be a doctor, but she was also a girl. That night, as she drifted off to sleep, Nate's face followed her into her dreams.

Chapter Twenty

—◦◦◦—

A S SHE LEANED INTO A BONE-CHILLING fifty mile per hour wind that threatened to knock her off her feet, Carrie held her scarf more tightly about her nose and mouth and soldiered on. It was only about five hundred feet from her car to the front door of the hospital, but she couldn't seem to walk in a straight line. The wind had been unrelenting all week.

February's gusty winds and heavy blowing snow meant frequent whiteouts. She could now better understand how easy it was to get disoriented and walk in a circle or off course. She had read stories about people—including a group of schoolchildren—found frozen after attempting to walk home from school during one of these all-too-frequent blizzards. Each morning, as she shoveled an oasis in the front yard for Annie, she thought about the loss of life and the hardships brought on by such harsh weather. She wasn't sure she could ever get used to this aspect of Montana living.

The lack of mobility brought feelings of intense isolation, often resulting in depression. You could either embrace indoor life by enjoying a good book or a card game or succumb to acute cabin fever. Carrie certainly wasn't immune to moments of occasional stir-craziness, so she made an effort to get outside as much as possible. When that wasn't possible, she took advantage of an old stationary bicycle Dr. Jim had left in the garage.

This winter, it wasn't snow that presented the biggest hazard. As people spent more time indoors together, the flu virus was spreading like a summer wildfire through entire families and across the reservation. Healthcare workers fell ill in droves, leaving the hospital short-staffed. Those few who remained healthy wore face masks and worked extra hours to help desperately ill patients, including their coworkers. Even Peg had suffered a bout of flu that kept her home for four days. So far, she and Nate had escaped the epidemic, but she knew it might only be a matter of time until one or both of them came down with it.

She had met with Medicine Owl to get her advice. She recommended a sweat and a combination of plants, including Echinacea and lobelia, to cleanse the body of the offending virus. Although the sweat lodge was undeniably useful in fighting a viral illness, doing a sweat wasn't practical in blizzard conditions.

"You can get into the bathtub in water as hot as you can stand. When you get out, wrap yourself in blankets and sweat out the sickness," Medicine Owl advised.

Carrie's notes read as follows:

> In addition to the use of Echinacea (also called purple coneflower) to strengthen the immune system, Medicine Owl makes a poultice of the Echinacea roots and applies it to injuries or swelling in her patients. The combination of yarrow and Echinacea are helpful, she says, in relieving fevers and shortening the duration of colds and flu. Yarrow, which she often recommends as a digestive aid, combined with mint, is helpful for those suffering seasonal allergies. I found this to be true, in my own experience. Congestion can be relieved with clary sage, eucalyptus, fennel, peppermint, and rosemary. Effective natural expectorants include basil, eucalyptus, ginger, peppermint, and thyme. Fever is reduced with basil, eucalyptus, and peppermint.

* * *

As Carrie saw patient after patient with high fevers, severe gastro-intestinal distress, body aches, and congestion of the upper and lower respiratory tracts, she knew that even anti-viral medications weren't doing much to halt the course of the virus. In this case, she realized, the remedies Medicine Owl recommended were not just complementary, they were just as effective. Those who went to Medicine Owl seemed to recover just as quickly as those who visited the clinic and took an anti-viral medication.

There was one weapon in Carrie's arsenal that she was confident would help. During the 1918 flu pandemic, anecdotal evidence had indicated that doctors who practiced muscular-skeletal manipulation had better patient outcomes than their medical colleagues who relied solely on the common medicines of the day. Manipulation had been shown to facilitate the body's natural ability to heal itself. Gran swore by it. Carrie intended to make sure all her patients received this specialized hands-on care.

In an email to her mother and Gran, she wrote:

It seems as if winter will never leave. Here on the reservation, like everywhere else, the flu is hitting us hard. I can barely keep up with the number of patients we're seeing, and we're limited in the number of hospital beds available. I continue to talk with Medicine Owl, who offers various remedies depending on the individual's symptoms and overall health.

Gran replied:

In addition to manipulation, eucalyptus oil, licorice root, Echinacea, and sweating are common treatments for colds and flu viruses. I'll be curious to hear about your results.

One evening later that week, as Carrie left the hospital, she saw John idling in his Jeep by the hospital's front door. He rolled down the window.

"I hope no one in your family is in the ER," she said.

"Many in our family have had flu, but all are recovering," John said. "I've been spared so far. I wish I could say the same for my students. So many are sick, I've cancelled classes for the rest of the week. Hopefully, it will keep other kids from getting sick, too."

"This particular virus comes on so fast that your students may not know they're sick until they've already spread it to their friends," she said. "How can I help?"

"I'll let you know. Hop in. Let's grab a bite to eat." He leaned over and opened the passenger door for her.

"Now that's an offer I won't refuse."

"Let's go to the taco place," John said. "I missed lunch."

They went to a tiny Tex-Mex place popular with locals. When they arrived, Carrie wondered what had led John to seek her out tonight. After they were seated at a booth in the corner, he picked up the menu and studied it. She glanced quickly at her menu and decided on a cheese enchilada and side order of guacamole and chips. John studied the menu as if it held important answers to all life's questions.

For a split second, she had a vision of him in traditional Native American attire—leather pants, a hand-woven shirt—wearing his hair long and sporting feathers and beads. No matter what his attire, John made a striking figure. If he and Gali married and had babies, they would be beautiful.

She played with a paper wrapper from her drink straw, rolling it into a tight ball and batting it around with her finger as she stared at his hands. His fingers were long and slender with short, square-cut nails—no sign of manual labor—the hands of an educated man. A thin, braided-leather band was tied around his left wrist. Other than this, he wore no watch or rings. His coarse black hair was salted with more white hair around the crown of his head. His deep-set dark eyes, every bit as intense as they had been the first time she met him, now appeared profoundly weary. He looked to be a man with far more concerns than joy in his life.

Still, there was something different in his demeanor tonight, a spark of light-heartedness. She hoped it had to do with Gali. She glanced down at her hands, the nails oval and petal pink with tiny white crescents at the tips. They were so small and fragile compared to John's larger, dark-skinned hands that she was suddenly aware of the vast differences between them. Without warning, an intense feeling of otherness washed over her. What was she doing here?

"Carrie," John said, "is anything the matter?"

His voice startled her, and she realized she'd been staring off into space. She was exhausted from seeing triple the usual number of patients. "Oh, sorry, did you say something just now?"

"Are you ready to order?" He smiled. "You look tired."

"I am, a little," she said. "I'll survive. How is Gali?"

"She's well. She sends her best. She asked how you're faring this winter. It isn't an easy life, especially the first winter you spend here. You are alone a lot."

"Tell her I think of her, too. And I'm not so alone," she said with a smile. "I have Annie with me, and I have my work." She stopped to consider his question. "It helps to stay busy. I can't deny I miss my family, but I'll be seeing them in March when I attend a conference. It's just another month—not long now."

"I was thinking it is good that you and Nate have each other for company." John averted his eyes as he said this.

"Yes, I see him at the hospital. He spends his time like I do—working, mostly. Oh, and playing hockey, of course. You probably see him more than I do."

"He is alone, too," John said. "He questions whether he ought to look for a woman to share his life with. I tell him that he must ask his spirit. Then he will know who is right for his life's journey." John might have been commenting on the weather, his tone was so matter-of-fact.

Nate was questioning that he was alone? She wanted to ask John about this, but didn't want to appear too curious. It was reassuring to hear him speak on matters of spirit. His comments about Nate were just as relevant to her life, and she wondered if the comment was for her benefit too. Nate was in her thoughts more and more. Did John sense this?

Carrie changed the subject; thoughts of Nate and romance were making her uncomfortable. "I've been wondering how things are going with you and Gali. Are you making any plans for the future?"

"We have decided to marry." John dabbed at his lips with a paper napkin. "I want to be with her. She is willing to move here."

"That's wonderful, but what about your family?"

"I have heard their thoughts. I cannot allow them to stop me from doing what I know is right."

"This was just what I needed to hear today," she said with a grin, putting down her fork, "good news. When will you get married?"

"Soon, I think."

"I'd better be invited to the wedding."

"It remains to be seen what we will do about a ceremony," he said. The server brought their check, and Carrie reached for her purse.

"Please. You do so much for our people," John said, waving off her attempt to pay.

"It's a privilege, John."

He insisted on paying, then with a smile, he helped her into her coat. After dropping her off beside her car in the hospital parking lot, he waited until she started the engine.

As she watched his taillights leave the parking lot, Carrie hoped that he and Gali would live happily on the reservation. Would the Leathers family eventually accept Gali as their daughter-in-law? Surely, a good woman so deeply loved by their son would win their hearts eventually.

Chapter Twenty-One

⚊\╎⁄⚊

O N THE DAY BEFORE VALENTINE'S DAY, Carrie summoned up the courage to try her hand at a pot roast for dinner. She had never made one, but it seemed easy enough. Buy a hunk of beef and stick it in a big pan in the oven with some water, salt, and pepper for whatever amount of time the internet recommended. She'd experiment on herself before inviting friends.

"I need a roast today, a small one. Could you make sure I get one that will fall apart?" she asked the butcher.

Behind her, she heard a snort, followed by a chuckle. "It's how you cook the roast."

She whirled around to find Nate pushing a shopping cart. "Oh, hi," she said, mortified that he had overheard her. "So you're giving cooking lessons now?"

He grinned and rubbed the stubble of beard on his chin. In his green scrubs that resembled baggy pajamas, Nate always managed to look like a sleepy teenager. "I can show you how. If you do it yourself, I can't promise you'll get the same results."

"Very funny. Tell you what: if you help me cook it, you can join me for dinner tonight. Are you that brave?"

"I'm not sure, actually." He stroked his chin, weighing the question. "Are you inviting anyone else?"

"No, it'll just be the two of us. To tell you the truth, I thought I should learn how to cook something other than spaghetti."

"Okay, I'm in. Don't touch that piece of meat until I get there." He gave her one of his irresistible dimpled grins. "You don't have the credentials."

"Ha-ha." As she watched his retreating figure, another thought came to mind. It brought fresh spots of rosy color to her cheeks.

Despite the teasing, running into Nate was a nice surprise. She hadn't seen him in two days. There had been a bad accident on a highway outside of town involving a carload of teenagers, none wearing seatbelts. Fortunately, the injuries weren't severe enough to warrant sending anyone by helicopter to a trauma center. Nate had been able to handle all the surgeries himself.

She made a mental note to consider a presentation to high school students about the realities of driving, as well as safe passenger rules for cars. Teenagers, regardless of where they lived, believed they were indestructible. It was lucky there had been so much snow piled up along the side of the road. The snowdrift slowed the car and kept it from rolling down the ravine. If it had rolled a few more times, there would have been fatalities.

When she got home from the grocery store, she changed out of her sweatpants and turtleneck sweater. Standing in the bathroom in front of the mirror in her white lace bra and panties, she applied mascara, a little blush, and rose-tinted lip gloss. Then she smoothed a fragrant floral moisturizer all over her body and turned this way and that, studying herself in a non-clinical way, hoping to observe herself the way a man might.

As a doctor, she gave little thought to naked bodies, even her own. Male and female medical students often practiced procedures on each other or changed clothes in communal locker rooms. Bodies were their business. But now, with Nate, it was different.

It had been a long time since she cared as much as she did right now about how she looked as a woman. *You're acting like a horny teenager. Get a grip.* Nevertheless, she chose a lavender silk blouse and matching amethyst teardrop earrings. Studying herself in front of the bathroom mirror, she unfastened one more button on the blouse and unfastened her French braid, releasing her hair in long, loose waves. Her hair needed a trim, but at least it was clean and shiny. A half hour later, she stood in the kitchen, hands on her hips, a terrycloth dishtowel tucked into her best-fitting jeans. She poured a small glass of red wine and took a sip, wondering what she should do ahead of time to prepare for Nate's cooking demonstration.

Annie woofed at the sound of Nate's knock and trotted to the front hallway, beating Carrie, who checked her reflection in the hall mirror before opening the door. Nate handed her a large box of chocolate-covered cherries.

"It's Valentine's Day tomorrow," he said. "It seems rude to show up at a woman's door without candy. I would have made you a card, too, but my art skills aren't that good."

"Chocolate-covered cherries are my favorite!" She accepted the box of chocolates and opened it, selected one of the candies, and bit into it. Thick, syrupy cherry juice dripped down her lower lip onto her chin in sticky beads. She laughed as she self-consciously dabbed at her chin with the kitchen towel. "Here, try one."

He separated a chocolate-covered cherry from its wrapper, popped the entire piece into his mouth, and chewed, licking his fingers. "Not a bad appetizer, if I do say so. We're off to a good start."

He had shaved and put on a sky-blue sweater and black jeans. He smelled enticingly of spicy aftershave with a hint of lavender or sandalwood.

They walked through the hallway into the kitchen. "Would you like a glass of wine?" she asked. "It's a zinfandel. I think it was a good year. Well, at least I remember it as a good year."

He looked at the bottle. "That year is one I'd rather forget, but sure." He handed her a plastic shopping bag filled with food. "I brought a few ingredients we'll need to cook this meal properly."

As she pawed through the bag, he snatched it from her hands. "No peeking." He pulled out several onions, a bunch of carrots, celery stalks, garlic cloves, and a plastic bag containing a mix of herbs. "These are essentials. I was pretty sure you didn't have any of this stuff."

"Did I forget something at the store?" She looked puzzled. "I bought meat and potatoes and a bagged salad and ice cream. What more do we need? It's a roast, not Julia Child's *boeuf bourguignon*. And you don't look anything like Julia Child, by the way."

Nate rolled his eyes and chucked her under the chin. "And Martha Stewart, you are not. I'll show you the best way to make a roast," he said. "It's my mother's recipe. The first thing we do is preheat the oven. Could you get me a cutting board and a sharp knife, please?"

She observed in fascination Nate's proficiency as a cook. "Clearly, you're a man of many talents."

"You have no idea," he said. He took a quick sip of wine and resumed chopping the onions and celery. He cut the green tops off a bunch of carrots before cutting them into bite-size chunks. Then he broke the garlic bulb into cloves, smashed the cloves with the side of the knife, and removed the skins.

"Nate! What you just did with that knife was so impressive!" She perched next to the counter on a kitchen stool. "I bet you didn't learn how to do that in your surgical residency."

"Surgeons can do more than operate, you know." He rubbed olive oil into the meat and seasoned it before sprinkling the herb mix over the roast. Then he lifted it from the cutting board and placed it in the center of the vegetables. "And there you have it."

"That didn't look so hard," she said. "I think I could handle that."

"Well, next time, I'll let you." He covered the roasting pan with aluminum foil and stuck it in the oven.

While the beef, potatoes, and vegetables roasted, they watched movies, including one of Carrie's favorites, *Shawshank Redemption*. Fortified with wine, cheddar cheese, and crackers, they found it to be the ideal Saturday afternoon activity. With Nate at one end of the sofa, Carrie on the other, their companionship seemed as natural as if they had been together for years.

When the movie credits rolled, she sat up. "It's great that after all those years in prison, Tim Robbins' character finally breaks free and finds his way to his dream spot. It's a metaphor for getting rid of all the stuff standing in the way of what you want."

"Getting metaphysical, are we?" Nate grinned. "Okay, so what about this? Even when things seem impossible, when it seems like there's no way for him to ever be free, he believes he'll get there. He envisions it in so much detail, he feels optimistic, and that helps him plan the perfect getaway. He even helps someone else believe in that dream, and that guy ends up in paradise, too."

"Now who's the philosopher?" she teased. But she understood his message. She had grown up believing that the mind was a powerful instrument, much more so than the body. What you truly believed could be achieved. Gran had taught her that.

Glancing at the clock, Nate stood up. "If you set the table, I'll take the roast out."

While Nate carved the roast, she arranged placemats, silverware, and cloth napkins on the table. As an afterthought, she moved a white candle from the kitchen countertop to the center of the table and lit it. With the roast perfectly cooked and seasoned, she poured a little more wine, resolving to stop after that glass. She needed to keep her wits about her.

As they dug into their salads, Nate said, "Tell me about your grandmother. It sounds like she's been a major role model."

"She still is. From the time I was little, I wanted to be just like her. I used to help her in the greenhouse. That was how I learned about plants that have medicinal value. 'Weeds and seeds,' my dad always said."

"I don't think I ever asked you this before. How did the daughter of an MD end up as a DO? Were you being rebellious?" He flashed a grin.

"I started out thinking I'd become an MD, but then I learned what made osteopathic medicine different, and it made so much sense from a holistic standpoint. Manipulation was the value-added part. Dad wanted me to go to Penn—that's his school. When I got accepted and didn't go, he was pretty steamed. He's also on the faculty, so that made it worse."

"Yikes."

Carrie twisted her mouth. "I know. I probably could have handled the whole thing better. But I don't think Dad has ever understood the reasons for what I do. He and I butt heads all the time. But at some point, he'll have to accept that I have a right to make my own choices."

"You're still going back to Philadelphia to join his practice?"

"Not until July. That's assuming his job offer still stands. To tell you the truth, the way I feel right now, if I could choose where to spend the rest of my life, it would be here."

He smiled. "I wish you would." His face reddened. "It's more fun with you here."

After they finished dinner, she made a pot of coffee. "Let's wait a little while for dessert. I'm stuffed."

Nate expertly rinsed the dishes and stacked them in the dishwasher. He scoured the roasting pan with a steel wool pad and dried it while she put away their leftovers. Then he wiped up all the kitchen counters and shined up the stove.

She couldn't conceal a smile as she watched him work, sweater sleeves pushed up, long arms immersed in hot sudsy water, scrubbing away at the dirty pan. She thought of her father, who had never washed a dish in his life. He assumed it was someone else's job. Carrie was utterly charmed that Nate cooked *and* cleaned up after himself. It was obvious that it wasn't a show for her benefit, either. How could any woman not feel lucky to have a man like Nate Holden?

"Thanks," she said, feeling suddenly shy, "for everything—for helping me." A blush that had nothing to do with the wine they had been drinking suffused her cheeks.

"I had fun," he said and turned back to the sink. "I like hanging out with you." He let the water out of the sink and dried his hands. Standing next to her under the kitchen light, Nate looked into her eyes. "Let's go sit by the fireplace."

Carrie nodded, her stomach flip-flopping. He indicated with the slightest movement of his chin for her to follow. She trailed behind him into the living room, swept along on a river of emotions she scarcely had time to analyze. She had a feeling that something more than friendship was about to happen.

"Carrie," Nate said, "I don't want this to sound like it's coming out of left field." He paused, looking unsure. "I really like you." He brushed his index finger along her jawline, sending a little shiver along Carrie's neck that traveled down her spine. It was such a tender gesture, incredibly sensual. As she reacted to his touch, a wisp of gold hair fell across her eye. Nate tucked it behind her ear, moving his head closer to hers.

"Nate, I …." She looked into those extraordinary blue eyes and knew that whatever happened next would alter their relationship forever. Good or bad, it was a point of no return.

He bent to kiss her, his lips fitting over hers in a way that felt oddly familiar, as though it had happened before. Or maybe, she thought afterward, they had envisioned kissing long enough that it felt like a natural next step. She parted her lips slightly as his mouth skimmed hers, and then touched her tongue to his as their kiss deepened and continued for another minute or more. Her arms crept around him as he pulled her close. It was the kiss she had always dreamed of, one she would not soon forget. It was the best kiss of her life.

She took a step back, hardly able to believe what had just happened. Clearly, there was more on his mind than friendship. So where would they go from here?

Nate put a finger to her lips and traced them, looking into her eyes. "And now," he said, "I don't have to wonder what it feels like to kiss you."

Chapter Twenty-Two

—◦◦◦—

Two days later, at three in the morning, Carrie woke from a fitful sleep with the worst headache of her life, a severe backache, chills, and painful limbs and skin. She went downstairs to the kitchen and started a kettle of hot water for tea, pulled out lemon juice and honey, and took her temperature. Her eyes widened with concern—102.2.

Fever was the body's natural way of defending itself from invasion, so unless her temperature went too high, she planned to take a more natural approach to her care. Holding her mug of lemony-sweet tea, she sat in the rocking chair, wrapped in blankets. It was rare for her to be sick, even with a cold. But all of the sick patients coupled with exhaustion had left her vulnerable. There would be no seeing patients for several days until she was well and free of fever for at least twenty-four hours. She would have to call in sick today, leaving the clinic without a physician. The timing couldn't have been worse.

At seven o'clock, after calling the hospital's main number to report her illness, she crawled back into bed with her laptop and emailed Gran.

> I'm now an official flu patient. I plan to consult Medicine Owl as soon as possible. Knowing that this just needs to run its course, I'd like to try the natural remedies she recommends. I'll keep a log of what I'm taking, in what doses, and how often, and note the results.

She had every intention of reaching out to Medicine Owl, but as her fever rose, it was easier to drift in and out of sleep. She was too weak to get out of bed and didn't see the text message Nate sent, asking if she was okay. When she finally heard her cell phone ring a short while later, she reached over on the bedside table to pick it up.

"Hello?" she asked in a near whisper, her throat burning.

"Carrie, this is John. I am outside your house. Open the door."

"I have the flu. I don't want to expose you. I need to reach Medicine Owl. She may be able to help."

"I have already spoken with her. Peg Bright Fish said you were sick and asked me to tell Medicine Owl. Nate is in surgery or he'd be here, too. Peg left a message for him."

"I don't want anyone exposed to this unnecessarily," she protested.

"I understand your concern, but you're sick. Medicine Owl has given me a package for you with instructions that I wrote out. The package is on the doormat."

"Thank you, John." Carrie was too ill to fully comprehend the series of steps that had been taken on her behalf by her concerned friends in the course of just two hours.

Wrapping herself in her warmest robe and slippers, she carefully made her way downstairs to the front door, opened it, and picked up the package John had left for her. She held on to the doorway for support, feeling lightheaded, and noticed John watching her from his car. She waved at him and he waved back. The instructions from Medicine Owl were written in John's neat handwriting, outlining clearly how to administer a cleansing of the body using the herbs and roots she had sent, along with instructions for a steaming.

The herbs Medicine Owl sent included Echinacea, lobelia, and licorice root. Licorice was good for throat discomfort and cough. Echinacea helped support the immune system. Since it wasn't just the head and chest that were affected by a virus, lobelia was a cleansing agent for the digestive system. There were also instructions to take a bath or shower in water as hot as she could stand, then wrap up in blankets to cause the body to sweat out the illness. Medicine Owl reminded her to drink plenty of water, juices, and tea with honey, which would aid her body, particularly the lymph system, in ridding itself of the invading virus.

Carrie dragged herself upstairs to the bathroom and lined the bathtub with the fluffiest towel that she could find to ease her aching back and limbs. She shut the bathroom door and filled the tub with hot water. Placing her cell phone within easy reach, she lowered herself into the water and remained there, dozing off and on, until the water became tepid. Then she slipped on a clean nightgown and wrapped herself in blankets, as Medicine Owl had advised, and sipped a tall glass of water.

Much later in the day, she heard rapid knocking on the front door. She stumbled to the landing at the top of the stairs, nearly fainting as she made her way down the stairs. She opened the door to find Nate, concern etched on his face.

"I heard you were sick, but I couldn't get away from surgery until a little while ago. Let me take a look at you."

"No," she said, stepping back from the door and covering her nose and mouth. "I don't want you exposed to this. I'm following Medicine Owl's instructions, and I'm beginning to feel better. You'll be no good to anyone if you get sick, too."

"Don't be ridiculous. I'm here to help."

"Do me a favor, then, and just keep checking via text messages, okay?"

"It's not okay! You are the most stubborn woman," Nate said, running his hand through his curls in frustration. "I understand that you're worried about giving me the flu, but you need help."

"And I'm getting it ... from Medicine Owl. I want to see the results of treatment using her methods. Nate, this is the perfect way to demonstrate the effectiveness of her herbal remedies."

"This is no time to be a guinea pig, Carrie. Dammit. At least let me bring you an anti-viral, in case you change your mind."

"Thanks, but I'm going to follow Medicine Owl's instructions. I want to see firsthand how her treatments affect my recovery versus what I've seen with an anti-viral or no treatment at all. I don't want to be tempted to take the anti-viral. What she is telling me to do *is* helping."

"I'll be checking on you often," he said. "Do you hear me?" His voice trailed off as she shut the door.

TWENTY-FOUR HOURS PASSED WHILE CARRIE CONTINUED with the herbal and steam treatments. By the next morning, she was feeling well enough to get out of bed. She had even managed to send an email to Gran.

> I'm feeling much better today. I can attest to the benefits of sweating and the herbal remedies provided by Medicine Owl. The only thing I lack is some soft-tissue massage and manipulation to make sure my body is operating at peak efficiency. Wish you were here. You were always the best at that.

She didn't hear back from Gran right away. But perhaps she was busy seeing patients. Late in the afternoon, as Carrie heated up a bowl of chicken noodle soup that Peg had dropped off for her, she heard a car in the driveway, followed by the sound of heavy steps on the front porch. It was either John or Nate. She wrapped her heavy robe around herself more tightly and went to answer the door. For a moment, she was sure she was hallucinating.

"Dad! What are you doing here?"

"Carrie, thank God! I was afraid of what I'd find when I got here," her father said as he pulled her to him in a fierce hug. After releasing her from what felt like a death grip, he held her at arm's length, studying her face. There were tears in his eyes.

While she took in her father's wild-eyed appearance—his gray hair sticking out in matted tufts, face unshaven, clothes rumpled in a most uncharacteristic way—she attempted to process this unexpected development. What was he doing here? He must have heard from Gran that she had the flu. But how had he gotten here so fast? It would have taken a super-human effort to make the trip from Philadelphia to Browning in the middle of winter.

"Dad, what in the world …?" She stepped back so he could enter. He stamped his boots on the rug in the entryway as Annie rushed from the kitchen to investigate.

"I found out you were sick and that you were planning to let the medicine woman take care of you," he said. "I just had to make sure you had the care you needed. You're my daughter."

"Dad, it means the world that you're here." She couldn't stop smiling. "I'm so much better now. Really, the difference is remarkable." She leaned in to him, sniffing the familiar scent of his wool coat. "How did you get here so fast?"

"Fast? It took forever," her father said, removing his overcoat and tossing it over the banister. "I caught the first plane out of Philadelphia to Chicago and then managed to fly standby to Denver. Then I had to catch another plane to Great Falls. After that, I rented a car and drove here." He stopped. "Stand still and let me look at you. I want to see for myself how you're doing."

As Carrie waited for her father to finish his visual inspection, which included a hand on her forehead to check for fever, Annie sniffed his pant leg. "This is Annie, your grand dog," she said.

Since Carrie usually boarded Annie or left her in the care of friends when she flew back and forth to Philadelphia, Annie had never met the rest of the family. Mark knelt down and held out his hand tentatively for her to sniff.

"Hello, girl," he said. He hadn't approved of Carrie's decision to adopt a dog while she was still in residency. Yet his eyes softened as Annie licked his cold hand.

"Why don't we sit down at the kitchen table? My nurse, Peg, brought over homemade chicken noodle soup this morning. Would you like some?"

Her father smiled. "That sounds great. I haven't eaten anything since last night except for peanuts on the plane. I'll run out and get whatever you need later on. For the next few days, I'm here to take care of you."

"And I'll let you," Carrie said. Really, this was beyond anything she would have believed possible.

He leaned against the kitchen counter, staring out the window at the mountains in the distance. "I've never been to a place like this. There isn't a building to block a single view, just wide open spaces. The mountains, the skies, the endless prairie …. They're just as you described them, and then some."

"I think it's as close to heaven as we can get." She set another bowl of soup and a spoon on the table.

"I must say, for someone who so recently came down with this flu, you look remarkably well," her father finally commented.

"At the beginning, it felt awful." She shook her head at the memory. "I was so weak and sore, I could hardly get out of bed. I'm sorry I scared you. Gran must have been really worried."

"Of course, your grandmother was concerned. She told me about your plans to consult the medicine woman. I can see now that I probably overreacted, but this flu has taken quite a few lives this year. I needed to make sure you were okay. Anyway, I was overdue for a chance to see you." He smiled, looking uncomfortable, then added, "I've missed you."

"I've missed you, too." She reached across the table and took his hand.

"Dad?" Carrie sat up in bed and threw off the covers. "Dad?"

From her room, she could hear muffled moans. In a few seconds, she was across the hall and at his side. He was thrashing around on the bed, mumbling incoherently.

She laid her hand on his forehead and flinched at the heat she felt rising from his skin. "Not you, too."

"I'm sick," he said.

"You sure are. Stay put." She went downstairs, returning with a glass of water. "Sip this," she said. She took his temperature, her fears confirmed.

She forced a reassuring smile. "I'd say you're officially my flu patient now. Don't worry. I've seen far worse."

"I don't think I've ever felt this bad." His voice was hoarse and she could hear a slight rattle in his breathing. "I need you to get me an anti-viral."

She didn't tell him the hospital was out of the medication. If he didn't start on an anti-viral within the first three days, it wouldn't do him any good. She patted his arm. "Dad, I'll take good care of you."

She went downstairs and called Nate. When he answered, she said, "My dad is pretty sick. I've given him something for aches and fever, but I was wondering if the hospital has gotten more anti-flu meds yet?"

"Not yet." He paused. "I've called around to the pharmacies in the area. They're out of stock, too."

"I'll do the best I can without it, then," she said. "I'll do manipulation, if he'll allow it."

"How are *you* doing?" he asked.

"I've been fever-free for almost twenty-four hours. I've still got a cough, but Medicine Owl's tea helps. I need to get more for my dad."

Nate chuckled. "Are you sure he'll go for that?"

"No, of course not. I'm doing what I have to do—what I believe works."

"I'll call if that shipment arrives. Make sure you're taking care of yourself, too. And, Carrie …?"

"What?"

"You know I'm here for you."

"I do know that, yes."

Chapter Twenty-Three

CARRIE DOZED IN THE ROCKING CHAIR by her father's bed, hyperaware of his every need. Still not feeling completely well herself, she had asked Nate to be on red-alert, in case help was needed transporting her father to a hospital. As his illness wore on, Carrie knew she needed assistance with his day-to-day care. She needed Gran. But of course, that wasn't possible. It was Medicine Owl who showed up at her door, taking over his care and allowing her to rest.

To Carrie, who was overwhelmed, exhausted, and frightened, the medicine woman could not have been more welcome. Medicine Owl removed the shawl she always wore and set down her bag.

"You rest, daughter," she said, leading Carrie by the arm to a chair. "We will work together for your father's healing. I will pray now."

For such a tiny, elderly woman, Medicine Owl was strong—as strong as most men. She helped Carrie move her father from his bed into the bathroom, where they shut the door and turned on a hot shower to create a sauna effect. They sat him on a bench and held him up as he slumped over, heavy as a stone statue. The temperature in the bathroom wasn't as hot as the sweat lodge, but the steam was still beneficial. In addition, Carrie kept up a routine of soft tissue massage and manipulation to aid his body in fighting off the virus.

By the third day, he was breathing easier. When his fever finally broke, it left him weak and drenched in sweat. She could hear that the congestion was easing in his lungs.

"Thank you, Medicine Owl," she said, letting out a long breath after taking his temperature and finding it normal. "He's better now."

"We are a good team." The medicine woman smiled and rose from the rocking chair. "I will leave now."

"It's probably good that Dad wasn't completely aware of what Medicine Owl was doing," Carrie reported to Gran by phone after the medicine woman left. "But I wish you could have been here. Maybe you would have known what he was talking about. He was saying things that scared me."

"Delirium can cause people to say strange things," Gran said. Carrie thought she heard fear in her voice.

As she served her father a cup of chicken broth and plumped his pillows, she wanted to ask him about the things she had heard him say. At one point, he had yelled, "Mother, Mother! Don't let him die!'"

"I think you're over the worst," she said, crawling onto the bed beside him and sipping from her own mug of soup. "You'll need to stay here for a few more days, though."

"I thought I was going to die," he said.

"The steam helped a lot—that and the tea Medicine Owl brewed for you. You should feel lucky that you got all the benefits of the sweat lodge without having to roll in the snow like I did." She grinned.

He chuckled. "I can see why so many people swear by it. I don't remember, though, how much of the anti-viral I took."

"Truthfully, I couldn't get any, and by the time it arrived, it wouldn't have done you much good, anyway. But I was kicking myself the entire time."

"Why?" He gave her a sidelong glance.

"It was my choice not to take any medication when Nate offered it to me. But if I had agreed to let him bring me some, I might have had it here for you. Just because I wanted to go the no-drug route didn't mean I was comfortable making that decision for you."

"All's well that ends well." Her father looked thoughtful. Then he grimaced. "While I was running such a high temp, I had the strangest dreams. There was someone chanting—oh, and drumbeats."

"You weren't dreaming. That was Medicine Owl. She was praying over you while she administered an herbal poultice treatment."

"You don't say." He chewed on his lower lip. "I honestly thought I was dying. As you know, I have experience losing someone from the flu—someone I loved."

"Did the flu kill your father? Was that what happened?"

"The flu was what led to his death, but that isn't the whole story." Mark looked off into space, picking at a corner of the quilt.

"What happened? No one ever talks about it—not you, not Gran, not even Mom." She laid her head on his shoulder.

He set down his cup of broth and took her hand, stroking her fingers. "I had a lot of time to think on the trip out here. Your grandmother says I need to deal with what happened the night he died."

"What do you think? Is she right?" Carrie sat up and turned toward him, her eyes meeting his. There she saw pain and regret. "I don't know the full story, but there has to be a reason why you've been so angry at Gran."

"I blamed her for letting my father die."

"Oh, Dad." Carrie leaned back against the pillows, stunned. This was worse than anything she had ever heard him say.

"He passed away about two hours after telling my mother he wasn't feeling well. He went to lie down. I was in my room playing. I was just a little guy—had just turned seven." He looked off into the distance. "It happened so fast. She went to check on him between patients and called for an ambulance. She kept working on him. It seemed like the ambulance would never get there. I remember screaming, begging her to do something. She finally said, 'There's nothing I can do, son. He's gone.' "

"That must have been so awful." She could envision the scene: Gran trying to resuscitate her young husband, the heartrending sounds of a child screaming, the horror and agony as Gran realized her husband was dead. "I remember reading about that flu. It was one of the worst for pneumonia. Is that what happened?"

Carrie watched as her father continued staring into space. He seemed lost in the memories of that night so long ago. Her heart ached for the frightened little boy who watched his father die, who begged his mother to save him.

"He had cardiomyopathy," Mark continued. "It hadn't yet been diagnosed. Apparently, Mother was worried about the arrhythmia, shortness of breath, the exhaustion. He balked at seeing a specialist, said he was just working too much. He was a trucker, and time off the road meant no pay. So he put her off. When he came down with the flu, he went downhill fast."

"He wouldn't have had the strength to fight the virus if his heart was already weakened."

"An autopsy confirmed cardiomyopathy. Of course, as a kid, I wouldn't have understood any of that. Everyone said my mother was the best doctor around. We had patients in and out of the house all the time. But she couldn't save her own husband."

"Dad, when did you learn about the cardiomyopathy?"

Mark let out a long breath. "I was in high school. By then, I wanted to be a doctor, too. Mother suggested cardiology. That was when she told me about my dad. I didn't fully understand his condition, of course, until I went to medical school. After that, it was all I could imagine doing with my life—saving people like my dad."

"But if you knew your father had cardiomyopathy, why did you still blame your mother? There wouldn't have been much she could do if he was already that sick."

"I know that." His eyes closed. "I needed to blame someone. It was easier to blame her." He shrugged. "I remember going to my room to play, so maybe I could have helped or alerted her earlier. I remember that now. But she and I had other issues, too. Seemed like I was always angry with her. And maybe I was angry at my father, too—who I didn't even get a chance to know—for not going to see that specialist."

"You and your mother could have grown closer as a result of what happened. She was all you had left. You were her only child."

"Mother was always working, always seeing patients. She wasn't like other mothers, and I thought she put her patients first, before Dad, before me."

"It's a delicate balancing act. You know that. But she worked out of her home office so she could be there for you."

Her father worried his lower lip, considering the question. "I didn't see it that way. For years, I've chewed on the memory of that night. She was so busy with her patients, she didn't check on my dad in time to save him. When she finally did, I heard her crying, begging God to help her. Yes, I thought maybe she could have saved him if she hadn't been so busy taking care of strangers. But I had my own guilt, too, wishing I had been there, watching over him." He let out a raspy laugh, devoid of humor. "I used to wonder if I might have been able to save him, somehow. I was so little. How could I have done anything? But I remember thinking that maybe a magic kiss could have made the difference, and that my mother should have tried that. But it was also when I gave up on my faith. God didn't help him, either."

Tears filled Carrie's eyes. "But surely by now, you know these things happen. We lose patients. No matter how hard you try, sometimes you can't save someone. No matter how much you know about a condition, it's not always in your hands. You've had to make choices about taking care of strangers, too. I remember growing up wishing you were home more. You did exactly what she did."

"I've come to realize that." Her father closed his eyes.

"Dad, I understand now."

"Someday, when you have children of your own, you'll have to deal with that challenge, too." He smiled. "One of these days."

"I hope so. And I hope when that happens, my kids know how much I love them. I always did know that, Dad. I've always known how much you love me."

He avoided her eyes. "I've been hard on you, Carrie. Sometimes parents mean well, but we make mistakes."

"Dad, there's so much I want to say. I don't know where to start."

"Before you say anything, I want to apologize for my heavy-handedness last summer. I didn't behave well when you couldn't come to work with me at my practice. I didn't even congratulate you on the award. It was wrong for me to interfere in your relationship with Tom. I shouldn't have given him money for that down payment. By the way, he insists he'll pay me back."

Carrie let out a deep breath, considering her response. "I think it just took me by surprise. He hadn't even bothered to tell me you offered him a job. He wasn't telling me much of anything. Then all of a sudden, I was getting a set of keys to a house I'd never seen."

Her father had the grace to look ashamed. "I know. Your mother pointed that out to me, and again, I'm sorry. I'm even sorrier that I allowed you to leave as you did without telling you …." He paused, looking again as if he might cry. "I should have told you that you have always been my pride and joy. I'm a stubborn man. I like things my own way, but my way doesn't have to be your way."

Carrie could hardly believe her ears. "Hearing you say that means a lot."

"If anything had happened to you … well, I never would have forgiven myself. I had to come."

"It's good you decided to check on me. I didn't realize until I saw you how much I needed my dad."

"Well, maybe not so much these days," her father said. "You seem to be doing fine on your own."

"I'll always need you," Carrie insisted. "What Medicine Owl did got me over the worst of it. "But seeing you," she touched her heart, "makes the place in here feel better."

"While your grandmother and I have our differences, we do agree on one thing: how precious you are to us. She told me immediately that you were sick. We had a rather heated discussion about what you were doing to help yourself and the merits of that kind of treatment. But in the end, she agreed it was important for me to come here and see you. I could hardly stop her from coming herself."

"It sounds like the two of you had another fight. I don't like to hear that. It mystifies me how two intelligent people—both doctors, and a mother and son, to boot—find it so difficult to see eye to eye on anything." Carrie stirred her soup. "You're more alike than you know."

"I can't imagine in what ways," Mark said, bristling. "We approach everything differently."

"You're both board-certified doctors. You've both had great careers. The truth is that I've taken the best from both of you in how I approach medicine."

Mark sat up straighter in the bed. "I didn't come here to discuss my mother and me. I came to see you and take care of you. Things didn't turn out quite the way I envisioned. You ended up taking care of me."

"We took care of each other," Carrie said. She hoped that he had not allowed too much time to pass in making things right with her grandmother. He still had some thinking to do where Gran was concerned.

As they rested together in the big bed, they heard the sound of drums in the distance. She smiled. "Each of us marches to our own drummer."

A smile flickered across his face. "I heard drums in the distance while I was sick. I don't think I imagined it. Do you hear them often?"

"All the time. It's how messages get delivered here."

"Interesting." He was silent for a moment, processing this information. "Do you know what they're saying now?"

"I think I do, actually. 'All is well.' "

A FEW DAYS LATER, THEY WENT TO the hospital to meet Peg and other colleagues, who flocked to Carrie, expressing their relief and joy that she was well. Her father was charmed when Peg said, "So you're the man responsible for giving us this wonderful woman. She's the answer to our prayers."

Emotion worked on his face as he thanked her. Then he said, "She was the answer to our prayers, too—her mother's and mine."

Carrie shot him a questioning look. On their way from the clinic to the emergency department to see Nate, her father asked, "Did you know we tried for three years to have a baby, without success? It was a miracle when your mother found out she was pregnant with you."

"That was before fertility drugs. Was it just that you relaxed and stopped trying, and then it finally happened?" Carrie teased.

She had never heard this version of events. She knew that her parents had been married after her father graduated from medical school and that she hadn't been born until a year after he completed his residency. But she didn't know they'd had difficulty conceiving.

"Your grandmother gave your mother treatments—manipulation and an herbal tea. I didn't know about the herbal tea until later or I would have questioned it. Of course, I wouldn't give my mother's efforts any credence, whatsoever. You came along later that year."

"What kind of herbal tea did Gran give Mom?"

"I don't remember. You'll have to ask her."

"But you didn't have any more kids. You stopped with me. Was I that much trouble?"

Her father sighed. "Your mother had a difficult time during delivery. She came dangerously close to needing an emergency C-section. She wanted my mother to stay and help her during labor. I wouldn't allow it. I wouldn't allow my own mother in the room with my wife while she struggled in labor." His voice cracked. "I have regrets about so many things I've said and done, Carrie."

"Dad, those are years we can't get back. But we can do things differently in the future." She took his arm as they continued walking through the hospital's corridors. "We're making a new start, you and me. Please do the same with Gran. Will you do that for me?"

He nodded. As they entered the ER, they found Nate between patients. When he saw Carrie, he broke into a wide grin. "Wow. You look a hundred percent better," he said. "You were definitely a paleface the last time I saw you." He looked over at Mark. "You must be Carrie's dad. I'm glad you're better, too, Doctor."

"I've made a miraculous recovery, as they say," her father said, stepping forward to shake Nate's hand. "Please call me Mark."

"It's good to meet you, Mark. It's really something that you came all this way just to check on your daughter."

"It wasn't exactly easy to get here, but where there's a will, there's a way."

Nate grinned. "That was some will, I'd say. Welcome to Blackfeet Community Hospital and my emergency department."

"I'm impressed with this facility," Mark said, looking around. "For such a small hospital, it seems to have everything you need to get the job done."

"Everything except enough doctors." Nate exchanged glances with Carrie. "With Carrie out sick this week, we've been hard-pressed to keep up with all the customers."

"Well, she's done enough lollygagging for one week. She'll be back to work tomorrow. I've got to get back to my own practice."

Carrie gave him a playful slap on the arm. "Lollygagging?" she said in mock outrage.

As they left the hospital, her father stopped and looked back. "I'm guessing you don't have a cardiologist on staff here."

"We don't. We sure could use one," Carrie said. "I was hoping you'd consider joining the volunteer medical corps this summer—maybe see a few of our sicker patients." She was thinking of Dancing Bird. She glanced out of the corner of her eye at him.

He got into the car and started the engine. "I'll give it some thought."

Chapter Twenty-Four

⁓⁓

"WHILE I'M IN PHILADELPHIA, JUST CALL or email if you need anything," Carrie told Peg as she left final orders for patients. "I'll check my phone as often as I can."

It was the second week in March, one day before her trip to Philadelphia. Although she had always enjoyed continuing education conferences, she'd never been quite this excited. She had prepared and practiced her breakfast presentation on the Roosevelt project several times—once for Nate—and felt confident. In addition to seeing classmates and colleagues in scientific sessions and at her medical school's alumni reception during the conference, she'd have plenty of time to spend with family. Now that she and her father had patched up their relationship, there was little to worry about in that regard. And weather in Montana was holding steady, ensuring she could get to Great Falls to catch her flight.

"You go and have fun. Don't worry about this place," Peg said. "We'll miss you, but we'll get along."

"Thanks for taking care of Annie."

"She's a good girl. Besides, if we keep Annie, you have to come back." She handed Carrie a chart. "I'm glad you're seeing Dancing Bird before you go. I don't like the looks of her today."

The first glimpse of the tiny woman in the examination room told Carrie everything she needed to know: her patient had taken a turn for the worse. Dancing Bird's hands and feet were swollen, and she wheezed with each breath. But she was cheerful and offered up a broad smile when she saw Carrie.

"Dancing Bird, how are you feeling?" she asked, holding her patient's hands in hers.

"My spirit is old," Dancing Bird replied, her dark eyes twinkling. "But I am still here."

"I'll be away for a week," Carrie said, a lump forming in her throat. "If you have more trouble breathing or you don't feel well, please go to the emergency room." She knew this turn of events was all too likely to happen. Whether Dancing Bird would listen was another issue entirely.

"I will see Medicine Owl."

"That's a good idea." Carrie listened intently to her patient's heart and lungs. She thought of hospitalizing her, but knew Dancing Bird preferred to remain at home. "I have seen Medicine Owl, too," Carrie said. "Has she given you anything to help you feel better?"

"She helps my spirit," the old woman said. "That is all I need now."

"Yes," Carrie answered quietly.

She drew Dancing Bird to her, making small adjustments to her spine in an attempt to ease her breathing. Holding her close felt like a hug. She now realized that Dancing Bird wouldn't survive the winter and guessed that she knew it, too.

"THERE SHE IS!" SHE HEARD HER mother's voice even before she caught sight of her in the crowded baggage area of Philadelphia International Airport.

"Mom!" Carrie broke into a dead run. Her mother was dressed in a grape-colored coat, her blonde hair swept up into a chignon, twinkling diamond studs on her ears.

Her father stood behind her, an expectant smile on his face, until Carrie released her mom and launched herself at him. "Dad!"

He kissed and hugged her, then stepped back to have a better look. "Your mother needs to make sure you get enough to eat while you're home. You still look too thin to me. Or maybe I should pick up some Philly cheese steaks and shoo-fly pie."

"I can't believe a cardiologist would say that." She laughed and shook her head. "Maybe I need to start paying attention to what Mom does in the kitchen and actually learn how to cook."

Linking arms, all three waited for Carrie's suitcase to come down the conveyor belt. Her father fetched the car while she and her mother waited outside in the passenger pick-up area. All around her, people scurried into waiting cars or hailed taxis, causing security guards to blow their whistles and yell out warnings. Accustomed to the quiet of life on the reservation, the cacophony of sounds nearly overwhelmed Carrie. She turned to her mother, who observed her with a thoughtful expression.

"Gran will be joining us for dinner tonight, but someone will have to drive over and pick her up," Lynne said. "She's had some numbness in one leg—

probably from that hip. Your dad doesn't want her driving."

"I'll go," Carrie agreed. "Walking with a different gait from that sore hip has surely thrown her spine out of alignment. Maybe she'll let me give her a treatment."

Carrie slid into the backseat while her father put her suitcase in the trunk of his SUV. As they made their way through heavy Philadelphia traffic, she updated her parents on the most recent news from Browning. The flu had petered out, although the cough lingered. Medicine Owl planned to stay in town until June, when she'd return to her hut in the foothills. Nate's emergency department was being remodeled. The hospital had a new program to limit overuse of antibiotics in an effort to curb superbug-resistant strains of bacteria—a step that Carrie had long thought necessary. Her father listened attentively and interrupted a few times with questions, having met the people she mentioned.

"How's Nate?" he finally asked. "I was glad I had a chance to meet him when I was there."

"Fine. Somehow, he managed to avoid the flu. Not sure how, not with all the flu patients they had streaming through the ER. If he had gotten sick, he would have had a backlog of surgeries until next year."

"He must be good, to do so many different procedures. And he's head of emergency medicine, too. That's quite a load." Her father whistled under his breath and shook his head. "I admire someone who is competent at so many things."

"He makes it look easy," Carrie said, the pride evident in her voice. "Nate can do anything."

They parked in the circular driveway of the Nelsons' two-story white Colonial, set back from the road on two wooded acres. Her father took Carrie's suitcase up to her room while she reacquainted herself with the elegant house she had grown up in. The formal dining room looked the same, with its dove-gray textured walls, glossy white woodwork, and crystal and gold chandelier. The mahogany dining room table was set for four with her mother's best white tablecloth, starched and pressed to perfection, and matching cloth napkins held with monogrammed gold napkin rings. A vase of yellow forsythia and pussy willows graced the center of the table.

"What are we having for dinner?" Carrie asked, appreciating the delicious scents that always pervaded her mother's kitchen.

"Turkey, mashed potatoes, dried-corn casserole, spinach salad, rolls, and pecan pie—all your favorites. I thought we'd make this our Thanksgiving and Christmas meal combined, since you weren't able to be with us."

"I want doubles on everything." Carrie stood at the huge bay window, looking outside at the enormous backyard with its kidney-shaped swimming pool now covered in a blue tarp. There was a large patio for entertaining and a small basketball court where her father had taught her how to shoot baskets. She had so many wonderful memories of growing up in this house. It was familiar … and yet not. With a smile, she realized that the place that now felt like home was 2,300 miles away.

"Have a cup of tea with me," her mother called to her. Carrie sank onto a bench at the trestle table while her mother brewed a pot of tea and arranged a small plate of raisin-filled cookies. "Tell me more about the people you spend time with." She handed her the small cream pitcher. "In your emails, they all sound so interesting. This John you talk about—the Blackfeet man—will he marry his girlfriend?"

"He says they will. No idea when. There are still a lot of family issues. John's grandfather is a tribal elder and would rather John marry someone from the Blackfeet Nation. There is a woman he was supposed to marry—the daughter of his mother's best friend. It's sort of an arranged marriage situation, I think. It remains to be seen how things will work themselves out."

"So, there are people you care about there and who care about you. You seem happy." Her mother's eyes were searching, beseeching her to say more.

"I am happy. It can be rough, at times. The people deserve more than they're getting. We need more doctors. Either that or I need to grow another pair of hands. But I've enjoyed every minute I've spent there." She paused. "Well, almost every minute. The flu was no fun."

"Do you get homesick?" Her mother reached out and touched Carrie's hair. "I worry about you."

"I think I'm always a little homesick," she admitted. "Thanksgiving and Christmas were hard. They were my first big holidays away from the family."

"They weren't much fun for us, either." Her mother wrapped both hands around her mug. "I want time alone with you this weekend—just the two of us. I scheduled girl time at the spa on Saturday—haircuts, mani/pedis, the works."

"I must look a mess," Carrie said, gingerly picking up a lock of her hair, which now reached the middle of her back.

"Nonsense. You're a beautiful girl. But I also know that you put your own needs last. Let me do what mothers do and take care of you."

Carrie knew the subject of Tom would come up, eventually, with her mother—maybe even her father. It was inevitable. She wasn't surprised when her mother worked Tom into their conversation. "Tom was here the other night for dinner and asked about you."

"It's nice that you continue to keep him fed, Mom. I'm sure he appreciates it. How is he?"

"He seems fine. He's living in that big house all by himself."

"I'm sure a lot of women would love to live in a house like that. Maybe he'll meet someone new and get married."

"You don't miss him?" Her mother bit into a cookie.

"I don't." Carrie looked directly into her mother's eyes. "I hope no one, especially Tom, thinks there's any chance we'll get back together."

"Ever since Dad got back from Montana, he hasn't spent much time with Tom outside the office. I wondered if the two of you talked about him at all."

"Dad apologized for lending Tom money for the house." She chose her words carefully. "Mom, I don't care if Tom and Dad remain friends outside of work. It's okay if you invite him over for dinner." She spoke slowly, hoping her words got through. "I would not have been happy with him. I hope I'll have another chance to marry. If not, I'll still know I made the right decision."

"I just want you to be happy. It's all I've ever wanted." Her mother rested her hand over Carrie's.

"I know that, and I promise I'll try to give you grandchildren someday, since that's at least some of your concern." She grinned. Glancing at the clock on the kitchen wall, she leaned over and kissed her mother on the cheek. "I'd better go get Gran now."

She picked up the keys to her mother's BMW off the rack by the back door and drove to Gran's house. Parking in the driveway, she peeked into the greenhouse at the profusion of plants growing there. As she walked up the steps of the white farmhouse, she noticed the aging porch furniture and the peeling paint on the steps and floor. Gran had always been so particular about caring for her property. But at her age, it would be difficult to handle all the maintenance on such a big place. The thought of Gran growing older, and the realization that she wouldn't be around forever brought a tightening to Carrie's heart. What would she do without Gran?

She rapped on the door, even though it was rarely locked. "Hello-o-o?" she called out, inhaling the tantalizing aroma of apples, sugar, and cinnamon. An apple pie sat cooling on the radiator cover, the edges of its crust perfectly browned. She heard a sound behind her and turned, her throat catching. Gran hobbled in, stooped over and leaning on her cane. She appeared years older than the last time Carrie had seen her, just eight months ago.

"Gran," she said, embracing her carefully. "I wanted to get a little time alone with you before dinner. How are you doing?"

"Fair to middlin'. I have a favor to ask you." Gran eased herself into a chair.

"Anything."

"I wondered if I can ride along with you to the conference every day. I've got a few more credits I need to earn this year. And of course, I wouldn't miss our alumni reception. I'm so proud of you, I'm likely to pop a few buttons while they brag about you!"

Carrie laughed. "It'll be weird to be standing there, hearing about myself, when I've only been out of school a few years. You should be the one they honor, if you ask me. Of course you can ride with me. What a thing to ask." Carrie smiled with relief that Gran was still keeping up her license to practice medicine. Besides, it would be fun to attend sessions with her. "Mom and Dad sent me a gift card for a plane ticket for Christmas, so I decided to use it to come to this conference."

"You'd probably have been better off using that ticket to go someplace sunny. But I must say you do seem to be enjoying your work there and your life on the reservation." Gran rested her cane against the table. She studied Carrie with her calm blue eyes. "Life agrees with you. I can see that."

"I love it there. And isn't it lucky that I've gotten to know the medicine woman? The two of you would get along well. She seems familiar to me, as if I've known her all my life."

"I'm glad." Gran was quiet for a moment before offering a weak smile. "Next time you see her, ask her if she has a remedy for old age."

"She might." Carrie smiled. She looked into Gran's sapphire blue eyes, as clear and direct as ever. "Medicine Owl is in her nineties and still going strong." She paused. "Gran, I can see how much that hip is bothering you, from the way you sit. Will you let me work on you?"

Gran nodded, brightening. "I knew there was a reason I wanted you to be an osteopath—free treatments." With difficulty, she rose and made her way to her office at the front of the house.

The two rooms where she saw patients looked the same to Carrie as they always had. Gran still had one of the first manipulation tables, heavy as a chest of drawers and made of oak. She had used it with countless patients over the years. Carrie performed about ten minutes of soft-tissue massage and then made several adjustments she felt certain would ease Gran's discomfort and make walking easier.

"There," she said. "I'll check this again before I leave. But that ought to get you on your way to feeling better."

"Couldn't have done a better job myself," Gran said, giving her a peck on the cheek.

They drove back to her parents' house. That evening, there was no medical or career discussion to create tension. Over dinner, she and her father laughed as easily together as they had during the five days he spent in Browning. The more remarkable change, however, was the easy, affectionate banter between Gran and her father.

"They're making up for lost time," her mother whispered as Carrie helped her bring in Gran's apple pie and coffee. It was a dinner like no other for this family, one of peace instead of conflict.

Over the next four days, Carrie and Gran attended the family medicine conference and enjoyed time with friends and colleagues. She gave Gran another treatment and was pleased to see further progress. Gran was now able to walk a few steps without her cane and claimed not to need any pain relievers or muscle relaxants to sleep.

"I feel like a new woman," she said, brandishing her cane like a sword. "By the time you see me again, I won't need this darn thing."

On Saturday, Carrie went with her mother to their favorite spa. Wrapped in soft white terrycloth robes, they sipped herbal tea and enjoyed facials, haircuts and styles, full-body massages, manicures, and pedicures. She felt rested and rejuvenated—almost but not quite ready to return to Montana. With her hair sleek and shiny from a deep conditioning treatment, she felt sexy for the first time in over a year. As she admired her reflection in the mirror at the salon, another thought occurred to her. *I can't wait for Nate to see me.*

That evening, they sat together in front of the fireplace, sipping wine. "Thanks for today, Mom."

"You may be a doctor now, but you're still a young woman. Don't let yourself get frumpy." Her mother put both feet up on the ottoman and yawned. "Has there been anyone nice on the reservation for you to see socially?" Her expression was all innocence, but Carrie knew better.

"Maybe. What have you heard?"

"Not much. I just remember that your father commented about someone he met there."

"I bet he did." Carrie chuckled. "I don't know what to say. I guess anything is possible."

"The surgeon?" Her mother suddenly looked alert. "Is there a spark there for him, too, do you think?"

Carrie blushed, remembering their first kiss. "Oh, yes. There's definitely chemistry between us. I like him a lot. I just don't know if it's a good idea, since I'm leaving in July."

"You've always had a sensible head on your shoulders. If he treats you well, and you have lots in common, don't let the opportunity pass for you to have some fun. From what you've told me, he sounds like a wonderful man. Maybe he could visit you here."

Carrie laughed. "Yes, maybe he could visit, and you could check him out."

"It's a mother's job." Her mother grinned. "I've been wondering if you're worried about having to work with Tom when you come back. Just in case that's a concern, he's opening a new satellite office out in Skippack for your father. You wouldn't have to work alongside him."

Carrie took in a sharp breath. Leave it to her mother to cut to the chase.

"That's some of my concern, yes. The bigger issue is that I can't be here and in Montana, too. Being there is everything I ever wanted professionally. Dad and I are getting along so well. I am not sure where this is leading for my career and personal life."

"Your father cherished the time he spent with you. It meant so much to him that he could take care of you when you were sick. And then you returned the favor." Her mother looked thoughtful. "He came back a different man."

"He told me what happened when his father died," Carrie said. "It's really good to see him and Gran in a better place."

"It makes life easier for both of them ... and for me." Her mother leaned her head back against the chair. "The day she told him you were sick, they had a terrible argument. She was proud of you for being so courageous and insisting that Native American medicine could help. She said you were smart and could draw from the best of both worlds. I tried not to get in the middle of it, but I could hear everything they were saying. It was getting out of hand."

"Dad said they really got into it."

"That's an understatement." Her mother frowned, recalling the scene. "He said if he allowed it, she'd let you die like she did her husband. I was stunned that he actually said that."

"Oh no!" Carrie bit her lip. "That must have devastated Gran. It was an awful thing to say and an even more terrible thing to hear, especially from your own son. There was nothing she could have done." Carrie shook her head, still amazed at the hurtful words family members could hurl at loved ones. And she was certain that, no matter what had happened, her father loved his mother.

"I know that. You know that. Even your dad knew it deep down. It was the saddest thing in the world. She finally looked at him and said, 'Don't you know he was the love of my life? He died in my arms! Don't you think I would have given my own life if it would have saved his?' "

Her mother dabbed at a tear. Carrie's own throat was constricted with emotion. She considered how much family strife there had been just beneath the surface all these years. The old injuries had festered for decades, creating a thick scarring of resentments. Yet forgiveness, surprisingly, had taken much less time, healing the divisions. Medicine Owl had been right. Forgiveness often started in the heart of one person, but could replicate through others in what often seemed a miraculous way.

"I've never heard her talk very much about him or her marriage." Carrie took a sip of her wine. "No one talks about him. There are no pictures of him here, no mementos of his life. Gran has that photo of them on their wedding day on her bedside table. That's all I've ever known of him. I always thought he looked like Dad."

"After he died, she had such a difficult time. She was a doctor, yes, but she was also a young wife with a child. She loved her husband very much. Then, suddenly, she was a young widow with a little boy who missed his dad. She told me she grieved for years and years. I think she also blamed herself. Hearing that accusation from her son reopened a wound."

"Dad said she was always busy helping other people. He resented that she put her patients first."

"In his mind, she did," her mother said. "Remember, in those days there weren't many female doctors. After her husband died, she threw herself into her work, and I think your dad's childhood was tougher for that. She had to support them both. But look at how he turned out. I'd say she did a good job."

Carrie nodded. "She worked out of their home and provided for him by doing something that was really important. I hope if I'm ever lucky enough to have children, they won't resent my career."

"On some level, I'm sure he knew how much her work mattered. When he and I were dating, she wanted him to go into practice with her, and he flat out told her no. By rejecting her invitation, it was as if he was rejecting her as his mother, too. Their relationship has only gotten more strained over the years ... well, until recently."

"She appears to have forgiven him," Carrie said.

"He's her child. As far as she was concerned, there was nothing to forgive."

ON HER LAST EVENING IN PHILADELPHIA, Carrie drove over to the house where Tom lived, intent on returning his engagement ring. It didn't seem right to keep it. She stood on the front porch and rang the doorbell, tempted to peer through the narrow cut-glass windows on either side of the door. Now that she was standing here, she wondered if this was such a good idea. She half hoped Tom wouldn't answer and she could leave the ring at her parents' house for him to pick up. Then, her heart pounding, she heard the sound of the deadbolt opening.

"Carrie." All the color drained from Tom's face when he saw her. "I wasn't expecting to see you. I mean, I hoped you'd call or stop by."

"Sorry I didn't ... call, that is. Am I interrupting anything?"

Tom cleared his throat. "Not at all. Please, come in. I was just, er, doing some laundry. Can I get you something to drink? I've got that chardonnay you like."

She entered the foyer, noting familiar pieces of furniture and a few items of bric-a-brac that her mother had given him. "Thanks, but I can't stay," she said. "I just wanted to make sure I gave you back the ring. It isn't right for me to keep it."

Tom's face reddened as he accepted the ring. "It doesn't belong to me. It belongs to you." He reached out and took her hand. Before she could withdraw her hand, he slipped the ring onto her fourth finger. "It belongs here, on your finger."

"Tom, no." She met his eyes. They were plaintive but hopeful.

"Carrie, I made mistakes, and I want things to be the way they used to be between us."

"I don't think—"

"Please let me finish." He was still grasping her hand. "I don't want to live in this house without you. I don't want to live my life without you. I am asking for another chance to make things right. I don't care if you stay on the reservation through July. I can wait until then."

Carrie shook her head. "So much has changed between us, Tom. I don't feel as I once did, and it wouldn't be fair for me to say that I do. Even when I move back here, I just don't see a future between us. I'm sorry. We're likely to see each other occasionally through work. I hope we can be friends."

Even as she said this, she knew it was unlikely. There was too much history between them to return to being friends. She knew him too well. Tom bowed his head as she removed the ring and handed it back to him. Eyes filled with compassion, she squeezed his arm, turned away, and let herself out.

FOLLOWING THE NIGHTLY NEWS, AS CARRIE and her parents sipped tea in front of the fireplace, she watched her parents exchange glances. Finally, her mother cleared her throat. "Dad and I have decided to come to Montana to visit you in July—the same week as those North American Indian Days you talk about. Can you help us find a place to stay on the reservation?"

"Really?" Carrie's eyes lit up. "We'll have such a good time! There are plenty of nice places: a big resort lodge, cottages …. I'll write down a few options for you. Things fill up early for summer, though. You'd better book something now."

"I hope I can find a place to hit some golf balls," Mark said.

"Dr. Jim would love to take you out on the course," she said. "I wish you'd still consider helping us out that week in the clinic. Nothing ventured, nothing gained, as they say."

"I suppose I could think about putting in a little time, if you need me."

Carrie jumped up from her chair and threw her arms around his neck, planting a huge kiss on his cheek. "Dad, that makes me so happy!"

"Send me the particulars," he said. "But remember, your mother and I will be there on vacation to spend time with you, too, not just to work with the Indians."

"The Indians definitely need a good cardiologist, and you'll never see more appreciative patients than the Blackfeet. But don't worry. We'll have plenty of time together." She grinned. It was as good as a promise from her father. He would never say that he actually wanted to volunteer with the medical corps, but Carrie knew she had him on the hook. Mark Nelson, MD, was going to have the time of his life. It would be a nice way to end her time on the reservation, too, before returning to Philadelphia. And maybe, just maybe, her father would agree to a flexible contract that would allow her to spend more time in Browning. Anything was possible.

He sat down on the sofa beside her and wrapped one arm around her neck. "After I got back from Montana, I learned something new."

"What's that?"

"Well, as you know, one of my partners is a DO. I told him what happened to me on the reservation and what you and the medicine woman did. He told me something about DOs, and about my mother, that I'd never heard before. Turns out, she was his family's doctor when he was a kid. He said people flocked to her during several bad flu seasons. She was doing something other doctors weren't."

Carrie listened with a smile. "Did he say what it was?"

"When she treated people for the flu, she also performed muscular and skeletal manipulation. For a long time, I didn't understand why you wanted to learn that. I didn't realize it had such value—or if I did, I rejected it outright because my mother thought it was important. Turns out, I was misinformed. He said that during the Spanish flu pandemic of 1918, osteopaths often had better patient outcomes than their other medical colleagues. They treated soldiers with the flu, and the soldiers recovered. Medical scholars theorized it was the manipulation that made the difference."

"It's one of the first things we learned in medical school. The body has the ability to heal itself if every system and organ is working at peak efficiency. I've seen it over and over in my career. It's why I use manipulation with so many of my patients, even if they come in for other conditions. I used manipulation on every flu patient I saw, including you."

"Carrie, with all that has gone on between us, especially some of the things I've said to you in recent years, can you ever forgive me?" Her father's eyes sought hers.

"You're my dad, so of course I forgive you. What I want to know is have you forgiven Gran? Have you been able to forgive yourself?"

"I'm well on my way. It wasn't until after I came out of that flu and all the crazy dreams I had that I could admit I was carrying around a load of guilt, too. Yes, yes, I know, I was just a kid, but children don't always comprehend the truth in situations. In my mind, I should have helped save my dad. After he died, I used to imagine he was with me in my room when I played. I'd talk to him and tell him how much he was missing. I was angry with him, too, for leaving us, and I thought that made me a bad person. That made the guilt even worse. I have talked with Gran about what I remember. I'm beginning to understand what she has been through, too."

"We're all making a fresh start. I like the way we are now." She burrowed into the big chair beside him, as close as she could get.

Her father put one arm around her. "You seemed a little quiet this evening. Is everything okay?"

"You might as well know. I went to see Tom today. I needed to return his ring. He asked me to give him another chance."

"I can't say I'm surprised. He asked me a few weeks ago about your plans. What did you say?"

She shook her head. "I said it wouldn't work between us. I don't feel about him the way I should feel … not anymore. It's too late for us to salvage this relationship."

Her father was quiet for a moment. Finally, he said, "I think you're right. I also think that somewhere out there is a man who is right for you. I think I might even know a good match."

Chapter Twenty-Five

T HE COMMUTER JET FROM DENVER LANDED in Great Falls late Monday afternoon. Carrie cleared a foot of snow from her car and began the drive back to Browning, a trip that would be longer and more treacherous on these snow-covered roads. She scanned the area, left and right, watching for racks of antlers on either side of the road. With nothing but white as far as the eye could see, it was easy to daydream and miss a warning sign of trouble ahead. Even so, her mind drifted to Nate. He was occupying more and more of her thoughts these days.

July would be here before she knew it, and her time on the reservation would be up. Although her heart yearned to remain in Browning with her patients, the decision about whether to stay or go was anything but simple. Yes, her father had visited the reservation and understood more about her life there, but he would still be disappointed if she didn't join his practice. On the other hand, if she left the reservation, she'd be leaving behind beloved patients and friends, including Peg, Ken, John, Gali ... and Nate.

Nate. She felt a flutter in her belly. If she left, she'd be leaving her heart behind—in more ways than one. A compromise might be possible—maybe she could take a week off every few months and return to the reservation. Her father might be more open to a split commitment between his practice and Blackfeet Community Hospital. It was worth further discussion. Why, then, had she avoided bringing up this touchy subject while she was in Philadelphia?

Even if a compromise could be reached, and she could be on the reservation on and off throughout the year, was it even a good idea to harbor romantic thoughts of Nate? She wanted more than a long-distance relationship. Maybe it was better to cut the cord and move on before someone got hurt.

As she turned from the moonlit road into the driveway, she pressed the garage door remote control on her windshield visor. Nothing happened. She hit it again before noticing that the lamp she had put on a timer in the front window was off. A feeling of dread gripped her.

"Terrific. No electricity."

She hauled her suitcase from the car over the deep snow and into the house, fearing the worst. Peering into darkened rooms, she stopped every so often to check the floors for water that would indicate a broken pipe. Everything appeared to be intact. She also had plenty of firewood. She lit a blaze in the fireplace and put on her ski pants and another sweater. Curled up on the floor by the fireplace, wrapped snugly in a cocoon of comforters and blankets, she fantasized about Nate until the fire (and her thoughts) warmed the room enough to permit sleep. Over the next few hours, she intermittently dozed and fed the fire with wood. Without Annie, who was snug and safe with the Bright Fishes, she had never felt more alone.

Snow fell throughout the night. This was followed by the clicking and scratching sound of icy pellets on glass. Things were going from bad to worse. When the alarm on her phone went off at six, she reluctantly threw back her cocoon of blankets and peered out the front window. An icy blue sheen like glass covered the snow, highlighted in eerily beautiful streaks by the light of the moon. As pretty as it appeared, the scene indicated dangerous driving and walking conditions.

She reluctantly made her way upstairs to the bathroom, shut the door, and lit two large, scented candles. Turning on the hot water, she realized that she'd have to be quick to take advantage of whatever heated water was left in the tank. She stepped under the shower, grateful for warmth. A heavy fog formed in the bathroom, causing her to fumble as she shivered, getting dressed in long thermal underwear beneath her scrubs, along with two pair of socks and a heavy cardigan. It was good that Annie was at Peg's house. The Bright Fishes had a wood-burning stove in their kitchen.

The drive to the hospital took longer than usual due to the ice on the road, which caused her car to slide this way and that. But when she arrived at the hospital, cheery warmth and the smell of baking cinnamon and fresh coffee greeted her. Following her nose, she took a quick detour to the kitchenette. There she received the warmest welcome she had ever had from coworkers.

"We were afraid you wouldn't come back," one of the nurses, Shirley, said with a shy smile as she retrieved cinnamon rolls from the oven.

"She had to come back. We have her dog," Peg said.

Carrie laughed. "Surely, you didn't really think I wouldn't come back. There's no place I'd rather be." She gave Shirley a quick hug. Taking a bite of a warm, spicy roll glazed with vanilla icing, she added, "Mm, this is just what I needed."

Despite the bad weather, which meant a lighter patient load than usual, three mothers arrived in active labor. They progressed rapidly, and she managed to deliver their babies in a matter of a few hours—two girls and a boy. *Good thing I came back when I did*, she thought. By four thirty, she was running on fumes. Closing her office door, she sat down at her desk, rested her head in her hands, and closed her eyes.

"Dr. Holden is looking for you." Peg cracked open the door and poked her head in.

"Oh? Did he need something?"

"I couldn't say. Maybe he just missed you." As Carrie looked up in surprise, Peg's eyes twinkled with mischief.

Carrie tried to appear stern but couldn't quite pull it off. "Dr. Holden is a *friend*, Peg."

"He might have other ideas. That's what I think." Peg pretended to recoil in fright. "Don't look at me like that. All of us hope you end up together. You'd have beautiful, golden-haired children."

Carrie shook her head, color rushing to her cheeks. "That's how rumors get started, Peg."

"Sometimes rumors end up being true."

"And sometimes rumors just cause trouble." She gave Peg a meaningful look and changed the subject. "Hey, I need to see if there is heat in the house before I pick up Annie. Would it be okay if I come over around seven, assuming the house is warm enough to take her home?"

"Suit yourself. I'll feed her before you get there. Hopefully, I can tear her away from Ken. I might have to let him get his own dog now." Peg's merry laugh rang out. "By the way, I didn't mean to upset you. I meant what I said about you and Dr. Nate. We're all so fond of both of you. We just want you to be happy."

"Well, that's sweet. I'm glad you like us, and I suppose people must gossip." Carrie was still trying to maintain her dignity and quell the rumors. "Remember, I'm leaving in July, right after Indian Days."

"I don't want to hear that," Peg said, her smile fading.

"Think of me as another Dr. Jim. I'll be back as often as I can," Carrie assured her. "This place is home, too."

When she arrived back at the house, the power was on, and the downstairs had started to warm up. She drove to the Bright Fishes' house to retrieve Annie, who greeted her at the door with yelps of happiness and wet kisses. Dancing in circles, Annie headed immediately for the front door.

"So much for appreciation." Peg stood in the doorway, drying her hands on a dishtowel. "She wants to go home with her mother."

"It's probably warm enough for her now," Carrie said. "Thanks again for taking such good care of my little girl while I was away."

"We love having her," Peg said. "She didn't lack for a thing."

"I didn't worry a bit." Carrie hugged Ken, who handed her Annie's blanket and dishes.

"I think the grandkids convinced her she's better off with you," Ken said. "She sure got a workout with the little ones."

Annie jumped eagerly into the front seat of Carrie's car, and they set off for home. Having already disposed of everything in the refrigerator and freezer, Carrie took stock of what remained in the pantry. She didn't particularly feel like going to the grocery store, but now it looked as if she had no choice. As she pulled her coat out of the closet, she heard loud knocking on the front door and hurried to open it. Nate stood there, stamping snow off his feet on the front doormat.

"Hey," she said, reaching out to give him a casual, one-armed hug. "Peg said you were looking for me today. What's up?"

"I still don't have power. Can I crash on your sofa tonight?"

"You don't have to crash on the sofa. There's another guest room," she said. "Come in. I was just about to go out and pick up a few things at the store."

"No need. I'll run out to the car and get everything." He returned with three plastic bags of food.

"You're like the perfect guest," Carrie said. "You even come with your own provisions."

"I brought wine, too."

"Isn't that how we ended up in a compromising position not so long ago?" she asked in her most innocent voice. "A little wine between friends ... and suddenly, we're more than friends."

"Um, well, yeah," he said. "I don't promise to behave myself tonight, either."

"You'd better. Annie is watching." She opened the bottle of chardonnay he handed her. It was already chilled. "I haven't had dinner yet. What should we fix from all this stuff you brought?"

"I have chicken in that bag. How about fried chicken and mashed potatoes? I'll make it." He pulled out a skillet. "Why don't you peel and dice a couple of potatoes?"

"I know how to make mashed potatoes now, just like Peg," Carrie said with pride. "Are you sure you just had all this stuff at your place? This looks like a well-laid plan. Maybe your heat isn't really off."

"You'll just have to trust me, I guess. Don't look a gift horse in the mouth. I just offered to cook for you."

"True." Carrie poured Nate a glass of wine and handed it to him. "I'm glad you're here."

He set down the glass and took her into his arms, tipped her chin up, and kissed her lightly. His lips were soft, the kiss gentle yet full of restrained passion. She closed her eyes and returned it, wrapping her arms around him, loving the feeling of being this close to him, this connected.

Reluctantly, they parted with two more quick kisses. He stroked her cheek. "If we keep this up, we'll never get dinner made. I'm starving."

While Carrie peeled and diced potatoes and then put them on to boil, she filled him in on the family medicine conference. Carrie lit a candle, and they worked side by side, smooth jazz in the background. Having set the mood for a romantic dinner, she suddenly recalled that Nate wouldn't be leaving after dinner tonight. Her sensible side said they were treading on dangerous ground. But as she watched him cook, her imagination ran wild. She thought about what it would be like to undress him. Clearly, the sensible part of her was losing this debate. And the wine wasn't helping.

"Other than the conference, and all the accolades I'm sure you collected, did you have a good time in Philadelphia?" Nate dipped the chicken pieces in egg wash and then in bread crumbs and herbs before laying them carefully in the skillet's hot oil.

"I had a great time. The whole family dynamic has changed since my dad came here."

"That's what you needed—time with your family, especially more time with your dad." Nate kissed her on the nose. "Watch out. I'm going to turn the chicken now." He lifted the golden-brown chicken pieces with tongs and turned them over. After a few minutes, he removed the pieces and laid them on a plate layered with paper towels. He moved the hot skillet to a back burner and watched with approval as Carrie mashed the potatoes, whipping them with the electric mixer until they were light as air. "Not bad," he said.

"I'm not a complete failure in the kitchen." She waved a wooden spoon at him.

"You're right. I couldn't have done better myself."

They sat down to eat with Annie plastered to the floor by Carrie's chair. She reached down and stroked the dog's velvet ears. "Peg and Ken took good care of Annie."

"I could've looked after her, you know. I've wanted to get a dog."

"I'll be glad to share her," Carrie said. "You can start by taking her out just before bedtime. I'll stay inside where it's nice and warm." She grinned at him and picked up a drumstick. Biting into it, she savored the blend of herbs in a perfect layer of crunch. "Mm, Nate, you are the most amazing cook."

"Glad you like it." He added another pat of butter to the potatoes on his plate, letting it pool in the center. "So, did you and your dad talk about … well, you know." He helped himself to more chicken.

"I know what you're getting at. We didn't talk specifically about the future, but I think the stage is set for a more serious discussion. He's coming here in July to volunteer … my mom, too. I'm almost ready to talk with him about a compromise—living and working there, but coming here regularly. I'm also happy to report that things have improved between Dad and Gran."

"You've never told me the whole story."

"I didn't really understand it myself until recently. It goes back to when my dad was a kid, and his father died. He blamed my grandmother, even though there was nothing she could have done. There was a blow-up between the two of them just before he came here, but at least it set the stage for a real discussion. They seem to have worked everything out."

"Most families have issues. That sounds more serious than most."

"The survivors suffered far longer than the actual victim, who died many years ago." Carrie took another sip of wine. "It would have been better if Dad and Gran could have talked long before they finally did. I guess the same thing could be said for Dad and me. We never *discussed*, we argued. I had my point of view. He had his. We were never able to move beyond the conflict to any kind of resolution." She paused. "In a way, that's still the case. He's assuming I'll be leaving here in July, for good. I'm still trying to figure out how to placate my dad and live the way I want to."

Nate shook his head. "Maybe your dad sees things differently now. He came here. He saw what you do. What if you just tell him what you want?"

"It won't be that easy. It never is."

"Maybe that's because you aren't sure what you want." He made direct eye contact.

"It isn't just my life we're talking about, you know. I have to make sure everyone else's life is okay, too."

"That's not up to you, Carrie. Yours is the only life you are responsible for."

She couldn't deny the truth in this statement. Having so recently won favor with her father, she feared losing it again. The flow of their relationship had always been complicated by undercurrents. Most of her life, she had fought to have him accept and respect her decisions.

Yet Nate was right. Suddenly, she saw the utter futility in continuing to mold her life to fit what someone else wanted. She and her father were different people. He had his career. She had hers. Now she needed to make what might be the most important decision of her life.

As she and Nate sat at the table, gazing at each other in the flickering candlelight, another thought crossed her mind. How much did she figure in his plans? Did he think about her the way she thought about him? She remembered what Peg had told her earlier that day. *All of us hope you end up together.* Watching him, she felt that familiar sensation in the pit of her stomach, the knowing. But this time, it didn't feel like a warning. It was acceptance of an inner truth about Nate. She had fallen for him.

Nate smiled. "You did something different to your hair. I like it."

"I thought I should make more of an effort not to look like a tired, overworked doctor." She patted her sleek hairstyle with its shiny layers. She was glad he had noticed. Rising from her chair, she carried their plates to the sink. "It's tough to be a girl here. Wearing scrubs is so asexual."

Nate joined her at the sink and began running hot water for dishes. "I've always thought you had that kind of natural beauty—what women like my ex try to achieve but never quite do. I never see you wearing much makeup or a bunch of jewelry. I like that. Don't try to be anyone other than who you are."

Carrie's heart leapt. She reached out and touched his arm. "You cooked. I'll clean up."

"I have a better idea. Let's go enjoy the fire."

Annie sat up and took notice when Nate and Carrie stretched out in front of the fireplace on mounds of soft pillows. Nate pulled a soft throw over them and began kissing her. The blazing flames brought a rosy glow to their skin. Carrie raised herself up on one elbow to take in the sight of Nate, so handsome that her breath caught in her chest. He looked like a Greek god with his golden curls and classic features. Everything about him was perfection.

He pulled her on top of him and caressed her face before kissing her again. As the kiss deepened, she felt his hands under her sweater, touching the sensitive skin on her back and sides. He continued to kiss her, more urgently now. As they lay side by side, he unfastened the buttons on her sweater. Expertly, he reached behind her and unhooked her bra, continuing his exploration of her body, running his fingers across her breasts and up and down her back until she let out a small cry of pleasure.

She reached for his sweater, but he beat her to it, raising it over his head and tossing it. Then he yanked his tee-shirt off, pulling her close. Skin to skin, they kissed until a less romantic thought occurred to her.

"Nate," she whispered.

"Mm, what?" He moved on top of her.

"Do you have protection?"

"No." He rolled off her and sat up, drawing his knees into a V. He looked at her and grinned. "We're like a couple of teenagers. We both know better."

She sat up and reached for her sweater. "You're right. We do know better. All we need right now is an unexpected, um, development. I delivered three of them today."

"To tell you the truth, I didn't intend to let it go that far. But I do want to make love to you, Carrie." The look on his face told her just how much.

"I want that, too. I just think—"

"You think we're rushing things."

"Maybe." She drew her arms through the sleeves of her sweater, fastening the buttons as quickly as she could. She was shaking, but not from the chill. "I want this as much as you do. But we haven't planned for this. We don't know what will happen."

Nate sat up, too. "Couldn't we figure it out as we go along?"

Her eyes opened wide. This was something she hadn't expected to hear from him, not tonight. "Nate, I'm a planner."

"Why don't you try living, instead of planning to live?"

She shook her head, shocked. His question felt like a slap. "I'm not sure what to say to that."

"You don't always know what's coming in life, Carrie. I had no idea how fast my life would change that day in the ER. I could have died. But I didn't. Now I'm choosing to live in a way that makes me happy. It's different than what I envisioned, but it works. I'm open to happiness." He pulled his tee-shirt and sweater on over his head. "Maybe I should sleep at my house tonight."

"No, don't go. Besides, you'll freeze." She reached out to touch his arm as he started to stand up. "I wish things were different. Both of us have ended engagements in the past year. I don't want to have to say goodbye again to someone I care about." She let her hand remain on his arm, feeling the warmth of his skin.

"Okay, I get that." He paused. "Look, I don't want you to think what happened tonight was some kind of booty call. I wouldn't do that to you. I was here because I want to be with you."

"I never thought it *was* a booty call, Nate," she said.

Nate blew out a whoosh of breath. "You're right. We shouldn't get carried away. Forget it happened."

"I don't want to forget it happened. Let's just wait and see, okay?"

"Are you suggesting that there's even a chance you might be staying?" He looked hopeful.

"I don't know what I'm saying." Carrie bit her lip. "Give me a little more time, okay?"

Nate turned and stood in front of the fireplace, poking the logs, his back to her. She watched him, wishing more than anything that she knew what the future held. Her desire for him was stronger than anything she had ever felt, even with Tom.

"Hey, I'm sorry. I didn't mean to ruin the moment." Behind him, Carrie laid her cheek on his back and wrapped her arms around his waist. "I want to make sure everything is right. Otherwise, we could hurt each another. You mean too much to me."

He turned and took her in his arms. "It's okay." He leaned in and kissed her. "Still friends?"

"Better than friends," she said, feeling that strange tug on her heart that happened so often with Nate.

She knew at that moment that she was deeply in love with him. The feeling was bittersweet. She wanted more than a spontaneous moment of passion, a night of intense lovemaking that, even if it *was* just what they both needed and wanted, might create confusion and set the stage for heartbreak. She couldn't do that to him. She also didn't want to be hurt or disappointed by love again.

As the fire ebbed to orange flickers, Nate poked the embers until they turned to ash. Picking up his glass, he swirled the last of the wine and finished it. He held out his hand and asked, "Ready to call it a night?"

Carrie took his hand and squeezed it. "In a minute."

She poured water from a bottle in the fridge and gazed out the window. The moon was the color of buttercream in a cobalt-blue and gray sky. From somewhere in the distance, she heard the cry of a wolf. Was it her wolf? Another joined in with its own mournful sound.

She remembered Dr. Jim's words to her so long ago. "They mate for life."

Longing for Nate with all her heart, she wondered if she had just missed her chance by not making love with him. She returned to the living room, wanting nothing more than to lie in his arms, to feel his body against hers, to sleep next to him. He took her hand and led her upstairs.

"Good night," he said, kissing her tenderly on the lips before going to the guestroom. "I'm locking this door. No monkey business."

Carrie laughed, relieved that he had made a joke. She brushed her teeth and put on a pair of flannel pajamas and thick socks. Then she invited Annie under the comforter and held her tight, breathing in the dog's familiar scent, stroking her soft ears until she heard the regular breathing that told her Annie was asleep.

She lay quietly, her thoughts like wayward children, each insisting on her undivided attention before losing interest and abandoning her when another demanded its turn. She wondered if the rumors at the hospital might escalate. Gossip was inevitable, especially in a place as small as Browning. And after all, why wouldn't people talk? The rumors were true. *I love Nate. He might love me, too.*

As if sensing that she had been displaced by the evening's activities between the two humans under her roof, Annie nestled her head in Carrie's neck as if to say, "I'm here, too."

"I love you, too," Carrie whispered, stroking Annie's soft fur, grateful for her presence.

As much as she wanted Nate, she had a decision to make first: whether to remain on the reservation or go back to Philadelphia. Seeing him a few weeks a year wasn't going to allow her to have the kind of relationship she wanted. It seemed either way she turned, each decision brought its own struggle with guilt and pain. Her leaving the Blackfeet people meant one less physician to care for them. Staying on the reservation meant abandoning her father and disappointing him again. What if a compromise wasn't possible?

The budding relationship with Nate had made her decision even more difficult. Whatever happened between them, it was important to take care. If a relationship wasn't meant to be, it was better to know now. But as she lay there in the silence, she was all too aware of Nate's proximity. She thought of what Dancing Bird had told her months earlier, that there was someone here for her to love.

Oh, please let Nate and me have our chance together. Let him be the one.

Chapter Twenty-Six

"**H**EY, CARRIE! WAIT UP!"

At the sound of Nate's voice in the hospital corridor, she stopped in her tracks. "Hi," she said. "I'm on my way over to the ER. I just got a call that my services are needed."

Nate fell in step with her as they headed to the ER. "I'm heading the same direction, probably for the same reason: possible abdominal surgery. Could be appendicitis."

As they approached the waiting area, they ran into John. He jumped to his feet, looking worried. "Am I ever glad to see you guys," he said, reaching out to shake Nate's hand. "One of my teachers has terrible stomach pain. Rather than wait for the ambulance, I brought her over."

"I'm on this," Carrie said to Nate. Patting John's forearm, she said, "Sit tight and relax."

She pushed open the door to the emergency room and headed to the bay where John's third-grade teacher, Raven Brown, lay in acute pain. There were any number of possibilities with severe stomach pain, including appendicitis, diverticulitis, and gall bladder disease. After assessing her patient's condition, she would know whether Nate needed to come in for a surgical consultation.

She looked at the vital signs a nurse had taken. "Hello, I'm Dr. Nelson. I hear you've got pain in your belly. When did you first notice it?"

"Last night around midnight," the young woman said. "It comes in waves. It's getting worse."

Carrie placed one hand on Raven's abdomen and exchanged glances with the nurse. Then she went to the sink to wash her hands. She knew the cause of the pain. As unbelievable as it seemed, her patient was unaware of what was happening with her body.

As she examined her, Carrie's suspicions were confirmed. "Raven, you're about to give birth. Did you have any idea you were pregnant?"

"No! This can't be happening!"

"It's about to happen. So, you had no missed periods? Nothing that felt like little gas bubbles moving around?"

"Nothing, I haven't felt anything. My husband and I aren't ready for this!" Raven screamed as the baby's head began to descend into the birth canal.

"Raven, you're doing great," Carrie said, coaching the frightened mother-to-be. As the nurses readied the area for an emergency birth, Carrie donned a gown and new gloves.

"Can you give me something for the pain? Please?" Raven begged.

"We can't. You're too close now. We'll help you through it. Breathe like this." Carrie demonstrated for Raven the way to breathe to help ease the pain.

As another strong contraction hit and Raven began pushing, two nurses stood on either side to assist with the birth. Carrie was concerned that the baby might be premature. Premature births without a neonatal intensive care unit or a pediatric specialist on hand were never an ideal situation in Browning. If the baby was more than a month or two early or in distress, she would need to stabilize the infant and arrange for immediate transport to another facility.

"Is your husband on his way, I hope?" Carrie asked. "We can hold on another minute or so for him to get here, but not too long. Your baby wants to be born now."

It was fortunate that Raven had called her husband before John drove her to the hospital. The shocked young father-to-be arrived in the nick of time. He was helped into a gown and stood at his wife's side as Raven pushed their baby into the world. Carrie caught the newborn and guided him out, breathing a sigh of relief. She looked up to watch the astonished father when he saw his son for the first time.

"You have a handsome boy," Carrie said, holding up the baby. "Would you like to cut the umbilical cord?" A nurse handed him a pair of scissors.

"Yes," the young man answered in a voice husky with emotion. He snipped the cord connecting his wife to their new son, his expression one of shock and growing delight. Carrie quickly examined the baby, relieved that he appeared to be a healthy weight and that his color was good. He was also howling in protest—a good sign that his lungs were mature. The nurse weighed and measured him before wrapping him in a receiving blanket. All the signs pointed to a full-term infant.

Carrie stayed with the new mother for a few minutes and encouraged her as she nursed her baby for the first time. Then she walked back out to the waiting area to talk with John. His hands were laced tightly together, his head bowed in prayer.

"I am happy to announce that your student body has just grown by one. Mrs. Brown has given birth to a healthy baby boy," she announced.

"*What?* I had no idea!" John raked his hands through his hair. "I drove her over here. What if the baby had been born in my car?"

"I'm sure you would have handled it just fine. But, thank goodness, you got her here quickly. She's fine, and so is the baby. I wonder if any of the other teachers suspected she might be pregnant. Sometimes other people are aware of things the mother doesn't notice."

"I don't think anyone noticed anything. She didn't look any different than she usually does."

"Well, I'd say you're going to need a substitute teacher pretty quickly." She grinned. "Or … can you handle a third-grade classroom for the rest of the semester?"

"Not third grade." He looked horrified. "Tell me how this can happen. I don't understand how a woman can give birth without knowing she's pregnant." He scratched his head. "The signs are fairly obvious, I'd think."

"You'd be surprised. It happens regularly enough that I've stopped questioning it."

"I'm just glad she and the baby are okay." John sat down, as shaken as the new father had been. Then he said, "I wonder if they have everything they need to bring the baby home."

This was the John Leathers Carrie loved best—a man who was always thinking of others. She smiled, guessing that he would make sure Raven and her husband had everything they needed for their new son. "Maybe the other teachers will want to throw her a surprise baby shower. It'll be even more fun since the baby is a surprise, too!"

"I'll go back to school and let everyone know." Instead he sank further into the chair.

Carrie sat down across from him. "Are *you* okay, John? You've had quite a shock today. It's not every day one of your teachers gives birth on the job."

"I'm fine. Actually, I feel as proud as if it was my own kid." John looked up and offered a weak smile.

"One of these days, it just might be you in the delivery room, you know." His eyes widened and an odd expression washed over his face.

"When that happens, you'd better be there, too," he said.

After the romantic interlude with Nate in her living room that night in March—when they had come so close to making love—Carrie sensed that he was detaching from her. Other than an occasional coffee break or consultation about a patient, she hadn't seen much of him at all. It was as if he had erected a wall between them. How could she blame him? What if he had decided that it was too difficult to be just friends with her? He wanted more, and she was holding him at arm's length. Perhaps he had given more thought to the very real possibility that she would leave and become an occasional volunteer at the hospital. They would hardly see each other. Another wave of sadness washed over her, tinged with regret.

On Sunday morning, she decided to take the bull by the horns and call him. Holding her phone in one hand while pressing her foot against the inner thigh of her opposite leg in a yoga tree pose, she waited for him to answer. When he did, she said, "Good morning. I'm going cross-country skiing today. Want to come along?"

"Sorry, I can't. I have to check on a patient. But why don't we get together for dinner tomorrow evening? We could run over to Two Medicine Grill."

"Okay." She paused and took a deep breath. "Nate, is anything wrong? I mean, between us?"

He hesitated before replying, "I wouldn't say anything is wrong. It's just that I got to thinking about what almost happened a few weeks ago. You were right. Until you make a decision, it's better if we stay friends." There was silence for a moment. "I've got to run," he said, finally. "See you tomorrow night."

"Bye." Carrie felt an ache in her throat so intense she couldn't speak. She ended the call and wiped away tears. Then she leaned against the wall, trying to get her bearings.

Placing a cold washcloth over her eyes, she waited for the worst of the sadness to pass. Maybe the loving spirit that Dancing Bird had mentioned so long ago hadn't been Nate, after all. Carrie had wanted so much for Nate to be the one.

Dancing Bird! Carrie suddenly had a sick feeling in her stomach. After a few months of improvement, Dancing Bird's congestive heart failure was progressing more rapidly, and Carrie was worried. She decided to check on her by phone the next morning—if there was a phone number listed on her patient record. If Dancing Bird wasn't feeling well enough to come in to the clinic, perhaps Carrie could drive over to her home to check on her. She wasn't supposed to make house calls, but a friendly visit surely wouldn't hurt. Maybe she could impress on Dancing Bird's family members the importance of a low-salt diet for her.

For now, though, she wanted to get out in the fresh air until the feelings of hurt and yearning over Nate abated. She grabbed her cross-country skis and poles. Since she was going farther into the fields and the snow was still much deeper there, she decided not to bring Annie. She would make it up to her later with a walk around the house in the safety of their backyard or up the road.

As she shushed across the field on her skis, she looked out on the magnificent scene in the distance: tall fir trees still adorned with white snow under a powder-blue sky. She glided to a stop and took a deep breath of clean air. The calendar might say it was April, but the temperature still hovered in the thirties. She covered her mouth with one of her gloved hands to warm the air as she took several breaths.

Reaching into her pocket, she pulled out her iPhone, taking a quick photo of the mountains to send to her parents. Day by day, moment by moment, she never grew tired of the scenery here—maybe because there was never a time when the land and sky looked exactly the same. Sometimes she grieved the setting of the sun as it disappeared behind the mountains in its neon stripes of orange, yellow, and pink. In the morning, she rushed to the window, watching in delight as the fiery sun appeared over the horizon and the sky changed from the darkest indigo to the lightest powder-blue. She took photo after photo, desperate to capture the images, certain that she'd never witness the same scene again. After she returned to Philadelphia, she would review the pictures every day and remember where she took each one and how she'd felt at the time.

On one such occasion, she had dropped to her knees on the ground, silent before the Great Creator that had gifted her with such spectacular sights. In these moments, as she experienced profound joy at the beauty surrounding her, Carrie understood why the Indians worshipped nature. To appreciate the warmth of the sun, express gratitude in song and dance, was to feel at one with the Source of everything.

As she put her phone back into her pocket and zipped it up, she caught sight of the wolf. The animal was standing in the snow about two hundred yards away, just watching her. *Hello.* Her knees turned to jelly. She knew that if she turned and attempted to ski away, the wolf might follow. *Never turn your back on a wild animal.* Standing still seemed the best course of action. In any case, she was powerless to move as her heart pounded with an equal measure of fear and excitement. Standing in that spot, admiring the animal, she offered up a silent prayer for protection. Yet in her heart, she knew the wolf meant her no harm.

"You come to see me often," she said in the most conversational tone she could muster. The wolf, with its keen hearing, surely could pick up the sound of her words. "If you're watching over Annie and me, thank you."

The wolf did not move but continued watching, panting. Its pink tongue was visible from where she stood. She took several shallow breaths, wishing for a deeper connection with the animal yet relieved that the wolf kept its distance. After a minute or two, the she-wolf turned and trotted off, disappearing into the dense foliage of a grove of firs.

Carrie wondered how old the wolf might be and if she had a mate. Was it the wolf and her partner that cried out in the night? She would never know. All she did know was that Medicine Owl was right: the wolf *was* kin. All creatures, man and beast alike, were interconnected in this circle of life, a medicine wheel of nature, of spirit. Far from feeling afraid now, she was comforted and reassured by the wolf's presence. No matter what else might be happening, there was a divine order to all of life. Reluctant to leave the peace of this place, she turned slowly on her skis, gave a backward glance over her shoulder, and headed home to another animal spirit that loved her, the one named Annie.

THE PHONE RANG AT TEN THIRTY as Carrie was preparing to call it a night. It was a nurse from the emergency room. "We have one of your patients here, Doctor. She isn't doing well. She is asking for you."

"Dancing Bird," Carrie breathed, the heaviness in her heart letting her know the end was near. "I'll be there as fast as I can."

She had been in the process of emailing Gran, who was doing much better and credited Carrie for her ability to walk without a cane. She quickly finished her email message. "Must go now, Gran. One of my patients is in trouble. I may lose her tonight." If anyone would understand, it was Gran. But now there was another family member who also would want to know, and who would care. Her father.

She arrived at the hospital to find Dancing Bird in respiratory distress, her heart failing. Oxygen had been administered, along with an intravenous drip. "Dancing Bird," she said, "I'm here."

The old woman's eyelashes fluttered and she made direct eye contact. "My spirit is ready to go home."

"Wherever you're going, we'll meet again," Carrie said. She sat at the edge of the bed and took Dancing Bird's hand. All she could do now was be with her patient and support her in the dying process. She leaned in closer and whispered, "You can go whenever you're ready."

"My Doctor Golden Hair," Dancing Bird said between labored breaths.

Her eyes closed. Within minutes, her heart rhythm faltered and she was gone. She had signed a do-not-resuscitate order, a formality that Carrie had confirmed recently, knowing the end was near.

A nurse opened the door and saw Carrie sitting on the bed. "I'll leave you alone, Doctor," she said in a quiet voice before shutting the door.

When a person dies, their spirit stays for a short time. She is still here.

Carrie stayed by Dancing Bird's bedside for another hour, studying the peaceful expression on her patient's face, the slight smile, as if she had just seen something too beautiful for words. It was a privilege to honor Dancing Bird's life and to have been with her during those final precious minutes.

Leaning over her, she said, "I'll miss you" and touched her lips to Dancing Bird's forehead.

THE NEXT MORNING, CARRIE WORKED AT a near feverish pace, seeing patients and trying not to think about the loss of one so dear. No matter how many years a physician practiced, it was never easy to lose a patient. Especially in family medicine, generations of family members became well-known and much-loved. But in any specialty, doctors loved and lost patients. Carrie knew that Mark had cardiovascular patients who had been in his care for many years. He knew their hopes and dreams, their moments of sadness and grief, as well as he understood their symptoms or their diagnoses.

Carrie thought about this—her father's legacy to her—and the countless times they had butted heads. Yes, her father could be intractable on issues that were Carrie's alone to discern. But she understood that his arguments with her were based more on love and concern for her welfare. Her father had made a brave and selfless move toward healing their troubled relationship by making the trip to Browning when she was so ill with the flu. He trusted her to care for him when he became ill, too. Whatever happened next, she knew how much he loved her.

"Hi, Dad," she said the next evening when he answered the phone. It was nine o'clock in Pennsylvania. Nate was picking her up in fifteen minutes to go out for a quick bite to eat. But she longed to talk with her father, to tell him about Dancing Bird.

"Well, well. It's good to hear your voice! Your mother and I were just discussing you at dinner tonight."

"Oh? You haven't changed your mind about coming in July, I hope."

"Nothing like that. We were wondering if the three of us could take a little excursion over to Essex to that Izaak Walton Resort. I want to stay in one of those old caboose cars! It's supposed to be a wonderful place to hike and look out at the mountains. Seems like a nice little side trip."

"What a great idea!" She was delighted at this turn of events. "Nate and I have been there for dinner. It would be fun to stay over and explore it with you and Mom."

"If you think you can spare the time away from the hospital, why don't you reserve a caboose for us for an overnight? We're going to be there ten days total. Did your mother tell you that? I'd like for us to see as much of the area as we can." Her father sounded enthused.

"With all the doctors who are volunteering this year, we'll definitely have time for fun. What does Gran always say? 'Many hands make light work.' "

He chuckled. "I've been hearing that since I was a boy. I hope everything is okay with you, honey. You sound tired."

"Actually, I am. I lost a patient last night—congestive heart failure. I was at the hospital until very late, just sitting with her. I was prepared for this to happen, of course. The last time I saw her, I knew it was a matter of time. But that doesn't make it any easier, does it?"

"No, no, it doesn't," Mark said. "I'm sorry to hear that. Was she the one you told me about, the one who called you Doctor Golden Hair?"

"Yes," she said, impressed that he would recall this detail. "I remember when you lost patients and how hard you took it. I always knew how much you cared about them. That's really stuck with me, Dad. It's why I'm in family medicine. Everything you taught me about being a physician is still with me. I am the way I am because of you."

He was quiet for a moment before clearing his throat. "You couldn't have said anything that would mean more to me. I'm proud of you and all you've accomplished. But you've done that on your own, my girl."

"Thanks, Dad. I love you."

"I love you, too, Carrie." There was a rustling on the phone line. "Your mother wants to talk to you now. You call me anytime."

Her mother took her turn on the phone. "Goodness, it seems like forever since you were here, and it's really only been a few weeks. We're really excited about our Montana trip. Your father won't tell you this, but he's already made his packing list."

Carrie stifled a giggle and sat back in her desk chair. "Imagine that. I can't wait to see you."

She hoped her parents would fall in love with the summer splendor of Glacier and understand why she loved it so. To see Montana in the warmer months was to know nature's perfection. There simply was no more beautiful place in the world—of that she was quite certain. And then it struck her with a force that almost knocked her over. At that moment, she knew what she had to do.

"Mom, could you put Dad back on the phone? There's something I need to tell him."

"There's something he'd like to tell you, too." Her mother's tone gave nothing away.

Carrie heard Nate's car in the driveway. As she waited for her father to return to the phone, she opened the door. "Would you mind waiting a few minutes?" she asked him. "I'm about to talk to my father."

THE DISCUSSION WITH HER FATHER WAS a bigger surprise to Carrie than seeing him show up on her doorstep that day in February. "Dad, I wanted to let you know that I want to stay here," she said. She looked at Nate, whose face broke into a wide grin.

"I guessed you would end up telling me that, especially when I saw how you interacted with people at the hospital and how much they like you. I knew you'd never be completely happy anywhere else." He paused, then added, "It's okay."

"Really? You aren't disappointed that I won't be joining you, after all?"

"Of course, I'm disappointed, but only because I won't get to work with you. So, now I want to say that I can do more to help. I'll be there in July to volunteer, but I'd like to begin offering my services more often. It's time for me to give back."

This was not at all what Carrie had expected to hear. "Dad, I don't know what to say, except thank you. Dr. Jim will be so glad to hear this."

"So, now we have a plan." He sounded jovial. "Tell Nate I said hello."

"I will, Dad. Thank you for understanding. I love you."

When she got off the phone, she walked straight into Nate's arms. She had never felt so light, so carefree. He kissed her and held her in place, keeping her rooted to earth.

"Nate, remember that night in March when we almost …?"

"How could I forget? What about it?" He cleared his throat, looking embarrassed.

"Well, after we have dinner, could we have a do-over?"

Nate blushed and raked his hands through his curls. "Why, why, why isn't there any fast food around here?"

"On second thought, never mind the food," she said, taking him by the hand. "We can figure that out later … much later."

THE FOLLOWING AFTERNOON, SHE CALLED DR. Jim to tell him that her father would be joining the volunteer medical corps on an as-needed basis starting in July. As expected, he was elated. "I knew he'd come around," Dr. Jim said. They talked for a few minutes before he added, "I'll be around more often, too, this year. I'm taking more time away from my practice. Believe it or not, I'm easing into retirement."

"I can't believe what I'm hearing," Carrie said. "You do know, don't you, that retirement doesn't mean changing practice locations and keeping up the same exhaustive pace? You ought to think about slowing down, playing more golf while you're here. You deserve it."

"Keep telling him that, Carrie," Lois chuckled from her place on the upstairs extension. "So far, my words have fallen on deaf ears."

Carrie told them about Dancing Bird's passing. "I know she was aware that her time was coming. I wasn't surprised to get the call that she was in the hospital. Still, it was hard. It was such a privilege to be with her at the end."

"You've had some incredible experiences this year on the rez," Dr. Jim said. "I didn't meet Medicine Owl until the sixth summer I was there."

"Yes, but the tribe hasn't made me an honorary Blackfeet member yet, Medicine Wolf," Carrie said with a chuckle, using the name she knew would please him most. "You're the only one who has earned that distinction. I'm just Doctor Golden Hair."

Later, she completed her notes from her most recent meeting with Medicine Owl.

Medicine Owl treats inflammation and muscle pain with a variety of plants—many that are common foods: blueberries, cherries, raspberries (and the leaves of the raspberry plant), broccoli, cauliflower, green beans—and salad greens, which provide magnesium. She often chews on flax seeds and pumpkin seeds. Hops are helpful, too. She said she would tell people to drink some beer, but she doesn't want patients to carry it to the extreme. "Chew rosemary," she says. In addition to arnica, which is generally recognized as safe and well-known for its anti-inflammatory properties, other herbs she commonly uses include goldenseal, chamomile, witch hazel, and white willow bark.

Chapter Twenty-Seven

⁓∖∕⁓

O N THE FIFTH OF MAY, CINCO de Mayo, Carrie left the clinic a little before
six o'clock and walked home, enjoying the first blush of true spring. The
days were growing noticeably milder, although she had been warned that Old
Man Winter might still have it in him for a last hurrah. She wanted to open
all the windows in the house and smell the night air. She would sit out on
the front porch with a glass of iced tea, lie in the soft green grass, and pick
a bouquet of wildflowers for the kitchen table. Now that she knew she was
staying on the reservation, she could celebrate the arrival of spring rather
than dread it.

Breathing in the fragrant air as she walked along the highway toward
home, she counted down the days until Dr. Jim and Lois arrived in Browning.
It would be nice to watch Dr. Jim putter around his garden again. She looked
forward to talks with Lois, too.

It had been a longer day than usual in the clinic, or so it seemed. To her
surprise, Gali was scheduled late that afternoon for a physical. Carrie hadn't
noticed her name on the schedule until Peg handed her the chart that read
Galilahi Leathers.

"This is a new patient. She is John Leathers' wife."

"I didn't realize they had gotten married." Carrie's brow furrowed.
Although John typically played things close to the vest, she wondered why
he hadn't mentioned his wedding. If not, it was likely his parents didn't know
about it yet. Yes, that had to be it.

She took a quick sip of lukewarm coffee and headed off to see Gali.
She rapped on the door of the examination room and entered. "Hello!
Congratulations on your recent marriage. I'm happy for both of you."

Gali's glossy black hair was tied back in a long braid. She wore jeans and a loose-fitting top. "I told John it was time to see you."

"I was hoping to be at the wedding ceremony. Or did you elope?"

"We had a simple ceremony in Kalispell, just the two of us, last weekend." Gali didn't wear the beaming smile of a new bride. Instead, she appeared sad.

"Please come into my office so we can talk first." Carrie beckoned for her to follow. "I've wanted to see you for months, but didn't expect it to be here in the clinic."

"Actually, I'm here because I'm pregnant," Gali said.

"Wow! Congratulations again." Carrie offered her a chair. "After we talk for a few minutes and I get some information from you, we'll send you down the hall for the usual lab work so we can know for sure. I bet John is excited!"

"John is taking his fatherly responsibilities very seriously," Gali said, worry giving way briefly to amusement. Then she grew serious again. "It's not ideal timing."

"Well, I can't tell you how many times I've heard that. But in the end, the timing usually ends up being just right." Carrie decided to ask a question that would give her a better picture of Gali's situation at home. "Have things improved with John's family, I hope?"

"I wouldn't say that." Gali frowned and took a deep breath. "We decided that under the circumstances, it was best to get married and keep things quiet a bit longer. The only one in the family who is supportive is Mike."

"He's a dear man."

"Dr. Carrie, I'll be honest with you. When John told his parents he had proposed to me, they made it clear we were not welcome together in their home." Gali's large brown eyes filled with tears. She struggled to regain her composure as Carrie slid the box of tissues toward her. "I don't think they'll ever accept me or our baby."

"I still hold out hope they will," Carrie said. "But I wish things could be different for you, especially now." She shook her head in sympathy. "Maybe the situation will improve after the baby is born. I've seen it happen before where a grandmother laid eyes on her first grandchild and it was love at first sight. Whatever you do, don't give up hope."

"I'm trying to remain positive, for John's sake. He's so sad about everything that has happened."

"But not about the baby, right?"

Gali smiled. "No, he's pleased about the baby."

"Well, let's confirm the pregnancy. I'm going to check on some other patients while you go to the lab."

She left Gali with Peg while she saw two other patients. Then she returned to the room where Gali was already waiting. Her patient appeared anxious, her lips set in a grim line.

"Congratulations. You're going to be a mom." She smiled.

Gali's eyes filled with tears that spilled down her cheeks. Shooting Carrie a concerned look, Peg quickly left the room. Putting her arms around Gali's thin shoulders, Carrie patted her back and handed her a tissue. "I know. This kind of news takes a little time to adjust to. Are you pleased, though?"

"Yes." But Gali continued dabbing at the corners of her eyes.

After several minutes, Carrie was able to proceed. She talked with Gali about the facilities for labor and delivery, birthing classes, and diet—normal discussion for a newly pregnant patient. Gali stared at the ceiling, sniffing back tears, answering in monosyllables. It was clear that she didn't want to talk about the baby or events to come.

"We can get into all this later," Carrie told her. "You're a little more than three months along. Everything looks good. I'd say the baby will be here around November fourth."

"Thank you," Gali said, averting her eyes.

"I wish I had words of wisdom to help you with the family stuff."

Gali dabbed at her nose again. "When they find out we're married, I'm afraid it will be the final straw. His mother acts like I don't exist. I thought I was prepared for this, but it is more difficult than I ever imagined."

Carrie washed her hands and smoothed on moisturizer as she considered the best response. John was her friend. Gali was his wife and the mother of his child. Now she was Gali's doctor. What, if anything, could she do? She would need to keep a professional distance, which would be difficult.

"If you have any questions or concerns, please let me know," she said, offering her hand to Gali as she got down from the table.

"Thank you. I will."

There really was no way to know if John's parents would relent and accept his new wife and the baby into their family. It seemed impossible to Carrie that a close family like the Leathers wouldn't come to accept the situation, in time. Families struggled and overcame their challenges together. If her father and grandmother could come to new understanding over a conflict that had evolved over fifty years, surely the Leathers family could accept John's choice of a wife and their baby.

She leaned against the sink. "I believe that when parents get angry, they don't really stay that way," she said. "Stubbornness or a lack of understanding about issues is what keeps us apart. John's mother may be working through that, even as we speak, just as you and John are. In this case, everyone has adjustments to make."

"I hope you're right," Gali said.

Carrie thought of the conversations with her father in recent months that had done so much toward healing the rift between them. "I have a particular reason for saying that I think things have a surprising way of working themselves out," she said. "Unfortunately, it isn't easy waiting and wondering." She patted Gali's shoulder. "Hang in there. I believe things will get better for you and John."

On Saturday, as she tapped out an email to Gran about a recent conversation with Medicine Owl, her phone rang.

"Hey," Nate said without preamble when she answered. "I wondered if you have plans for later this evening."

"Not really. What's up?" She hit send on the email to Gran.

"I wanted to talk to you about something. I'll bring pizza."

"Okay," she said. "If you bring the pizza, I'll unscrew the cap on a new bottle of wine."

Nate chuckled. "Nothing pretentious about *you*."

At seven o'clock that night, she heard his shave-and-a-haircut knock at the front door. When she opened it, he was holding a large pizza box that reeked of pepperoni. A grease stain was already spreading across the box bottom and lid.

"Here, let me take that," she said and gingerly deposited it on the kitchen counter.

Nate removed his jacket and slung it over a kitchen chair. "I've been thinking," he said, kissing her.

"About what?" she asked when she was able to talk again.

"I know what we said a few weeks ago about not rushing things. But I think we're wasting time. I mean, we should really be together."

"Well, I like how you think," Carrie said, smiling. "What did you have in mind?"

Holding her face between his hands, he kissed her again. She felt the tension in her body drain out. All she could think, at that moment, was how right it felt to be in his arms. She wanted to spend every day of her life with this man.

"Carrie, you and I came here to do something that matters. It isn't easy living and working here, but we're committed to this place. It seems like we were drawn here. I believe we were meant to be together."

"Medicine Owl said you and I were together in a previous lifetime—that we were Blackfeet ... and healers," Carrie said, smiling at the memory.

Nate's forehead creased. "She did?" He considered this for a moment. "I believe that. There's something so familiar about this place and the people. And last summer, when we met, I felt as if I already knew you."

"I don't close my mind to anything anymore. The Blackfeet believe in reincarnation. Now it makes sense to me. You and I have been reunited."

"It's possible. I've been feeling restless, like there is something I was supposed to know. I kept wracking my brain. It was something important ... about you. It was right *here*." He tapped on his forehead. "I couldn't stop thinking about you. I still can't." He paused and took a deep breath before moving closer and wrapping his arms around her waist. "I want us to live together, work together. I love you, Carrie."

She could barely speak for the lightness that filled her. "That sounds like a proposal. Was it?"

Nate laughed. "You're right, it wasn't a very good one. I promise I'll do it better when the time is right. I'm just stating my intention to be with you."

"That's good enough for now. But, Nate ...?"

"What?"

"Let's not live in your house."

He looked into her eyes. "You're right. We need a place of our own."

"HELLO, IS ANYBODY THERE?" PEG ASKED, snapping her fingers in front of Carrie's face. She'd been staring at the same screen on the electronic medical records program for several minutes. "You've been walking around here all day in a definite moony state."

"I do not moon."

"You're not fooling me. Something's up."

Carrie saw that the jig was up. "Oh, okay. I suppose you'd figure it out soon enough, anyway. Nate and I are seeing each other now. "

"I hope you're seeing more of him than we get to see."

"Peg!" Carrie laughed as a blush ran from her neck up into her cheeks.

"I knew it! That man has been head over heels for you for months. Everyone knows it." Peg was beaming. "I just hope you and Dr. Nate will end up as happy as Ken and me, although Lord knows I've had my share of headaches with that man. Men are a different breed of cat. That's for sure."

"Well, when I think of happy couples, I think of you and Ken, Dr. Jim and Lois, and my parents. I hope Nate and I will be as happy as all of you are." Carrie slung her stethoscope around her neck. It was time to get to work.

"Oh, and speaking of someone else who worships the ground you walk on, there is a patient waiting in Room Three to see you. I think he might have brought you something." Peg pointed to the examination room where Mike Leathers was waiting. "He looks real good today, by the way."

"Mike, how are you?" Carrie greeted her patient. He was the picture of health in a sky-blue tee-shirt and black jeans. He had lost weight, but was obviously in good shape. "You look great."

Mike nodded his thanks and broke into a beaming smile. Holding a large, flat parcel wrapped in brown paper and tied with twine, he seemed both nervous and excited.

"For me?" Carrie accepted the package and tore into the paper. When she saw what was inside, she gulped back the emotion that welled within her. "She's beautiful."

A watercolor painting of Carrie's wolf was displayed in a simple handmade pine frame, polished until it shone. The wolf sat in the foreground of a field with patches of bare ground, sparse wheat-colored grass, and snow. Behind the wolf, the Shining Mountains rose in the distance, majestic in blue, lavender, and white under a light-blue sky streaked with wisps of white clouds.

"I wanted you to be able to see her every day." Mike looked pleased and self-conscious as Carrie admired his work.

"Every detail is perfect." She continued studying the painting. "My wolf looks exactly like that. You even captured her silver face on the gray body."

"That is the only way a wolf should be captured, in a painting or photograph." Mike spoke with a fierceness Carrie had never heard from this quiet man.

"You ought to have your paintings in the museum, like your father," Carrie said. "I bet you could have an exhibit, too."

Mike flashed her a smile. He looked away as he spoke, but Carrie could see the pleasure in his expression. "My father and I will have an exhibit together during Indian Days. I have many paintings to finish before then."

Chapter Twenty-Eight

—⟩⟨—

"**W**ELCOME HOME!" HEARING FOOTSTEPS ON THE front porch and voices, Carrie hurried from the kitchen to greet Dr. Jim and Lois as they made their way to the door. Annie barked in excitement, dancing in circles. "I thought you'd never get here! Let me take that suitcase."

It was the third Sunday in June, a week later than Lois had said they would arrive. In a phone call two weeks earlier, she had told Carrie that Dr. Jim was under the weather, so they were changing their flights. When Carrie saw Dr. Jim, she suspected it had been more than a virus, as Lois had implied.

"Our flight out of Denver got delayed," Lois said, huffing as she entered the house, carrying three grocery sacks. "I made Jim put the pedal to the metal when we got to Kalispell. Hard to believe there's fresh snow on the mountain. But it just goes to show, we aren't in Kansas anymore."

"It's been really warm here the past week, and it stays light way longer in the evening." Carrie grabbed two of the bags of food from Lois and headed for the kitchen. "I thought we could have dinner on the patio tonight."

"That sounds ideal." Lois arranged their two suitcases by the stairs. "Jim, don't you dare take both these suitcases upstairs at once."

Carrie observed Dr. Jim with concern. What was the matter? His color wasn't good, and he had lost a noticeable amount of weight from a body that was already on the lean side.

She decided not to comment on his appearance. There would be time later to find out what was going on. "John and Gali are stopping by after dinner. I can't wait for you to meet her. Did I tell you she's expecting? Due in November. They just got married."

"Lots happened this year on the rez," Dr. Jim chuckled, plunking down in his favorite easy chair, out of breath. "Never knew this place could be so full of drama."

"For a small town, it's definitely got its share," Carrie said. "I feel sorry for John right now. I hope his parents will eventually relent and accept Gali and this baby."

"It's a shame Nadie and Earl Leathers still aren't willing to recognize this girl as John's wife. But John knew all along it would be an issue if he married her." Dr. Jim shook his head. "It isn't like their relationship was a secret or anything. Everyone on the rez knew about it. But he's the first one in his family to marry outside the tribe. It'll take some time for the family to process that."

"Well, I think it's marvelous that John finally tied the knot. He needed to settle down and get started on a family of his own." Lois bustled out to the kitchen and began putting away the groceries.

"You're next." Dr. Jim winked at Carrie. "You just have to meet the right guy."

Carrie's face turned beet red. "I wanted to wait until you got here to tell you. Nate and I are together now. It's serious."

"Whaaaat?" Lois's eyes were as wide as silver dollars. "You'd better tell us everything. Don't leave out a single detail."

Dr. Jim chuckled. "I had a funny feeling that would happen. Winters here are long, and people have needs."

"Oh, Jim." Lois glared at her husband and rolled her eyes. "Carrie and Nate will make a lovely couple. Really, I can't believe you just said that. I must admit, though, I had a similar thought about what might happen if the two of you were free to be together. *Not* that I would've put it the way Jim just did. I just said a few prayers to help things along some."

"Well, thanks for that extra boost of faith," Carrie said, laughing. "We had our issues for a while, trying to decide whether or not it was a good idea to move beyond friendship. In the end, I don't know that we had a choice. It just happened. But honestly, I can't imagine anyone more perfect for me than Nate. Even if we didn't live and work here, I think we'd still be right for each other."

"What do your parents think?" Dr. Jim asked.

"My dad says he knew when he saw Nate and me together at the hospital that there was 'a spark,' as he put it. My mom says she knew from my expression—even before I told her Nate was special. They're happy for us."

"And your dad is okay with your decision to stay here?"

"I thought he'd be upset, but he said he was expecting it. After he came here in February, he could tell this was where I wanted and needed to be."

"Well, good for him for figuring that out and supporting you," Lois said. "I can't wait to meet your parents."

"They'll be here soon," Carrie said, rubbing her hands together in anticipation.

"Speaking of the course of true love, I would imagine that with a baby on the way, Nadie and Earl have to at least consider what the future will look like in their family," Dr. Jim said.

Carrie twisted her mouth in sympathy. "The hardest part is that John's mother acts like Gali doesn't exist. I talked to John early this week, and he doesn't hold out much hope that things will change any time soon."

She thought back to her conversation earlier in the week with John, who had stopped by her office on his way home from work. She was glad to see him, but suspected from the look on his face that he needed to talk. She was honored that he trusted her enough to confide in her.

"Congratulations! Gali tells me you're married," she had said, giving him a hug. "I'm happy for you. Now tell me how your family is taking the news."

"I waited a little while to tell them." He shifted from one foot to the other.

"What's 'a little while'?"

"I just told them last weekend." John wearily rubbed his eyes with his fists. "I still haven't been able to have an actual discussion with my mother."

"Do you mean you haven't *seen* her to have a conversation, or she won't talk about it?"

"I mean, she is acting as if nothing has changed. She doesn't acknowledge that Gali and I live together as man and wife now."

Carrie shook her head, disbelieving. "But when the baby is born …."

"We're taking this one day at a time," John said in a terse voice. "My parents are behaving as I expected, as if nothing has happened. That is their way."

"But surely, your mother wants to be part of the baby's life. That means accepting Gali as its mother, as your wife."

"Our baby won't be a full-blooded Blackfeet. That is all there is to say."

"John, that baby will be your mother's first grandchild."

"Yes, and I know she'll come around eventually and want to see the baby. But when I drop by to see my parents or pick up Mike to go somewhere, my mother behaves as if there's nothing different at all going on. She doesn't ask about Gali. That's how she lets me know what she thinks: by saying nothing. It looks as if Mike is the favored son now."

Carrie smiled gently. "I know you don't begrudge Mike that kind of positive reinforcement. He deserves credit for turning his life around."

"He's getting all the attention now for being an artist like Dad. I got my girlfriend pregnant and went against my family and the entire Blackfeet Nation by marrying a Cherokee woman. I'm now the black sheep of the family."

"What you're talking about is called *love*. It matters more than laws or bloodlines. At least, I think so."

"Sometimes I wonder if I did the right thing, returning here," he said, his eyes sad. He leaned back in the chair in front of Carrie's desk. "Can someone who went off to a university for four years, lived in a city like Boston, and even lived abroad, return here and be satisfied? I'm not sure anymore. If I hadn't left the rez to begin with, maybe life would have been different—easier in some ways. I wouldn't have had such high expectations of myself or anything else. I would've married a Blackfeet girl, like my mother wanted."

"And you'd probably be fighting wildfires, living just above poverty level with a bunch of kids and no prospects for a better life," she reminded him. "John, I see how the majority of people live on the reservation. Their options are limited. You have dedicated yourself to giving these kids better lives. What you do matters. How could you even think something like that?"

John blinked, his expression grim. "It's hard to explain to someone like you who isn't from the reservation. It's difficult, no matter what I do. The first year I was in college, I missed my family and what was familiar to me here. But I didn't miss it as much as I thought I would. In fact, I only came back twice in the entire four years I was in college. I got accustomed to being away. For a while, I even looked down my nose at life here, at the things that were problems that never seem to be resolved. Even worse, I stopped talking about my life as a Blackfeet."

"That's understandable. At some point, everyone questions their past and wants to shake things up. But you knew you had something important to offer your people. What you have is more than a job. It's a calling."

From frustration to anger, from pain to something she couldn't quite identify, she had seen the gamut of emotions cross John's face this afternoon. He was usually a hard man to read. Today he was an open book.

"While I was living abroad," he said, "I started to understand what was important about my people. It's this place, our connection to the land. In Europe, your country of origin and your culture are everything. There are buildings that have stood for thousands of years. People know their lineage and are proud of it. A lot of Americans don't know their genealogy much past their great-grandparents. I know who I am. I know who came before me for hundreds of years and what we stand for."

When John spoke about his people, Carrie caught a glimpse into his nature, the passion burning in him that surely could withstand any hardship. He might be ostracized for a life choice, but he was unlikely to back down from what he knew to be right. He was here to serve his people, to help his students have a better life. No matter whether others agreed with his decision to marry Gali, Carrie felt certain that John Leathers was making a difference and that he would continue to work hard to make life better for the Blackfeet.

She listened, absorbing his words, trying to empathize fully. It was impossible to understand what he was going through—not completely. She was still an outsider to the reservation—more of an outsider than Gali, who was at least Native American. No matter how long Carrie lived in Browning, she would always be a white woman from Philadelphia.

"I don't understand everything you're going through. I know that," she said. "Maybe I never will. But the more I come to know you, the more I see that you're working really hard to make sure children understand what it means to be members of the Blackfeet Nation. Your grandfather has to be proud and grateful for that."

John's face grew more serious. "Carrie, he worries because he is one of only a handful of men who still speak the language. He doesn't want us to lose what makes us Blackfeet. I've just compromised our race."

He stared at a place on the wall behind her, deep in thought. Then he began again, "While I lived away from the reservation, I thought about the fact that I'm a member of one of the oldest Indian Nations in North America. I was lucky. I was given an education. It was time to come home and put it to use for my people. That's why I came back. But I knew it would be difficult and that I might have regrets. Today is one of those days. Thank you for listening."

"I still believe everything will turn out okay. Give it time." Carrie leaned back in her desk chair. "I'm always here for you."

He nodded. "As I am for you."

She had another thought. "Why don't you bring Gali by on Saturday so she can meet Dr. Jim and Lois? They're here for you, too."

"We will come on Saturday," he promised.

To her surprise, he leaned in for a quick hug and then held on for a moment longer. To Carrie, it felt as if he was reaching for a lifeline and didn't want to let go. She held him close, wishing she could do more.

"Will you be here for Gali's ultrasound next week?" she asked before letting go and stepping back. "I might be able to tell whether you have a son or daughter."

John's face registered surprise, along with something she suspected might be the first stirrings of delight. She cleared her throat. "All we know now is there's a baby in there, and it's yours."

Later she made her notes on her most recent visit with Medicine Owl:

> Medicine Owl wanted me to know about her uses for chokecherries. She pits them since the pits are poisonous. The berries, when crushed or dried, can be used in a tea to treat coughs and colds, flu symptoms, and nausea. Prepared as a poultice, chokecherries are used to treat wounds. She also spoke about Wild Carrot, commonly known as Queen Anne's Lace. While I've noticed that the plant has a distinctive

aroma, she said the root is edible and even tastes like carrots. It is very important, she said, that the plant have a distinctive carrot aroma because similar species are highly toxic.

* * *

VIOLET HIGHTOWER WAS CARRIE'S FIRST PATIENT the next morning. Carrie was delighted to see her looking leaner and more fit than she had on previous visits. "Well, look at you!"

"I've lost weight," Violet said, spinning slowly in place to show off her slimmer body.

"I can see that," Carrie said, glancing over the chart. "That's a pretty dress. I'm happy to report your blood pressure is in a good range, and your lab work shows that your kidney function is still holding steady. I'm comfortable with what I see. How are you feeling? Any more pain in your back?"

"Not as much. I feel better," Violet said. "My son and I are walking outside whenever we can, I am drinking water all the time, and we are eating more vegetables. I learned to make ranch dip with Greek yogurt."

"Did you get the recipe from the dietician?" Carrie sat down on a chair to give her full attention to Violet. "That sounds like something I need to try."

"My son is looking up recipes on the computer at school," she answered. "He brings me things he wants to try. Then we make them together."

"That sounds like fun." Carrie smiled at her patient. "It's such a good way to get kids interested in healthy foods. I was wondering if you'd seen Medicine Owl lately."

"I see her, yes." Violet looked as though Carrie might not approve of this.

"I'm glad. Medicine Owl does a lot of good. She and I work together."

Violet smiled. "Medicine Owl said prayers for me," Violet said. "I know she is helping."

"I can see how well you're doing," Carrie said. "Keep up the good work."

Once again, she had seen for herself that the medicine she practiced—medications, manipulation, along with nutritional recommendations for a plant-based diet and the spiritual component espoused by the medicine woman—was producing a good outcome for patients like Violet.

Just a few days earlier, she had started a chapter outline for a book on the confluence between modern medicine and Native American medicine. As she compiled all the notes from her visits with the medicine woman, she was aware of how this knowledge had changed her as a person and contributed to making her a better doctor.

Chapter Twenty-Nine

⁓∖⁄⁓

L OOKING OUTSIDE HER OFFICE WINDOW ON the first of July, Carrie saw two horses tethered to a pole in the parking lot. An entire family—father, mother, and three children, including a brand new infant—had traveled on horseback to the clinic. Just as it had nearly a year ago, the sight of this scene brought joy to Carrie's heart. It felt like an anniversary of sorts—a celebration of belonging. What a difference a year made: from anxiety and uncertainty about working at the hospital to career fulfillment, from insecurities about the differences between her and the Blackfeet to Dr. Golden Hair, from misery over an ill-fated romantic relationship to true love with the right man.

Months ago, she had started an official countdown, crossing off the days until her parents' visit the second week of July. To her delight, when Dr. Jim arrived at the clinic that morning, he told her that her father had completed the required paperwork and was already approved to work in the federal hospital. That he had tackled the daunting process of applying to work on an Indian reservation was proof that Mark was serious about wanting to serve.

"I already like him," Dr. Jim said. "He's got a good grasp of what we need here."

Even her mother had signed up for the volunteer corps, promising to help Lois cook and arrange social activities. Carrie wished Gran could be part of the medical corps, but suspected the trip would be too hard on her.

Now that the weather had warmed up, it was possible for Carrie to take Annie on her early morning runs. The old dog seemed as relieved as any human that winter was finally over. Carrie, Nate, and Annie often took long walks on the weekends, enjoying the splendor of their Northwest Montana homeland. But on July third, dark clouds formed and there was a snow squall.

"I guess Old Man Winter just had to have the last word," Carrie grumbled to Peg. She had dared to wear a sleeveless dress to work.

"We've had snow on the Fourth of July here," Peg pointed out. "You learn to be ready for anything. Get yourself some cowboy boots to wear with that dress."

Dr. Jim worked regular days at the clinic, always willing to see as many patients as necessary. He also pitched in to help at the clinic in Heart Butte. But Carrie could see that he seemed to tire more easily and often took a nap after lunch. She caught Lois watching him, concern etched on her face, and decided to broach the topic that seemed off limits.

"What's the matter with Dr. Jim? He doesn't seem as chipper as usual."

Lois blanched and plunged her hands into the dishwater, furiously scrubbing a pot. She seemed irritated by Carrie's question, almost defensive in her response. "He's fine. At his age, don't you think he has a right to be a little tired?"

Carrie persisted. "Whatever virus he had earlier must still be hanging on. Did he end up with walking pneumonia again?"

"No." Lois hesitated and then turned to face Carrie, wiping her hands on the dishtowel. "Whatever you do, please don't tell him I said anything. If you do, he'll think I'm scared. I probably should have told you before." Her face looked drawn. "He's been through a real tough time."

"What is it?" Carrie gripped the back of a kitchen chair. "Lois, whatever you tell me, it can't possibly be as bad as what I'm imagining."

"It is, honey. He just finished radiation treatments, and he's still going through chemo for prostate cancer. He started treatment in October, right after we went back to Kansas City. He had surgery and then chemo and radiation. He doesn't sleep all that well, and he's still healing from the radiation. All in all, it was about eight weeks of radiation treatment every day. His oncologist says everything looks good now. But as you can see, the combination of the chemo and radiation has taken some of the wind out of his sails. He's getting better every day, but I still worry."

"Of course you do. I can only imagine." Carrie laid a comforting hand on Lois's arm. "He doesn't need to keep up such a demanding schedule at the hospital. I hope he knows that. Whatever he feels like doing is still a big help."

Lois sighed. "He knows that, but after so many years of busting his tail, it's hard for him to slow down. He's a work horse. You know that. As long as there are patients needing care, he'll soldier on."

"When my dad gets here, I hope the two of them can take a day or two and play golf together. They both deserve some down time."

Carrie pursed her lips, hoping that Dr. Jim would tell her about his cancer. But he might decide to keep the news to himself. She had always agreed with his philosophy that it was better to focus on good health than to relive tales of bad health.

"How long will it be until he can retire?" She found a fresh dishtowel and began drying pots and pans.

"With everything that's happened this year with the cancer, I want him to taper off so we can start spending the entire warm season here, June through September." Lois shook her head as if doubting that would be possible. She bent her head over the sink and shook her head. When she looked at Carrie, tears brimmed in her eyes. "I was scared I'd lose him." Lois wiped her eyes with her dishtowel. "I want us to be able to retire and enjoy life together, whatever time we have left."

Carrie wrapped her arms around her while she cried. She had rarely seen Lois with anything other than a smile on her face. "Maybe he just needs permission to slow down," she suggested. "Let's figure out a way to convince him that it's okay to enjoy life, for a change."

"Your presence is all he needs, dear girl. Now that you're here, he can relax. His people are in good hands. You know, don't you, that he thinks of them as *his* people?"

"They think of him that way, too."

Lois wiped her eyes and let out an abrupt laugh, more brave than humorous. "I need a dry dishtowel out of that drawer. I soaked through this one with my boo-hoos. Whatever you do, please don't let Jim know I cried. He doesn't need that. I have to be strong for him the way he's always been for me."

"NATE?" CARRIE ROLLED ONTO HER SIDE and ran her fingernails lightly across Nate's chest until he shivered.

"Hmm, what?" he mumbled, half asleep. "That tickles."

She rested her head on his chest, listening to the steady beat of his heart. "I love you so much."

Nate pulled her close. "I love you, too." He kissed the top of her head and combed his fingers through her silky hair.

"I think we should build a house of our own." Carrie had been thinking about this for a few weeks. She knew that she wanted to be married to Nate, and it seemed to make sense to build a house together. Having agreed not to live in Nate's rental house, they were weighing their options. Although she had dutifully sent sums of money to Philadelphia to repay her father, who finally insisted that she stop, she had saved a considerable sum over the past year, thanks to rent-free living. Dr. Jim and Lois were going to be spending more time in their house now. It was time to think about a place for her and Nate to call their own.

"We *could* build our own place." Nate rose up on one elbow, facing her. "What did you have in mind?"

"I was thinking we could build something similar to what Dr. Jim and Lois own—at least three bedrooms, a house that can grow with us. We could get new pine furniture, something rustic and handmade. A sleigh bed, maybe, and a big trestle table with benches and captain's chairs for the dining room. I'd like a big colorful woven rug for underneath the table. We could put a sectional sofa in front of the fireplace so we can sit by the fire and drink wine."

"For someone who claims not to be domestic, you sound like you've given some serious thought to the whole home-design thing." Nate sounded interested, though.

She laughed quietly. "Maybe I can learn to cook, too."

"Thought you'd scale two mountains in one climb, eh?"

She squeezed his arm playfully. "Stop. I'm a little late to the game, not completely hopeless."

"That lasagna you made tonight was pretty good."

"It was Stouffer's and you know it. Don't tease me. You know I'm trying. I don't have much time to do complicated stuff."

"Stouffer's is fine, Carrie. By the time we get home from work, as long as whatever I'm eating doesn't bite me back, it's all good. I don't care if you cook. I can cook." He stroked her back with his fingers. "You know what I like even more?"

"What?"

"This." He arranged himself on top of her. "And this," he murmured, kissing her until he felt her body, always so tense, relax under his hands. "And this." He kissed her again, raising the covers over their heads before working his way from her neck down her torso.

"I thought you were playing hockey later."

"This is my warm-up."

"No time for a hat-trick."

Nate chuckled. "Sure there is."

THE CALL FROM HER MOTHER CAME late in the afternoon that Thursday as Carrie was finishing up her day at the clinic. "We're here!" her mother said. "And we have a surprise for you."

"What is it?" Carrie asked.

"Not telling you. You'll just have to wait and see."

"Mom, you know I'm not good with surprises."

"This one you'll like."

After she saw her last patient, she hurried home to shower and change. When she saw her parents' rental car pull into the driveway, she rushed outside to greet them. There was someone in the backseat with snow-white hair. Carrie whooped with joy.

"Gran, I can't believe you didn't tell me you were coming!"

Gran stepped out of the car into Carrie's arms. "Well, when you're my age, you can't be sure of anything. I thought it was better to play it safe and not get your hopes up." She took Carrie's hand. "Lord, child, I can see why you're so happy here. It's breathtaking."

"Yes, my goodness, what a gorgeous place!" her mother exclaimed. "The mountains are spectacular. There's so much sky."

"I sure am glad to be back," her father declared. "It's even more beautiful than I remembered."

Carrie felt a wet nose against her knee. "Mom, Gran, this is Annie."

"Oh, aren't you sweet?" Her mother bent down on one knee to pet their four-legged family member. "Her name suits her. Hello, Annie. I'm your grandma."

Gran sat down on the front-porch swing and motioned to Annie, who jumped up with her and settled down to be petted. "Now I see why they're called the Shining Mountains," Gran said. "We city folks never get to see views like this."

Carrie shook her head, still amazed to see her. "I wondered why you didn't respond to my last email." She laughed knowingly. "You couldn't keep a secret from me."

"Frankly, we can't believe she didn't tell you, either," her mother said. "She wasn't going to be left behind, no matter what. She also signed up to volunteer at the clinic."

Now it all made sense. Earlier that morning, Dr. Jim hadn't wanted her to see the list of physicians in the corps. He had been sworn to secrecy.

Without her cane, Gran looked years younger in a denim dress, her figure still trim and petite. Her mother and father were decked out in high-end rugged outdoor clothing. She had a feeling a certain retailer would have a better fiscal quarter than usual.

"Carrie, I hope I'll have a chance to meet the medicine woman," Gran said. "I'd like to talk with her about the indigenous plants she uses—the ones I've never seen before."

"That can be arranged. I'm sure she'd like to meet you, too."

After a few minutes, Dr. Jim and Lois came outside to greet their guests, and introductions and more hugs were exchanged.

"I can't thank you and Lois enough for all you've done for Carrie," her mother said, embracing them.

"Doctor Nelson, may I call you Nanette?" Dr. Jim turned to Gran and took her hands. "It's an honor to finally meet you."

"Call me Nanette ... or Gran. I answer to both," she said with a laugh. "I feel as if I already know you."

Dr. Jim shook Mark's hand. "I hope you brought your golf clubs."

"They're in the back of the car. Carrie said you've got a great course here. Hope you and I can get out a few times this week when we're not serving the Indians ... I mean, Native Americans." Her father's face flushed red.

"The Indians will keep us plenty busy," Dr. Jim said, putting him at ease. "But there'll be plenty of time for eighteen holes. We like our visiting doctors to have a good time while they're here. We want to make sure you come back."

"I think you can count on that."

"By the way, we have our welcome dinner tonight," Dr. Jim said. "After everyone gets acquainted, we'll head over to the powwow grounds to watch competitive dancing. It's one of the biggest events of the week."

"Will we have an opportunity to meet Nate this evening?" Gran asked as she and Carrie sat together on the sofa, sipping glasses of sweet tea.

"That depends. His surgical load was pretty heavy today. But he'll probably show up at some point."

"It'll be nice to spend more time with him," her father said, making twinkling eye contact with Dr. Jim. "Carrie may be a doctor now, but she's still my daughter. Now that I know she and this surgeon are serious about each other, I need to make sure he's good enough for her."

"I think you'll find him suitable," Dr. Jim said. "He has some bad habits: boarding other hockey players, not shaving when he does three or four surgeries in a row—that kind of thing. But for the most part, he's civilized. He certainly loves Carrie. They make quite a team."

Carrie laughed. "Mom was concerned that I'd end up a spinster, wearing leather garments I made myself and communicating by drum."

"I just want you to be happy. That's all," her mother said. "If you choose to live in a tipi or play a drum, it's fine with me. But it puts a mother's heart at ease knowing you've found a nice man."

While Carrie and Gran sat together on the swing, Lois and her mother discussed the next day's lunch for the volunteers. "Put me to work," her mother said. She pulled a barrette out of her handbag and pulled her golden hair into a low ponytail. Her blue eyes, like Carrie's, were alight with enthusiasm. "I'm so glad we can be part of this! I told my husband it will be the experience of a lifetime. And it's wonderful to be here with Carrie, learning about her life. I've been imagining it all year, but now we can see for ourselves."

Carrie went into the living room with Dr. Jim and her dad. She could see that the two men already liked each other. As she watched Dr. Jim talk easily with her father, she wondered if he would confide in another male physician about his health issues. Perhaps it would be easier for him to talk with her dad than with her about his cancer treatment and prognosis.

THAT EVENING, AFTER THE WELCOME DINNER for volunteers, members of the medical corps went to the powwow grounds. As Carrie stood with her father on the sidelines, watching the dancing, she glanced every so often at his expression. He was watching the scene intently, as if mesmerized.

"It's really something, isn't it?" she asked, linking her arm in his, resting her head against his shoulder.

"I feel each of those drumbeats right here," her father said, touching the center of his chest. "They're like heartbeats, as if my rhythm is in sync with theirs. It takes me someplace else, somewhere outside myself."

"I've always felt that way, too."

"Funny, but the song is familiar, too, although I can't imagine how that could be possible."

Carrie smiled to herself. She had often thought the same thing. They stood together watching the dancers, taking in the sight of the Blackfeet celebrating their heritage as they had for centuries. From children to the very elderly, each Blackfeet understood the message shared by the drummers. It was as if the collective unconscious instilled in each of them contained these drumbeats and songs.

As the dancing began, Nate threaded through the crowd to join them and took Carrie's hand. She turned to find her parents and Gran watching her and Nate with delight.

Her father extended his hand to Nate. "Nice to see you again."

"Thank you, sir. We're glad you're back," Nate said, shaking his hand. "Thanks for helping us out this week."

"I look forward to it." Mark smiled and placed a hand on Nate's shoulder.

"I'd appreciate your opinion on a case I've got," Nate said. "Surgery doesn't seem to be the best option at this time."

"Happy to help. Were you aware that my mother also signed up this week?"

Nate turned to Gran and took her hand, giving it a gentle squeeze. "I can't thank you enough, Dr. Nelson."

"Oh, please. Call me Gran. Everyone else does." Gran's blue eyes twinkled.

Carrie beamed at her mother, who touched her cheek to Nate's. "I'm so glad to finally meet you," she said.

Throughout the evening, Carrie kept an eye out for John and Gali. The Leathers family had relatives visiting from Canada. For John and Gali's sake, she hoped there would be family harmony this week. The last time she had seen Gali at the clinic, Carrie had advised her to keep her anxiety level down.

Perhaps, in this case, staying away from family gatherings was the wisest course.

"When John and I are alone together in our home, everything is fine," Gali said. "John's brother and sister are on our side. It's the older generation that won't accept us."

"Maybe the younger generation can help smooth over issues with your in-laws," Carrie said. "Times are changing, even here."

JOHN AND GALI STOPPED BY THE Millers' house later that evening, just in time for dessert. When John rapped on the front screen door, Carrie invited them in and made introductions.

"Gali, right here in this room is the nicest group of people you'll ever meet," Carrie said. "Dr. Jim and Lois Miller; my parents, Dr. Mark and Lynne Nelson; my grandmother, Dr. Nanette Nelson; and my ... um ... Dr. Nate Holden." She blushed.

"I'm her surgeon," Nate said, earning hearty laughter all around.

Gali wore a hand-embroidered maternity smock. The baby boy growing inside her rested near his mother's heart. She appeared healthy as she stood arm in arm with her husband.

"It's a real family affair with all three Nelson doctors here this week," Dr. Jim said. "I think that in itself is a reason for celebration."

"We hope you'll find time to enjoy the reservation, maybe get over to see some of Glacier National Park," John said. "I'd be glad to go with you."

"That's very nice of you," Mark said. "If not this week, sometime later. From what we've all seen so far, this won't be our last visit."

JUST BEFORE SUNDOWN THE NEXT EVENING, Carrie and Gran walked around the house, investigating the variety of native plants that grew around the property. Gran recognized most of them and guessed at a few others, noting their historical uses. "This is comfrey. It helps heal bruises just like arnica. Comfrey clears up digestive disorders, too. And that over there is some nice bee balm. I bet the medicine woman uses that to break up fevers. It brings on sweating. And that's thistle, of course—good for the liver. Oh, and you have a nice patch of Echinacea for flu and colds. Why, you've got your very own pharmacy right outside your door."

Out of habit, Carrie surveyed the fields around the house, looking for her wolf. She hadn't seen the animal since just before Dancing Bird died in March. Every time she thought about the wolf, she wondered if the she-wolf had died at the same time as Dancing Bird. In her mind, Dancing Bird and the wolf were somehow linked.

But after about five minutes, she caught sight of the wolf, lying in the grass and watching them. "Gran, there she is. There's the wolf I've been telling you about—the one who visits me."

"I see her. She's a beauty." Far from showing fear, Gran appeared quite comfortable, even eager, to move nearer to the animal. "She's an old one. But look how regally she holds herself."

"Medicine Owl said she's kin," Carrie said. "She feels like kin to me. I've missed seeing her."

"We honor you, sister." Gran said in a voice loud enough to carry across the field. Turning to Carrie, she took her arm. "I do believe she watches over you."

Chapter Thirty

⸺⟩❘⟨⸺

AS THE WEEK SPED BY, CARRIE could hardly believe when it came time for the volunteers to leave the reservation. She was glad that her parents and Gran planned to stay several more days so that they could take a side trip to the Izaak Walton Hotel in Essex. Her father had asked Carrie to reserve an antique caboose car for their stay—a treat for everyone. Carrie wanted Nate to come along, but he insisted that she ought to have special time alone with her family.

"You hardly ever see them. You and I can fly to Philadelphia over the holidays and spend more time together," he promised.

Essex boasted spectacular mountain views. In addition to the caboose cars, because the hotel was located adjacent to the railroad tracks and served as a depot, the décor was a railroader's delight. Passing trains were part of the fun. For Carrie, so unaccustomed to time away from work, those two days gave her time to think. Her Roosevelt report and the book were foremost on her mind now. She felt compelled to share what she had learned from the medicine woman. Giving urgency to the book's central theme, one of these days Medicine Owl would be gone. Through the book, the medicine woman's work would live on.

They returned to Browning on Monday, just in time for dinner. As Lois and her mother prepared to serve the meal, Carrie sat with Dr. Jim, her dad, and Gran at the dining room table. Nate was working late in the ER.

Her father was still feeling the high from his week of volunteer service. "I'll definitely be back," he said. "In fact, I'll do what I can to get here at least one or two other times."

Carrie's eyes lit up. "If you managed to get here in February when you did,

I don't doubt that nothing can stop you." She held up her glass of iced tea. "I'd like to make a toast to my father, mother, and grandmother, the newest members of the volunteer medical corps."

"Here, here!" Dr. Jim said, raising his glass, a broad smile on his face. "Thank you again for joining us this year. Mark, there isn't a single cardiac patient who didn't get what they needed this week. Nanette, we hope you'll be back, too. Thanks for doing that update on kidney health and hypertension for our hospital staff."

"You're most welcome," Gran said. "I enjoyed it."

Carrie looked over to see her dad hold up his glass of iced tea in a toast to his mother. His first experience volunteering at the hospital had had a tremendous impact on him. He had helped out in the clinic many more hours than initially promised. He also had consulted with Nate on several cardiac cases.

"Your dad needed this," her mother said quietly to Carrie. "He's at a time in his life when it's important for him to remember why he became a doctor."

Even more amazing to Carrie was that earlier that day, her father had allowed Dr. Jim to treat him for a twisted knee that occurred during an unfortunate golf swing earlier in the week. When Dr. Jim saw her dad limping, he offered to see what he could do. Her father was impressed with his first osteopathic treatment and asked so many questions of Dr. Jim that Carrie couldn't resist teasing him. "Maybe you ought to take a class in manipulation, Dad."

"Maybe I will. I could barely walk without considerable pain before he did, well, whatever he did," her dad said. "It worked."

Carrie and Gran exchanged amazed looks.

"Your daughter is really the expert," Dr. Jim said. "She's the one who needs to show you some of the fancier stuff. My training was years ago, so I just keep up on the basics."

Her dad turned to Carrie, his expression both curious and humble. "What do you say? Want to teach an old dog some new tricks?"

"I'd love to." Carrie turned just in time to see the beaming smile that lit up Gran's face.

As LOIS SERVED COFFEE AND SLICES of warm cherry pie, they heard heavy steps on the front porch and then a male voice. "Help! I need help!"

Carrie, Dr. Jim, and Mark rushed to the front door, where they found Mike Leathers bleeding heavily from a head wound. His left arm dangled by his side, broken. He looked ready to collapse.

"Mike!" Carrie threw open the screen door and caught her patient before his knees gave way.

She and Mark lowered him to the floor and she began assessing his injuries. Dr. Jim ran for his medical bag while Lois produced a blanket. Mike was sweating profusely, barely able to speak. Between gasps, he managed to get out the sketchy details.

"I'm not sure if he's still alive!" He stopped to catch his breath while Carrie applied the pressure bandage Dr. Jim handed her to the wound above his left eye. "He was alive when I left him."

"Who?" Carrie asked as a sick feeling engulfed her.

"John. My brother John." A tear trailed down Mike's cheek.

"What happened?" Carrie's heart dropped.

"A deer ran in front of us, and the car rolled. John's trapped inside."

"I'll call 911," Dr. Jim said and went to the phone. "We'll need ambulances for both guys."

"Was Gali in the car, too?" Carrie prayed not.

"It was just John and me," Mike said and flinched as she adjusted his arm and began cutting away his shirt. Mike's arm was swollen and bruised, but there was no sign of fractured bone protruding through the skin. As she attended to his head wound, which was still bleeding profusely, Gran brought another blanket and arranged it under Mike's head. Getting down on her knees, she checked his vital signs. Anyone watching would never have guessed she was eighty-five.

"Was John moving when you left him?" Mark asked.

"No. I thought he was dead, but then I saw him breathing. I couldn't get him to wake up or move."

"Lie still, son. We need to see about that arm," Mark said while Carrie and Gran immobilized Mike's forearm using a ruler Lois supplied. Gran wrapped the arm with gauze to hold it securely in place.

"Dad, we need to find John fast." Carrie was on her feet, grabbing her car keys.

Mike gave them the location of the accident. "I need to go with you!" he said, struggling to get up from the floor.

"It's better if you stay here. We don't know the extent of your injuries." Carrie watched Dr. Jim apply a sterile dressing to the laceration on Mike's head. The wound would need stitches. "Dr. Jim and Gran, please see to Mike until the ambulance gets here. Dad and I will find John."

Gran nodded as she stroked Mike's hair, speaking soothing words in her calm voice, continuing to monitor his vital signs. Carrie had never seen Gran in action in an emergency. Watching her, she felt proud. After calling for ambulances, Dr. Jim said, "I'll call Gali ... oh, and Nadie and Earl Leathers, too. They'll want to be at the hospital for their boys."

Carrie grabbed her medical bag, and she and her father sprinted to the car. She sped out of the driveway and down the highway as fast as she dared, praying that John was alive and not too badly hurt. But when she saw the car, which Mike had told them rolled more than once and was completely demolished, she gasped. "Oh my God," she said. "How Mike walked away from this, I have no idea. This is bad."

She ran from the car, with her father just steps behind her. He tried to open the driver's side door, but it wouldn't budge. They raced around to the passenger side, which was still open from Mike's escape. She felt for a pulse on John's neck.

"He's alive. Would you grab the blanket from my backseat? I'll get him covered up."

She unbuttoned John's shirt and pressed her stethoscope to his chest, assessing his vital signs. There were no visible lacerations on his face or body, but there was a lot of bruising on his chest and abdomen, indicating the likelihood of life-threatening internal injuries. She opened his eyes and found the pupils fixed and dilated. Her father retrieved the blanket from Carrie's car, and she wrapped it around John, hoping to alleviate traumatic shock.

Mark took Carrie's stethoscope and listened, his face grim. "He's bleeding somewhere in there."

They were relieved to hear the ambulance siren. "I'm not moving him until they bring a backboard," Carrie said. She continued monitoring John's pulse at the wrist as she listened to his heart rate with her stethoscope. She leaned farther inside the car and stroked his hair. "John, it's me, Carrie. Can you hear me?"

There was no response. Her father ran to meet the ambulance as it skidded to a stop on loose stones near the crash site. Carrie remained at John's side, continuing to reassure him that everything was fine and that she was there for him.

"I'm Dr. Nelson. This patient has probable internal injuries," she told the paramedics.

With difficulty, the crew opened the driver's side door and painstakingly removed John from the vehicle on a backboard. Carrie examined him and found that his leg was broken in two places. Her father stood nearby as the paramedic started an IV and oxygen flow for John. Carrie continued to assess his condition and to confer with her dad. From his vital signs, she guessed there was significant internal bleeding. She hoped he didn't have a rare blood type.

"Nate will need to get ready for this guy," her father said, frowning.

She raced to her car to call him, but the signal on her cell phone wasn't strong enough this far out of town, and the call wouldn't go through. "Dammit," she muttered.

As the ambulance sped down the highway to the hospital, Carrie and her father followed. She was terrified for John. Would he even make it to the hospital? She glanced out of the corner of her eye at her father, whose eyes were closed, his hands folded on his lap. He appeared to be .... Was he praying?

By the time they arrived at the hospital, she was glad to see that every member of the Leathers family was in the waiting area. When Gali saw Carrie, she ran to her, tears streaming down her face. "Can you tell us how he is?" she asked. "No one is telling us anything."

Carrie led her to a chair as she checked her pulse rate. With such a traumatic event this early in her pregnancy, there was a chance of stress-induced early labor. "It's good that John is such a strong man. They're doing everything possible for him in there. Gali, you remember my father, Mark Nelson. Dad, will you stay with Gali while I go in and see about John?"

She hurried down the hall and through the entrance to the emergency room. All hands were on deck, evaluating and treating John and Mike. Mike was awake and alert, far more concerned about John than himself. The physician assistant on duty was preparing Mike for an X-ray.

"Any sign of internal injuries?" she asked the PA.

"Not that I can tell. There's no pain in the belly," he said.

"Good. Let's watch him closely," Carrie said. "That car rolled more than once. I want to make sure he doesn't have undetected internal injuries. I want him admitted overnight."

"Will do," the PA said. "His vitals are good. I'll stitch up that laceration, unless you want to do it, Doctor."

"You go ahead," she said. "I may need to be available for his brother." She took Mike's hand as she spoke. "You're going to get a few stitches to close that cut. After an X-ray, you'll get a cast, unless Dr. Holden needs to do more to fix the arm. It looks like a simple break to me, though. I'm going to check on John now." She released his hand.

Mike looked up at her, fear in his eyes. "Will my brother live?"

"He's alive now, Mike, thanks to you. If you hadn't run so far to get help, it might be a different story. We'll do everything we can to help. Pray. That's what you can do."

John was hooked up to a heart monitor, oxygen, and an IV. His color was so bad that Carrie gasped. Nate was in the cubicle, working to stabilize him.

"Am I ever glad to see you," he said. "I'm heading upstairs to scrub. Come with me. I could use an extra hand in the OR."

"I'll be right back." Carrie went to find her father and Gali to tell them that she would be assisting Nate in surgery. "I'll let you know as soon as the surgery is complete," she promised.

Considering her close friendship with John, she would need to remain detached, despite her fears for his survival. Nate and John were close friends, too. Watching Nate scrub up, as calm as if he were about to perform a routine tonsillectomy, she swallowed hard and scrubbed her hands and arms thoroughly. Then she held them out as a nurse helped her into a surgical gown, shoe covers, mask, and gloves.

"I need a second set of eyes when I open him up," Nate said. "I don't want to miss any bleeders."

The surgery took a little over four hours as Nate inspected and repaired internal injuries caused by three broken ribs and removed John's damaged spleen. Carrie marveled at his skill as he repaired the damage. He closed up the abdominal incision with skillful sutures and then set the fibula in John's leg.

"I think he'll do fine," Nate said. "He's lucky he didn't have a punctured lung."

After John was wheeled into the recovery area, she and Nate walked arm in arm out of the operating room and into the hall, where they embraced. "We almost lost our friend tonight," Carrie said.

Nate yanked off his surgical cap and wiped his brow. "He's a strong guy, but he's going to need help for a while. I hope Gali can handle him."

"I think from what I saw in the waiting area, the family will all help out." Carrie felt certain that given the extraordinary nature of the problem, the Leathers family would pull together. "Let's go find Gali and John's parents. Thank God, there is good news about two sons tonight."

They walked down the hall, still dressed in their surgical scrubs and shoe covers, to let Gali know that her husband was resting and the surgery had gone well. Gali sat red-eyed next to Nadie and Earl Leathers. When the family saw both doctors walking down the hall, they stood up, their faces anxious.

"This is Dr. Holden, our surgeon," Carrie said. "She glanced at Nate, allowing him to provide the surgical update.

"I had to repair some internal bleeding, and we had to give him a couple of units of blood. He also has a broken left leg—not the most serious I've seen. The leg will heal nicely. He'll be in the recovery room for a little while yet. When he wakes up, you can see him." Nate made eye contact with Carrie. "I'm going over there to check on him now. I'll call you later."

Carrie turned, intending to make a brief comment about the importance of family support, and was amazed to see Nadie Leathers embrace Gali. Then Earl hugged his new daughter-in-law and put an arm around his wife. The three of them stood together, holding on to one another for dear life. Then

Nadie patted the baby bump visible through Gali's dress and smiled. When Nadie finally spoke, Carrie knew all was well with this family.

"Welcome, Daughter."

Chapter Thirty-One

—◦—

THE ALARM ON CARRIE'S CELLPHONE WENT off at six o'clock, the same time it always did. But this morning, it felt as if she hadn't slept at all. "Nooo, not yet," she groaned, rolling over to shut it off. She was exhausted, but knew she had a full patient schedule that day.

She had finally gone to bed at two in the morning after spending over an hour downstairs in the living room with her father. When she returned from the hospital, Dr. Jim and Mark were sitting by the fireplace, sipping a fine Scotch and waiting for her. She was grateful for their company.

"Here, I think you might need one of these," Dr. Jim said and poured Carrie two fingers of the Scotch.

She took a sip and coughed. "That might be way more than I need." Settling into the couch, she gave them an update. "The good news is that John tolerated the surgery well. When I left, he was awake. Mike is doing well, too. I've got to say it: Nate did an unbelievable job of putting Humpty Dumpty back together again. John was a mess inside. The bad news is he'll be laid up for a while."

"Was Nate able to fix that leg, too?" her father asked. "I was worried about that."

"He set the leg while John was still under."

"Thank God. Carrie, you did one heckuva job tonight. I'm proud of you." He leaned over to give her a peck on the forehead. They embraced, and Carrie relaxed into her father's arms.

"Having you there helped," she said. "Thanks, Dad."

"If you two will excuse me, I think I'll head up to bed now," Dr. Jim said.

Carrie and her dad continued talking about John's condition, the pros and cons of healthcare in Browning, and Mark's thoughts about his work in the clinic until Carrie glanced at the clock above the fireplace. "I need to be at the hospital in a few hours. I'd better get some sleep."

They stood up together, and her dad pulled her to him, kissing the top of her head. "What you did tonight, Carrie," he cleared his throat, "well, any time there is that kind of traumatic injury, you need a cool head to manage all the possibilities. You knew exactly what you were doing, and John is alive because of it." Carrie started to speak, but he stopped her. "Let me say my piece. I know you and I haven't always agreed, especially when it came to your career. But I want you to know, I get it now. After spending a week here, seeing what you do on a daily basis, experiencing it for myself ... well, I couldn't be more proud of you and your decision to work here."

This was something she had never thought she would hear from him. It was more than an apology or an agreement that she should continue serving here. It was a validation of her life and work. Stepping back, she looked into his eyes.

"When I was a little girl, I remember how many times I thought about what you did every day, everyone you helped." Carrie smiled at the memory of running to greet her father when he came home from work after a long day. "You made people's hearts better, and everyone said you were the best at what you did. I wanted to be just like you. And now, I think maybe there's a chance of that." She kissed him on the cheek. "I couldn't love you more than I do right this minute. And having a chance to work with you this week ... well, it's been the greatest experience of my life."

"Maybe we're a lot more alike than we are different." He smiled.

"Could be. Wouldn't Mom and Gran be amazed to hear us now?"

NATE TEXTED CARRIE AS SHE WAS getting out of the shower. John is doing well. Gali is there with him. Home to bed. Love you.

Carrie wrapped her wet hair in a towel and sat in the rocking chair, setting it into a slow motion. She stroked Annie's soft fur and sat quietly, thinking about the events that had transpired over the past year and altered her life forever. She remembered the anxious young woman who had arrived on the reservation with her dog, questioning nearly everything, unsure of how to proceed, afraid of missing out. The life she lived now bore little resemblance to what it had been just a year ago.

She recalled the challenges, large and small, that she had faced over the past year—anxiety over career choices, fears that she might not be accepted on the reservation, and heartbreak over the events that led to her broken engagement. She had worried that she'd miss out entirely on a loving marriage and family. And then, of course, there were the seemingly insurmountable troubles with her father. All that was in the past. Just as she had weathered a year in Northwest Montana, she had also survived storms that threatened to tear apart her family relationships.

After living on the reservation and observing the way the Blackfeet lived in harmony with the four seasons—measuring their time in *now moments* rather than stressing about the future—she had begun her own transformation. She was different now, less prone to fears. When she was tense or under stress, she remembered that all she had to do was breathe and trust. She had become acutely aware of the bond she shared with others. The process had been gradual and deeply spiritual. In miraculous ways, situations had been resolved, as if a larger hand had taken control. Although she was not a member of the Blackfeet Tribe, she was part of a greater whole, made up of people, animals, and the vast land that was theirs to love and honor.

Through determination, hard work, and faith—in something bigger than herself—she had begun to concentrate more on those who needed her, less on her own concerns. She had sought the wisdom and knowledge of the ages—information others in her position might have rejected outright. Most of all, she had opened her heart to the possibility of new love and had found someone to share her spirit journey, just as Dancing Bird had predicted.

That evening, she and her family gathered at the Millers' home for a farewell dinner. Her parents and Gran were scheduled to leave the next morning. As everyone sat down to a meal made even more sumptuous by the combined cooking talents of new friends Lois and Lynne, Carrie couldn't imagine a more perfect way to end a week none of them would ever forget.

After dinner, while coffee and dessert were being served, she excused herself. "I'm going over to see Nate for a few minutes," she said.

"Give him our love," her mom said. "It would be wonderful to say goodbye in person, but we understand how busy he is."

As her parents exchanged smiles, Carrie slipped out the door. "I won't be long."

Nate was sitting on the front step of his house when she parked in his driveway. With his curls still wet from a shower, he stood and walked toward her. She still thought he was the most beautiful man she had ever seen.

"Your mom and dad haven't left already, have they?" he asked. "I was on my way over to say goodbye."

"They're still here and they'd love to see you. I needed to see you more." She tilted her face up to meet his kiss. She held onto him, knowing they were already bound by more than fate, more than common interests or shared passions.

"You go ahead. I'll be right behind you," he said and went back in the house.

Driving to the Millers' house with Nate following in his car, she thought about their future. It would be wonderful to introduce Nate to other family members and friends. They had begun making plans to build their own home and would soon go through the process of finding suitable land. They would marry and start a family of their own. The future was theirs to imagine and create together.

Everyone looked up from the dinner table when they walked in. Lois said, "Hi, you two. Nate, would you like some dessert and coffee? This is Gran's homemade apple pie. I've never known you to turn down pie."

"Don't mind if I do," Nate said. "But first, I have something I need to say." He turned to Carrie. "I've already gotten permission from your parents." He knelt down on one knee and handed her a black velvet box containing a perfect, glistening, princess-cut diamond ring. "Carrie, will you marry me?"

Carrie tried to speak, but couldn't manage anything. Finally, she said, "Yes!" as everyone clapped.

She looked at him curiously. "But Nate, when did you talk to my parents?"

"He asked our permission the other night while you were out delivering a baby," her father said. "Your mother and I hope you'll be as happy together as we've been all these years."

"We hope you'll be as happy as *we've* been, too," Dr. Jim said, his arm around Lois's waist.

Nate slid the ring onto Carrie's finger. "I'm sure Carrie has a dream wedding in mind. I'm okay with whatever she wants."

"Oh, we'll have such fun planning a wedding!" Her mom's eyes shone with excitement. "Come to Philadelphia for the holidays. We can pick out a dress and look at venues for the reception. You want a traditional Quaker wedding, right?"

"What does that mean?" Nate looked a little wary. "We're allowed to speak, right?"

"It just means that we'll simply state our intention to be husband and wife. We can say whatever else we want," Carrie explained as his eyes widened. "But I have an idea, and I don't think anyone will find it too surprising. I want to have the ceremony here with everyone we know and love. If we get married in Philly, none of our Blackfeet friends or our coworkers from the hospital can be there." She turned to her parents and Gran. "Will you come back next July so we can get married here?"

"I think that's the best idea of all." Her father reached for the chilled bottle of Champagne that Dr. Jim handed him.

"Champagne, too?" she asked incredulously. "So, everyone knew about this?"

"We're glad we could be part of this occasion. It was Nate's idea to ask you with all of us here," Gran said. "We know you're not big on surprises, but some surprises are good, right?"

"He was probably afraid you'd say no. He thought his chances were better with an audience," Dr. Jim joked.

Nate admired the colorful, fiery diamond in its elegant setting on Carrie's finger. "Do you like it?" he asked. "I had to borrow one of your other rings to make sure I got the size right."

"I love it," she said and wrapped her arms around his neck, kissing him. "It's perfect. *You're* perfect."

Her father held a dishtowel over the cork on the Champagne bottle and popped it while Lois held out flutes for him to fill. Then she passed them around, and everyone toasted the newly engaged couple.

"To my beautiful daughter and her husband-to-be," he said. "Cheers! And to a Montana wedding next July. I can't wait to come back to this place. It's a slice of heaven on earth."

Carrie and Nate linked fingers as they sipped their Champagne. Her eyes met his. It had been a year to remember. She and Nate were where they belonged, doing work they loved and beginning their lives together. Anything was possible, if you believed.

"To you, Carrie," Nate said, toasting her.

In the distance, they heard the sound of drums. Carrie smiled. "I think I know what they're saying."

"What?" Nate asked. They listened for a few minutes in silence.

"Welcome. Welcome home."

Photo by D'Lara Photography

ROBIN STRACHAN'S POETRY, FICTION, AND NONFICTION have been published in local, regional, and national publications for over thirty years. Born in Johnstown, Pennsylvania, she began her writing career as a reporter doing features. Her personality feature stories for the newspaper and its sister magazine, coupled with her love of Maeve Binchy novels and all things related to the British Isles, eventually led to a decision to write fiction that includes strong individual character stories.

Listening for Drums is her third novel. Her second novel, *Designing Hearts*, was published by Camel Press in 2015. Her first, *Manifesting Dreams*, was released in 2011. A sequel to *Listening for Drums* is in progress.

Since 1981, Ms. Strachan has served in executive and development roles in higher education, health care, and medical research. She holds a bachelor of arts degree with dual majors in English and philosophy. She is also a published poet and a professional artist. She makes her home in the Chicago area.

For more information, go to: robinstrachanauthor.com.

From Robin Strachan
and Camel Press

‿֊◟◞֊‿

Thank you for reading *Listening for Drums*. We are so grateful for you, our readers. If you enjoyed this book, here are some steps you can take that could help contribute to its success and the success of this series.

- Post a review on Amazon, BN.com, and/or GoodReads.
- Check out www.RobinStrachanAuthor.com or blog and send a comment or ask to be put on her mailing list.
- Spread the word on social media, especially Facebook, Twitter, and Pinterest.
- Like the Facebook author page (AuthorStrachan) and publisher page (CamelPressBooks).
- Follow the author (@AuthorStrachan) and publisher (@CamelPressBooks) on Twitter.
- Ask for this book at your local library or request it on their online portal.

Good books and authors from small presses are often overlooked. Your comments and reviews can make an enormous difference.

Designing Hearts

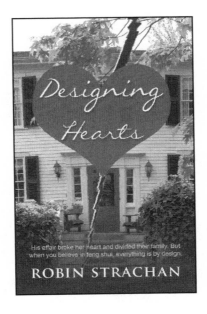

Jill has the perfect life: a celebrity husband, twin sons, and a flourishing design business. Then her husband David's affair hits the tabloids. As Jill struggles to adjust, David pours on the charm. Can she forgive him even if it means losing Denny, an artist who may be her soul mate? Jill has made feng shui work for others; now it's time to see if she can use it to put her own life to rights.

42902123R00163